W9-BMT-577

The

Harvest

Books by Robert Charles Wilson

Bantam Books

New York   Toronto

London   Sydney

Auckland

Robert

Charles

Wilson

The
Harvest

THE HARVEST
A Bantam Spectra Book / January 1993

Published simultaneously in hardcover and trade paperback.

BOOK DESIGN BY MARIA CARELLA

Library of Congress Cataloging-in-Publication Data
Wilson, Robert Charles, 1953–
  The harvest / Robert Charles Wilson.
    p.   cm.
  ISBN 0-553-09123-9 (hc)
  ISBN 0-553-37110-X (tp)
  I. Title.
PR9199.3.W4987H37   1992
813'.54—dc20   92-14430
                             CIP

Published simultaneously in the United States and Canada

Bantam Books are published by Bantam Books, a division of Bantam Doubleday Dell Publishing Group,
Inc. Its trademark, consisting of the words "Bantam Books" and the portrayal of a rooster, is Registered in
U.S. Patent and Trademark Office and in other countries. Marca Registrada. Bantam Books, 666 Fifth
Avenue, New York, New York 10103.

PRINTED IN THE UNITED STATES OF AMERICA

FFG   0 9 8 7 6 5 4 3 2 1

93-04767

For Devon . . . the best I can
do right now.

———

And, belatedly,
for my parents.

The

Harvest

Prologue

"*Tonight,*" the President of the United States said, "*as we gaze at the sky and wonder at what we see there, our minds are crowded with questions.*"

It was an Everest of understatement, Matt Wheeler thought.

He regarded the President's solemn face as it flickered in the blue aura of the TV screen. The man had aged in office, as presidents often do. Much of that aging, it seemed to Matt, had occurred in the past two weeks.

He turned up the volume and opened the patio doors.

Cool air spilled into the living room. The thermostat kicked over and the baseboard heaters began to warm up. Matt listened to the tick of hot metal in the President's long pauses.

The air outside was cold, but the night sky had cleared for the first time this rainy March. For the first time, Matt would get his own look at the phenomenon that had been terrifying the rest of the world for most of a week. He'd seen pictures, of course, on the screen of his nineteen-inch Sony. But that was TV. This was his backyard. This was the sky above Buchanan, Oregon: moonless, dark, and cut with bright scatters of stars.

He checked his watch. Five minutes after ten o'clock. Back east, in the nation's capital, it was past one in the morning. The President had delivered this speech hours ago. Matt's daughter Rachel had been at band practice during the first broadcast . . . rehearsing Sousa marches at the announcement of what might, after all, be Armageddon. Matt had taped the whole thing. The networks were running excerpts at the top of every hour, but he thought she should hear all of it. Especially tonight. When the sky was clear.

He turned back briefly into the warm shell of the house. "Rachel? About time, honey."

Rachel had been holed up in her bedroom since dinner, rearranging photos in the family album. Whenever she was unhappy, Rachel would deal out these old photographs across her bedspread, stare at them for a time, then shuffle them back into the vinyl-bound album in some new and presumably meaningful order. Matt had never interfered, although it troubled him when she disappeared into the past like this—unfolding family history like a road map, as if she'd taken a wrong turn somewhere.

But it was a soothing ritual, too, and he didn't want to deny her any scrap of consolation. Rachel had been seven when Celeste died, and Matt supposed the memory of her mother, sad as it might be, might also help sustain her through this crisis. He hoped so.

She came out of her room dressed for bed: a nightie and a pink flannel robe. Comfort clothes. Rachel was sixteen, and he was occasionally startled that she had matured so fast—it was every parent's lament, but he felt as if she'd grown up in an eyeblink. Not tonight, though. Tonight—in this old robe—she could have passed for twelve. Her eyes were shadowed, maybe a little resentful as she looked at him. Maybe she *felt* twelve. *Don't make me see this. I'm only a kid.*

They stepped out together into the night air.

"*For the first time in human history,*" the President said, "*we stand in the light of a new moon.*"

"Sky sure looks big," Rachel observed.

Bigger than it had ever looked, Matt thought. More hostile. But he couldn't say that. "It's a pretty night."

"Chilly." She hugged herself.

The house stood at the crest of a hill, and Matt had always appreciated this downslope view. He pointed east across a dozen dark rooftops to a ridge where a stand of Douglas firs tangled with the stars. "We should see it about there."

"*Many of us have reacted to recent events with fear. I have on my desk reports of rioting and looting. Perhaps this is unsurprising, but it does us all a great disservice. We are traditionally a strong and levelheaded nation. If we survived Pearl Harbor, if we kept our wits about us at Bull Run, it would be absurd—it would be un-American—to surrender to hopelessness now.*"

But the Pacific Fleet had been decimated at Pearl Harbor, the Union Army had panicked at Bull Run, and anyway, Matt thought, this wasn't a war. It was something else. Something unprecedented.

Rachel pressed tight against his side. He said, "Are you scared?"

She nodded.

"It's okay. We're all a little scared."

She gripped his hand fiercely, and Matt felt a cold rush of anger. *Goddamn you*, he thought at the empty sky. *Goddamn you for frightening my daughter like this.*

The President's voice was clangorous and strange under all these springtime stars.

"*Our scientists tell us we've travelled a long evolutionary road from the beginning of life on this planet. Whoever our visitors are, they must have travelled a similar road. Perhaps we seem as strange to them as they seem to us . . . or perhaps not. Perhaps they recognize us as their own kin. Distant cousins, perhaps. Perhaps unimaginably distant, but not entirely foreign. I hope this is the case.*"

But you don't know, Matt thought. It was a pious, happy sentiment. But nobody knows.

A screen door wheezed open and clattered shut: Nancy Causgrove, their neighbor, stepping outside. The yellow buglight in the Causgroves' backyard made her skin look pale and unhealthy. She poured out a saucer of milk for Sookie, a fat tabby cat. Sookie was nowhere to be seen.

"Hi," Rachel said unhappily. Mrs. Causgrove nodded . . . then paused. And looked up.

"*When I was a child,*" the President said, "*we took our family vacation one summer in the Adirondacks. We owned a cabin by a river there. It was a wide, slow river—I don't recall its name. That summer, when I was ten years old, I believed we were all alone, about as far from civilization as it was possible to get. But that river took me by surprise. It wasn't crowded . . . but every once in a while someone would come by, a hiker along the shore or a canoe out in the river where the current ran fast. I was shy about these visitors, but in time I learned to smile and wave, and they always smiled and waved back. Sometimes they stopped, and we would offer them a cup of coffee or a bite of lunch.*"

The President paused, and for a moment there was only the creak of frogs from the cold marshland down in the valley.

"*I am convinced our Earth is like that cabin. We have been alone a long time, but it seems a river runs past our habitation, and there are people on that river. Our first instinct is to shrink back—we are a little shy after such a long time by ourselves. But we also feel the impulse to smile and say hello and trust that the stranger is friendly, and I think that is a strength. I think that impulse is what will carry us through this crisis, and I urge all of you to cultivate it in your hearts. I believe that when the story of our time is written, historians will say we were generous, and we were open, and that what might*" *have seemed at first like the end of the world was simply the beginning of a new friendship.*

"I urge you all—"

But the President's words were lost in Rachel's gasp.

Nancy Causgrove fumbled her grip on the milk bottle. It shattered on the stone patio, a wet explosion.

Matt stared at the sky.

Above the western horizon—stark behind the silhouette of the Douglas firs—the bone-white orb of the alien spaceship had begun to rise.

▪   ▪   ▪

There were three things in this world Matt Wheeler loved above all else: his daughter, his work, and the town of Buchanan, Oregon.

Gazing at this blank and unimaginably large structure as it glided above the trees, as it eclipsed Orion and wheeled toward Gemini, he was struck with a sudden conviction: *All three of those things are in danger.*

It was a thought born in the animal fear of this new thing in the sky, and Matt worked to suppress it.

But the thought would recur. Everything he loved was fragile. Everything he loved might be forfeit to this nameless new moon.

The thought was persistent. The thought was true.

▪   ▪   ▪

A year passed.

Part

One

New

Moon

Chapter 1

August

The crisis some people call "Contact" continues to preoccupy Congress and the Administration as elections approach.

We *call* it "Contact," but as Senator Russell Welland (R., Iowa) observed last week, contact is the thing most conspicuously lacking. The spacecraft—if it *is* a spacecraft—has circled the Earth for more than a year without attempting any kind of signal. On the sole occasion when it displayed a sign of life—when it emitted the structures that occupy our major cities like so many monuments to the ineffectiveness of our air defenses—it was an event impossible to interpret. It's as if we have been invaded by a troop of extraterrestrial mimes, deranged but very powerful.

Or so the conventional wisdom would have us believe. In the City of Rumors, nothing is taken for granted. Recent high-level international summits—including several underreported jaunts by the Secretary of State—have sparked suspicion that genuine "contact" of some kind may be imminent. According to unofficial White House sources, back-channel lines to the Germans, the Russians, and the Chinese—among others—have been buzzing with traffic for at least a week. Coincidence?

Who knows? Clearly, however, *something* is afoot. And Congressional leaders of both parties are demanding to be let in on it.

> —*August 10 installment of the*
> *nationally syndicated column* Washington Insider
> *(from the scrapbook of Miss Miriam Flett,*
> *Buchanan, Oregon)*

A year and some months after the immense alien Artifact parked itself in a close orbit of the Earth, Matt Wheeler spent an afternoon wondering how to invite Annie Gates to the party he was hosting Friday night.

The question was not *whether* to invite her—obviously he would—but *how*. More precisely, what would the invitation suggest about their relationship? And what did he want it to suggest?

Pondering the question, he washed his hands and prepared to see the last two patients of the day.

▪ ▪ ▪

In a town the size of Buchanan a doctor ends up treating the people he sees at backyard barbecues. His last patients were Beth Porter, daughter of Billy, a sometimes-patient; and Lillian Bix, wife of his friend Jim.

The two women, Beth and Lillian, were posed at opposite ends of the waiting-room sofa like mismatched bookends. Lillian paged through a *Reader's Digest* and dabbed her nose with a hankie. Beth stared at the far wall, absorbed in the music that seeped from the headphones of her Walkman like the rhythmic rattling of a pressed tin pie plate. A few more years of this, Matt thought, and he'd be treating her for hearing loss.

The teenager was first up. "Beth," he said.

She gazed into space.

"Beth. Beth!"

She looked up with the resentment of someone startled out of a dream. The resentment faded when she recognized Matt. She thumbed a switch on the cassette player and pried the phones out of her ears.

"Thank you," he said. "Come on in."

As he turned, Annie Gates stepped out of her consulting room with a file folder in hand. She glanced at Beth, shot him a look: *Good luck!* Matt returned a smile.

Annie Gates wore medical whites and a stethoscope around her neck. Unlike Beth and Lillian, Annie and Matt were a matched set. They were business partners. They were professionals. He was sort of in love with her. He had been sort of in love with her for most of a decade.

▪ ▪ ▪

Matt Wheeler had been practicing primary-care medicine in this building for fifteen years. He had grown up in Buchanan, developed what he thought of as "the medical impulse" in Buchanan, and after serving his residency in a Seattle hospital and passing his general boards he had hightailed it back to Buchanan to open a private practice. His partner then had been Bob Scott, a dark-haired and high-strung Denverite who had interned with him. Together they had rented this suite, a waiting room and three consulting rooms on the seventh floor of the Marshall Building, a sandstone legacy of the Hoover era planted firmly at the intersection of Marina and Grove.

Matt and his partner had understood the perils of family practice, or thought they did. The real money was in specialties, in "doing procedures"; the hassles were in family practice. Not just patient hassles—those they had been prepared for. But insurance hassles, Medicare and Medicaid hassles, paperwork hassles . . . in time, a crippling, skyrocketing overhead. Dr. Scott, professing a nostalgia for city life, bailed out and left for L.A. in 1992. Last Matt heard, he was working at the kind of corporate storefront clinic sometimes called a "Doc-in-the-Box." Bye-bye hassles. Bye-bye independence.

Matt persevered. He couldn't imagine a life outside of Buchanan, and he couldn't imagine any work more satisfying than the work he did, at least when he was allowed to do it. Celeste had died around the time Bob left for California, and the new demands on his time had been, perhaps, a blessing in disguise.

Bob Scott's replacement showed up in June of that year: a young female internist named Anne Gates. Matt had not expected a woman to show interest in the partnership, particularly not a young blond woman in a businesslike skirt and a pair of black-rimmed glasses that amplified her eyes into something owlish and fiercely solemn. He told her she'd have to put in long hours, make house calls, cover at the local ER, and expect nothing spectacular in the way of remuneration. "It's not city work," he said, thinking of Bob Scott's defection and the cut of that Perry Ellis skirt.

Whereupon Anne Gates informed him that she had grown up in a farm town on the prairies of southern Manitoba; she knew what small towns were like and Buchanan didn't look so damn small to *her* (though it did look *decent*). She had survived a residency in an inner-city hospital where most of the ER patients had been gunshot wounds, knife wounds, and drug ODs. She had emerged from this ordeal still believing in the fundamental value of primary-care medicine, and as far as "remuneration" went, she would be happy to live in the absence of cockroaches, get more than five hours' sleep in a given week, and treat at least the occasional patient who didn't initiate the relationship by vomiting on her.

Whereupon Matt Wheeler discovered he had a new partner.

They had worked together for nearly a year before they discovered each other as human beings. He was recovering from Celeste's death and what interested him about Anne Gates in that unhappy time was, for instance, her remarkable finesse with fiber-optic sigmoidoscopy, a procedure he loathed and dreaded, or her uneasiness with cranial injuries of any kind. They shifted patients according to each other's weaknesses and strengths; Anne ended up with many of his geriatric patients, and he took an extra share of pediatrics. But she was also a woman and Matt was a widower and there were days when the vector of that equation did not escape him. On the first anniversary of her arrival in Buchanan, he took her to dinner at the Fishin' Boat, a restaurant by the marina. Soft-shell crab, shallots in butter, margueritas, and a prearranged ban on doc-speak. By the end of the evening he was calling her Annie. They went to bed for the first time the week after that.

They were passionately involved for most of that year. The year after, they seemed to drift apart. No arguments, but fewer dates, fewer nights together. Then the pace picked up for another six months. Then another hiatus.

They never talked about it. Matt wasn't certain whether these peaks and valleys were his fault or hers. Whether they were even a bad thing. He knew for a fact, however, that a pattern had been established. Nearly ten years had passed since Annie Gates stepped through that office door for the first time. Matt's hair had grayed at the temples and run back a little from his brow, and Annie had developed frown lines at the corners of her eyes, but ten years was an eyeblink, really, and at no point in that time had they ever been entirely separate . . . or entirely together.

Lately they had drifted through another vacuum, and he wondered how she would take this invitation for Friday evening. As a courtesy? Or as a suggestion to spend the night?

And which did he prefer?

The question lingered.

■ ■ ■

He showed Beth Porter into his consulting room, down the hall from Anne's.

The consulting room was Matt's enclave, a space of his own creation. Its centerpiece was a set of authentic Victorian oak medical cabinets, purchased at a rural auction in 1985. Behind his desk was a creaking leather chair that had formed itself to the precise contour of his behind. The window looked crosstown, beyond the sweltering marina to the open sea.

Beth Porter took her place in the patient chair while Matt adjusted the blinds to keep out the afternoon sun. Annie had recently equipped her office with vertical blinds, covered in cloth, which looked exactly sideways to Matt. His consultancy announced: *Tradition*. Annie's replied: *Progress*. Maybe that was the invisible hand that conspired to pull them apart.

She was on his mind today, though, wasn't she?

He took his seat and looked across the desk at Beth Porter.

He had examined her file before he called her in. Matt had been Beth's regular doctor since her eleventh birthday, when her mother had dragged her into the waiting room: a sullen child wearing a cardboard party hat over a face swollen to the proportions of a jack-o'-lantern. Between rounds of birthday cake and ice cream, Beth had somehow disturbed a hornet nest in the cherry tree in the Porters' backyard. The histamine reaction had been so sudden and so intense that her mother hadn't even tried to pry off the party hat. The string was embedded in the swollen flesh under her chin.

Nine years ago. Since then he'd seen her only sporadically, and not at all since she turned fifteen. Here was another trick of time: Beth wasn't a child anymore. She was a chunky, potentially attractive twenty-year-old who had chosen to wear her sexuality as a badge of defiance. She was dressed in blue jeans and a tight T-shirt, and Matt noticed a blue mark periodically visible as her collar dipped below the left shoulder: a tattoo, he thought, God help us all.

"What brings you in today, Beth?"

"A cold," she said.

Matt pretended to take a note. Years in the practice of medicine had taught him that people preferred to make their confessions to a man with a pen in his hand. The lab coat didn't hurt, either. "Bad cold?"

"I guess . . . not especially."

"Well, you're hardly unique. I think everybody's got a cold this week." This was true. Annie had come to work snuffling. Lillian Bix, in the waiting room, had been doing her polite best to suppress a runny nose. Matt himself had swallowed an antihistamine at lunch. "There's not much we can do for a cold. Is your chest congested?"

She hesitated, then nodded. "A little."

"Let's listen to it."

Beth sat tensely upright while he applied his stethoscope to the pale contour of her back. No significant congestion, but Matt was certain it wasn't a cold that had brought her in. The ritual of listening to her lungs simply established a doctorly relationship. A medical intimacy. He palpated her throat and found the lymph nodes slightly enlarged—hard pebbles under the flesh—which raised a small flag of concern.

He leaned against the edge of his desk. "Nothing too much out of the ordinary."

Beth inspected the floor and seemed unsurprised.

"Maybe it isn't a cold you're worried about. Beth? Is that a possibility?"

"I think I have gonorrhea," Beth Porter announced.

Matt made a note.

▪ ▪ ▪

She surprised him by reciting her symptoms without blushing. She added, "I looked this up in a medical book. It sounded like gonorrhea, which is kind of serious. So I made an appointment. What do you think?"

"I think you made a reasonable diagnosis. Maybe you ought to be a doctor." She actually smiled. "We'll know more when the test comes back."

The smile faded. "Test?"

Annie came in to chaperon and distract Beth while Matt took a cervical culture. There was the inevitable joke about whether he kept his speculum in a deep-freeze. Then Annie and Beth chatted about Beth's job at the 7-Eleven, which was, Beth said, as boring as you might think, selling frozen pies and microwave burritos until practically midnight and catching a ride home with the manager, usually, when there was nothing on the highway but logging trucks and semitrailers.

Matt took the cervical swab and labeled it. Beth climbed down from the table; Annie excused herself.

Beth said, "How soon do we know?"

"Probably tomorrow afternoon, unless the lab's stacked up. I can call you."

"At home?"

Matt understood the question. Beth still lived with her father, a man Matt had treated for his recurring prostatitis. Billy Porter was not a bad man, but he was a reticent and old-fashioned man who had never struck Matt as the forgiving type. "I can phone you at work if you leave the number."

"How about if I call here?"

"All right. Tomorrow around four? I'll have the receptionist switch you through."

That seemed to calm her down. She nodded and began to ask questions: What if it *was* gonorrhea? How long would she have to take the antibiotics? Would she have to tell—you know, her lover?

She paid careful attention to the answers. Now that she had popped the cassette out of her Walkman, Beth Porter began to impress him as a fairly alert young woman.

Alert but, to use the old psychiatric rubric, "troubled." Enduring some difficult passage in her life. And tired of it, by the pinch of weariness that sometimes narrowed her eyes.

She was twenty years old, Matt thought, and seemed both much older and much younger.

He said, "If you need to talk—"

"Don't ask me to talk. I mean, thank you. I'll take the medicine or whatever. Whatever I have to do. But I don't want to talk about it."

A little bit of steel there.

He said, "All right. But remember to phone tomorrow. You'll probably have to come by for the prescription. And we'll need a follow-up when the medication runs out."

She understood. "Thank you, Dr. Wheeler."

He dated the entry in her file and tucked it into his "done" basket. Then he washed his hands and called in Lillian Bix, his last patient of the day.

▪   ▪   ▪

Lillian had skipped a period and thought she might be pregnant.

She was the thirty-nine-year-old wife of Matt's closest friend. The conversation was genial, rendered a little awkward by Lillian's tongue-numbing shyness. She came to the point at last; Matt gave her a sample cup and directed her to the bathroom. Lillian blushed profoundly but followed instructions. When she came back, he labeled the sample for an HCG.

Lillian sat opposite him with her small purse clutched in her lap. It often seemed to Matt that everything about Lillian was small: her purse, her figure, her presence in a room. Maybe that was why she took such pleasure in her marriage to Jim Bix, a large and boisterous man whose attention she had somehow commanded.

They had been childless for years, and Matt had never commented on it to either of them. Now—armored in medical whites—he asked Lillian whether that had been deliberate.

"More or less." She spoke with great concentration. "Well. More Jim's doing than mine. He always took care of . . . you know. Contraception."

"And you didn't object?"

"No."

"But contraception has been known to fail."

"Yes," Lillian said.

"How do you feel about the possibility of being pregnant?"

"Good." Her smile was genuine but not vigorous. "It's something I've thought about for a long time."

"Really thought about? Diapers, midnight feedings, skinned knees, stretch marks?"

"It's never real till it's real. I know, Matt. But yes, I've imagined it often."

"Talked to Jim about any of this?"

"Haven't even mentioned the possibility. I don't want to tell him until we're certain." She looked at Matt with a crease of concern above her small eyebrows. "*You* won't tell him, will you?"

He said, "I can't unless you want me to. Confidentiality."

"Confidentiality even between doctors?"

"Honor among thieves," Matt said.

She showed her brief smile again. It was there and gone. "But you have lunch with him all the time."

Jim was a pathologist at the hospital; they had done premed together. They liked to meet for lunch at the Chinese café two blocks up Grove. "It could make for an uncomfortable lunch, sure. But it's a quick test. We should have a verdict before very long." He pretended to make a note. "You know, Lillian, sometimes, in a woman who's a little bit older, there can be complications—"

"I know. I know all about that. But I've heard there are ways of finding certain things out. In advance."

He understood her anxiety and tried to soothe it. "If you're having a baby, we'll keep a close eye on everything. I wouldn't anticipate trouble." That wasn't all there was to it . . . but at the moment it was all Lillian needed to know.

"That's good," she said.

But her frown had crept back. She wasn't reassured, and she was far from happy. He wondered whether he ought to probe this discontent or leave it alone.

He put down his pen. "Something's bothering you."

"Well . . . three things, really." She tucked her handkerchief into her purse. "What we talked about. My age. That worries me. And Jim, of course. I wonder how he'll react. I'm afraid it might seem to him like . . . I don't know. Giving up his youth. He might not want the responsibility."

"He might not," Matt said. "But it would surprise me if he didn't adapt. Jim likes to shock people, but he comes into work every day. He's serious about his work and he shows up on time. That sounds like responsibility to me."

She nodded and seemed to draw some reassurance from the thought.

Matt said, "The third thing?"

"I'm sorry?"

"You said three things bothered you. Your age, and Jim, and—what?"

"Isn't it obvious?" She looked at him steadily across the desk. "Some nights I open the window . . . and I see that *thing* in the sky. And it frightens me. And now what they've put in the cities. Those big blocks or buildings or whatever they are. I see that on television. It doesn't make any kind of sense, Matt. What's the name of that shape? An 'octahedron.' A word you shouldn't have to use after you leave high school. An octahedron the size of an ocean liner sitting in Central Park. I can't turn on the TV without seeing that. And no one knows what it means. They talk about it and talk about it and none of the talk amounts to more than a whistle in the dark. So of course you wonder. I mean, what happens *next*? Maybe getting pregnant is just a kind of wishful thinking. Or a new way to panic." She sat with her purse nestled in her lap and looked fiercely at him. "You're a parent, Matt. You must know what I mean."

■   ■   ■

He did, of course. The same doubts were written in Beth Porter's withdrawal into her Walkman, in the way his daughter Rachel came home from school and watched the network newscasts with her knees pulled up to her chin.

He calmed Lillian Bix and sent her home, did a little tidying up while Anne finished with her own last patient. Then he opened the blinds and let the sunlight flood in, a long bright beam of it across the tiled floor, the oak cabinets. He peered out at the town.

From the seventh floor of the Marshall Building, Buchanan was a long flat smudgepot in a blue angle of ocean. Still a fairly quiet lumber port, not as small as it had been when he opened the practice fifteen years ago. Many changes since then. Fifteen years ago he'd been fresh out of residency. Rachel had been a toddler, Celeste had been alive, and the community of Buchanan had been smaller by several thousand souls.

Time, cruel son of a bitch, had revised all that. Now Matt's fortieth birthday was three months behind him, his daughter was looking at college brochures, Celeste was ten years in her grave at the Brookside Cemetery . . . and a spacecraft the color of cold concrete had been orbiting the earth for more than a year.

It occurred to Matt, also not for the first time, how much he hated that ugly Damoclean presence in the night sky.

How much he still loved this town. He believed he had always loved it, that he had been born loving it. It was funny how that worked. Some people have no sense of place at all; they can park at a Motel 6 and call it home. And some people, many of them his friends, had grown up hating the provincialism of Buchanan. But for Matt, Buchanan was a map of himself—as essential as his heart or his liver.

He had been a solitary, often lonely child, and he had learned the intimate secrets of the marina, the main street, and the Little Duncan River long before he acquired a best friend. He had folded this town, its potholed roads and Douglas firs, its foggy winters and the Gold Rush facades of its crumbling downtown, deep into the substance of himself.

His wife was buried here. Celeste had been committed to the earth at Brookside Cemetery, a stone's throw from the estuary of the Little Duncan, where the chapel rang its small carillon of bells every Sunday noon. His parents were buried here.

He had always believed that one day *he* would be buried here . . . but lately that conviction had begun to falter.

He had deposited flowers on Celeste's grave at Brookside just last week, and as he passed through the cemetery gates he was possessed of a dour conviction that some wind of destiny would sweep him elsewhere, that he would die in a very different place.

Like Lillian Bix—like everybody else—Matt had fallen prey to premonitions.

That ugly white ghost ship floating on the deep of every clear night.

Of course Lillian was scared. Who the hell *wasn't* scared?

But you go on, Matt Wheeler thought. You do what you do, and you go on. It was the decent thing.

▪ ▪ ▪

He heard Annie dismissing her last patient, and he was about to step into the hallway and offer his invitation when the phone rang: an after-hours call from Jim Bix that did nothing to dispel his uneasiness. "We need to talk," Jim said.

Matt's first thought was that this had something to do with Lillian's visit. He said, cautiously, "What's the problem?"

"I don't want to talk about it over the phone. Can you stop by the hospital after work?"

This wasn't about Lillian. Jim sounded too disturbed. Not having-a-baby disturbed. There was a darker note in his voice.

Matt checked his watch. "Rachel's home from school and she said she'd fix dinner tonight. Maybe we could have lunch tomorrow?"

"I'd prefer tonight." Pause. "I'm working shift hours, but how would it be if I stopped by on my way home?"

"How late?"

"Eleven, say. Eleven-thirty."

"It's important?"

"Yes."

Not *maybe* or *sort of,* Matt thought. Flat *yes.* It made the small hairs on his neck stand up.

"Well, yeah," he said. "I'll be looking for you."

"Good," Jim said, and promptly hung up the phone.

▪   ▪   ▪

He caught Annie as she headed out the door.

When he told her about the party Friday night, she smiled and said she'd be there. It was the familiar Annie Gates smile. She thanked him, touched his arm. He walked her to the parking lot.

By God, Matt thought, we may be on-again-off-again, but I do believe at the moment we are definitely on.

He was surprised by the pleasure he took from the thought.

She gave him a brief hug as she climbed into her Honda. The touch was therapeutic. It wasn't good to be alone, Matt thought, when the world had taken such a curious turn.

Chapter
2
Brookside

In December 1843, when the explorer John Fremont was mapping what would become the state of Oregon, he descended in a single day from a howling snowstorm in the high Cascades to a lake surrounded by soft green grass—from winter into summer. Winter Rim, he called his starting point, and Summer Lake, where his party pitched camp for the night.

A century and a half later, the state was still defined by its geography. The Willamette Valley, heartland and breadbasket, ran between the Cascades and the Coast Range for 180 miles south of Portland. East of the Cascades was a parched, cold desert. West of the Coast Range was coastal Oregon, 280 x 25 miles of farmland, forest land, and isolated fishing villages.

Buchanan was the largest of the coastal towns, a forest port situated on a broad, shallow bay. It had grown with the Dunsmuir Pulp and Paper Mill (est. 1895) to a population approaching 40,000 at the end of the twentieth century. Its shipping docks handled a respectable Pacific Rim trade, and its fishing fleet was the largest south of Astoria.

Buchanan had begun to cross the demarcation point between *town* and *city*, with all the possibilities and problems that implied: diversity, employment, anonymity, crime. But the municipality still held its Fishing and Logging Festival every July, and the local radio station still broadcast tide tables and Salmon Bulletins between sessions of softcore C&W.

Like every town on the Oregon coast, Buchanan was accustomed to rain. Each winter, the ocean seemed to infiltrate the air. There was not just rain, there was a complex palette of mist, drizzle, fog, woodsmoke, and low clouds. Winter was the slow season, the melancholy season.

But even Buchanan occasionally saw a blue sky, and this summer had been drier than most. Ever since Independence Day, the town had basked under a dome of clear Pacific air. Reservoirs were low and a fire watch had been declared in the deep coastal forests. Crickets ratcheted in the brown fingers of dry lawns.

Afternoons evolved into long summer evenings.

Matt Wheeler's thoughts had turned to Brookside Cemetery that afternoon, lingered a moment and turned away. Tonight he sat down to a meal of pan-fried steak and pondered a more immediate problem: that troublesome phone call from Jim Bix. Brookside had fled his attention.

It lingered in the minds of others.

Miriam Flett, for one.

Beth Porter and Joey Commoner, for two more.

■   ■   ■

SPEECH PROMISED ON SPACECRAFT

announced the headline in the *Buchanan Observer*.

Miriam Flett spread the front page across the kitchen table and attacked it with the pocket razor she had purchased this morning at Delisle's Stationery in the Ferry Park Mall.

Miriam appreciated these disposable pocket cutters, a tongue of stainless steel that slid in and out of a round plastic sheath as you touched a button on the side. They were 59¢ each in a bin on the counter at Delisle's, and they came in different colors. Miriam bought one every week. This week, she had chosen blue—a calming color.

The blade, not calming, was as bright and sharp as a claw.

Miriam attacked the newspaper. Four neat slashes separated SPEECH PROMISED from the lesser SHELLFISH POISONING SUSPECTED and LUMBER INDUSTRY FORESEES SLUMP.

She inspected the bottom-right corner of the article for a *continued p.* 6 or similar words—*continueds* were always annoying. But there was no such notice.

Good, Miriam thought. A good omen.

Miriam did not precisely understand the nature of the work she had undertaken, but she understood two things about it. One: It was important. And two: Neatness counts.

■   ■   ■

If Beth Porter and Joey Commoner had come roaring along Bellfountain Avenue on Joey's Yamaha motorcycle—but they didn't, not until later—they might have seen Miriam outlined in the window of her small bungalow, clipping newspapers as the sun eased down, a compact gray-haired shape hunched over a scarred kitchen table.

Miriam had lived all her fifty-six years in the town of Buchanan. For nearly half of those years she had presided over the reception desk in the principal's office at the James Buchanan Public School. Last year Miriam had been reprimanded for handing out religious tracts to the children waiting to be scolded by Principal Clay. Principal Clay (whose first name was Marion, and heaven help him if the truth behind "M. Jonathan Clay" ever escaped into the playground) had hinted to Miriam that early retirement might be a wise option. Miriam Flett didn't have to be told twice.

Once upon a time she might have held on to that job with both hands—gripped it until her fingernails tore free. Miriam was not fond of changes in her life. But she supposed the Miriam who couldn't tolerate time and change had died last year, when the Eye of God appeared in the sky.

The message in that advent had seemed quite clear.

Places change. People pass on. Love dies. The world becomes, in time, almost uninhabitably strange.

Faith abides.

She seldom attended church. It was Miriam's opinion that the local churches—even the Truth Baptist, which people thought of as a fundamentalist church—misrepresented the Bible. Miriam believed in God, but she did not have what the television evangelists called "a personal relationship" with Him. The very idea frightened her. The churches made much of redemption and forgiveness, but Miriam had read the Bible three times through without discovering much evidence in those pages of a loving God. Merciful—perhaps. On occasion. But Miriam believed most profoundly in the scary God of Abraham and Isaac, the God who demanded his sacrifices in flesh and blood; who swept aside humanity, when humanity displeased Him, the way a farmer might spray his crops with Malathion to eradicate a persistent infestation of beetles.

These thoughts were vaguely on her mind as Miriam directed her eyes to the clipping before her.

The White House announced today that the President would address the nation amidst growing rumors of a new breakthrough in communication with the so-called alien spacecraft orbiting the Earth.

Similar announcements have been made by the leaders of several major powers, including President Yudenich of the Russian Republic and Prime Minister Walker of Britain.

These announcements have led to accusations of a high-level conspiracy to conceal information. In a speech to Congress, Republican Whip Robert Mayhew accused the President of—

But Miriam sighed and pushed the scrap of paper away. Tonight she seemed to have no relish for the news, particularly political news. She settled her bifocals on the table and rubbed her eyes.

The kitchen table had been much eroded by Miriam's work. Over the course of a year, her cutter blades—bearing down a little too hard on this clipping or that—had stripped away slivers of Formica. The table had come to look like a butcher block, and Miriam regretted it. The kitchen, otherwise, was quite tidy. She had always believed in a tidy kitchen.

She picked up her eyeglasses and pulled her scrapbook closer.

This was the current volume, Volume Ten. The other nine were stacked on a hutch beside the table. The upper shelf held spice bottles and cookbooks; the lower shelf, her work.

It was not long after she left the school board's employ—shortly after the Eye of God appeared—that Miriam began to understand that she was quite alone in the world: friendless in Buchanan, considered an eccentric even by the churches. Of her family, only her father had remained alive—and that barely. He had been living in the Mount Bailiwick Care Community, incontinent and incoherent, but Miriam had visited him every day, had talked to him even when his pupils dilated with foggy disinterest. She told him about her project.

"I've started clipping the papers," she said, and watched him carefully for some tic of surprise or discouragement. There was none. Unshaven, he sat in bed and looked at Miriam with the same passive stare he directed at the TV set as soon as Miriam left the room, or before she arrived.

Emboldened, she went on. "I think it's what I'm *supposed* to do. I can't explain how I know that. I don't suppose anybody told me to do it. But I will take all the newspaper writing about the Eye of God and I'll put those clippings in a book. And at the end of all this it will remind someone what happened. I don't know what the end will be, or who will need to be reminded. But that's what I'll do."

In the old days, Daddy would have had some answer. He used to have quite a lot to say about Miriam's projects, almost always disparaging. Miriam had never quite lived up to Daddy's expectations.

Since the stroke, however, Daddy had had no expectations whatsoever. Miriam could say and do what she wished—even in this room.

She had wished to quit her job when Principal Clay accused her of fanaticism. She had done so. She had wished to keep a scrapbook. So Miriam had done so.

She pulled down Volume One from the shelf. It was little more than a year old, but the newsprint inside had already begun to turn brittle and yellow.

All these clippings were from the *Observer,* mostly labeled UPI or Reuters. Miriam could have had more clippings if she'd taken a Portland paper or gone down to Duffy's for *The New York Times.* But the point of the exercise wasn't *more.* The point was *enough.*

NASA MYSTIFIED BY OBJECT IN SKY

Her first and fondly remembered. Miriam turned a page.

NOT NECESSARILY HOSTILE SAYS U.N. COMMITTEE

FEAR SWEEPS WORLD

MOBS TOPPLE GOVERNMENTS IN JORDAN, ANGOLA

Miriam turned a whole sheaf of pages.

NEW YORK CITY RESCINDS CURFEW; PANIC
HAS SUBSIDED SAYS MAYOR

Such a sweep of history enclosed in these books! She skipped ahead to Volume Three. By Volume Three, the screaming headlines were more sparse. Many of the clippings were from the Features section. So-called opinion pieces. In Miriam's opinion, worthless. But she had collated them faithfully.

LIFE IN UNIVERSE INEVITABLE: SAGAN

Astronomer and popular writer Carl Sagan argues that the events of the past six months were "inevitable, in one form or another, given over-whelming odds that life has evolved elsewhere in the galaxy. We ought to be grateful that this has happened in our lifetime."

Sagan does not see the artifact as a threat. "It's true that no attempt at communication has been made. But recall that any journey between stars must take an immensely long time. The entities responsible must be capable of exercising an enormous patience. We should try to do the same."

But Miriam recognized that song: it was a lullaby, whistled in the dark. Clipping the *Observer,* Miriam had grown tired of Sagan and all the other pundits to whom the media had so eagerly flocked. In the end, they were as plainly ignorant as everyone else. And as plainly misguided.

It is an Eye, Miriam thought, and was there any question just Who was peering through it? And an Eye must have a Hand: of Judgment.

Volume Six.

April and May of this year. A very fat volume indeed.

ALIEN ARTIFACTS IN MAJOR CITIES

But the photographs told the tale best. Here was a telescopic view of the so-called Artifact, starry dots emerging from it like so much confetti or winter snow, a snow of some two hundred flakes dispersed equivalently across the world. Then, in the later pictures, not flakes of snow any longer but faceted obsidian structures hanging above all the world's proud hives—New York, Los Angeles, London; and Moscow, and Mexico City, and Amsterdam; and Johannesburg and Baghdad and Jerusalem and too many others, all marked on a newsprint map of the world dated April 16. Grim octahedral slabs. Inhumanly perfect. They did not fly, veer, dash, dart, or glide; simply fell through the atmosphere like so many precisely aimed bubbles. They landed with the gentility of butterflies in available open spaces, and when they had landed they did not move. No visitors emerged. Having arrived, the octahedrons did nothing more spectacular than cast their own immense shadows.

Miriam supposed Mr. Sagan was continuing to advise patience.

It was not the Eye but these several Fingers of God that seemed to have worked an effect on the people of Buchanan. Miriam knew people had begun to take the Eye for granted, as people will take anything for granted if it stands still long enough. But the Fingers were a message. They said: *Yes, I've come for a purpose. No, I'm not finished with you. And: I move slowly but inexorably and you may not lift a hand against me.* It was a truth that penetrated the idiotic cheerfulness of her neighbors, a truth that bent the backs of the proud and softened the voices of the mighty. The town of Buchanan seemed to acknowledge at last that this was the Endtime, or something like it—that nothing predictable would happen anymore.

Miriam opened Volume Ten to the first blank page and installed SPEECH PROMISED ON SPACECRAFT with a few dabs of her Glu-Stik, also from Delisle's.

She hoped this was the only clipping from the *Observer* tonight. Miriam was tired. She had shopped for the week's groceries today and felt worn out, maybe even a little feverish. Light-headed. The check-out girl at Delisle's had sneezed three times into her hankie as Miriam was purchasing her cutter blade today. Miriam had paid with a one-dollar bill and hoped she hadn't been handed a case of influenza along with her change. What were they calling it? Taiwan Flu? That was all she needed . . . what with the difficult times ahead of her.

But Miriam was dutiful and didn't go directly to bed. Instead she turned the pages of the *Observer* and frowned through her bifocals at every article. There was nothing more for her collation in the first section. She observed with pleasure that Perdy's, the big department store at the Ferry Park Mall, had stopped running their NEW MOON MADNESS sale ads with that ridiculous drawing of the Eye of God beaming at a Kenmore washing machine. Maybe Perdy's advertising department had been talked out of this sacrilege. Or maybe they were just nervous—like everybody else.

Skimming Section Two, the only other section the *Observer* possessed, Miriam was startled by something she had *not* expected:

It was her father's obituary.

Silly to be surprised. She had arranged for it herself. Daddy had been a respected instructor in lathe mechanics at the community college and Miriam thought his passing deserved notice in the *Observer*.

But the impending publication of the obituary, like so many of the other occasions and observances surrounding his death, had slipped from Miriam's mind like a dew drop falling from a leaf.

Seeing the notice brought it all back. She had marked appointments on her calendar: a meeting Saturday with Rev. Ackroyd to arrange details of the memorial service. A check to the funeral director at Brookside. Notices to Daddy's friends and colleagues, of whom only a handful were still living.

He had died Monday night in his sleep. The doctor at Mount Bailiwick said Daddy's heart had simply stopped, like a weary soldier surrendering the flag. But she had not witnessed the death and still couldn't encompass the simple fact of his absence.

There would be no more painful, wordless visits to his room. No more of the awful suspicion that his body had been vacant since the stroke—that he had been replaced by some respirating automaton.

But no more Daddy calling her name, either: not even the hope of it ever again. No smell of shaving soap and the razor white of starched collars.

No more his *Try to do better today, Miriam*, as she trudged out the door to school, woman and child.

Since the stroke, Daddy had been a ghost in a hospital bed. In death, he had evolved. When the man at Mount Bailiwick called to tell her Daddy died, Miriam had been startled by an involuntary memory of *places*: the house on Cameron Avenue where they had lived so many years, her room in it, her bedspread and her books, the way the lace curtains moved and sighed when she opened the windows on summer nights.

Things she had not thought about for thirty years.

In death, Daddy had entered into the world of all those lost things.

Sorely missed by his daughter Miriam, said the obituary. But that was only half a truth. All the unfulfilled expectations that had dogged her even in his hospital room—all those were gone, too. She had mourned him with tears the night he died . . . but mourned him also with secret relief and a childish, hidden glee.

She kept these feelings to herself, of course.

But the Eye—of course—could See.

■   ■   ■

She put the eviscerated newspaper in a pile to be bundled for the garbage. She filed Volume Ten in its place on the shelf.

She made a cup of tea. The sun was well down now. The sky was a transparent inky blue, the Eye already peeking through the big back window.

Miriam pulled the drapes.

She turned on the television and watched the ten o'clock news show, a Portland program on cable. But the anchors, a man and a woman, looked like children to her. Children playing dress-up. Where were the adults? Dead, probably.

She touched her forehead with the back of her hand.

I really am feverish, Miriam thought. *At least a little.*

She turned out the lights, checked the lock on the front door, and retired to bed.

She was asleep as soon as she pulled the quilt around her shoulders.

She stirred only once—after midnight, when Joey Commoner's motorcycle sped past the house, the sound of Beth Porter's laughter mingling with the roar of the engine.

Miriam turned once restlessly and went back to sleep as the noise faded. But her sleep was not dreamless.

She dreamed of Brookside Cemetery.

■   ■   ■

At sunset, as Miriam Flett was gazing absently into the many volumes of her Work, Beth Porter stood at the south end of the parking lot of the Ferry Park Mall wiping her nose and waiting for Joey Commoner to show up.

She wondered whether she ought to be here at all. She felt hot and stupid in her leather jacket. She probably should be home lying down. She was sick, after all. Dr. Wheeler had said so.

The parking lot was empty—a lonely vastness in the last blue daylight.

The air was still hot, but the sky had a deep and vacant look, and by midnight there would be a cool wind running in from the sea.

Beth checked her watch. He was late, of course. Joey Commoner! she thought. You asshole! *Be* here.

But she still didn't know what to do when he came.

Tell him to fuck off?

Maybe.

Go with him?

Maybe.

To Brookside? In the dark, with a motorcycle and this can of spray paint she had bought for no better reason than because he told her to?

Well . . . well, *maybe*.

▪   ▪   ▪

Ten minutes later, she recognized his bike making a noisy exit from the highway.

He zoomed across the parking lot driving gleeful S-curves, leaning with the motorcycle until it looked like his elbows would scrape the blacktop.

He wore a black helmet and a black T-shirt. The shirt was from Larry's Gifts and Novelties on Marina, downtown. Larry's had been what used to be called a head shop until they took away all the drug paraphernalia a few years ago. No more waterpipes, no more grow-your-own manuals. Now Larry's specialized in leather pants, T-shirts illustrated with the gaudy iconography of heavy metal bands, and a few brass belt buckles in the shape of marijuana leaves.

Joey Commoner's T-shirt showed a neon-blue screaming skull on a bed of blood-red roses. Beth couldn't remember which band it was supposed to represent. She wasn't into heavy metal or the Dead. Neither was Joey, really. She was willing to bet he'd chosen this shirt because he liked the picture. It was the kind of picture Joey would like.

He came to a stop a yard away with the engine roaring and bucking. What struck Beth as really bizarre was the combination of that shirt and his helmet. The helmet was gloss black and the visor was mirrored. It made him look utterly insectile. For lack of a face to focus on, your attention strayed to the shirt. To the skull.

Then he pried the helmet off his head and Beth relaxed. Just Joey. His long blond hair was matted by the helmet, but it came free in a gust of wind and trailed around his shoulders. He was nineteen years old, but his face looked younger. He had round cheeks and a lingering case of adolescent acne. Joey would have loved to look dangerous, Beth thought, but nature hadn't cooperated. Nature had conspired to make Joey's anger look like petulance and his hostility resemble a pout.

He stood with his bike between his legs and the setting sun behind him, waiting for her to say something.

Beth discovered her heart was beating hard. She felt as if she'd had too much coffee. Light-headed. Nervous.

The silence stretched until Joey took the initiative. "You sounded pissed off on the phone."

Beth summoned all the blistering accusations she had rehearsed since she left Dr. Wheeler's office. Eloquence fled. She struck to the heart of the matter. "You gave me the clap, you asshole!"

Incredibly, he smiled. "No shit?"

"Yeah, no shit, you made me sick, no shit!"

He stood there absorbing the information with his lip still curled in that faintly insolent smile. "You know, I wondered . . ."

"You *wondered?*"

"Well, it kind of hurts. . . ."

"*What* hurts?"

He was beginning to sound like a twelve-year-old. "When I pee."

Beth rolled her eyes. He was hopeless, he was really completely hopeless. *It hurts when I pee.* Well, damn! Was she supposed to feel *sorry* for him?

"So who have you been screwing, Joey?"

He looked faintly hurt. "Nobody!"

"Nobody? You don't get the clap from nobody."

He thought about it. "Last year," he said. "My cousin took me to a place. In Tacoma."

"A place? What, a whorehouse?"

"I guess."

"A whorehouse in Tacoma?"

"Yeah, I guess. Do we have to talk about this?"

She felt she could only repeat these verbal impossibilities he was pronouncing. She nearly said, "Do we have to *talk* about this?" Instead she gathered what was left of her composure. "Joey, you screwed a prostitute in Tacoma and gave me gonorrhea. I'm not happy."

"It was before I met you," he said. He added—grudgingly, Beth thought—"I'm sorry."

"Sorry doesn't pay for the antibiotics." She looked away. "It's degrading."

"I'm sorry. All right? What am I supposed to say? I'm sorry." He pushed forward on the Yamaha's seat. "Climb on."

No, she wanted to tell him. It's not that easy. Not just *I'm sorry. Climb on.* You can't get away with that.

But maybe it *was* that easy, and maybe he *could* get away with it.

She felt something shift inside herself, the tumbling of a weight in the hollow of her stomach.

"You got the paint?" Joey asked.

She was condemned by the weight of the bag in her hand. She held it up to show him.

"Good." He stepped on the starter until the motor caught and screamed. He lowered his helmet over his head. There was a second helmet strapped to the bike; Beth put it over her head and tucked her hair underneath.

Climbing onto the bike, she felt a sudden burst of something she realized was joy . . . the mysterious, dizzying pleasure of doing something she knew was wrong. Making a serious mistake, making it *deliberately.*

"Hurry up." Joey's voice was muffled by his visor and the roar of the bike. "Almost dark."

She put the motorcycle between her legs and her arms around the bone and sinew of his hips.

■ ■ ■

He smelled like leather and grease and sweat and wind.

Beth remembered schoolgirl gab sessions, steamy telephone conversations, the inevitable question: *But do you love him?* The same question rattled in her head now, high-pitched and girlish and embarrassing. *But do you love him, do you love him, do you love him?*

Her first instinct was that the whole idea was ridiculous, even offensive. Love Joey Commoner? The words didn't connect. It seemed to Beth that he was an inherently unlovable object, like . . . oh, a garter snake, for instance, or a bait shop, or a can of motor oil. Something only a grubby little boy could approach with affection.

But that was not the whole answer. If the question had truly been asked, Beth's truest answer would have been something like: *Yes, I do love him . . . but only sometimes, and I don't know why.*

She had met him last year during her first month at the 7-Eleven up the highway. Beth had divided the clientele into five basic types: little kids, high-schoolers, suburban family types, bikers, and "Pickup Petes"—the guys who drove pickup trucks with strange accouterments, roll bars or banks of what looked like kleig lights, and who wore those duckbill caps day and night. Joey didn't fit any of these categories, not even "biker." He didn't ride a muscle bike and he didn't travel with the bike crowd. He always came alone. He shopped for snack food: quarts of ice cream and frozen pies, usually, and almost always on a Friday night. She learned to expect him.

One Friday he got into an argument with a Pickup Pete who had parked his rig practically on top of Joey's Yamaha. No damage had been done to anything but Joey's sense of dignity and proportion, but Joey called the guy a "cross-eyed asshole" and spat out the words with such acidic clarity that Beth was able to hear him quite clearly through the window glass next to the checkout counter. The pickup guy's response was inaudible but obviously obscene.

She had watched with startled interest as Joey hurled himself at the man, who must have been twice his age and nearly twice his weight. Suicide, she thought. He's fucking crazy. But the boy moved like a whirlwind.

By the time she remembered to ring for the night manager, the fight was over.

Joey, needless to say, had lost.

When she went off-shift at midnight, he was still sitting on the cracked sidewalk outside. His upper lip was split and dripping blood onto the dusty concrete. In the green-and-white glare of the illuminated 7-Eleven sign, the spatters of blood looked both ghastly and unreal—like alien blood.

She could not say why she stopped and spoke to him. It had seemed like a bad idea even at the time.

But, like many bad ideas, it had a powerful momentum of its own. Her feet paused and her mouth opened. "No ice cream tonight, huh?"

He looked up sullenly. "You saw that guy?"

She nodded.

"He was fat," Joey said with a shudder of distaste. She learned later that this was one of Joey's pet horrors: he was disgusted by fat people.

"Yeah," Beth said, "he was." She remembered the guy as a steady customer—remembered the distinctive way his jeans sagged below the cleavage of his rump. "Gross," she contributed.

Joey's look turned to cautious gratitude.

Later, Beth would realize that she had seen both sides of Joey Commoner that night. Joey the authentically dangerous: Joey who had called that impressive wall of flesh "a cross-eyed asshole" and leapt at him like a crazed monkey attacking a rhino. Joey had been all fingernails and spit and bony knees and her first fear had been for the bigger man.

And Joey the vulnerable, Joey the little boy. Joey bleeding on the sidewalk.

She wanted to mother him and she wanted to offer herself to him. The combination of impulses made her feel like the sidewalk was spinning.

"How about a ride home," she said.

"What?"

"Ride me home and I'll fix up those cuts for you. I have Band-Aids and things. My name is Beth Porter."

He climbed onto his motorcycle. "I know. I've heard of you."

Well, Beth thought, that fucks *that* up.

Same story all over again. She was inured to it; nevertheless it hurt. But he scooted forward. "Climb on," he said.

She didn't hesitate and she concealed her surprise. She climbed on and felt the leather seat press up between her legs.

"Joey Commoner," he said.

"Hi, Joey."

Zoom.

■ ■ ■

Tonight he took her south along the highway and across the bridge that spanned the Little Duncan River. He turned off the highway and circled back through a raw development of frame houses to the river's edge. Beth hopped off the bike. Joey cut the motor and wheeled the vehicle down the embankment behind the concrete pilings of the bridge.

The air was quiet here. Beth listened as the crickets resumed their creaking along the riverside.

The Little Duncan followed this stony bed to the sea. South across an open field, beyond the hydroelectric towers, the lights of the houses looked too far to reach—the last margin of civilization. North beyond the river was only weeds and the greasy back lots of businesses fronting on the highway. East: the Duncan River cutting back into the foothills of Mt. Buchanan. West: the cemetery.

Joey knew what most high school graduates in the south end of Buchanan knew, that if you followed the Little Duncan beyond this rockfall and through the duckweed flats, you could sneak into Brookside Cemetery after the main gates were locked.

Joey took the can of cherry-red aerosol spray paint out of the bag. He balled up the bag and threw it into the moonlit flow of the creek. He tucked the can under his belt, to keep his hands free.

Beth followed him along the riverbank. She understood Joey well enough to know that talking was over: there would be no talking now, only motion.

She had the idea that Joey was a reservoir of motions, that he did much of his thinking with his body. She had to work to stay close to him as he scrambled among the weeds and rocks up to the grassy margin of the cemetery. He moved with a feverish agility. If his motions were ideas, Beth thought, they would be strange ones—deft, delirious, and unexpected.

Maybe they would be dreams. The night had begun to seem dreamlike even to Beth. The Artifact had risen in the sky like a big backward moon. It looked faintly yellow tonight, a harvest-moon color. Beth was as frightened of the Artifact as everybody else, but she took from it, too, a curious exaltation. Hanging in the sky above her, casting its light across the trim grass and gravestones, the Artifact was a refutation of all things safe and secure. People lived their stupid lives in their stupid houses, Beth thought, but this new moon had come to remind them that they lived on the edge of an abyss. It restored vertigo to everyday life. That was why people hated it.

Joey had gotten ahead of her. He moved in the shadows of the trees, uphill to the three stone mausoleums where Buchanan's best families had once interred their dead. Too good for burial, the bodies had been enclosed in these stone boxes. To Beth it seemed doubly macabre. She had stood once on a hot spring afternoon and peered through the small barred opening into the darkness inside one of these tombs, a garage-sized building inscribed with the name of the JORGENSON family. The mausoleum had been frigid with undisturbed winter air. She felt it on her face like a breath. It must be winter in there always, she thought. And backed away with a shuddery, instinctive reverence.

It was a reverence Joey obviously didn't share. He raised the can of cherry-red spray paint to the wall of the building and began to work the nozzle.

He worked fast. Beth stood back and watched. He covered the east exterior wall of the mausoleum with a motley collection of words and symbols like a machine printing some indecipherable code. The symbols were commonplace but Joey made them his own: swastikas, skulls, Stars of David, crosses, ankhs, peace symbols. She couldn't guess what they meant to him. Maybe nothing. It was an act of pure defilement, empty of meaning. The hiss of the spray can sounded like leaves tossing in the night wind.

He turned to the gravestones then, moving along the hillside so fast that Beth had to run to keep up. He made red Xs across the engraved names and dates. Now and then he would pause long enough to make a skull or a question mark. In the light of the Artifact, the red paint looked darker— brown or black on these chill white slabs.

It must be like sex for him, Beth thought. This frantic motion. This ejaculation of paint.

It was a funny thought but truer than she realized. When the can was empty Joey threw it at the sky—at the Artifact, maybe. The can looped high up and came down noiselessly among the graves. Beth approached him, and as he turned she saw the outline of his erection pressing against his jeans. She felt a shiver that was both attraction and revulsion.

He pushed her down—she let herself tumble—into the high grass at the edge of the woods. It was late, they were alone, and the air was full of scary electricity. A cool wind came in from the ocean with the battery odor of midnight and salt. She let him pull up her skirt. He was like a shape above her, something out of the sky. She lifted up for him as he tugged her underpants away. He breathed in curt, hard gasps. His penis was as hard and as chilly as the night. It hurt for a minute. And then didn't.

▪   ▪   ▪

Was this what she wanted from him? Was this why she had adopted Joey Commoner the way an alcoholic adopts the bottle?

No, not just this. Not just this push and shove and brief oblivion and sticky aftermath.

Joey was dangerous.

She wanted him—not *in spite* of that—but *because* of it.

This was a bad and troubling thought, allowable only in the neutral calm that came after fucking.

He pulled his pants up and sat beside her. Suddenly embarrassed by her own nakedness, Beth smoothed her skirt. Fucking in a graveyard, she thought. Christ.

She followed Joey's gaze out across the night. From this hill she could see the lights of downtown Buchanan and the night shimmer of the sea.

"Someday we'll do something big," Joey said.

Joey often made this ponderous statement. Beth knew what he meant by it. Something *really* dangerous. Something *really* bad.

He put his arm around her. "You and me," he said.

He's like some kind of wild animal, Beth thought. A wild horse maybe. A wild horse you befriended and who lets you ride him. Ride him at night. To some wild place. To the edge of a cliff. She closed her eyes and saw it. Saw herself riding Joey the wild horse to the brink of a limestone butte. Long drop to the desert floor. Some starry night like this. Just Beth and her wild horse and that soaring emptiness.

And she spurs him with her heels.

And he jumps.

▪   ▪   ▪

Later they saw the lights of the little golf cart the security guard rode through Brookside every night, and they ran down the hill and across the graves to the duckweeds and into the dark ravine where the river flowed. Beth imagined she could hear the guard's hoots of surprise as he discovered the vandalism, but that was probably her imagination. Still, the idea was funny; she laughed.

Joey sped away past these houses full of sleeping people, wending a crooked path down Buchanan's side streets . . . past the house of Miriam Flett, who turned in her bed at the sound of a motor and Beth Porter's wild laugh, and thought in her sleep of how strange the town had lately become.

Chapter
3
Machines

Jim Bix was ugly the way President Lincoln was said to have been ugly: profoundly, distinctively.

His face was long and pockmarked. His eyes, when he focused the full beam of his considerable powers of attention, resembled poached eggs cradled in cups of bone and skin. He wore a brush cut that emphasized his ears, which stood out not merely like jug handles—the image that sprang to mind—but like the handles on a kindergartener's clay jug, or the discarded work of a tremulous potter.

It was also a face transparent to emotion. When Jim Bix smiled, you wanted to smile along with him. When he grinned, you wanted to laugh. He was conscious of his own guilelessness, Matt knew, and oddly ashamed of it. He avoided poker games. He told lies seldom and never successfully. Matt had once witnessed Jim Bix attempting a lie: He told Lillian he had broken one of her Hummel figurines, protecting the guilty party, the family dog, whom Lillian despised. The lie had been so incoherent, so patently manufactured, and so blindingly obvious that everyone present had laughed—including Lillian but excepting Jim himself, who blushed and clenched his teeth.

Jim Bix, in other words, was a nearly unimpeachable witness. Matt kept that in mind as he listened to what his friend had to say. From anyone else, it would have been unbelievable. Absurd. From Jim . . .

Belief, that cautious juror, withheld a verdict.

● ● ●

Matt opened the door a quarter of an hour before midnight that August evening and welcomed in this ugly and obvious man, his friend, who was also one of the best and most scrupulous pathologists Matt had encountered. Jim accepted Matt's offer of coffee and settled leadenly into the living room sofa. He was 6'3" from toe to crewcut, and he dominated any room he inhabited, but tonight, Matt thought, he looked smaller—a sag had crept into his shoulders, and his frown hung on his face like a weight. He took the coffee wordlessly and cradled the cup in his hands.

Matt interpreted all this as fatigue. Early in the year, Buchanan General had been certified as a regional trauma center. This was good news for the administration; it meant prestige and more reliable funding. Among staff, the reaction was mixed. They were handed a wish-list of technological goodies—respirators, bronchoscopes, a new pediatric ICU. But they also inherited a number of difficult cases that would ordinarily have been transferred to Portland. For Pathology, it had meant a huge new work load without the prospect of additional staff. Jim had been working evenings for most of two months now. Of course he was tired.

Rachel had gone to bed, and the house, with its curtains drawn against the dark, seemed uneasy in its own silence. Jim cleared his throat. Matt said, "How is Lillian?"—disguising the fact that he'd seen her this afternoon.

"Seems fine," Jim said. "Kind of quiet." He ran a large hand through his stubble hair. "We don't see much of you and Annie lately."

"Lousy hours. Yours and mine. I hope you can make it on Friday."

"Friday?"

"Friday night. A little get-together. I called about it last week."

"Yeah, of course. I'm sorry, Matt. Yeah, we'll try to be here."

Matt said, "You look punch-drunk." No argument. "Is it that serious?"

A nod.

"Then you better tell me about it. And drink your damn coffee before it gets cold."

"Something's fucked up at the hospital," Jim said, "and nobody wants to listen to me."

▪   ▪   ▪

It had all happened, he said, very quickly.

It started earlier in the week. He took a couple of complaints from the staff doctors that hematology results were coming back funny. Standard tests: Smack 24s, red counts, white counts. Patients with borderline anemia were showing radically low hemoglobin totals, for instance.

New blood was drawn, new tests ordered, and he promised to oversee the results personally.

"Everything was kosher. I made sure of it. But the results . . . were *worse*."

Matt said, "Significantly worse?"

"I couldn't go to staff with these numbers. What was I supposed to say? I'm sorry, Doctor, but according to the lab your patient is dead. When the patient is actually sitting in the dayroom watching *Days of Our Lives*. And the bad thing is, it's not just a few samples now—now *everything* is coming up fucked. Hematology, hemostasis, immune response, blood typing. Suddenly we can't run *any* kind of blood assay without getting completely Martian numbers out of it."

"A lab problem," Matt said.

"Can you think of any kind of problem that would screw up *all* these results? Neither could I. But I thought about it. I talked to the chief resident, and he agreed we should farm out the most urgent tests to other labs until we track down the problem. Okay, we do that. This was a couple of days ago. We start looking at everything. Some weird contamination coming through the air ducts. Bad sterilization. Voltage spikes on the A.C. lines. We clean it all up. We try some basic tests on a sample of whole blood from the freezer. And everything comes out within reasonable limits."

"So far so good."

"Exactly. But I'm not entirely convinced. So we draw some *fresh* blood from a *healthy* donor, and we put it through the cell counts, hemoglobin counts, reticulocyte counts—plasma fibrinogen, platelet counts, one-stage assays—"

"And it comes up fucked," Matt guessed.

"It not only comes up fucked," Jim said, "it comes up so *completely* fucked that we might as well have been running tests on a glass of tepid well water."

■   ■   ■

Matt felt a touch of fear, as tentative as a cold hand stroking the back of his neck.

If there was some new pathology out there, and if it was common enough to be manifesting in all of Jim's blood samples . . . but why hadn't anyone else seen it? "What about the tests you farmed out?"

"They're not back. We phone the private labs. They're sorry, but the results don't seem quite . . . plausible. They want to know if the samples were damaged in some way, maybe contaminated in transit. Meanwhile, the chief resident gets a call from the hospital in Astoria. Are we having blood-count problems? Because they are. And so is Portland."

"Jesus," Matt said.

"That's the situation this morning. Everybody's going crazy, of course. Phone lines to the CDC are jammed. This afternoon, I take some fresh blood and I put it under a microscope. Has anything changed? Well, yeah. Suddenly there's foreign bodies there. Like nothing I've ever seen before."

Matt put aside his coffee cup, which had grown cold in his hands. "Foreign bodies? What—viral bodies? Bacteria?"

"On a slide they look kind of like platelets. Roughly that dimension."

"You're sure you're *not* looking at platelets? Maybe deformed in some way?"

"I'm not that stupid. They don't aggregate. They stain differently—"

"I'm not questioning your competence."

"Fuck, go ahead. I would, in your place. The weird thing is that these organisms *weren't there the day before*. I mean, do they reproduce that fast? Or what, were they *hiding*?"

"It's just so bizarre. If you were looking at blood from patients with a common pathology, okay, but—the patients are healthy?"

"Far as I can tell, the condition is not making anyone particularly sick."

"How could it not? White counts are low?"

"White counts are *missing*."

"This is ludicrous."

"Obviously! I know that! I've been reminded of it at great length. If you want me to make sense of it for you, I can't."

"But it's harmless?"

"I'm not saying that. I'm not saying that at all. It's an ongoing situation. It scares the shit out of me, actually. You know what I notice? Everybody I run into seems to have a case of the sniffles. You see that in your work, Matt? Nothing serious. But everybody, every individual. Walk into a crowded room and count the Kleenex. Check out a drugstore. Big run on OTC decongestants. My pharmacist says he can't keep aspirin in stock. Is this a coincidence?"

Matt said, "Well, Christ—I've got a bottle of Dristan half-empty in the bathroom cupboard."

"Uh-huh," Jim said. "Me too."

Annie had been sniffling at work. And Lillian, come to that. Beth Porter.

And Rachel. My God, he thought. Rachel.

■　■　■

The two men looked at each other in the sudden silence of shared fears. Matt said, "What do you want?"

"I just want to talk. Everybody I talk to at the hospital, everybody on staff—either they want a quick fix or they just don't want to know, period. And I want us to drink. Not this fucking coffee, either."

"I'll break out a bottle," Matt said.

"Thank you." Jim seemed to relax minutely. "You know why I *really* came here?"

"Why?"

"Because there are very few sane people on this planet. And you happen to be one of them."

"You got a head start drinking?"

"I mean it. I always thought that about you. Matt Wheeler, one sane individual. Never said it. Why wait?"

Why wait? This was more of an admission than he might have intended. Matt did not pause on his way to the liquor cabinet, but he asked, as casually as he could manage, "You think we're all dying?"

"It's a possibility," Jim Bix said.

■   ■   ■

They talked it through several rounds of drinks, covering the same territory, deciding nothing, speculating, probing, perhaps, the limits of each other's credulity. It was Jim, drunk and tired, who first used the word "machines."

Matt thought he'd misunderstood. "Machines?"

"You've heard of nanotechnology? They move around atoms, make little gears and levers and things? They can do that now."

"You have some reason to think that's what you're looking at?"

"Who knows? It doesn't look like a machine, but it doesn't look like a cell, either. Looks kind of like a spiky black ball bearing. There's no nucleus, no mitochondria, no internal structure I can look at with the equipment at the hospital. I wonder what a good research lab would find if they took one apart." He showed a thin smile. "Gears and levers. Betcha. Or little computers. Little subatomic integrated circuits. Running algorithms on nucleotides. Or something we can't even see. Circuits smaller than the orbit of an electron. Machines made out of neutrinos. Held together with gluons."

He grinned, not a happy expression. Matt said, "Sounds like Jack Daniel's talking."

"Two advantages to getting drunk. You can say ridiculous things. And you can say the obvious thing."

"What's the obvious thing?"

"That this is not entirely unconnected with that fucking unnatural object in the sky."

Maybe, Matt thought. But he had heard everything from hot weather to diaper rash blamed on the Artifact, and he was wary of that line of thinking. "There's no evidence . . ."

"I know what organic disease looks like. This is something altogether else. This didn't happen over the course of a month, Matt. We're talking about days. Practically hours. Bacteria can reproduce that quickly. But if these were bacteria they would have killed us all by now."

But if that were true— "No," he said. "Uh-uh. I don't want to think about that."

"You and the rest of the world."

"I mean it. It's too frightening." He looked into his glass, vaguely ashamed. "I accept what you're telling me. But if it's somehow connected with the Artifact—if these things are already *inside us*—then it's game over, isn't it? Whatever they want—it's theirs. We're helpless."

There was a silence. Then Jim put his glass on the side table and sat up. "I'm sorry, Matt. I did a shitty thing. I came here and dumped my problems in your lap. Not fair."

"I'd rather be scared than ignorant." But it was late. They had gone beyond productive conversation. Matt was afraid to check his watch; he had office hours to keep in the morning. Plague or no plague. "I need to sleep."

"I can let myself out."

"You can sleep on the sofa, you asshole. Is Lillian waiting up?"

"I told her I might spend the night at the office."

"Spend some time with her tomorrow."

Jim nodded.

Matt gave him a blanket from the closet in the hall. "We're in some pretty deep shit here, aren't we?"

"Pretty deep." Jim stretched out on the sofa. He put his glasses on the table and closed his eyes. His unhandsome face looked pale. "Matt—?"

"Hm?"

"The blood I took? The fresh sample? The blood I looked at under the microscope?"

"What about it?"

"It was mine."

∎   ∎   ∎

Matt allowed his alarm clock to wake him—savoring a long moment of twilight sleep, when the things Jim had told him were still submerged, a presence felt but not explicit. Then woke to a raw headache and terrible knowledge.

It was a fine, sunlit morning. He forced himself through a shower and put on clothes that felt like 100-grit sandpaper. Rachel was in the kitchen fixing breakfast. Fried eggs. Matt looked at his plate. Only looked.

"Are you sick?" his daughter asked.

"No." Unless we all are.

She sniffled. "Dr. Bix is asleep on the sofa."

"He's not due at the hospital until noon. We should let him sleep. He needs it."

She shot him a quizzical look but let the subject rest.

Rachel believed in the power of a home-cooked breakfast, and she insisted on cooking it herself. The pattern had been established during Celeste's illness and continued after her death, when Matt had been inclined to leave breakfast and dinner in the hands of McDonald's and Pizza Hut, respectively. Matt had supposed it was Rachel's way of mourning, packaging her grief in these daily rituals. By now it had become simply habit. But she did the work solemnly and always had. More than solemnly. Sadly.

Since last year, that sadness had seemed to infect all the other aspects of her life—the way she walked, the way she dressed, the mournful music she played on the stereo Matt had given her for Christmas. In her final year of high school, she had pulled a perfunctory B average—her aptitude for schoolwork tempered by a blossoming despair.

He picked at the eggs while she dressed for the day. When he saw Rachel again she was heading out the door, meeting some friends, she said, at the mall. She smiled distantly. "Dinner the usual time?"

"Maybe we'll go out," Matt said. "Dos Aguilas. Or maybe the Golden Lotus."

She nodded.

"I love you," he said. He told her so often. Today, it came out sounding awkward and ineffectual.

She gave him a curious look. "You too, Daddy," she said. And smiled again.

It wasn't a happy smile. It said, *Are things really as bad as that?*

Matt tried to smile back. He guessed it was an appropriate answer. A brave but unconvincing grin. *Yes, Rachel. Things are at least as bad as that.*

Chapter
4

Headlines

COUP ATTEMPT RUMORS DENIED

White House sources and a spokesman for the Joint Chiefs of Staff issued a statement today denying that a military coup d'état against the administration was in the making.

Unusual movements of airborne and infantry battalions around Washington, D.C., had roused speculation in some quarters. Publication in *The Washington Post* of a document allegedly leaked from the office of Air Force General Robert Osmond fueled rumors earlier in the week.

Asked whether the President would address these developments in his Friday speech to the nation, a White House spokesman suggested the topic didn't warrant further comment.

VANDALISM AT BROOKSIDE

Police are investigating extensive acts of vandalism that occurred last night at Brookside Cemetery.

Vandals apparently entered the cemetery after dark and left several monuments defaced with spray paint. Swastikas and skulls were among the crude emblems left behind.

Cemetery Director William Spung told the *Observer* that cleaning the headstones will take at least a week and will be "very costly."

Police Chief Terence McKenna admits such cases are often difficult to solve. "Acts like this are usually committed by adolescents," McKenna said. Police are considering a "Vandalism Awareness" program for local public schools.

No motive has been suggested for the crime.

"TAIWAN FLU" ON MARCH

According to the Centers for Disease Control in Atlanta, the nation is in the grip of a flu epidemic.

Cases of the so-called "Taiwan Flu" have been reported from all over the country.

The disease is a mild strain of influenza and is not considered dangerous.

"You might consider stocking up on Kleenex," a spokesman said.

Chapter
5
D.C.

The President adopted a posture of calm repose—elbows on desk, fingers steepled beneath his chin—as the Secretary of Defense was admitted into the Oval Office. "You're looking well, Charlie," the President said.

"And yourself, sir," Charles Atwater Boyle responded . . . perhaps, the President thought, with just a touch of genuine surprise.

The truth was that Charlie Boyle did not, in fact, look remotely well. His cheeks were patchy red, as if he were running a mild fever—no doubt he was. And he appeared to be nervous about this nighttime meeting, to which the President had summoned him without explanation. Charlie Boyle had matriculated through two bastions of poker-faced reserve, the Marine Corps and the banking industry, and had kept his political balance as well as any member of the Cabinet—at least until now—but the blank exterior was itself a clue to the struggle beneath. His notoriously chilly blue eyes darted periodically to the left, as if he was consulting some presence in the air—a cue card, perhaps. Or wishing for one.

The question becomes, the President thought, of whom is he afraid? Of me—or his dubious allies in this conspiracy?

"Charlie," the President said, "I want to talk to you about your coup d'état."

To his credit, the Secretary of Defense did not so much as blink.

"Sir?" Charlie said mildly.

"Sit down," the President said.

Charlie sat.

"I shouldn't call it *your* coup, should I? I know your position is ambiguous. And I don't expect you to admit complicity in a plot to overthrow the civilian government. It was General Chafee, wasn't it, who approached you with the idea that you might act as President *pro tem*? A Cabinet member, a civilian—an ideal front man. You'd lend them an air of legitimacy in a country where the words 'military junta' still have a nasty ring to them." The President put his palms flat on the desk and leaned forward. The gesture, he knew, was aggressive, imperial. "Quite honestly, Charlie, my sources don't know how you responded to the offer—only that it was made. And that General Chafee was smiling when he shook your hand."

"For the record," Charlie Boyle said, "I deny all this."

"Noted. But that's beside the point. Your loyalty is in question, but it's also immaterial."

The Secretary of Defense frowned. He can't decide, the President thought, whether he's been insulted. But he's curious, too.

"In that case," Charlie said stiffly, "what is the purpose of this meeting?"

"It's late," the President admitted. "You probably want to be home with Evelyn and the kids. I can't say I blame you. But in times like these I think we can be forgiven for some long hours." He tapped his desk with the point of a fountain pen while Charlie squirmed. "I've known you for five years and I've studied your career. You were the Cabinet appointment I was most proud of, Charlie, did you know that? I'm not suggesting you're a scoundrel. Only that your loyalties may be divided. Is that so far off the mark?"

"You're asking for a statement I can't make. For the record, I resent the implication."

"Forget the record. There *is* no record. This is *in camera*."

"I'm supposed to believe that?"

"You're supposed to listen." The President allowed an edge into his voice. The essential fact about Charlie Boyle was that he recognized authority. His life was a long hymn to authority: recognizing it, respecting it, acquiring it. *I know you*, the President thought. *I know your poor-boy Tidewater roots, and I know what the Marine Corps must have meant to the rootless child you once were.* More than a stepping-stone into civilian respectability, though it had been that too. All the old totems retained their magic. Charlie may have decided the man in the President's office was expendable, but the office itself, the *idea* of the office, the Commander in Chief, still carried a ponderous symbolic weight. And for the moment, at least, the President thought, that weight is mine to wield.

He chose his words carefully.

"I want you to consider that this effort might be futile. Worse, doomed. I want you to consider that the impressive people the JCS may have lined up are not the only impressive people in the country, military or civilian. There is still a powerful sentiment on behalf of representative government. Your uprising would not be unopposed and it would not be bloodless. And it would not be worthwhile."

Charlie Boyle sat for a long time in the ticking silence. When at last he spoke, he spoke cautiously. "People say you're in contact with the Artifact. They say you know something you're not telling. And there are rumors about some kind of disease. There's been a lid on the CDC since last week. You and the brass at the NIH and nobody's talking."

"Maybe I do know something. Maybe I'm preparing to communicate that knowledge in my own good time. That's my prerogative, is it not?"

"You haven't said one fucking word to the Cabinet. Even your own advisors, the NSC—"

"Given the climate of the times, is that surprising?"

"People want to know who's governing the country."

"Damn it, Charlie, *I* am!"

"People debate that. People think you might be a fifth-columnist."

"People who are compelled to seek power are prone to say any damn thing. Political campaigns aren't conducted without lies. Neither are military uprisings."

"You could put these rumors to rest."

"I'm addressing the nation in two days. Isn't that sufficient?"

"Maybe not." Lured into too many tacit admissions, Charlie sat stiffly in his chair—the offended Puritan. "You admit you know something."

"That's right. I know insubordination when I see it. And I know how to respond to it."

Charlie wavered but did not quite abandon his hostile stare. "You have no allies. Sir."

"Are you banking on that?"

There was no response.

"Tell them I'm aware of what's happening," the President said. "That's your task, Charlie. Tell General Chafee and General Weismann and that Pentagon cabal that their plans have been under scrutiny in this office for quite a while. Tell him they can't get what they want without a great deal of bloodshed." The President focused on the Secretary of Defense—caught his eyes and held them. "You've served this country faithfully for most of your life. Do you really want to plunge it into civil war? Do you really want to be the next Jefferson Davis—and go down the same way?"

The Secretary of Defense opened his mouth and closed it.

"Tell General Chafee—" This was the hardest part. "Tell him negotiation is not out of the question. But violence will be met with violence. And Charlie?"

"Sir?"

"Thank you for your time."

■　■　■

The Secret Service contingent had been doubled in the halls of the White House. The President wondered if that was a good idea. Too many unfamiliar faces about. It was a risk in itself. And it created an atmosphere of crisis—but perhaps that was unavoidable. He thought of Lincoln arriving in disguise for his inauguration, sharpshooters stationed around the Capitol dome. Times were bad, but times had been worse. Though, it was true, times had never been *stranger*.

Much of what he had said to Charlie Boyle was bluff, and the generals would know it; but it might be enough to cast doubt in certain quarters. It was a delay he was after here, not a resolution. The next few days were vital. It would be tragic if internecine squabbles such as this one caused unnecessary bloodshed, because those lives . . . well, they would be unrecoverable.

If it came to that, the President had decided he would issue the necessary orders and surrender his office, minimizing losses. But there were those who would fight on, for the best of reasons; and fighting, they would die; and dead, they would not be resurrected.

The crises we administer, the President thought, are never the ones we expect.

He did not consider himself a man especially well-equipped to administer this one. His career had been enormously successful but in every other respect ordinary. Scion of a New England political family, groomed from childhood for public service, he had graduated from Harvard with a law degree, reliable connections, and enough ambition to light up a city block. But it was an ambition hoarded; he was not impatient. He had moved through the ranks of the Democratic Party with grace, made more friends than enemies. He had run for public office first in his home state, defeating an incumbent Republican so decisively that the Party seriously began to consider his presidential mettle. And still he bided his time. He cultivated acquaintances in the Party hierarchy and among the baronial eminences of oil, law, manufacturing.

He had lost the nomination by a narrow margin in one primary but won it handily four years later. Western oil interests had defected from the complacent Republicans that year, and the South, reeling from the flight of industry to Mexico, had come back into the Democratic fold. And at the level of the ballot box, perhaps personalities had something to do with it. The President was a large man, easy with a crowd, ebullient, humorous. His opponent had been lean to the point of emaciation, prim, and too easily confused. Television debates had amounted to a rout; the Republican campaign tried to withdraw from the last of the three.

There was no suspense on election night, only the pleasure of watching CNN commentators find new ways to repeat the basic datum, that a long Republican ascendancy over the White House had come to an end.

Then the Artifact had arrived in orbit and every other issue dissolved in the immediacies of that almost incomprehensible event. He had spent most of his time in office struggling with it. Ineffectually, of course. It was a crisis that couldn't be addressed. Its secondary effects—the political instability, the sinking national morale—could. In that respect, he felt he had done some good. What an unexpected opportunity for a twentieth-century political figure: to do good. How Victorian. But he had grasped the unlikely nettle.

And there was still a chance to save some lives; and perhaps his interview with Charlie Boyle had helped. The next few days were critical. *We'll see*, he thought.

Beyond that—

Well, it was a new world, wasn't it?

He could feel the shape of the future, but only dimly. He suspected it did not contain a place for kings, conquerors, aristocrats; nor even parliaments, congresses, presidents.

■   ■   ■

Elizabeth was awake, reading a book as he entered the bedroom. She looked up sleepily. "How did it go?"

The President began to undress. "You know Charlie. Stiff-necked. A little dim. Self-preservation at all costs. But I think he'll be more cautious now."

"Is that good enough?"

He shrugged. "It's good. It may not be enough."

"Poor Charlie. He just doesn't *understand*."

"We're privileged," the President reminded his wife. "We were approached first. We're among the few." He had a curious thought. "The last aristocracy the world will see."

"I suppose we are. But if we had Charlie, too, and General Chafee—"

"That will come. Though I wouldn't count on Chafee. He strikes me as the type who might refuse."

"I wish it would all happen faster."

"It's happening as fast as it can. I only hope that no one dies. Even the generals would come to regret that, I think."

"They don't realize what they're fighting against. The death of Death."

The President slipped into bed beside his wife. He had brought a slender intelligence document, this morning's *For The President Only*, meaning to reread it—but what was the point? He took his wife's hand and turned off the light.

When he married Elizabeth Bonner, she had been trim, attractive, connected to a powerful Eastern family. In the thirty years since, she had grown ebulliently fat. There had been jokes during the campaign—unkind jokes, cruel jokes. But Elizabeth had not seemed to mind—she did not deign to acknowledge such peccadilloes. And the President was only mildly perturbed. Perturbed because he loved her, not because he objected to her exuberant size. He understood the secret: She had gained weight as she had gained wisdom; it was the weight of their marriage, an alliance well-anchored and substantial.

The bedsheets were pleasingly cool. "'The death of Death,'" he said. "That's an odd thought."

"But that's what it is," Elizabeth said.

The idea was comforting. And true, of course. Trust her to find the most succinct way of putting it.

And Death shall have no dominion. Was that the Bible? Tennyson? He couldn't recall.

In any event, the President thought, the time has come.

Chapter
6

Fever

Matt was a doctor because he had been seduced by the idea of healing.

A dozen TV series and a handful of movies had convinced him that the heart of the practice of medicine was the act of healing. He managed to carry this fragile idea through med school, but it didn't survive internship. His internship drove home the fact that a doctor's purpose is bound up with death—its postponement, at best; its amelioration, often; its inevitability, always. Death was the gray eminence behind the caduceus. Healing was why people paid their doctors. Death was why they were afraid of them.

Contrary to myth, the med degree conferred no emotional invulnerability. Even doctors feared death—even successful doctors. Feared it and avoided it. Sometimes neurotically. During his residency, Matt had worked with an oncologist who hated his patients. He was a good doctor, unflaggingly professional, but in a lounge or a cafeteria or a bar—among colleagues—he would explain at length what weaklings people were. "They *invite* their tumors. They're lazy or fat or they smoke, or they inebriate themselves with alcohol or lie in the sun with their skin exposed. Then they bring their abused bodies to me. 'Cure this, please, doctor.' Sickening."

"Maybe they're just unlucky," Matt had ventured. "Some of them, at least."

"The more time you spend on my floor, Dr. Wheeler, the less inclined you will be to believe that."

Maybe so, Matt thought. The contempt was not reasonable, but it

served a purpose. It kept death at arm's length. Open the door to sympathy—
even a crack—and grief might crowd in behind it.

It was not an attitude Matt could adopt, however, which helped steer
him into family practice. His daily work was leavened with mumps, measles,
minor wounds stitched, infections knocked out with antibiotics. Healing, in
other words. Small benevolent acts. He was a bit player in the minor dramas
of ordinary lives, a good guy, not a death angel presiding at the gateway to
oblivion.

Seldom, at least.

But Cindy Rhee was dying, and there was nothing he could do about it.

▪ ▪ ▪

He had told the Rhees he would stop in to see their daughter Friday
morning.

David Rhee was a forklift driver at the mill south of town. His parents
were Korean immigrants living in Portland; David had married a pretty
Buchanan girl named Ellen Drew and twelve years ago Ellen had borne him
a daughter, Cindy.

Cindy was a delicate, thin child with just a touch of her father's
complexion. Her eyes were large, mysterious, brown. She was suffering from
a neuroblastoma, a cancer of the nervous system.

She fell down walking to school one autumn morning. She stood up,
brushed the leaf debris off her jacket, carried on. Next week, she fell again.
And the week after. Then twice in a week. Twice in a day. Finally her
mother brought her in to see Matt.

He found gross anomalies in her reflexes and a pronounced papille-
dema. He told Mrs. Rhee he couldn't make a diagnosis and referred Cindy
to a neurologist at the hospital, but his suspicions were grave. A benign and
operable tumor of the brain might be the girl's best hope. There were other
possibilities, even less pleasant.

He attended her while she was admitted for tests. Cindy was immensely
patient in the face of the unavoidable indignities, almost supernaturally so.
It occurred to Matt to wonder where such people came from: the obviously
good and decent souls who endure hardship without complaint and cause
duty-hardened nurses to weep for them in the hallways.

He was with the Rhees when the neurologist explained that their
daughter was suffering from a neuroblastoma. David and Ellen Rhee listened
with ferocious concentration as the specialist described the hardships and
benefits, the pluses and minuses, of chemotherapy. David spoke first: "But
will it *cure* her?"

"It might prolong her life. It might send the tumor into remission. We don't use the word 'cure.' We would have to keep a close watch on her even in the best case."

David Rhee nodded, a gesture not of acquiescence but of brokenhearted acknowledgment. His daughter might not get well. His daughter might die.

I could have been a plumber, Matt thought, an electrician, an accountant, anything, dear God, not to be in this room at this moment. He couldn't meet Ellen's eyes when she left with her husband. He was afraid she would see his craven helplessness.

Cindy responded to the chemotherapy. She lost some hair but recovered her sense of balance; she went home from the hospital skinny but optimistic.

She was back six months later. Her tumor, inoperable to begin with, had disseminated. Her speech was slurred and her eyesight had begun to tunnel. Matt canvassed the hospital's specialists: surely *some* kind of operation. . . . But the malignancy had colonized her brain too deeply; the X-rays were eloquent, merciless. Surgery, if anyone had been mad enough to attempt it, would have left her speechless, sightless, possibly soulless.

Now she was home to die. The Rhees understood this. In a way, the prognosis was kind; she was functional enough to leave the hospital and with any luck she wouldn't end up DNR in some pitiless white room. Now Cindy was blind and could form only the most rudimentary words, but Ellen Rhee continued to care for her daughter with a relentless heroism that Matt found humbling.

He had promised he would stop by this morning, but he didn't relish the task. It was hard not to care about Cindy Rhee, hard not to hate the disease that was torturing her to death. There was a state of mind Matt called "being the doctor machine," in which he kept his emotions filed for later reference . . . but that was a difficult balancing act at the best of times, and this morning he was feverish and disoriented. He popped a decongestant and drove to the Rhees' house in a grim mood.

There was the question, too, of what Jim Bix had told him. He carried it like a stone, a weight he could neither dislodge nor easily bear. Jim was sincere, but he might still be mistaken. Or crazy. Or maybe this really was the beginning of the end . . . in which case, as indecent as the thought sounded, maybe Cindy Rhee was the lucky one.

He parked in the driveway at the Rhees' modest two-bedroom house. Ellen Rhee opened the door for him. She wore a yellow housedress with her hair tied away from her neck. The air in the living room smelled of Pine-Sol; an old upright vacuum cleaner stood sentinel on the carpet. It was Matt's experience that in the homes of the dying, housework is performed religiously or not at all. Ellen Rhee had taken to frantic cleaning. In the last few months he had seldom seen her without her apron on.

But she was smiling. That was odd, Matt thought. And the radio was playing. Some AM station. Cheerful pop music.

"Come in, Matt," Ellen said.

He stepped inside. The house was not as dim as he remembered it; she had opened all the blinds and pulled back all the drapes. A summer-morning breeze swept the odor of antiseptic past him, and a more delicate waft of roses from the backyard garden.

"I'm sorry," she said. "The house is kind of chaotic. I'm in the middle of cleaning up. I guess I forgot you were coming."

She sniffed and dabbed her nose with a Kleenex. The Taiwan Flu, Matt thought. Wasn't that what the papers were calling it?

He said, "I can come back another time—"

"No. Please. Come in." Her smile had not faded.

The clinical word for this kind of behavior was "denial." But maybe it was simply her way of coping. Carry on, smile, and welcome the guest. A new wrinkle in the etiology of Ellen Rhee's grief. But it seemed to Matt she *looked* different. Less burdened. Was that possible?

"Is David home?"

"Early shift at the mill. Would you like a coffee?"

"No, thank you, Ellen." He looked toward Cindy's bedroom. "How is she today?"

"Better," Ellen said. Matt's surprise must have been too obvious. "No, really! She's feeling much better. You can ask her yourself."

It was a macabre joke. "Ellen—"

Her smile softened. She touched his arm. "Go see her, Matt. Go ahead."

■　■　■

Cindy was sitting up in bed, a small miracle in itself. Matt's first astonished thought was: She *did* look better. She was still brutally thin—the delicate bone-and-parchment emaciation of the terminal cancer patient. But her eyes were wide and appeared lucid. The last time he stopped by, she hadn't seemed to recognize him.

Matt parked his medical bag on the bedside table and told her hello. He made it a point to talk to her, though the neurologist had assured him she couldn't understand. She might still take some solace from the tone of his voice. "I came by to see how you're doing today."

Cindy blinked. "Thank you, Dr. Wheeler," she said. "I'm doing fine."

■   ■   ■

"You look like you've seen a ghost," Ellen said when he emerged from the girl's bedroom. "Come on. Sit down."

He sat at the kitchen table and allowed Ellen to pour him a glass of 7-Up.

"She really is better," Ellen said. "I told you so."

Matt struggled to form his thoughts.

"She spoke," he said. "She was lucid. She understood what I said to her. She's weak and a little feverish, but I believe she may even have gained some weight." He looked at Ellen. "None of that should be possible."

"It's a miracle," Ellen said firmly. "At least that's what I believe." She laughed. "I'm a little feverish myself."

"Ellen, listen. I'm pleased about this. I couldn't be happier. But I don't understand it."

And truly, he did not. Yes, there was such a thing as a remission. He had once seen a lung tumor remit in a way that could be called "miraculous." But Cindy was a vastly different case. Brain tissue had been destroyed. Even if the tumors had somehow vanished, *she should not have been able to speak*. That part of her brain was simply missing. Even without the tumors, she would have been in the position of someone who had suffered a severe stroke. Some recovery of faculties might be possible; certainly not a complete cure . . . certainly not what he had witnessed in the bedroom.

He did not say any of this to Ellen. Instead, he offered: "I want to be sure. I want the hospital to look at her."

Ellen frowned for the first time this morning. "Maybe when she's stronger, Matt. I don't know, though. I hate to put her through all that again."

"I don't want us to have false hopes."

"You think she might get worse?" Ellen shook her head. "She won't. I can't tell you how I know that. But I do. The sickness is gone, Dr. Wheeler."

He couldn't bring himself to argue. "I hope you're right. Cindy said something similar."

"Did she?"

The girl had spoken with deliberation, as if the framing of the words still required enormous effort, but succinctly and clearly.

"Poor Dr. Wheeler," this emaciated child had said to him. "We're putting you out of business."

■   ■   ■

Strange as the incident was, here was something even stranger: He did not dwell on it or even think about it much after he left the Rhees' house.

He drove downtown along Promenade Street where the road followed the curve of the bay. There wasn't much traffic. It was an easy drive, the ocean still and blue under a feathery wash of sky. Hot August noon and nothing stirring.

He felt as strangely placid as Buchanan looked. Matt had blamed it on the fever—this empty calm, his own, the town's—but then it occurred to him to wonder.

Maybe Jim is right, he thought. We're all infected. Machines in the blood. A sort of plague. The Taiwan Flu . . . hadn't he dreamed about it?

But these thoughts, too, slipped away beneath the glassy surface of the day.

It turned out that Jill, the receptionist, hadn't shown up for work—phoned in sick—but Annie was at the office, sitting in Reception fielding calls, mainly cancelled appointments. She put down the receiver and transferred queries to the service for an hour so she could break for lunch; Matt brought up food from the first-floor coffee shop—which was under-staffed. Plastic-wrapped salads and ham sandwiches on white. Annie Gates picked at hers, eyes distantly focused. "Strange day," she mused.

Matt told her about Cindy Rhee, but the story felt distant, curiously immaterial, even as he told it.

Annie frowned. Wrinkle of brow and purse of lips. Trying to fathom all this but meeting some internal resistance. "Maybe that's why nobody's keeping their appointments. They're all—well, *better*."

Poor Dr. Wheeler. We're putting you out of business.

Maybe not better, Matt thought. Maybe sicker.

He told Annie what Jim Bix had said about foreign bodies in the blood of his hospital samples, in his own blood. He hadn't intended to tell her this, at least not yet—hadn't wanted to worry her needlessly. But she nodded. "I heard something about it at the hospital. Had lunch with a staff nurse from the path lab. She was scared spitless. So was I, by the time she finished. So I called the hematology resident at the Dallas hospital where I interned. He didn't want to talk about it, but when I told him what I'd heard he pretty much confirmed it."

So we were keeping this from each other, Matt thought. It was like an O. Henry story. How many other people were in on this secret?

He said, "That means it's not local."

"No. Are you surprised?"

"No."

"The CDC must have known about it at least as long as Jim Bix." She sipped her Pepsi. "I guess the clamps came down hard. There hasn't been a hint of it in the papers. I suppose the thinking is, why worry people? A disease with no symptoms, a disease with no epidemiology because everybody already has it—so why start a panic?"

"Surely they can't keep it a secret much longer."

"Maybe they won't have to."

He felt enclosed in a dome of feverish tranquillity. Part of him was conducting this conversation quite reasonably; another part was encapsulated, silent, but frightened by what Annie had said. These were thoughts he had not yet allowed himself.

A distant, dreamy note crept into her voice. "If this infection has a purpose—and I think it does—we'll all know pretty soon what it is."

He gave her a sharp look. "What makes you think it has a purpose?"

"Just a feeling." She shrugged. "Don't you think that?"

Not a question he wanted to answer.

"Annie, can I ask you something? You said when you heard about this from your friend you were scared. At the time."

"Yes."

"But not now?"

Her frown deepened. "No . . . not now. I'm not scared now."

"Why not?"

"I don't know, Matt." She regarded him solemnly across the remains of lunch. "I don't honestly know."

■　■　■

He spent the afternoon cleaning up paperwork and attending a single patient: a thirty-year-old housewife keeping an appointment to monitor her blood pressure. Yes, she was sticking to her diet. Yes, she was taking her medication.

Her pressure was a textbook-normal 120 over 80 despite a degree and a half of fever. She seemed absentminded but she smiled as she left. Thank you, Dr. Wheeler.

Matt pulled his chair to the window and watched shade and light mark time in the street beyond.

We're being sedated.

The town was quiescent. Every motion seemed isolated, a unique event. A car crawled along the hot blacktop in slow motion. An elderly man, his collar open and his suitcoat over his shoulder, stepped out of the Bargain Cuts Uni-Sex Barber Shop and paused to run a bony hand across his stubbled head. Sunlight winked on windshields, softened road tar, and lifted haze from the blank and distant ocean.

I should be terrified, Matt thought. And I'm not. And *that* should be terrifying, too. But it wasn't.

Sedation. What else to call this clinical calm? We should be screaming. We should be outraged. We should feel violated. Because this was—

Was *what?*

The end of the world?

Yes, Matt thought. Probably the end of the world. That was probably what this was.

■ ■ ■

At three o'clock a courier came upstairs with a folder of test results from the private med lab on the third floor. The blood results might be skewed, but apparently they could still sort out gonadotropin from a few CCs of urine. Matt gave the dossier a quick perusal. Then he phoned Lillian Bix and told her she was pregnant.

■ ■ ■

They closed the empty office at four.

"I walked to work," Annie said. "Maybe you can drive me back to your place." Matt looked blank. "Your dinner party. Remember?"

He almost laughed. The idea was ludicrous. How was he supposed to conduct a dinner party? Serve salt peanuts and play "Nearer My God to Thee?"

Annie smiled. "It's okay, Matt. Some cancellations phoned in this morning. Check your memo pad. There are probably more on your machine at home. You can call it off if you want. . . . I'll get dinner at a restaurant."

He shook his head. "No. Annie, I want you to come home with me. But there might not be anybody else."

"I know."

"Nothing to celebrate."

"I know, Matt. Maybe we can have a drink. Watch the lights."

"I'd like that," Matt said.

■ ■ ■

She was right about the party, of course. Everybody had canceled— most citing the flu—except for Jim and Lillian Bix, who showed up with a bottle of wine.

The mood was not celebratory, though Lillian had announced her pregnancy to Jim and Jim announced it to Annie. It was obvious from their slightly dazed expressions that his friends felt the way Matt did: fenced off, somehow, from the significance of all these strange events. "Like a patient etherized upon a table"—T. S. Eliot, if Matt recalled correctly. The phrase echoed in his head as the four of them fumbled around the kitchen, improvising dinner, while Rachel watched a TV newscast in the next room. The President, Rachel said, had canceled his Friday night speech. But everything was quiet in Washington.

Later, Matt switched off the air conditioning and the adults adjourned to the backyard deck. Lawn chairs in a cooling breeze, wine in stemmed glasses. Sunset faded; the first stars emerged. The breeze swayed the big Douglas fir at the back of the yard and Matt listened to the sound of its branches stirring, as gentle in the dusk as the rustling of a woman's skirt. "My God," he said, "it's—*quiet*."

Jim looked quizzical. "What do they say in the movies? *Too* quiet."

"Seriously," Matt said. "Listen. You can hear the trees."

Now they crooked their heads at the evening and grew attentive.

"I can hear the frogs," Annie marveled. "From the river, I guess. My gosh. Way down the valley."

"And that ringing sound," Lillian said. "I know what that is! The flagpole over at the elementary school. I walk by there some mornings. The rope bangs against the staff when the wind blows. It always reminds me of a bell."

A distant, random tolling. Matt heard it, too.

Jim said, "Is all this so odd?"

"Friday night," Matt said. "The highway runs along the river. You can usually hear the traffic. Usually nothing but. People going to the movies, guys out at the bars, maybe a lumber truck roaring by. It's the kind of sound you can put out of your mind, but you notice it when it's gone. There's always some kind of noise up here, even after midnight. A train whistle. A siren once in a while. Or—"

"TV," Annie said. "Everybody in the neighborhood with their TV turned up. On a summer night like this? With the windows open?" She shivered, a tiny motion; Matt felt it when he took her hand. She said, "I guess hardly anybody's watching TV tonight."

Matt glanced back at the house, where Rachel had switched off the TV and was standing at the window of her room, the light behind her, gazing moodily into the twilight.

"So everybody went to bed early," Jim offered. "The flu."

This offended Lillian, who sat upright in her chair. "You don't have to protect me. I know what's happening."

Matt and Jim exchanged glances. Matt said gently, "If you know what's happening, Lillian, you're one up on the rest of us."

Her voice was raw, her eyes mournful. "Everything's changing. That's what's happening. That's why there's nobody here tonight but us."

There followed a silence, which Matt guessed was acquiescence, then Jim raised his glass: "To us, then. The hardy few."

Lillian drank to show she wasn't angry. "But I shouldn't," she said. "Wine puts me to sleep. Oh, and the baby. It's bad for the baby, isn't it? But I suppose just a sip."

Tang, clang, said the distant flagpole.

▪ ▪ ▪

Matt stopped to say goodnight to Rachel and found her already dozing, tucked in a pink bedsheet, the window open to admit a breath of night air.

He pulled up a chair beside the bed, mindful of its creak as he sat.

Rachel hadn't changed her room significantly since her mother died. It was still very much a child's bedroom, lace blinds on the window and stuffed animals on the dresser. Matt knew for a fact that she still owned all her old toys: a vanity chest full of My Little Ponies and Jem; of miniature stoves, TV sets, refrigerators; a complete Barbie Camper set neatly folded and stored. The chest was seldom opened, but he supposed it served its purpose as a shrine: to Rachel's mother, or just to childhood, security, the kingdom of lost things.

He looked at his daughter, and the thought of the toy chest made him suddenly, inconsolably sad.

I would give it all back if I could, Rache. Everything the world stole from you.

Everything the world is stealing.

She turned on her side and opened her eyes. "Daddy?"

"Yes, Rache?"

"I heard you come in."

"Just wanted to say goodnight."

"Is Annie staying over?"

"I think so."

"Good. I like it when she's here in the morning." She yawned. Matt put a hand on her forehead. She was a little warm.

A troubling thought seemed to hold her attention for a moment. "Daddy? Is everything going to be all right?"

Lie to her, Matt thought. Lie and make her believe it.

"Yes, Rache," he said.

She nodded and closed her eyes. "I thought so."

▪   ▪   ▪

He unwound the studio bed in the basement for Jim and Lillian, who had both had too much wine, or were otherwise "etherized": too dazed, in any case, to drive.

I know how they feel, Matt thought. Bound up in cotton. Buoyant but sleepy. There had been occasions, as a college student, when he had smoked marijuana in a friend's dorm room. It had sometimes made him feel like this . . . encased in a protective and faintly luminescent fog . . . afloat, after he had found his way home, on the gently undulating surface of his bed.

Tonight he climbed into bed beside Annie.

It had been a while since they'd slept together, and now he wondered why. He'd missed this, the presence of her, her warmth and what he thought of as her "Annie-ness." She was a small woman, all her vivid energies and enigmatic silences packaged tightly together. She rolled on her side but snuggled closer; he curled himself around her.

The first time Annie came home with him Matt had been guilt-ridden—this had still been very much Celeste's house and Annie an intruder in it, an insult, he worried, to her memory. And he had wondered how Rachel might take it. A rivalry between Annie and his daughter was a complication he had dreaded.

But Rachel had taken to Annie at once, accepted her presence without question. "Because she mourned," Annie suggested later. "She mourned for her mother and I think in some ways she's still mourning, but she isn't hiding it from herself. She's letting go of it. She knows it's all right for me to be here because Celeste isn't coming back."

Matt winced.

Annie said, "But you, Matt, you don't like letting go. You're a collector. You hoard things. Your childhood. This town. Your idealism. Your marriage. You can't bear the idea of giving any of it up."

This was both true and maddening. "I gave Celeste up," he said. "I didn't have a choice."

"It's not that simple. There's a certain way you *shouldn't* let her go—she's a part of you, after all. And there's the giving up you couldn't help, which is her dying. And there's the space in between. Not a very big space right now. But that's the space where I fit in."

Matt wondered, holding Annie close to him, what had provoked this old memory.

You're a collector. You don't like letting go.

He guessed it was true.

Clinging to Annie now. Clinging to Rachel. Clinging to Jim and Lillian and the practice of medicine and the town of Buchanan.

Everything's changing, Lillian had said.

But it was too much to let go of.

A cool finger of air touched the skin of his shoulder, and Matt pulled up the bedsheet and closed his eyes in the summer dark; and then, like Annie, like Rachel, like Jim and Lillian and everyone else in Buchanan and in the sleeping world, he began to dream.

Chapter 7

The Quiet

A wave of sleep crossed the globe like the shadow of the sun, a line of dreaming that lagged only a few hours behind the border of the night.

It was a sleep more complete than the planet had known since the human species migrated out of Africa. Sleep tracked across North America from the tip of Labrador westward, and it possessed almost everyone equally: possessed the shift workers, the insomniacs, the wealthy, and the homeless; possessed the alcoholic and the amphetamine addict alike.

It possessed farmers, fishermen, the inmates of penitentiaries, and penitentiary guards. It possessed Methedrine-saturated truckers spinning Waylon Jennings tapes in the cabs of eighteen-wheelers, who pulled into the breakdown lanes of empty highways and slept in their rigs; possessed airline pilots, who landed 747s on the tarmac of sleeping airports under the direction of air-traffic controllers who methodically emptied the sky, and then slept.

There were isolated, and temporary, exceptions. Medical emergencies were rare, but telephone lines were maintained by a few dazed workers (who slept later); ambulances evacuated injuries to hospitals, where a few residents, functional but dazed beyond wondering at the events that had overtaken them, stanched the few wounds of a few sleeping patients . . . whose injuries, in any case, seemed to heal without much intervention. Fire crews remained functionally alert, though curiously sedated. No one slept until they had attended—without much conscious thought—to the obvious dangers: cigarettes were extinguished, ovens switched off, fireplaces damped.

The fires that did break out were accidents of nature, not humanity. In Chicago, a welfare mother named Aggie Langois woke from a powerful and incomplete dream—which was not a dream—to find flames licking out of a 1925-vintage wall socket and kindling the paper curtains of her two-room apartment. She took her sleeping baby and her wakeful but calm three-year-old and hurried them downstairs, two flights to the sidewalk . . . and was surprised to find the other occupants of the building calmly filing out behind her. The crack dealer from 3-A was carrying the legless old man from 4-B; and Aggie's personal nemesis, the neighbor girl who was a cocktail waitress and who liked to party after hours when the children were trying to sleep, had brought out a score of blankets and handed three of them to Aggie without comment.

Someone had paused long enough to dial 911. The fire engines arrived, not just promptly, but in eerie silence; the crew hooked up their hoses with an easy, economical motion. It was as if only a part of them was awake: the fraction necessary to do this job and do it efficiently. A man from the building next door—a stranger—offered Aggie a sofa to sleep on and a bedroll for her babies. Aggie accepted. "It's an unusual night," the man said, and Aggie nodded, mute with wonder. Before an hour had passed, the fire was extinguished and the occupants of the building had been dispersed to new locations, all in a strange and dignified silence. Safe and with her children safe beside her, Aggie began once more to dream.

Apart from the telephone exchanges, local communications dwindled and international networks began to fail. Within hours, the Earth had dimmed appreciably in the radio and microwave frequencies. Night overtook the western cities of Lima, Los Angeles, and Anchorage, and began to darken the ocean, while Israelis watched their CNN satellite feed shutting down due to "unexpected staff shortages," according to one weary Atlanta announcer; and then there was only a static logo, then only static—as overseas subscribers blinked at the horizon and guessed something was wrong, something must be seriously wrong, and it was odd how *calm* they felt, and later sleepy.

■　■　■

Some resisted longer than others. By some quirk of will or constitution, a few individuals were able to shake off their sedation, or at least postpone it a few moments, a few hours.

A sales rep for the Benevolent Shoe Company of Abbotsford, Michigan, driving a rental Chrysler northbound on 87 from the Denver airport, pondered the miracle that had overtaken him in the darkness. He was due to check in at a Marriott in Fort Collins and face a convention of western footware retailers, beginning with a "reception buffet" at seven, for Christ's sake, in the morning. The miracle was that some kind of formless disaster had spared him the necessity of scrambled eggs and bacon with a bunch of sleepy entrepreneurs wearing "Hello My Name Is" stickers.

The miracle had seemed to commence sometime after sunset, when his flight landed at Stapleton. The airport was nearly empty despite the fact that its gates were crowded with motionless aircraft. At least half the passengers on his flight stayed aboard, curled up in their seats . . . flying on to some other destination, he supposed, but it struck him as peculiar nonetheless. The terminal itself was cavernous and weirdly silent; his luggage was a long time arriving and the woman at the Hertz booth was so spaced out he had trouble holding her attention long enough to arrange a rental. Driving north, he was startled by the emptiness of the highway . . . cars pulling over into the emergency lane until his was the last mobile vehicle on the road, humming along like a sleepy wraith, listening to a Eurythmics tune that seemed to rattle in his head like a loose pea. Then the Denver oldies station abruptly signed off, and when he tried to find something else there was only one other signal, a country-and-western station, which promptly faded. Not normal, he admitted to himself. No, more than that. This was *way past* not normal, and it should have been scarier than it was. He pulled into the emergency lane, like everybody else, and climbed out of the car. Then he climbed up *on top* of the car and sat on the roof with his heels kicking at the passenger door, because—well, why not? Because he understood, in a feverish flash, that the world was ending. Ending in some strange and unanticipated and curiously sedate fashion, but ending, and he was alive at the end of it, sitting on top of this dung-colored Chrysler in a cheap suit and hearing for the first time the quiet of an abandoned night, a night without human noises. His own scuffles on the car top seemed achingly loud, and the wind made a hushed sound coming over farmland through the grain, and the smell of growing things mixed with the hot-engine smell of his car and his own rank sweat, and a dog barked somewhere, and the stars were bright as sparks overhead . . . and it was all a single phenomenon, *the quiet*, he named it, and it was awesome, frightening. He thought of his wife, of his seven-year-old son. He knew—another sourceless "knowing"—that whatever this was, it had overtaken them, too. Which made it a little easier to cooperate with the inevitable. He felt suddenly light-headed, too much alone on this immense table of sleeping farmland, so he climbed down and scurried back inside the womb of the car, where the silence was even louder, and curled up on the upholstery and obeyed a sudden and belated urge to sleep.

Among many other things, he dreamed that a mountain had begun to grow from the prairie not far from his car—a mountain as big as any mountain on the Earth, and as perfectly round as a pearl.

■ ■ ■

A thousand miles south, Maria Montoya, an expensive private escort, as she thought of herself—or whore, as her customers were occasionally unwise enough to whisper (or shout) in the transport of their passions—attempted to keep an appointment with a German businessman at one of the tourist hotels on Avenida Juárez in the Zócalo district of Mexico City.

Keeping the appointment proved mysteriously difficult. For one thing, there were no taxis that evening. Which was, as the Americans would say, a bitch. She depended on taxis. She had an arrangement with one company, *Taxi Metro:* She took a 10 percent fare cut in exchange for leaving the company's business card on her clients' hotel bureaus. Tonight the taxis were absent, the dispatchers failed to answer their phones, and the streets, in any case, were full of traffic that had parked along the sidewalks like clotted blood in an aging artery. The whole city was in this stalled condition. As bad as an earthquake! Of course, there hadn't been an earthquake or any other discernible disaster; the nature of this confusion was much more mysterious . . . but Maria didn't care about the details. She felt feverish, dazed, uneasy. She fixed her attention entirely on the need to meet this client. An important man, a wealthy man. She tried phoning to say she'd be late; the phones seemed to work but the hotel switchboard refused to answer. At last, Maria cursed and went out from her rented room into the unpleasantly hot night, the air glutinous and stagnant, and walked ten long blocks to the hotel district past all these stalled cars . . . but not stalled, exactly, because the drivers had pulled to the side of the road, sometimes onto the sidewalk, leaving a neat lane down the middle of the street, and they had turned their engines off, and all the lights. The cars had become dark caverns, and through their windows, mostly open, Maria saw the slumped shapes of sleeping passengers. Not dead—that would have worried her—just sleeping. How did she know? It was impossible to say. But the knowledge was inside her.

It was a harrowing journey. She almost fell asleep on her feet. She took a wrong turn and found herself wandering past the Palacio Nacional, its ugly *tezontle* masonry brooding over the motionless plaza and a hundred stalled cars. Her shoes clicked on the sidewalk, and an echo came rattling back.

She arrived at the hotel an hour late and with a broken heel. Her determination had wavered during the long walk and she was sleepy herself.

But she rode the elevator to the fourteenth floor, negotiated the pine-smelling and air-conditioned hallway to the room marked 1413, knocked and then opened the unlocked door when no one answered. Her client was inside—asleep, of course. A fat German snoring on the bedspread in his underwear, skin pale as eggshell and unpleasantly hairy. She felt a wave of contempt, an occupational hazard, and suppressed it. Obviously, she wasn't needed here. Not a chance of waking this man, who had made such an issue of her promptness. She ought to go home . . . but the thought of the journey made her weary.

Conscientious to the last, Maria placed a *Taxi Metro* card on the nightstand and lay down beside the sleeping German, a stranger, with whom she chastely slept, and with whom she dreamed.

■   ■   ■

Dreaming marched westward. Dreaming crossed the Aleutians from Alaska into Siberia. Dreaming descended on ancient Asian cities: on Hanoi, Hong Kong, Bangkok. Tokyo slept with such condensed uniformity that it seemed to Hiroshi Michio, the last traffic cop to close his eyes on the cloistered neon of the Akihabara, that so much sleep, like a fog, might rise up and obscure the stars.

Sleep followed night across the Russian steppes, across rusting collective farms and lightless arctic forests, across the Urals and the Caucasus, sleep like an army moving west until it crossed the Finnish border, marched into Ukraine and then Romania, then Poland, where it met no opposition but the cool night air.

Sleep conquered China and rolled into Tibet, Pakistan, India, swept from Calcutta across two longitudes to Hyderabad.

Sleep took Africa in a space of hours. It moved westward from the Gulf of Aden into the dry hinterlands, took the dying children in the refugee camps and suspended them in darkness; followed the equator through jungles and grasslands and consumed the stony deserts of Egypt, Libya, Algeria; took its final subject in a fish shop in Dakar.

Dreaming unwound the cities of Europe, interrupting a river of human night noise that had run without surcease since the founding of Rome. Dreaming silenced Berlin and Leipzig; captured Naples and Milan; shut down the humming grids of Paris and Amsterdam; crossed the English Channel and conquered, finally, London, where a few frightened individuals had monitored the systematic dysfunction of the world with their shortwave radios, silent now, but who slept at last with everyone else, and with everyone else dreamed.

▪ ▪ ▪

It was the same dream for everyone. The dream was complex, but the dream in its most fundamental form was a single thought, a question posed in six billion human skulls and more than three thousand languages.

The question was: *Do you want to live?*

Part

Two

One

in

Ten

Thousand

Chapter
8

Buchanan
Awake

Simon Ackroyd, D.D., Rector of St. James Episcopal Church since his appointment to Buchanan in 1987, woke from a long sleep thinking about the Aztecs.

By the end of the fifteenth century, the Aztec Empire had brought the practice of ritual sacrifice to such a pinnacle of efficiency that on one occasion in 1487 eighty thousand individuals—prisoners of war—were systematically killed, their beating hearts extracted with obsidian knives. The lines of victims stretched for miles. They had been caged, fattened, and sedated with a plant drug called *toloatzin* so they would endure the nightmare without struggling.

The Aztecs, when Simon read about them in college, had been the first real test of his faith. He had grown up with what he recognized now as a sanitized Christianity, a pastel Sunday School faith in which a gentle Jesus had redeemed humanity from the adoration of similarly pastel pagan idols—Athena and Dionysus worshiped in a glade. The problem of evil, in this diorama, was small and abstract.

There was the Holocaust, of course, but Simon had been able to rationalize that as a terrible aberration, the horrendous face of a world in which Christ commanded but did not compel.

The Aztecs, however . . . the Aztecs had lodged in his mind like a burning cinder.

He could not dispel the persistent, horrible vision of those lines of prisoners snaking through angular stone colonnades to the temple at

Tenochtitlan. It suggested whole worlds of unredeemed history: centuries fathomless, Christless, and unimaginably cruel. He envisioned the sacrificial victims and thought: These were men. These were human beings. These were their lives, alien and terrible and brief.

And then, one night in Episcopal Seminary, he had dreamed himself talking with an Aztec priest—a bony, nut-brown man in a feathered headdress, who had misunderstood his horror as religious awe and who responded with his own attempt at a compliment. Our knives are trivial, the priest had said. See what your people have achieved. All your missile silos, your invisible bombers, each one an obsidian knife aimed at the hearts of tens of millions of men and women and children; each one a temple, painstaking, ingenious, the work of an army of engineers, contractors, politicians, taxpayers. We have nothing to compare, the Aztec priest had said.

And Simon had awakened with the chilly suspicion that his own life, his own culture, everything familiar and dear, might in its essence be as twisted and cruel as the stone altars and kaleidoscopic deities of the Aztecs.

His faith sustained him through college, through his divinity degree, through his appointment to this parish. He was a thoughtful Christian, and on his good days he suspected his doubts only made him stronger. Other times—when the winter fogs enclosed Buchanan, or on moonless summer nights when the pines seemed to take on the barbed and thorny aspect of Tlaloc, the Aztec god of the underworld, in the repulsive mural of Tepantitla—he wished his doubts could be abolished, annihilated in a light of faith so intense it would wash away all these shadows.

Then—last night—he had had a very different dream.

▪ ▪ ▪

He woke tentatively, as if exploring a world made new and unpredictable. Which perhaps it was.

Simon felt the world wake up around him. It was waking, he knew, from a very dramatic and peculiar kind of sleep.

But the immediate world, his world, was still the same: same bed, same bedroom, same creaking wooden floors.

The fair weather had not broken. Simon opened the bedroom drapes. The rectory was a wood-frame house erected in the boom years after the Second World War, next door to the church, in the old part of Buchanan riding up the foothills from the bay. A modest house: its luxury was this view. The morning sky was luminous above blue ocean water. Wind stirred up foam on the crests of the waves.

The world was transformed but not new, Simon thought. Or rather, it was the human landscape that had been transformed.

They are at work inside us now.

He shaved and wondered at his reflection in the bathroom mirror. Here was a gaunt forty-five-year-old man, receding hair and graying beard, quite ordinary, but all of us, he thought, have become remarkable *underneath*. He dressed and padded downstairs in his bare feet. It was Simon's special indulgence to go barefoot around the house on pleasant summer mornings. His housekeeper, Mary Park, disapproved. She would glare at his feet as if they were a display of obstinence or bad taste, then shake her head. In fact, Simon rather admired his feet. His feet were unpretentious, unadorned, unbeautiful. They appealed to his Protestant impulses. They were "plain" feet, as the Amish might say.

Mrs. Park knocked and entered as Simon was tuning his small television set in the parlor—actually the church's television set, usually appropriated by the Sunday School for audiovisual displays. The rectory had been connected to cable last June at Simon's expense and for the purpose of indulging his addiction to news broadcasts and PBS. He tuned in CNN this morning, where a dazed female announcer was describing the events of the last thirty-two hours in baffled generalities. Apparently Western Europe was still asleep. Simon had a momentary vision of the Earth as an animal, a bear perhaps, groggy after a winter's hibernation, stumbling toward the light.

Mrs. Park offered a distracted "Good morning." She ignored his bare feet for once and began to assemble his breakfast—two eggs, bacon, and buttered toast. It was a cholesterol sin he could never bring himself to renounce. In any case, he was hungry this morning: He had slept for a night, a day, and another night. He thought with some awe of the morning he had missed, of the silent afternoon no human being had seen.

Mrs. Park seemed to be keeping an eye on the television through the kitchen doorway. Simon turned up the volume for her.

"Evidence of this 'enforced sleep' is inescapable," the newswoman was saying. "Reports of injuries, remarkably, are nil. Reports of the subjective experience suggest a direct, almost telepathic, contact with the orbiting Artifact."

And so on. Simon wondered how long this pretense at objectivity would be maintained. Good grief, he thought, we *know* all this.

No one wanted to name what was looming in the future. Elysium, he thought. Jerusalem. The *illud tempus.*

He adjourned to the kitchen when Mrs. Park summoned him. Had breakfast ever smelled this good before? Or was his body already different in some way?

She hovered at his shoulder. "Dr. Ackroyd—"

"Yes, Mary?"

"You had the dream?"

"We all did."

His housekeeper confessed: "I told them—I told them *yes*."

"Yes, Mary. So did I."

She was obviously surprised. "But you were religious!"

"Why, Mary, I still am. I *think* I still am."

"But then how could you answer them yes? If it's all right to ask, I mean."

He considered the question. Not a simple one. Many of his deepest beliefs had been challenged in the last thirty-odd hours. Some had been abrogated. Had he been tempted? Had he yielded to temptation?

He pictured the temple at Tenochtitlan, the arc and fall of the obsidian knives.

"Because of the Aztecs," he said.

"Sir?"

"Because there won't be any Aztecs in the world anymore," the Rector said. "That's all finished now."

■ ■ ■

The question had been posed in democratic fashion and it was becoming obvious that the yeas outnumbered the nays.

Mary Park had said yes, and so had her husband Ira; and they had known this about each other as soon as they woke and exchanged glances across the bedsheets. Ira was sixty this year, seven years older than Mary. All spring and all summer his emphysema had kept him housebound and weak as a child—his day a slow rotation of morning game shows, afternoon movies, evenings rereading the sports magazines that came in the mail. This morning he sat up and took a deep, experimental breath . . . then coughed, but not as deeply or painfully as the morning before. The air felt good. Sweet summer morning air, fresher than hospital oxygen. It was like a memory long forgotten and suddenly recalled. *Do you want to live?* Yes, by God! This morning he wanted very much to live. Even if it meant—in the long run—a certain *strangeness*.

Lingering in bed, Ira Park thought briefly about the possibility of going back to work at Harvest Hardware, where he had labored behind the counter for twenty-five years. Then he figured not. He had spent twenty-five years in retail sales and that was enough for one lifetime. Find something new to do for the next twenty-five years. Or twenty-five hundred.

· · ·

He had been replaced at Harvest by Ted Keening, eighteen, who had been described by his high-school guidance counselor (in a private joke in the teachers' lounge) as "not exactly college material. Too dumb for an academic scholarship, too fat for a sports scholarship, and too poor to buy his way in."

Ted was a television junkie and still some twenty pounds bigger than he'd like, but he'd lost weight since he started working at the store. There was a fair amount of physical labor involved, hauling stock up from the basement and so forth. But Ted was beginning to realize that his future contained more than a career in measuring chain and weighing nails. He had awakened this morning with the knowledge that he didn't have to die and that pretty soon no one would be liable to call him fat or stupid—which was how he had thought of himself even before he paused by the east window of the teacher's lounge and overheard his guidance counselor's joke. His reaction to this morning's revelation wasn't triumphant or gloating, just . . . he guessed "astonished" might be the best word. He didn't completely understand what was happening. It was *too big* to understand. But he felt the future. His own. The world's. The future had become a curious and wonderful thing. It shimmered on the horizon like a heat mirage, as hard to see, as achingly bright, but much more real.

■ ■ ■

He told his boss he might not be working at Harvest much longer. Mr. Webster, who had also said yes to an unvoiced question during his long sleep, told him he understood and that, as far as he could tell, there might not *be* hardware stores much longer. Which would be kind of a shame, given the years and money he had invested in this place. "But what the hell. I'm sixty-five years old. I'd have to give up the store one way or another. I guess I'd sooner walk away from it than get shut in a coffin. Ted, I think we're all bound for something we can't even guess at. It's as strange a thing as I have encountered, and you probably feel the same. But unless you're done with us already, would you mind ringing up these items for Mr. Porter?"

■ ■ ■

Billy Porter, Beth's father, was a fairly steady customer. Usually he came in for car parts from the automotive section. Billy was always fiddling with his ten-year-old Subaru, a car that stalled at intersections no matter what he did to the choke or the idle or any other part he could get his hands on. Or he came in to buy shells for his hunting rifle, Billy being an occasional hunter whenever his friends offered to drive him up into the mountains. Today he had bellied up to the checkout with a selection of garden tools, which Mr. Webster found vaguely amusing: The idea of Billy down on his hands and knees in the mulch . . . planting tulips, maybe . . .

But maybe it wasn't so funny. "Becky always kept the garden in such fine shape," Billy said. "I'm ashamed how I let it go. I thought it wouldn't take much cleaning up. A little work, what the hell."

"Taking the day off?" Mr. Webster asked.

"Taking an easy shift, anyhow. I don't know how much longer they'll need me down at the mill."

Billy had also said *yes*.

■　■　■

Some few had not.

Billy's daughter Beth had answered *No!*—had understood the offer and rejected it. She couldn't say exactly why. Something in her had grown sullen and hard and had drawn away from this alien touch. No, not me. You won't steal from me my dying.

But she woke knowing what she had turned down and it made her a little sad. The real question was, *What next?* What threats and possibilities lurked in this soon-to-be-new world?

She hiked down to the mall and called Joey Commoner from a pay phone.

Joey didn't want to talk about it, but Beth understood from his cryptic responses to her careful questions that Joey had also said *No*.

Wouldn't you know it? Birds of a feather, thought Beth. Well, damn. The last real people.

The last Aztecs, Rector Ackroyd might have said.

■　■　■

There were others.

Miriam Flett, who woke that morning with her agonies and virtues intact, but with a new idea of whose Hand had touched her during the night.

Tom Kindle, who had lived on the slopes of Mt. Buchanan for five years in a cabin without city electricity. He came into town summer weekends, when he operated a private ferry to the bay islands, but he spent his winters alone and liked it that way. What he didn't like was the shape of the miracle he had been offered in the night. A lemming future, Kindle thought. No damn privacy.

One junior member of the City Council and one city clerk.

A salesman at Highway Five Buick.

Matt Wheeler.

Chapter 9

Many Mansions

When he woke, Matt's first observation was that his fever had broken. He felt clearheaded and alert—there was nothing left of the sedation of the night before. But something was wrong.

He rolled over and reached for Annie, but his hand touched empty sheets.

Like everyone else, he had spent the night dreaming. His dream had seemed vividly real . . . *was real*, some part of him insisted. But Matt was equally determined that it *must not* be real, and he screwed down that determination like a carpenter's clamp over all errant and contrary thoughts. A dream, he instructed himself, was only a dream.

The house smelled of frying bacon and buttered toast. Matt dressed in weekend clothes, Levi's and a sweatshirt, and headed for the kitchen. A bar of sunlight crossed the tiled mosaic floor. A window stood open and morning air plucked at the curtains.

Annie and Rachel were collaborating on breakfast. Matt stood in the doorway a moment before they noticed him. They were giggling at some joke, heads together, Rachel in shorts and an old khaki shirt, Annie still in her nightgown. They cracked eggs into a blue plastic bowl.

It was Annie who turned and saw him. Her smile didn't fade, exactly. But there was a hitch in it—a blink of uncertainty.

"Breakfast coming up," she said. "For late risers. Jim and Lillian left early, by the way. They said thanks for the party and they'd stop for food at McDonald's."

"Wasn't much of a party," Matt said.

"Some wine, some friends. What else do you need?" Annie shooed him toward the table. "Go on, Matt, sit down. If you try to help you'll just get in the way."

He watched her move around the kitchen, tousle-haired and pretty in her nightgown. They hadn't made love last night. Blame it on the Taiwan Flu. But it had been much, much too long since the last time. Matt recalled five separate occasions when he had considered asking Annie to marry him, and each time he had shied away from the question, diverted by some lingering guilt or just a fear of disturbing the status quo, their fragile dalliance. Should have asked her, he thought. We'd have had more of these mornings. More nights in bed.

Rachel was curiously cheerful serving up the scrambled eggs. It was a rare pleasure to see her smiling. When she was a toddler, that grin had been big and infectious. Celeste would take her shopping and strangers would offer compliments—"Such a happy baby." She'd been a happy baby, happy toddler, happy little girl. It had taken Celeste's death to erase that smile, and Matt was surprised at the depth of his own reaction now that he was seeing it again. How long since she'd smiled like that? Not a brave smile or a halfhearted smile but a big Rachel grin?

But this was a thought both maudlin and dangerous, and Matt suppressed it and focused his eyes willfully on the varnished tabletop.

Rachel joined him at the table; Annie did not. He said, "You're not eating?"

"I ate. I have to dress. You two take your time."

She left the room, but not before Matt noticed a glance that traveled between Annie and Rachel like a semaphore signal.

He looked at his watch and saw that the date crept ahead an extra day. How had that happened? In his dream he had seemed to sleep much too long—but that was only a dream. Focus, Matt thought. He suffered a momentary fear that the world might fade around him, the walls of reality shatter to reveal . . . a void.

"Want to hear the radio?" Rachel asked.

Christ, no, Matt thought. "No—please." He was afraid, for reasons he could not admit, of what the radio might say.

She recoiled a little. "Sorry, Daddy."

"It's all right."

She picked at her eggs. The silence in the room was suddenly weighty, and Rachel's smile had faded.

"Daddy," she said, "I'm okay. Really."

"Of course you are."

"You're worried about me. But I'm fine. I really am. Daddy?" She looked at him intently. "Daddy, did you dream last night?"

He would not endure the weight of the question. He fought a childish urge to close his eyes and cover his ears. He looked away from Rachel and said, through a wave of shame that seemed to thicken his tongue, "No, honey, I didn't. I didn't dream at all."

▪ ▪ ▪

He drove Annie home along the bay shore.

Buchanan was quiet again today, but it was a normal Saturday quiet, not yesterday's odd and uneasy tranquillity. Folks were out in the morning cool, mowing lawns, weeding, making grocery runs. Matt allowed himself a moment's appreciation of all this suburban peace.

A blue haze rode up the slope of the mountain. The air through the wing window carried a rich bouquet of pine resin and sun-warmed asphalt. Matt followed the lazy curve of the road past the commercial dock, where a trawler stood in rust-colored repose, through the business district and beyond a high bluff of land to the apartment complex where Annie lived.

He had never understood why she chose to live in this down-at-the-heels corner of town, in an old walk-up building with pasteboard walls. She had never explained. There were a lot of things Annie had never explained. Where she disappeared to the second Saturday of every month, for instance; or why she had never replaced her genteel but ancient furniture.

But she invited him up, and he accepted the invitation. For all its apparent poverty, this was still very much an Annie kind of place: a bedroom and a big living room overlooking the bay, sparsely furnished, clean wooden floors, the elderly tabby-cat Beulah snoozing in a patch of sunlight. The apartment was as economical as a haiku: Every detail mattered.

Annie spooned out coffee into the basket of her coffee maker. Beulah had been fed by a neighbor; she paid no attention to the kitchen noises. The machine began to burble. Annie said, "We have to talk, Matt."

He knew that "we have to talk" was polite code for an impending emotional meltdown, and he didn't like it. He stood at the window and watched the ocean roll out blue and calm to the horizon. *Did* they have to talk? Was silence such a bad thing?

"Matt?" she said. "Did you dream last night?"

It was almost possible to hate her for the question.

He said, "Rachel asked me the same thing."

"Oh? What did you tell her?"

"I told her no."

"I don't think she believed you."

"She didn't say."

"*I* don't believe you."

He turned away with enormous reluctance from his view of the sunlit sea. "What's this about, Annie?"

"I had a dream," she said. "Rachel had a dream. I think every living human being on the surface of the Earth had that dream. Even you."

He fought an urge to bolt for the door. He was sweating, he was tense, and he couldn't resist his own diagnosis: *Denial*, announced the premed hotshot inside him. *You're denying what you don't want to face.*

He sat down at Annie's lacquered pine dinner table and closed his eyes. Beulah bumped against his leg. He picked her up. Beulah began to purr.

"All right," he said flatly. "Tell me what you dreamed."

•   •   •

But it wasn't a dream, Annie said, not really. It was a *visitation*, and the agency of that visitation had been the microorganisms—or machines—Jim Bix had warned him about.

("No, Matt, don't ask me how I know these things. I just do. Let me finish.")

The microbes were neither organism nor mechanism, Annie said; they were an amalgam of both, or something beyond either. They were capable of reproduction and were even, in their own dim way, intelligent. They had been distributed into the atmosphere by the trillions upon trillions, had ridden the jet stream to the extremities of the Earth, and by the end of July they had colonized every human organism on the surface of the planet. Within the last week they had begun to reproduce; their growth and their activity was what had produced the alarming hematology results.

Their job was to function as the voice of the Artifact. That is, of the Travellers.

Annie called them "Travellers" because that was their name for themselves: It defined them. Like the microbes they created, they were not organic beings. Unlike their creations, they once had been. They had been both organic and planetbound: creatures like ambulatory sponges, building their cities in the methane-rich tidal sinks of an Earth-sized moon orbiting a Jovian planet of an unimaginably distant star.

They had outgrown their world. They had poisoned it with organic and machine wastes, a catastrophe averted only by their abandonment of both organism and mechanism. In the wake of that crisis they became Travellers: planetless, bodiless.

The Artifact was their world now. It was both a physical structure and a much larger virtual environment. They inhabited it, a greater number of souls than the Earth contained human beings, but only a few of them occupied physical bodies at any given time, and then only for the purpose of repairing and maintaining the Artifact itself.

They were, she told Matt, not a hive or a computer or any such easily imagined thing; they were separate creatures, individuals, unique—but *capable* of so much more, being immaterial; of complex joinings and indefinite sleeps, of enduring the long journeys between stars without boredom or decline, of learning without ending. Their lifespan was indefinite, unlimited. They had achieved a kind of immortality.

They had been Travellers, Annie said—knowing some of these things only as she said them—since the Earth was a whirl of dust and the sun a hot new star, and they had forgotten nothing of what they had seen in those millennia. They were a vast library of inconceivably ancient wisdom, and they had arrived at the Earth at what they considered a critical and fortuitous moment, because, Annie said, *we are what they had once been*: intelligent, planetbound, and poisoning a world with our waste products.

It was obvious, she said, why they hadn't communicated with governments or world leaders. They had a better means of communication, the cybernetic microbes, a kind of arm of themselves with which they could touch each human being individually. This more intimate contact was the only communication worthy of the word. The microbes, which might be called *neocytes*, interfaced with nervous tissue, touching but not changing it. At the brink of Contact they had soothed the frightened population of the Earth—sedated us, Annie said, yes, but only long enough and deeply enough to prevent panic. Then they had induced a kind of long, deep sleep, and in that sleep the Travellers had spoken. They had spoken to six billion human beings over the course of the next thirty hours, and what they spoke was not merely language but a complex of, for lack of a better word, *understandings*, deeper and more profound than language could ever be. And they had explained all this and more, much more than Annie could tell.

But Matt, she said, you *must* have felt it: All the possibilities . . . the literally infinite possibilities . . . the lives they led . . . and their place, the Artifact, like a nautilus shell, not dead, as it had seemed, but filled with lives strange and various beyond belief. They must have showed you that.

They must have offered it to you, Annie said. Because they offered it to me.

They said I could have it, too.

Do you want to live? they had asked. *Live without dying? Live, in effect, forever?*

And Annie had said yes.

Do you want to live, they had asked, *even if you change? Even if you become, in time, something no longer entirely human?*

And that had given her pause; but she thought again of their long, complex, interesting lives; she understood that *everything* changed, that death itself was a kind of change, that *of course* it was impossible to live forever without changing—change was to be expected.

And again she said yes.

■ ■ ■

She poured coffee and put the cup in front of Matt. Matt examined the cup. It was a solid thing, gratifyingly real. A familiar thing.

Beulah yawned and jumped out of his lap; preferred, apparently, the sunlit floor.

Annie put her hand on his shoulder. "What did you tell them, Matt?" He pulled away from her touch. "I told them no."

Chapter
10
Etiquette

The President, whose given name was William, did what he had not done in quite this way for many years: he took a walk.

He left the White House by the Main Portico and crossed Pennsylvania Avenue into Lafayette Square. He walked alone.

It was a fine September morning. The air was cool, but a gentle sunlight warmed his hands and face. The President paused as he entered the park. Then he smiled and shrugged off his jacket. He unbuttoned his collar and pulled off his tie. He folded the black silk tie into a square and tucked it absentmindedly into his hip pocket.

No etiquette in the new world, he thought.

He was reminded of the story about Calvin Coolidge, who had shocked the fashionable guests at a White House breakfast by pouring his heavily creamed coffee into a saucer. Shocked but unfailingly polite, Coolidge's guests had done the same. They waited wide-eyed for the President to take the first sip. At which point Coolidge picked up the saucer, leaned over, and presented it to the White House cat.

The story was funny, but it seemed to William there was something ugly about it, too—too much of the ancient vertebrate politics of dominance and submission. After all, what was a President that anyone should be frightened of one? Only a title. A suit of clothes—and not a particularly comfortable one.

He was ashamed that there had been times when he thought *of himself* as "the President"—as a sort of icon, less man than emblem. He supposed that was how the Roman emperors might have felt, anointed by the gods; or their Chinese counterparts ruling under the Mandate of Heaven. These are dream-names we give ourselves, he thought; indeed, much of his life seemed like a dream, a dream he had been dreaming too deeply and for too long.

A dream from which he had been awakened by a dream.

The morning air made him feel young. He remembered a summer his family had spent at a beach resort in Maine. Not the riverside cabin he had recalled in that long-ago address to the nation. That had been an isolated July in the Adirondacks, much embroidered by his speechwriter. The family's summer place in William's twelfth year had been a fabulous old resort hotel, erected in the Gilded Age and preserved against the solvent properties of salt air and progress. Its attractions were its fine linens, its European cuisine, and its two miles of wild Atlantic beach. William's mother had admired the linen. William had admired the beach.

He had been allowed to explore the beach by himself as long as he promised to stay out of the water, which was, in any case, too chilly and violent for his liking. He loved the ocean from a cautious distance, but he loved it nonetheless. All that summer, every morning, he would choke down breakfast and bolt from the hotel like a wild horse vaulting a fence. He ran where the sand was packed and hard, ran until his side stitched and his lungs felt raw. And when he couldn't run anymore he would take off his shoes and explore the wetter margin of the beach, where water oozed between his toes and odd things lived in the tide pools and among the rocks.

When he tired of that, he would sit in the high salt grass and gaze at the juncture of ocean and sky for as much as an hour at a time. England was across that water. England, where American flyers had gone to join the battle against the Luftwaffe. Beyond England, Vichy France. Europe under the heel of the Nazis; embattled Stalingrad.

He watched the great clouds roll along the ocean rim, clouds that might have come from war-torn Europe, but more likely from the tropics, from seas that still carried a whiff of Joseph Conrad and H. Rider Haggard when he saw their names on a map: the Indian Ocean, the Arabian Sea, the Bay of Bengal. He would dream in such a fashion, and then he would eat his lunch: cold roast beef from the hotel kitchen and a thermos of sweet iced tea.

I was once as alive as that.

What fairy tales our lives are, William thought. How strange that that child could have conceived an ambition to rule the United States—could have pursued his ambition so relentlessly that he became something stony and patrician. It seemed to him now that he had fallen into a kind of trance, though he could not say exactly when. In law school? When he first ran for office? He had folded himself into the cloak of his career until it dimmed his urge to run away down some sunny summer beach. What a shame.

He drifted into sleep, sun-warmed on a park bench by the statue of Rochambeau . . . but the touch of the pistol barrel on his neck woke him instantly.

▪ ▪ ▪

The steel barrel was pressed against a space two inches below his left ear, sliding minutely against a knot of muscle under the skin.

William turned his head cautiously away from the pressure and looked up.

He did not immediately recognize the man who was holding the pistol. He was a tall man with a neat brush of white hair. A strong man, but not a young man—on the shy side of sixty, the President guessed. He was wearing an immaculate three-piece suit with the jacket open. William saw all this in the blink of an eye.

The face was startlingly handsome. And not completely unfamiliar.

He probed his memory. "Ah," he said at last. "Colonel Tyler."

John Tyler kept his body tight against the weapon to disguise it from the few tourists strolling in the park. He slid the barrel across William's collarbone and into his belly as he sat beside him on the bench.

John Tyler's name had cropped up every so often in the *National Intelligence Daily* or the President's *FTPO* briefings. Tyler had been a minor player in the planned coup d'état, which had been derailed, of course, by Contact. He was one of those ex–military men who lead odd little careers in the defense lobby, the so-called Iron Triangle. Revolving-door connections with—who was it? Ford Aerospace? General Dynamics? In exchange for some ground-floor lobbying with the House Armed Services Committee or the Subcommittee on Procurement. A man with contacts at the Pentagon, and Langley, and at certain banks. Tyler was an educated man and a convincing public speaker, and his prospects might have been brighter if not for the hint of a scandal that had ended his military career—some sexual impropriety, as William recalled.

He knew one other thing about John Tyler. A small piece of intelligence from a loyalist Air Force general. The architects of the coup had had a particular role in mind for Colonel Tyler: If William had refused to retire peaceably to some country dacha, it was John Tyler who was to put a bullet in his brain.

"I watched you," Tyler said. His voice was quiet but bitter. "I watched you leave the White House. My God, it's startling to see a President in public without a Secret Service escort. Did you think it was all over? You didn't need the bodyguards anymore?"

"It *is* over. The guards all went home, Colonel." He looked at Tyler's pistol. An ugly little machine. "Is this your revolution? I thought that was over, too."

"Keep your hands down," Tyler said. "I should kill you right now."

"Is that what you mean to do?"

"Most likely."

"What would be the point, Colonel Tyler?"

"The point, sir, would be that a dead President is better than a live traitor."

"I see."

In fact, William understood several things from this small speech:

He understood that the coup was a thing of the past; that Colonel Tyler had come here representing no one but himself.

He understood that Tyler had said *no* to the Travellers and was only beginning to grasp the significance of Contact.

And he understood that beneath his rigid calm, the Colonel was teetering on the brink of panic and madness. *Would* Tyler shoot him? He might or might not. It was an open question. It would be decided by impulse.

Choose your words carefully, William told himself.

"You had friends," he said to Tyler, "but they all changed their minds. They woke up and saw that the world is a different place now. Not you, Colonel?"

"You can bank on that."

"That was a week ago. Did you wait all this time to see me?" William nodded at the White House behind its spiked fence. "You could have walked in the front door, Colonel. No one would have stopped you."

"I talked to your friend Charlie Boyle yesterday. He told me the same thing. I didn't believe him." Tyler shrugged. "But maybe it's true. I mean, if you're out taking a goddamn stroll."

Charlie Boyle has only been my friend since he woke up immortal, William thought; but yes, Charlie had been telling the truth. The White House was open to the public. Like any other museum.

There was a twitch of impatience from Tyler, a slight pursing of the lips. William drew a slow breath.

"Colonel Tyler, surely you know what's happening. Even if you don't want any part of it. Even if you said no to it. This isn't an alien invasion. The flying saucers haven't landed. The Earth hasn't been occupied by a hostile military force. Look around."

Tyler's frown deepened, and for a space of some seconds his finger tightened on the trigger. William felt the barrel of the gun pulse against his body with the beating of Tyler's heart.

Death hovered over the park bench like a third presence.

That shouldn't frighten me anymore, William thought. But it does. Yes, it still does.

"What I think," Tyler said, "is that everybody has been infected with a hallucination. The hallucination is that we can live forever. That we can cohabit like the lamb and the lion in a Baptist psalm book. I think most people succumbed to this disease. But some of us didn't. Some of us recovered from it. I think I'm a well man, Mr. President. And I think you're very sick."

"Not a traitor? Just sick?"

"Maybe both. You collaborated—for whatever reason. You're not qualified to hold office any longer."

"*Am* I sick? You're the one with the pistol, Colonel Tyler."

"A weapon in the right hands is hardly a sign of illness."

How strange it was to be having this conversation on such a gentle day. He looked away from Colonel Tyler and saw a ten-year-old attempting to fly a kite from the foot of the statue of Andrew Jackson. The breeze was fitful. The kite flailed and sank. The boy's skin was dark and gleaming in the sunlight. The kite was a beauty, William thought. A black-and-yellow bat wing.

For a moment the boy's eyes caught his and there was a flash of communication—an acknowledgment in the Greater World of each other's difficulties.

I may yet talk my way out of this, William thought.

"Colonel Tyler, suppose I admit I'm unqualified to hold the office of President of the United States."

"I have a gun on you. You might admit any damn thing."

"Nonetheless, I *do* admit it. I'm not qualified. I say it without reservation, and I'll continue to say it when you put the gun away. I'll sign a paper if you like. Colonel, would you care to help me nominate a successor?"

For the first time, Tyler seemed uncertain.

"I'm quite sincere," William hurried on. "I want your advice. Whom did you have in mind? Charlie Boyle? But he's not trustworthy anymore, is he? He's 'diseased.' The Vice-President? The same, I'm afraid. The Speaker of the House?"

"This is contentious bullshit," Tyler said, but he looked suddenly miserable and distracted.

"Colonel Tyler, it would not surprise me if you were the highest-ranking military officer not under the influence of what you call a disease. I don't know how the chain of command operates in a case like this. It's something the Constitution doesn't anticipate. But if you want the job—"

"My Christ, you're completely insane," Tyler said. But the gun wavered in his hand.

"It's a question of constituency. That's the fundamental problem. Colonel, do you know how many people turned down the opportunity to live forever? Roughly one in ten thousand."

"You can't possibly know that."

"For the sake of argument, let's assume I do. The population of the Earth is roughly six billion, which yields six hundred million individuals who are not, as you say, diseased. Quite a number. But not all of them are Americans—not by a long shot. Colonel Tyler, do you recall the last census estimate of the American population? It's vague in my mind. Something on the order of three hundred million. That would give you a constituency of roughly thirty thousand people. The size of a large town. Quite an amenable size for a democracy, in my opinion. Under ideal circumstances, you could establish direct representative government . . . if you mean to continue holding elections."

Colonel Tyler's eyes had begun to glaze. "I can't accept that. I—"

"Can't accept what? My argument? Or the Presidency?"

"You can't confer that on me! You can't hand it to me like some kind of Cracker Jack prize!"

"But you were willing to take it away with a gun—you and your allies."

"That's different!"

"Is it? It's not exactly due process."

"I'm not the fucking President! *You're* the fucking President!"

"You can shoot me if you want, Colonel Tyler." He stood up, a calculated risk, and made his voice imperious. He became the President of the United States—as Tyler had insisted—one more weary time. "If you shoot me once or twice I might survive. I understand this body of mine is a little tougher than it used to be. If you shoot me repeatedly, the body will be beyond repair. Though it seems a shame to clutter Lafayette Square with a corpse on such a fine sunny morning."

Colonel Tyler stood up and kept the pistol against William's belly. "If you can die, you're not immortal."

"The body is mortal. I'm not. There is a portion of the Artifact that contains my—I suppose *essence* is the best word. I am as much there as I am here. I am *awake* here, Colonel, and I am *asleep* there . . . but if you shoot me you'll only reverse the equation."

A wind swept through the park. A dozen yards away, the boy's kite flapped and hesitated. *Pull*, William thought. *Work the string.*

The kite soared, black and yellow in a blue sky.

"Let's take a walk, Colonel," William said. "My legs cramp if I don't stretch them once in a while."

▪ ▪ ▪

They walked along 17th toward Potomac Park, past the Corcoran Art Gallery and the offices of the OAS, the blind jumble of Washington architecture.

The city's most revealing buildings were still its monuments, William thought. The Lincoln Memorial, the Jefferson Memorial. An American idea of a British idea of a Roman idea of the civic architecture of the Greeks.

But the Athenians had operated their democracy in the agora. We should have copied their marketplaces, not their temples. Should have moved in some fruit stands, William thought. A rug vendor or two. Called Congress to session among the peanut carts on Constitution Avenue.

He had once loved the idea of democracy. He had loved it the way he loved his beach in Maine. Like his love of the beach, he had misplaced his love of democracy in the long journey to the White House.

Oh, he mentioned the word in speeches. But all the juice had gone out of it.

He wondered if Colonel Tyler had ever really loved democracy. He suspected the Colonel had never loved a beach.

"You gave all this away," Tyler was saying. "It went without a battle. Not a raised fist, Mr. President. It's a crime worth a bullet, don't you think?"

The gun had retreated into a holster under the Colonel's jacket, but William was still acutely aware of its presence.

"What are you suggesting I gave away, Colonel?"

"America," Tyler said. "The nation. It's sovereignty."

"Hardly mine to give up."

"But you collaborated."

"Only if you persist in seeing this as an invasion. Well. I suppose I *did* collaborate, in a certain way." It was true, the President's significant dream had come a few nights before the rest. Early Contacts fell into two categories: the very ill and the very powerful. The ill, so their diseases wouldn't carry them off at the eleventh hour. The powerful, so dangerous mistakes might not be made. "I think of it as cooperation, not collaboration."

"I think of it as treason," Tyler said flatly.

"Is it? What choice did I have? Was there some way to resist? Would a panic have changed anything?"

"We'll never know."

"No, I don't suppose we will. But, Colonel, the process has been democratic. I think you have to admit that much. The question—the question of living forever and all that it entails—was asked of everyone. You think I should have spoken for America. But I couldn't, and I didn't have to. America spoke for itself. Colonel, it's obvious *you* were able to turn down that offer. Others could have made the same choice. By and large, they didn't."

"Absurd," Tyler said. "Do you really believe that? You think creatures who can invade your metabolism and occupy your brain can't *lie* about it?"

"But did they? You were as 'invaded' as everyone else. And yet, here we are."

"I said I might be immune."

"To the compulsion but not to the asking? It's an odd kind of immunity, Colonel."

They settled on a bench in the Constitution Gardens where pigeons worried the grass for crumbs. William wondered what the pigeons had made of all these sweeping changes in the human *epistemos*. Fewer tourists. But the few were more generous.

He should have brought something to feed the birds.

"Think about what you're telling me," Tyler said. "They approached *everyone*? Every human being on the surface of the earth? Including infants? Senile cripples in rest homes? Criminals? The feebleminded?"

"I'm given to understand, Colonel, that the children *always* said yes. They don't believe in death, I think. An infant, a baby, might not have the language—but the question was not posed entirely in language. The infants and the senile share a will to live, even if they can't articulate it. Similarly the mentally ill. There is a nugget of self that understands and responds. Even the criminals, Colonel, though it is a long journey for them even if they accept this gift, because it comes with the burden of understanding, and they have many terrible things they may not want to know about themselves. Some of the worst of them will have turned down the offer."

The Colonel laughed a wild and unpleasant laugh. "You know what you're saying? You're telling me I'm the unelected President of a nation of homicidal maniacs."

"Hardly. People have other reasons for not wanting immortality. Such as your reason, I presume."

The Colonel scowled. Here was dangerous territory, William thought. He took a breath and persisted: "It's like looking into a mirror, isn't it? When the Travellers talk, they talk to the root of you. Not the picture of yourself you carry around in your head. The heart. The soul. The self that is everything you've done and wanted to do and refrained from doing. One's truest self isn't always a handsome sight, is it, Colonel? Mine was not, certainly."

Colonel Tyler had no response except a haggard exhalation of breath.

The pigeons didn't like this sound and they rose up in a cloud, to settle some distance away by the Reflecting Pool, where the image of the sky was pleasant in the cool wind-rippled water.

■   ■   ■

Over the past week, traffic inside the Beltway had been light. Official Washington had begun to close up shop, in a mutual consensus that required no debate. Capitol Hill had become a ghost town—just yesterday, William had stood in the Rotunda and listened to his footsteps echo in the dome above his head. But there were still tourists in the city, if you could call them tourists—people who had come for a last look at the governing apparatus of a nation.

Some of these people passed quietly along the Mall. William did not feel misplaced among them, though they seemed to make Colonel Tyler nervous.

"I want to ask you a question," Tyler said.

"I'm a politician, Colonel. We're notorious for dodging the hard ones."

"I think you ought to take this more seriously, Mr. President." Tyler touched the bulge of the pistol almost absently. His eyes were unfocused. And William reminded himself that the Colonel's madness might not be new; it might be an old madness that Contact had simply aroused and let loose. It was as if Tyler generated a kind of heat. The heat was danger, and the temperature might rise at any provocation.

"I'm sorry if I seemed flippant. Go on."

"What happens next? According to your scenario, I mean."

William pondered the question. "Colonel, don't you have anyone else to ask? A wife, a girlfriend? Some member of your family? I have no official standing—my information is no better than anyone else's."

"I'm not married," Tyler said. "I have no living family."

And here was another piece of the John Tyler puzzle: a grievous, ancient loneliness. Tyler was a solitary man for whom Contact must have seemed like a final exclusion from the human race.

It was a bleak and terrible thought.

"In all seriousness, Colonel, it's a difficult question. You don't need me to tell you everything is changing. People have new needs, and they've abandoned some old ones—and we're all still coming to terms with that. I think . . . in time, these cumbersome bodies will have to go. But not for a while yet." It was an honest answer.

Tyler fixed him with a terrible look—equal parts fear, outrage, and contempt. "And after that?"

"I don't know. It needs a decision—a collective decision. But I have an inkling. I think our battered planet deserves a renewal. I think, very soon, it might get one."

■ ■ ■

They had made a circle; they stood now outside the gates of the White House, and the day had grown warm as it edged toward noon.

Despite the threat, William was tired of dueling with John Tyler. He felt like a schoolboy waiting for some long detention to grind to an end. "Well, Colonel?" He looked Tyler in the eye. "Have you decided to shoot me?"

"I would if I thought it would help. If I thought it would win back even an inch of this country—dear God, I'd kill you without blinking." Tyler reached beneath his suitcoat and scratched himself. "But you're not much of a threat. As quislings go, you're merely pathetic."

William concealed his relief. Immortal I may be, he thought. But I'm not finished with this incarnation.

Besides, how would he have explained his death to Elizabeth? She would accuse him of clumsiness—perhaps rightly so.

"You think this conflict is over," Tyler said. "I don't grant that. Some of us are still willing to fight for our country."

But why fight, William thought. The country is yours! Colonel Tyler—take it!

But he kept these thoughts to himself.

"I only hope," Tyler said as he turned away, "the rest of the geldings are as docile as you."

■ ■ ■

William watched the Colonel walk away.

Tyler was a man on a terrible brink, William thought. He was alone and vastly outnumbered and carrying some ghastly cargo of old sin. The world he lived in was receding beyond the limits of his comprehension.

And it need not have been that way. Maybe that was the worst part.

You could have said yes, Colonel. And you know that, whether you choose to admit it or not.

■   ■   ■

William experienced this sadness for Colonel Tyler, then folded it into memory the way he had folded his silk tie into his pocket.

He might not have seen the last of Colonel Tyler—but that was tomorrow's worry.

Today was still pretty and fresh. He had fifteen minutes to spare before lunch. And no one had killed him.

He considered the White House lawn. Scene of countless Easter egg hunts, diplomatic photo opportunities, presentations of awards. Had he ever really looked at it? The groundskeepers did excellent work. The grass was verdant and still sparkling with morning dew.

He wondered how it would feel to unlace his shoes and peel off his socks and walk barefoot over that green and gentle surface.

He decided it was time to find out.

Chapter 11

Kindle

The dream, in Tom Kindle's opinion, was just what it appeared to be: an invitation to submerge himself in a cozy, communal immortality. And while Kindle found the idea repulsive, he harbored no illusions about the attraction it would hold for his fellow men.

Therefore, in the two weeks and some days since that peculiar night, Kindle had stayed out of town. He wasn't sure what Buchanan would look like when he saw it again. He wasn't sure he wanted to know.

He had hoped to postpone any journey into town as long as possible, but that desire became academic when he slipped on a muddy hiking trail and came to rest twenty vertical feet down the west slope of Mt. Buchanan, his left leg broken at the hip.

■　■　■

Maybe he shouldn't have been on the trail at all. Nothing had forced him out here. His cabin was well-stocked and he had plenty to read. Currently he was working his way through Gibbon's *History of the Decline and Fall of the Roman Empire*. The book was not much more entertaining than yesterday's dishwater, but Kindle had bought it as part of a five-foot shelf of the Classics of Western Literature, and he was determined to get his money's worth.

Nor had claustrophobia driven him out. The cabin was spacious enough. He had bought this little property—some miles from Buchanan up an old logging road—in 1990. The cabin itself was a kit-built project he had put up with the help of a few friends, one a building contractor with access to quality tools. Since then, every penny that didn't maintain his boat or buy food had gone into improving the property.

He paid for town water, since the municipality had run a public works line up here during the real-estate rush of the eighties. But his only electric power came from a gasoline generator in a shed out back. Winters were sometimes snowy, but Kindle had insulated the building and installed a woodstove to keep himself warm. No need for that this time of year, not just yet.

It was a cabin—not quite big enough to be called a house—but it was a *comfortable* cabin, and he wasn't suffering from cabin fever. The impulse to take a long walk up these back trails had been only that, an impulse, obviously a stupid one. The dry spell had broken last week; rain had fallen for three consecutive days and the trails were wet. The trails were also, in places, steep.

And Kindle was, he hated to admit, not awfully young anymore. When asked, he gave his age as "about fifty." In truth, he paid little attention to his age and disliked doing the calculation. When you live alone and work alone, who gives a doughnut hole about birthdays? Who *counts* 'em?

But he had turned fifty-three in January and wasn't as agile as he used to be. Consequently, when he came up a muddy switchback where a fallen pine had carried off a square yard of the hiking trail, he wasn't quick or canny enough to grab at the nearest root or sapling as his boots rolled under him and the world turned suddenly vertical.

He lost consciousness when the leg snapped.

▪   ▪   ▪

When he woke again, some vital instinct kept him immobile. He did not dare to move, only blinked up at a sky crowded with moist conifers and worked at interpreting this sensation of something gone terribly wrong.

He was light-headed and not ashamed of talking to himself—not that he ever had been.

"You fell down." The basic datum. "You slipped off the trail, you asshole."

He swiveled his head and saw his own flight path traced in broken saplings and churned topsoil. Long way down. He had fetched up here: in a sort of gully in the hillside, his ass soaking in a cold stream and his legs curled at the trunk of a mossy old hemlock.

He took particular note of something he did not like at all: the way his left knee had rotated at such a peculiar crooked angle.

"Well, shit!" Kindle said. The sight of his broken leg made him feel both frightened and angry. Of the two, the anger was more vocal. He cursed eloquently and loudly, and when he was finished the forest fell silent—blushing, perhaps. And then there was the new and essential question that had to be faced, like it or not: "Tom Kindle, have you killed your idiotic self?"

Maybe he had. The cabin was a quarter-mile downslope—more like a mile by trail. Suppose he made it back: The cabin lacked a telephone. Help was in Buchanan, or anyway no nearer than the closest neighbor—another three miles downhill on a dirt and gravel road.

And there was no guarantee he could move even as far as the next sapling without passing out again.

He shifted his body experimentally and nearly did pass out. The pain when he moved was a brand-new thing, a burning stick thrust into his leg all the way up to the small of his back. He let out a shriek that sent birds wheeling from a nearby tree. When he was still, the agony subsided but did not entirely retreat. It was concentrated in his left leg between hip and knee; everything below that was numb.

The leg needed a splint. It needed to be immobilized, or he simply could not move.

He raised his head and inspected the injury. There seemed to be no blood, no exposed bone; and that, at least, was good. Kindle had once worked at a logging camp in British Columbia, and he had seen a man suffer a leg injury that left his femur projecting from his thigh like six inches of bloody chalk.

The bad news was that this might not be a simple fracture; the knee might be involved. If Kindle recalled his first aid correctly, you don't try to realign a joint injury. You immobilize it and "transport to medical care."

He scanned the immediate area and located the burled walnut walking stick he always carried on these hikes. Good old stick. Friendly presence. Sturdy enough to splint a bad break. *It'll do*, he thought. But it was about a foot and a half out of easy reach.

He pulled himself toward it, screaming.

He screamed throughout the process of binding his leg, an act that seemed to progress in waves. The waves were of pain, and when they crested—when he felt consciousness begin to slip away—he would lie still, panting and dazed, until his vision cleared; then he would work at the splint a while longer.

In the end, after a measureless time, the walnut walking stick was lashed around his thigh and lower leg with torn strips of his cotton shirt—a job he admired as if someone else had done it.

And if he moved?

The splint kept the leg more or less still and minimized the pain. Kindle dragged himself a short distance along the wet bed of the stream. The water was only a trickle, inches deep, but very cold. Not too bad on a warm afternoon like this . . . but it was *late* afternoon, and some of these end-of-summer nights got chilly when the sky was as clear and high as it was today. All this heat would leak away after the sun went down. And then he'd be wet and cold. "Hypothermia," Kindle said out loud. Not to mention shock. Maybe he was in shock already. He was shivering and he was sweating, both at once.

He inched downhill along the bed of the stream. The stream crossed a trail some yards down. Then he could get out of the water. But not until then. There was no way he could drag his fiery, useless leg through the undergrowth of this dense Pacific Coast forest.

It occurred to him as he crawled along the rocky creek bed that if he had accepted the offer of the aliens he might not be in this position. He would be immortal. There would be a Place Prepared For Him, as Kindle's mother used to say. His mother had been religious. Dakota Baptist. Cold winter Baptist. Her philosophy went something like: Kick me till I go to heaven. Kindle's natural father had died of a heart attack while he was driving a snow plow for the municipality; two years later his mother married a carpet installer who got drunk every Saturday night. Oscar was his name. On the coldest Saturday night of a cold Dakota winter, Oscar had been seen, and become famous for, pissing out the second-story bedroom window while singing the Hank Williams tune "I Heard That Lonesome Whistle Blow." Which was all well and good, and nothing Kindle would hold against a man, but Oscar was also a mean and petty drunk who used his fists more than once on Kindle's mother. It was all right, she said, marriage was always a rough road and anyhow there was a Place Prepared For Her. Kindle, who was fifteen, put up with six months of this before he decided that if there was a place prepared for *him*, it was somewhere outside the city limits. He rode to New York City on a Greyhound bus, lied about his age, and served an apprenticeship as a merchant seaman. Five years later he took a trip back home. Oscar was unemployed, drinking Tokay on the steps of the Armory, not worth beating up even for the cold comfort of revenge. His mother had left long since. No forwarding address, which was probably a smart move on her part.

Thus Kindle was alone and suspected there was no Place Prepared For

Him, a suspicion the following thirty-three years had done nothing to dispel. He did not believe in heaven, and he had turned it down when it was offered. Now, however, he wondered if he'd been too hasty.

A Place Prepared might be better than this damp forest, which was getting darker, now that he noticed.

The sky had turned a deep and luminous blue. Had the sun set? Yes, it had, but only just. These old firs and hemlocks were heavy with shadow.

And he was on the trail now, inching along the dirt, caked with mud. When had that happened?

And his throat was raw with screaming, though he did not remember screaming. He wasn't screaming now. The sound he was making was more like a moan. It was a kind of song, not entirely tuneless. It reminded him of the song the flying monkeys sang in the movie *The Wizard of Oz*.

This thought made Kindle feel almost jaunty. He looked up at the stars—now there were stars—and wondered if he could sing a real song. Somewhere under all this pain, he had developed a conviction that everything was actually very funny. This was a funny position to be in. Singing would make it even funnier.

The trouble was, he didn't know very many songs. Oscar's bedroom aria aside, he had never paid attention to songs. He had learned "Jesus Loves Me" at the Baptist Sunday School, but he was damned if he'd sing a Sunday School song when there wasn't even a Place Prepared For Him. He knew "The Streets of Laredo," but only one verse. Maybe one verse was enough.

"As I went out walking the streets of Laredo—"

Mind you, he *shouldn't* have gone out walking.

"As I went out walking in Laredo one day—"

No longer day, but night.

"I met a young cowboy all dressed in white linen—"

He began to wonder if he liked the direction this song had taken.

"All dressed in white linen and cold as the clay."

No, it was the wrong song entirely.

But he went on singing it, and his sense of giddy detachment failed him, and he grew miserable with the thought that he couldn't even decide for himself what song he ought to sing.

• • •

He came within sight of his cabin as the Artifact rose in the western sky.

A kind of moon, it cast a little light. That helped. But the sight of it was a fearful thing for Kindle.

He couldn't say he hated the Artifact. It hadn't given him any cause for hatred. But he had always been suspicious of it. Well, so had everyone else; but Kindle's suspicions had been broader than most. Most people suspected it was an alien spaceship come to wage war or blow up the earth or some such thing. Kindle had doubted that. His experience of the passage of time was that the thing that happened was never the thing you expected. Whatever came of this Artifact, Kindle had thought, it would not be the monster-movie scenario everyone feared. It would be something, certainly not better, but surely *different*—new, unexpected.

And hadn't events proved him right? No one had expected this visitation in the dark, this whisper in the ear about Life Eternal.

Certainly Kindle had never guessed that tiny machines in his nervous tissue would ask him whether he wanted to give up his body and certain habits of mind and grow beyond Kindle into something that was both Kindle and much more than Kindle.

His answer had been immediate. No, by God. He had clung to his aging body and intemperate ego all these years and he wasn't eager to give them up. He disliked the idea of his soul mingling with other souls. He was alone by choice and by nature, and he wanted to keep it that way.

But he wanted to live, too. It was not a love of dying that made him turn down the offer. He wanted desperately to survive. But on his own terms.

He wanted to live, and that was why he was here, prostrate at the door of his thirteen-year-old Ford pickup truck, singing "The Streets of Laredo" in a faint raw voice and wondering how to endure the thing he must do next.

▪ ▪ ▪

To enter a vehicle one must stand up.

Even a one-legged man can stand, Kindle thought.

Unless his pain prevents him.

Unless the act of pulling himself up by the door handle of an old pickup truck grinds bone against ragged bone and causes him to stop singing and makes him scream again instead.

Unless he passes out.

But Kindle remained conscious even as the landscape performed a pirouette around the fiery axis of his spine.

His useless leg, bound and curled at the knee like the leg of a dead fly, flopped against the door of the truck.

Key! Kindle shrieked to himself.

He carried his keys with him always. He braced himself with his right hand and fished in his pocket with his left. Maybe it was stupid to lock up his truck when he lived this far from people. Who would come out here to steal such a wreck? But it was his habit to lock up the things he owned: his truck, his boat, his cabin.

He found the key, transferred it to his right hand, somehow fumbled it into the lock without moving the rest of his body.

Then he took a deep breath, slid away from the door and opened it a crack.

Good work.

But his left leg was splinted, and he dared not tamper with the splint—so how was he supposed to cram himself behind the wheel?

Once behind the wheel—what *then*?

He took the key from the door and clasped it tight in his right hand.

"Tom," he said in a hoarse whisper, "this is the hard part. That other part was easy. This is the hard part."

Easier still to lie down and go to sleep.

Drive in the morning.

Or die before dawn.

More likely that second possibility, Kindle thought. Dying would be the easiest thing of all. Maybe he could even drag himself to the cabin and die on his own sofa, which would at least lend some dignity to the event. People would find him after a while. Maybe they would find his worm-track leading down from the mountain. Goddamn, they would say, look at what this man did! What an admirable man whose corpse is lying on this sofa!

Was this his sofa? Nope, Kindle realized: This was the front seat of the old Ford pickup, and he was stretched out across the length of it.

■   ■   ■

These memory lapses were disturbing, but he imagined he could hear the echo of his own screams fading down the hillside. So perhaps it was better not to dwell on the past.

He pulled himself into a sitting position with his back against the driver's-side door and both legs stretched out across the seat. He could see over the dash well enough. But there was no way to get a foot down to the floor pedals.

At least he was out of the wind. That was no mean accomplishment.

He looked around for a way to push the pedals.

His resources were meager. Within reach: an empty styrofoam cup, a snow brush, and a copy of *Guns and Ammo*. Not too helpful.

Oh, and one other thing. The walking stick he had used to splint his leg.

The leg had swollen enormously. From crotch to knee, it looked like a cased sausage. The rags he had used to bind the splint were deeply embedded, the knots pulled tight by the pressure.

Don't make me do this, Kindle thought. No, this is too much. I can't even begin to do this.

But his traitorous hands were already fumbling against the feverish flesh down there.

■   ■   ■

When he came to himself again, he found the walking stick clutched in his trembling left hand.

It was still nighttime, though the Artifact had set. Maybe it was coming on toward morning. Kindle didn't know; he didn't wear a watch. The stars looked like morning stars.

He was shaking like a sick animal. This shaking was a bad thing, it seemed to him. Made it hard to keep the broad end of his walking stick secure against the floor pedals. And it would only get harder when the truck was moving.

He put the key into the ignition, pumped the gas pedal twice and turned the key.

The engine coughed but didn't catch.

That was normal. Kindle sometimes thought of this old Ford as his "hiccup truck" for the way its engine fought him. It would catch, run, stall; or nearly stall, misfire, rattle and bounce for a time before it settled down. "Come on, you sack of shit," Kindle whispered. "Come on, you lazy turd."

The engine caught and lurched and Kindle screamed as the truck jogged on its ancient shocks. His broken leg was braced against the seat, but there was nothing to hold it and no way to prevent it flopping around in that sickening, loose way.

Kindle tried to sing "The Streets of Laredo" as he put the truck into gear and pressed the gas—a terrible stagger forward—and steered out of this dirt turnoff away from the cabin toward the logging road.

He switched on the lights. The pines crowding the roadside loomed in eerie grids of shadow.

He was sitting sideways and a little low. He wasn't accustomed to steering with his left hand and his reflexes were shot, but he managed to aim the Ford approximately midway down this column of spooky-looking trees. God help anybody coming uphill, but who would be, at this hour?

From here into the outskirts of Buchanan was mainly a downhill ride, and Kindle found he didn't have to work the gas pedal much; it was struggle enough to keep the walking stick pressed against the brake to impede the acceleration of the truck. It occurred to him he'd be in some profound trouble if he passed out again. "So stay awake," he told himself. He remembered that a Place Had Been Prepared For Him in the regional hospital as long as he didn't run his hiccup truck off the Streets of Laredo.

He passed two other cabins—the property of men as solitary as himself—but he didn't stop. If he stopped, nobody might be home; and Kindle did not relish the prospect of starting up this truck again. Better to drive as far as possible toward Buchanan, or at least down to where the streetlights began.

But then—in a wash of fear that took him by surprise—Kindle remembered that Buchanan might not be the Buchanan he remembered.

Last week, the monsters had come to Buchanan.

Curious ambulatory sponge-things who had infected everybody's blood.

Was this a real memory or some kind of trauma hallucination? Well, Kindle thought, it sure *felt* like a real memory.

Still: Monsters?

And if that was true . . .

He did not summon the images, but here they came: Monsters out of comic books, tentacle-headed things unloading from a flying saucer; or the zombie-eyed human eunuchs out of a dozen movies, slaves of the Overmasters and hungry for human flesh. They had Prepared a Place For Him on the communal barbecue.

Kindle shook his head. He couldn't decide whether this was funny or scary. Maybe it would be smart just to press on the brakes and die in the dark up this mountain.

(He did, in fact, apply a sudden pressure there, because the truck had picked up a great deal of speed without his noticing.)

No, Kindle told himself sternly. No dying allowed. Go for help. Follow the plan.

See the monsters if you must.

The truck rattled on.

▪   ▪   ▪

He had reached the suburban margin of the town just inside the city-limits sign when his pain and fatigue crested, and the truck rolled into an embankment and came to rest with its headlights pointed at Orion.

The impact dashed Kindle against the steering wheel, causing the horn to emit a squawk; then he rolled back, semiconscious, into the seat. The truck's motor rumbled on.

The sound of the horn and the grinding engine woke a thirty-year-old insurance investigator named Buddy Winkler, who had recently become immortal but who still liked to get a good night's sleep. He went to the window of his two-year-old tract house and gazed with sleepy astonishment at the semivertical Ford riding a dirt bank in the vacant lot next door. Then he phoned 911. He gathered up a blanket and hurried out to the accident, where he quickly surmised there was nothing he could do to help the injured man inside—a screaming and broken mortal man whose eyes rolled wildly at the sight of him.

Monsters, Kindle thought—dimly, when he thought at all.

Monsters leering down at him.

He screamed until he was mute.

▪ ▪ ▪

And after a dark time he recognized hospital corridors, and understood for one lucid moment that he was lying on a gurney cart with medical staff bustling around him.

A frowning face lofted into proximity, and Kindle reached up with what remained of his strength and took this person by the collar of his gown.

"Get me," Kindle gasped, "a human doctor."

"Relax," the entity pronounced. "I am human."

"You know what I mean, you alien shitsack! Get me a *human* doctor, you monster!"

Kindle fell back gasping.

The man looming over him turned away. "Can we have some sedation here? The patient's hysterical. Oh, and somebody call Matt Wheeler."

Now I think maybe I am safe, Kindle thought, and embarked upon a sleep that would last for two days running.

▪ ▪ ▪

Giddy light-headedness and fog.

Kindle awoke once again.

He was in bed. His leg was bound and in traction. It hurt, but only a little. Kindle guessed he was sedated and that right now nothing would hurt very much.

He felt distant and vague, and he supposed if you tore off his arm and beat him with it that would be okay, too. Probably a nice opiate drip on that IV.

But the main thing was that he had made it to the hospital. He took a certain pride in that. His memory was fuzzy, but he recalled that it had been a long and harrowing journey.

A man in medical whites approached. Kindle watched this process with languorous detachment. He managed, "You must be the doctor."

"That's right, Mr. Kindle."

"I asked for a human being."

"You got one. My name is Matt Wheeler."

Matthew Wheeler was an ordinary-looking man with a woebegone face. He's too young, Kindle thought idly, for all those frown lines.

"You're human, Dr. Wheeler?"

"As human as you are, Mr. Kindle."

"Not one of *them*?"

"No. But they can treat you as well as I can. There's no need to worry."

"Maybe," Kindle said. "Has the town changed much? I've been up in the hills since, since—" Since what was it called? Contact.

"Not much." Dr. Wheeler looked uncomfortable. "Not yet."

"How's my leg?"

"It should mend reasonably well. In time. May I ask how you broke it?"

"Walking out back of my cabin. Fell in the fuckin' mud."

"How did you get into town?"

"Dragged my ass down to my truck." The memory was a little clearer now. "Then I drove." He shrugged.

"That's remarkable. That's quite an accomplishment."

Kindle was alert enough to recognize a compliment. "I guess I'm hard to kill, huh?"

"I guess you are. You were a sorry mess when the ambulance brought you in, or so I'm told. The leg will heal, Mr. Kindle, but you're going to be here for a while." The doctor made a notation on his clipboard. "I understand your attitude about . . . human beings. But I can't be in the room twenty-four hours a day. You'll have to cooperate with the hospital staff. Will you do that for me?"

"You'll be around, though?"

"I'll be around. I'll make a point of it."

Kindle nodded agreement.

"You'll probably want some more sleep." The doctor turned to leave the room.

Kindle closed his eyes, then opened them. "Dr. Wheeler?"

"Yes, Mr. Kindle?"

"How many of us are there? I mean—there *are* more of us in town, aren't there?"

The doctor looked even wearier. "A few. I want to get us all together in a couple of weeks. Kind of a town meeting. Maybe you can be there. If you lie still and let that bone mend."

Kindle nodded, but vaguely; he had already forgotten the question, was already easing back into sleep.

Chapter 12

Brookside (II)

For the memorial service Miriam picked out what she still thought of as her church clothes, though she hadn't been to church for years: black dress and hat, white gloves, an unscuffed pair of orthopedic shoes.

She adjusted the hat a final time in the mirror by the front door, then stepped out into a hazy summer morning.

More than two weeks had passed since the night she was touched by the Thing.

No longer the Eye of God—what a mistake *that* had been! It was, Miriam supposed, still the *agency* of God, as a plague of locusts might be His agency; but it was alien, insinuating, false, and quite un-Godlike in its offer of unconditional absolution. Miriam supposed she would recognize God easily enough when she faced Him: God was Justice, and carried a sword. The Thing, contrarily, had spoken in the plangent and intimate voice of a lover. It offered too much and did not hate sufficiently.

But the world was a different place for its coming. Even over the course of two weeks, Miriam had seen the changes.

The news, for instance. The news wasn't worth the paper it was printed on or the time it displaced on TV. In a handful of days, the *Buchanan Observer* had shrunk to a few negligible pages—mostly cooking columns, gardening tips, and a few syndicated columns. Large stories had made small headlines: undeclared but universal ceasefire in all the world's wars, presidents and premiers unavailable for comment, no film at eleven. What they ought to have, Miriam thought, is a generic headline. NOTHING HAPPENS. NOBODY CARES.

At least the memorial service was still on schedule. Her father's body had been committed to the earth a day before Contact, but the service had been postponed to allow Miriam's uncle, a man she had never met, to fly in from Norway, where he worked. Naturally, the flight had been canceled— there had been something in the news about civilian aircraft commandeered for relief flights into the African famine zones. So the service would go on this afternoon with or without Uncle Edward.

Or so Miriam hoped. Was *anything* certain these days?

Dr. Ackroyd had been willing to go ahead with the service, but even the Rector had changed. Last week, Simon Ackroyd had confessed to being one of *them*. The Rector was engaged in the same transformation that had overtaken the rest of the world, and Miriam was not at all sure she would like what the man had turned into, or that *he* would like *her*, or that she would be safe at the end of the world's strange new evolution.

■   ■   ■

She didn't think of herself as an Episcopalian, but her father had called himself that even though he seldom attended services. She suspected he'd picked the Episcopalians because they were the most upscale congregation in town; barring the Catholics, whom Daddy had regarded as a fanatical sect, like Shiites or Communists.

The Episcopal Church squatted like a gray stone bulldog on its acre of lawn and peered across a long slope of rooftops to the sea. Miriam parked and climbed the stairs to the parish office. Dr. Ackroyd had said he would meet her here and they would drive together to Brookside Cemetery.

The Rector was waiting in his office with a concerned expression on his homely face. "Sit down, Miriam," he said.

She listened as he explained how the memorial service would proceed, though they had arranged all this in advance. Does he think I'm senile? Miriam wondered. Or had the ministry lowered his expectations? Perhaps he often dealt with stupid people.

The ceremony would be outdoors, at the graveside. It was to be simple and brief. Above all, Miriam hoped, brief. She hated all mumbling over the dead and would never have agreed even to this much if Uncle Edward, the hypocrite, hadn't insisted.

"I didn't know your father very well," the Rector was saying, "but there are people in my congregation who did, and they tell me he was a good man. A loss like this is never easy. I know you're going through a difficult time,

Miriam—for this and other reasons. I want you to know I'm here if you need to talk."

The offer struck Miriam as both laughable and strange. Her response was spontaneous: "All I want to know is—how you can *do* this?"

"I'm sorry?"

"After what happened that night. You know what I mean."

He drew back. "This is my job. That hasn't changed."

"You were touched by the Thing."

He looked bewildered. "You mean Contact?"

"Nobody calls anything by its right name. Doesn't matter. I'm a Christian woman, Rector. When the Thing touched me I knew it was nothing a Christian should have anything to do with, and I gave it a Christian response. I don't see the point of immortality outside the Throne of God. But you. You shook hands with it—am I right? And yet, there you sit. Prepared to read Scripture over the body of my father. How can you do that?"

Dr. Ackroyd seemed dismayed; he took a long time answering.

"Miriam," he said finally, "you may be right." He paused as if to summon thoughts. "I'm not sure I know what a Christian is. I've thought about this a great deal since Contact. The harder I look for Christianity, Miriam, the more it evaporates before my eyes. Is it Martin Luther or is it Johann Eck? Is it Augustine, or is it John Chrysostom? Is it Constantine? Is it Matthew and Mark and Luke, and did they write the Scriptures we call by their names? Or was Christianity buried along with the apocrypha at Nag Hammadi?"

Now it was Miriam's turn to be bewildered.

"I simply don't know," the Rector confessed. "I think I never did know. I think there is something in the Artifact nearly as rich and strange as all our earthly religions put together. Nearly. Miriam, when I spoke with the Travellers I put some of these questions to them. I have a sense of what their spirituality consists of . . . and I think it may not be incompatible with ours. They don't claim to have unraveled every mystery. In fact, they're quite humble about their ignorance. They think consciousness might have some special relationship to the hidden order of the universe, even a persistence after absolute death. I'm not sure whether this ought to be called religion or cosmology. But they acknowledge that some subtlety of mind may be bound into the functioning of stars and time.

"They didn't ask me to abandon my Christianity, Miriam. It's only that I've had to be more honest with myself about the things I know and the things I don't. The divinity of Christ, the extrinsic nature of God . . . maybe I was never really convinced of those things. Only wanted to believe them.

"So you're right, Miriam. I don't guess I'm entitled to call myself a Christian any longer. But I can perform the memorial service. I can help you say goodbye to your father, and I can mark the mystery of death, and I can honor it—perhaps more sincerely than ever before. I would be pleased to perform that service for you. But if you feel I'm unqualified, I'll step aside. Maybe we can find someone else, maybe even here in town."

Miriam was stunned. She gazed at the Rector, then shook her head. "No . . . that's all right. You do it."

"Thank you, Miriam."

"It's not a vote of confidence. I don't think it matters who says the words. If there's a Heaven, it's beyond our commanding, and if there's a Hell, our prayers won't keep us out of it." She looked at her watch. "Shouldn't we leave? It's getting late."

■   ■   ■

She drove with him to Brookside Cemetery, through the gates and up a winding road to the graveside. She had wanted an outdoor service. Miriam hated chapels. They smelled like overripe sachets, like decaying lavender.

Mist still lingered in the lowlands and across the water, but the sun had burned the sky blue overhead. Mt. Buchanan rose up behind the cemetery like the shoulders of a green and granite colossus. This was a hillside plot, and it was pleasant to see the rows of graves running down to the main gate and the road.

From this hillside Miriam watched the crowd begin to gather.

She had mailed an announcement of the memorial service to those few of Daddy's friends still living, mainly retired staff from the Community College and the members of the Bridge Club whose company he had enjoyed before his stroke. She was surprised by the relative youth of the crowd beginning to gather—too many strangers, faces she did not recognize—and by its size.

Cars had filled the chapel parking lot at the foot of the hill, and more cars had begun to park along the road, all the way down to the intersection and out of sight.

Troubled and vaguely frightened, Miriam turned to Rector Ackroyd. "Daddy didn't know all these people."

"The service was announced in the *Observer*."

She knew that; she had clipped the announcement. "But why are they here? What for?"

"To mark a solemn occasion. Miriam, your father was the last man in

Buchanan to die before Contact. Do you know what that means? His was the last involuntary death in this town."

But it was a reasoning that made Miriam hostile, for reasons she didn't wholly understand.

"I don't want strangers here."

"I'm sorry you feel that way. But it's not a joke. They're sincere—their feelings are genuine."

"*How could you possibly know that?*"

"I know," the Rector said simply.

Miriam frowned but acquiesced. She was beginning to feel numbed by the morning's events. Rector Ackroyd read the service and Miriam listened distantly, unable to associate this ceremony with her father; he had become intangible, a fading memory of a pleasanter time. *I'm here to mourn*, she reminded herself sternly. But what about all these other people?

The hillside was covered with people, all silent and attentive, even those who must be too far away to hear the service.

Half the population of Buchanan must have come here, Miriam thought.

Maybe they had also come to mourn.

Not for her father. For something they had lost or given up. For what they couldn't have back.

For a way of life.

For the town, the country—for the planet, Miriam thought.

Chapter 13

Arguments and Unwindings

When Lillian refused to see him for a physical exam—despite his nudging, his cajoling, and at last his ill-concealed anger—Matt decided enough was enough. Extraterrestrial mysticism was one thing; jeopardizing her health and the health of her unborn child was quite another.

He arranged to have lunch with Jim, see if he could attack the problem from that angle.

A few weeks ago, it might have been hard to fit lunch into his schedule. Today, free time was easy to come by. His office consultations had dropped to a trickle. He spent most of his time at the hospital doing shifts for absentee residents, and much of that time convincing Tom Kindle to submit to physical therapy. He had not seen a new patient, nor more than a handful of his reliables, since what they were starting to call "Contact."

Nor, despite the hours at Buchanan General, had he seen much of Jim Bix. Jim—like Lillian, like Annie Gates, like so many others—had accepted the promise of immortality that night in August.

Matt had still not developed a strategy for talking to such people.

Jim had been his closest friend. Contact had turned him into a stranger.

■ ■ ■

They met in the cafeteria. The staff cafeteria was a basement room the size of a basketball court, and today it was almost deserted. The ventilators hummed like meditating monks and the air smelled faintly of cabbage.

Jim sat at a corner table picking at salad and rice pilaf. Matt pulled up another chair and regarded his friend. Same old ugly son of a bitch he ever was, Matt thought.

But the conversation was like an old car on a cold day, hard to start and hard to keep running.

"You don't look like you're sleeping much," Jim said.

In fact he hadn't been. Too much to think about. Too many things he didn't *want* to think about. His days were either empty or surrealistic and his nights were often sleepless. But he didn't want to say that. "I didn't come to complain. Actually, I wanted to talk about Lillian. She refused to come in for monitoring. I wondered if you knew that. I don't anticipate any problems with the pregnancy, but it seems like a bad precedent."

Jim listened carefully. Then he wiped his chin with a paper napkin and shrugged. "If she says she doesn't need to see you, and there's no pressing problem, maybe we ought to leave it at that."

"There isn't *currently* a problem. But she's pregnant and forty, and that's hardly a risk-free scenario. And you know it, Jim. If she wants to change doctors—for whatever reason—okay. Fine. We'll set her up with a specialist. But she has to see *somebody*."

"Does she?"

"Christ's sake, Jim!"

His exclamation echoed around the empty room.

"All I'm saying, Matt, is that she has more access to her internal condition than she used to. It sounds strange, but it's true. She knows things you might not expect her to know."

"I'm skeptical of that."

"I guess I would be too, in your position. I don't know what I can say to convince you. If it means anything, *I'm* convinced."

"Convinced of what? That Lillian doesn't need medical care?"

"That she knows whether she needs it or not. If she did, Matt, I'm sure she'd come to you." He folded the napkin. "We miss seeing you. Why don't you stop by the house sometime? Talk to her yourself. She'd be happy to talk."

"Can she perform an ultrasound on herself? Can she diagnose an ectopic pregnancy?"

"I believe she can."

"Jesus!"

"Matt, would you calm down? I can explain it . . . but not if you're raving."

He wondered if he ought to simply leave the table. But Jim was his friend, or had been his friend; maybe he was obliged to listen a while longer.

"It feels like a century since we talked about this. That night at your house. Less than a month ago. Remember that? Just before Contact. We got drunk."

"You were talking about machines in the blood."

"Neocytes."

"Is that what you call them?"

"It's the consensus name."

Matt let this pass.

"The point is," Jim said, "they're still here. Not in you. You sent 'em packing. Your blood is original stock—and I guess you know that, since I haven't seen you down in the path lab doing your own smears."

True. The Travellers, as Annie called them, had told Matt they would leave his body, and he had believed it—he had never questioned the matter.

"But the rest of us are still carrying neocytes," Jim said, "and they're doing some work. Nothing too obvious yet. But take Lillian. If she was ectopic, or preeclamptic, or anything like that, the neocytes would deal with it. Or they would let her know so she could take the appropriate steps. I'm not sitting here telling you Lillian should go through this pregnancy unmonitored. The point is, she *is* monitored. She's getting better attention than you or I could give her, and she's getting it twenty-four hours a day."

"And that's . . ." He couldn't contain his horror. "That's *okay* with you?"

"It's a benevolent process, Matt. There's nothing wrong with it."

"My God. My God. What about the fetus? We're talking about your child. Are they working on it, too? Is the child full of . . . neocytes?"

"Yes, it is."

Matt stood up too quickly. The table rocked and an empty cafeteria glass dropped and shattered on the floor.

Jim bent to pick up the pieces. He put two daggerlike shards on the table, out of harm's way. He said, "I didn't mean to upset you."

"You're bleeding," Matt said.

He'd cut his hand. The blood that oozed out was thick. It was the color and consistency, Matt thought, of hot blackstrap molasses.

▪   ▪   ▪

Later in the afternoon, he stopped by Tom Kindle's room.

The floor nurse called Kindle "a handful," her code word for a patient who was uncooperative but good-humored about it. Kindle, who had lived alone on the slopes of Mt. Buchanan for some years, seemed to be adjusting fairly well to the new situation—his injury, Contact. Matt guessed he had the advantage of not feeling suddenly like an outsider . . . he had been an outsider all along.

When Matt entered the room, Kindle was watching TV; when he noticed Matt, he hit the mute button on the remote control.

"They moved in the TV this morning. I said I didn't want to pay for it. They said I didn't have to. Nobody else using it. It's been years since I watched TV much." Kindle shook his head. "Now I get a chance and there's nothing good on. Nothing but the news."

"Last time I looked," Matt said, "there *wasn't* any news. Not the kind of news I'm used to. All the armies went home and nobody robbed the grocery store."

"I think that *is* news," Kindle said.

"Seems like it's a more peaceful world."

"Shit on that. The *graveyard* is peaceful." Kindle turned back to the TV screen. "Have you seen this?"

Matt looked at the picture. It was the octahedron in Central Park. There was a CNN logo in the lower-left corner of the screen.

"I've seen it before." He remembered when the octahedrons came out of the sky last spring, all those dark and ominous shapes—how Rachel had watched the videotape replays almost obsessively. Everybody had been afraid of the octahedrons, which had functioned, as far as Matt knew, mainly as monuments, or at most as a diversion. The real war had been microscopic and brief. Why invade the Earth when you can invade the bloodstream? A question of scale.

"I've seen the fuckin' thing a dozen times too," Kindle said. "That's not the point. Watch!"

And with a deep reluctance Matt took a second look at the TV screen.

This was videotape, but recent.

Kindle said he'd been watching it all day, over and over again.

Matt stared without comprehension as the octahedron—that vast black shape featureless and tall as a ten-story building—somehow *unwound itself*.

The motion was difficult to focus on even in slow-motion playback. It reminded him of a spring uncoiling. It was that kind of action . . . but multidimensional and terrifyingly fast.

Nothing decent moved like that. It made him think of a trap sprung, a cannon fired, a rattlesnake striking, every fast and deadly thing.

He blinked at the screen with his mouth open.

Kindle laughed. "Amazing, isn't it?"

No. It was frightening. He felt nauseated.

The octahedron unwound into countless smaller shapes. The CNN camera zoomed closer, and Matt was able to see that each shape was the same, a bulbous saucer mounted on a truncated cone. Perhaps about the size of a person, though it was difficult to judge. He couldn't tell whether these devices touched the ground or hovered above it.

"Thousands of 'em," Kindle said. "More."

They began to move, radiating away from their point of origin through the trees and along the bike paths like an obscenely strange mass of strolling tourists.

Like a nest of ants, Matt thought, swarming out of its hole.

"One for every town and city in North America," Kindle said.

"How do you know that?"

"The guy on the newscast said so. Don't ask me how *he* knows."

"What are they?"

Kindle shrugged. "Helpers. So the TV says."

"*'Helpers'?*"

"That's what CNN is calling them. Don't blame me, Matthew—I don't write the news."

He looked at the screen. There was a Helper in close focus now. It was a featureless matte-black object, and it looked about as helpful as a mace, a claymore, or a ballistic missile.

"Sit down, Matthew," Kindle said gently. "You don't look too well."

■　■　■

Later—when the shock wore off—Matt told Kindle some of the things Jim Bix had said, about "neocytes" and the possibility of physical changes in the body.

Kindle absorbed all this with a thoughtful expression. "Matthew," he said, "did you ever hear of a nurse log?"

Matt said he hadn't—did it have something to do with the floor nurse, Miss Jefferson?

"No, not that kind of nurse. Back in the eighties, I worked for a while in Canada. Logging on the west coast of Vancouver Island. I got to know some of the forest there, what they call climax forest, meaning a forest that hasn't been burned for a long time. Centuries. They have some 800-year-old cedars over there. Amazing trees. And it rains nonstop half the year, so in places you get what they call a temperate rain forest. Very dense vegetation, very wet.

"Decay is one of the main things that happens in a place like that. Every time one of these huge hemlocks falls down, or a cedar, say, or an amabilis fir, it's not just a dead tree. It's *food*. It turns into what's called a nurse log, because it's nursing new trees, among other things. When it's rotting, that log might contain more organisms than there are people on the surface of the Earth. It's so full of life it actually heats up—as much as five or six degrees warmer than the air."

"This is interesting," Matt said, "but—"

"I'm almost finished. Shit, you doctors are impatient people! All I mean to say is that it strikes me maybe the Earth is like a nurse log. All that talk about pollution, global warming, and so on. People used to say, Are we killing the Earth? My theory is, we already killed it. It's dead. Like a nurse log. So all these decay organisms just arrowed in on it. Maybe humanity was already the first stage of decay, like a fungus growing in the heartwood. Then the insects move in to eat the wood rot, and the birds eat the insects. . . ."

"That's disgusting," Matt said.

"A little. It's how nature works, though. Why should it be different when we're talking about the whole planet? This thing in space, the Artifact, the octahedrons, these Helpers—" Kindle shrugged. "They just smell a rotting log, that's all."

■   ■   ■

Matt wasn't cheered by these speculations, and he left the room sour-minded and unhappy. It was almost six o'clock—he'd wasted an afternoon staring at the horrors on Tom Kindle's TV set. Time to go home.

Dinner with Rachel. Another evening to endure.

He had come to dread this time of day.

Worse, Kindle's forest analogy haunted him during the drive home. Maybe the Earth *was* a nurse log; maybe the old hermit was right.

But he thought about Jim Bix, his smile fixed in place, his blood the color of thirty-weight motor oil.

A worse thought: Maybe Jim was a nurse log.

Something new growing in the hollow shell of him.

Maybe Lillian was a nurse log.

Maybe they all were.

Chapter
14

B&E

Beth Porter was accustomed to seeing the Artifact suspended in every clear night sky and seldom gave it much thought. It was something people talked about on TV, like war or the economy. About as insubstantial as that. There had never been a war in Buchanan; the economy just meant people getting laid off, or not, at the pulp mill; and the Artifact was a light in the sky, as alarming as a streetlamp.

Or so she had thought.

Now, Beth had to admit, things were changing. Now things were beginning to get . . . well, *scary.*

.   .   .

She spent Friday night at Joey Commoner's before they decided to do the B&E.

Joey lived with his father, who was divorced and worked part-time for a building contractor; but Joey's father had taken off in July to spend a couple of months on a Seattle job and to shack up for a while with his girlfriend, a Canadian-born typesetter who used to secretary for a drywall firm in Buchanan. So Joey had had the house to himself for the summer.

Labor Day had come and gone, but Joey wasn't sure when his father would be back. His old man had telephoned three times since Contact, but Joey wouldn't talk about what he said. Joey, Beth knew, was also a little scared of what had been happening since that feverish Friday night.

So they sat in the basement, which was Joey's private apartment, with its own bathroom and even a little kitchenette; and they watched a rental movie and smoked dope.

Joey was a cautious doper. He was wary of drugs, in a strange way, and limited himself to a once-a-week smokathon, usually Friday night. That was why he always showed up at the 7-Eleven Friday nights, buying frozen pies and ice cream. Marijuana, microwave cherry pies, and vanilla ice cream were Joey's customary vices. After they got to know each other he had invited Beth to join him in the ritual. When she was transferred to the day shift, she did.

Beth herself was careful about drugs. Contrary to her high-school reputation, she was not keen to break the law . . . or hadn't been, in those days. But she soon learned that this Friday night dope binge wasn't the scariest thing about Joey—in a way, it was the *least* scary thing about him. Joey Commoner in a stoned condition was accessible, in some ways even a little more human. He'd kick back and laugh at some TV movie, and they would feast on reconstituted cherry pie and ice cream until their lips looked rouged, and sooner or later they would make love. Stoned, Joey made love to her. Other times they simply fucked.

So Beth learned to look forward to Friday nights, and would have enjoyed this one except for what they saw on TV.

The rental movie ended and when Joey hit the rewind button the network came back on: a picture of an octahedron unwinding, this one somewhere in Europe.

Beth set aside her 7-Eleven cherry pie, and Joey put down the 1970's-vintage blue plastic bong he had ripped off from one of his cousins, and the two of them gawked at the screen.

"Holy shit," Joey said, with what sounded to Beth like a combination of awe and deep discomfort.

Beth, thoroughly stoned, was especially impressed with a close-up still of what the announcer called a Helper. She remembered her last year of high-school biology, peering through a microscope at a bread mold, black pin-shaped structures called "sporangiophores," a word that had eluded her during the final exam but that came back now with the odd precision of a dope revery. That's what these Helpers looked like. A crowd of sporangiophores spreading over the landscape. Coming soon to *your* town, if she understood the commentary correctly.

It was too much. Joey hit the off button and turned his back on the screen.

Joey was very much into not believing what was happening around him. For instance, Joey did hobby electronics, built hi-fi gear and radios and things, and this had fascinated Beth at first, because—like everybody else—she had Joey pegged as being a little stupid. It turned out he read circuit diagrams better than he read English. There was always a tangle of wire and junk parts in one corner of the basement and often the air reeked of solder. Which was okay; it was interesting. But Beth had come to realize that electronics wasn't just a skill Joey had—it was a wall, a moat, a hiding place. It shut out everything scary. It even shut out Beth.

And now, scared by what they'd seen on TV, he began to look restless—like if Beth cleared out he might dip another circuit board in aluminum sulfate or something. Fuck, not tonight, Beth thought. She didn't want to be alone tonight.

That was when the idea of the B&E occurred to her.

She thought of it strictly as a means of holding his attention. In the old days Beth had been more or less indifferent to Joey's attention. Now, suddenly, helplessly, she was hungry for it. Not that there was anyone competing with her; Joey had never shown much interest in other women, perhaps excluding that night with the hooker in Tacoma. What she was competing with was the dense forest inside Joey's own head. Where he liked to get lost. Where she couldn't go.

But the cemetery vandalism last month had seemed to keep him interested—so why not a similar adventure? Similar but more daring? Why not a B&E, in fact?

She posed the question. Joey looked thoughtful.

"Where?" he asked.

"The Newcomb house," Beth said. Sudden inspiration. "You know the place? House up on View Ridge with two lawn jockeys in front? Bob Newcomb used to be my father's boss at the mill. He's been on vacation since August first. Some place in Mexico. My father thinks anybody who goes to Mexico in August is an idiot."

"Long vacation," Joey said.

"They might not be coming back at all." Because of Contact. But she didn't say that.

"Two lawn jockeys and a garden with a sun clock," Joey said.

"That house, right."

"Stupid fuckin'-looking house, Beth."

"There might be something inside."

He shrugged. "What do we want?"

"I don't know!"

"We can't fence anything. Do you know how to fence stolen property?"

She didn't. "We could just mess it up. Or take whatever we liked. The stereo."

"Or cameras," Joey said, warming to the idea. "Or even a videocamera or something like that. Except if they're on vacation they probably took it with them. "

Suddenly he was hooked. Switched on like a light.

There was a well of restless anger inside Joey, and she had tapped it . . . but it was a strange talent, the ability to wind up Joey Commoner toward petty crime, and something she was only intermittently proud of.

The horse, the spur.

Dangerous, Beth.

Did she really want to do this? Maybe it was an idea that only made sense in dope-logic, one of those smoke-ring thoughts with no real beginning or end. Or just a dumb, transient impulse.

Too late for second thoughts, however. Joey was already putting on his motorcycle jacket.

■ ■ ■

He drove north along the coast in a misty rain.

The night had turned cool. The motorcycle stitched through valleys of fog, Beth with her visor down and everything blue with rain. Streetlights seemed dim, the white line tentative.

There was no traffic. Since Contact, people didn't go out so much. They stayed inside, especially in bad weather.

The things in their brains had made them cautious—meek, in Beth's opinion. Wasn't it the meek who were supposed to inherit the Earth?

Now is the hour.

Joey wasn't meek. The sound of the motorcycle bounced around these sodden hillsides like an announcement of Armageddon. He drove recklessly fast.

She tightened her grip on his waist and squeezed her thighs around the saddle. Wet face, wet hair, Joey's leather jacket wet and slippery in the rain.

He drove to the top of View Ridge and killed the engine.

Beth, still stoned, was suddenly absorbed in the view: tumbling clouds and the foggy ocean downslope to the west. Everything in shades of night gray or night blue except the buzzing amber streetlights. A paper flapped on a telephone pole, a wet photocopied announcement of a meeting of regular human people at the hospital next Wednesday night, Dr. Matthew Wheeler presiding, an event Beth had already marked on her calendar. She thought she might attend, might bring along Joey, see who was left. But that was a daylight plan for the daylight world.

Joey wheeled his motorcycle down the rain-slick sidewalk, quietly, not talking. Beth felt alternately conspicuous and fog-hidden, paranoid and fuzzily excited. No one seemed to be watching. There were only a few lights in these big hillside houses. But these weren't normal houses anymore, or at least not normal *homes*; the people inside weren't normal. Maybe, Beth thought, they can see us with some kind of third eye. Maybe they don't need to look.

Joey took the Yamaha up the Newcombs' long driveway and stood it in the shadows behind the garage. The Newcomb house had a light in it, too, the token light people leave on when they're out of town, supposed to frighten burglars, who are supposed to be that stupid. Beth followed Joey into the backyard. Nothing but shadows and wet grass here. Smell of lawn clippings, garden loam, rain.

Beth's paranoia began to peak. The trouble with getting stoned was that sometimes it opened a moment of great clarity, like a window. Too much clarity was a bad thing. She didn't always like what she saw.

Tonight she saw herself alone. She felt herself alone on this dark lawn and alone on the planet, as alone as she had ever been.

She knew about being alone. She had known about it ever since her fourteenth birthday, when her mother sent her to a clinic in Portland to defuse a little ovarian timebomb set ticking by Martin Blair, her then-boyfriend, fifteen, saved from reproach by the status of his family, the Blair Realty Blairs—Martin who had actually bragged some to his friends: Yeah, he *got a girl pregnant*. . . . Alone on the suction table and alone when she came back to school, Buchanan's youngest suburban slut, according to Martin's schoolyard testimony. Alone sitting by herself at an empty cafeteria table. Alone but daggered with stares, sniggered at in hallways, propositioned in corners by boys who lacked the courage to speak to anyone real. Alone with shame so intense that after a while she lost the ability to blush.

But that was one kind of alone, and this was another.

All these houses, Beth thought . . . empty of families, empty of people, full of something else, something that only looked human.

Joey broke a pane of glass in the back door of the Newcomb house and reached inside to open the lock. To Beth it sounded like a cymbal crash, a shrieking announcement of their presence.

Suddenly this wasn't what she wanted. Not at all.

Maybe to have a normal life, do normal things . . . she had never let herself even imagine that. But it would be better than this. Better than breaking into an empty house on a rainy night. Better than riding Joey Commoner's motorcycle down some dark highway. Better than any future she could imagine for herself now that the monsters had taken over the world.

■　■　■

The house smelled like a stranger's house. Broadloom, air freshener, old cooking. She felt uninvited, unwanted, criminal.

Joey seemed to thrive on the sensation. His eyes were alert, his steps small and agile. The light the Newcombs had left burning was a lamp in the downstairs bedroom; it made long shadows through the doorway. Joey headed for this room first, where he pulled open dresser drawers and tossed their contents, picking out nothing in particular: a handful of twenty dollar bills, probably Mrs. Newcomb's mad money; an empty keychain with a Volvo tag. Beth was mute, immobilized by her own guilty presence in a bedroom where she didn't belong. Her eyes registered details she wished she could forget: the Japanese print over the bed, birds on ink-line trees; the oak dresser with cigarette burns clustered at one end; worst of all, Mrs. Newcomb's nightgowns and Mr. Newcomb's jockey shorts tumbled together and soaking in the contents of an overturned perfume bottle. Seeing all this was the real theft, Beth thought.

She said, "This is too weird. I don't like this."

"It was your idea."

"I know, but . . ."

But it didn't matter. He wasn't listening. He was gone, vanished into the dimmer light outside the bedroom, and Beth was forced to hurry after or be left here with no company but her conscience.

■　■　■

The worst part was yet to come.

She lost track of time as Joey rummaged through the house. He turned on no lights, seemed to navigate by instinct or animal vision. He wasn't robbing the house so much as *possessing* it, Beth thought—making it his own through an act of violation. He was fucking it. No, raping it. He left his mark everywhere: tables overturned, doors flung open, closets stripped. She followed in a daze, inarticulate even in the space of her own skull, waiting for him to finish, waiting until they could leave.

In a hallway closet, Joey found his prize, a palm-size camcorder—since when had he cared about video?—small enough to slip into his leather jacket, which he zipped up around it. *Take it*, she thought. *Then, Christ, let's go!*

She turned away. Turning, she saw red light wash shadows of raindrops against the wall . . . saw this light blink on and off and on again . . .

Her terror began before she could pin a word on it and name the dreaded thing. She tugged Joey's arm, almost pulled him off balance. "Joey, the *police*—a *police car*—"

He took her by the wrist and pulled her away from the window. Things were happening too quickly now; there wasn't time to think. She followed Joey out the back door into the rainy yard. Joey inched along the wall toward the corner of the garage. She kept a hand on his jacket.

We'll be arrested, Beth thought. Put on trial. Sent to jail.

Or—

Or something worse.

Something *new*.

Please let it be prison, Beth thought. Not some unhuman thing, bugs in the brain, alien punishment.

Her breath hitched, and she wondered if she might begin to cry. But Joey took her hand and pulled her forward, and she was suddenly too busy for that.

He jumped onto the motorcycle and kicked over the engine while Beth scurried on behind.

From here in the shadow of the garage, protected from streetlights, perhaps invisible, Beth had a clear view of the cop car. It was parked at an angle in the street, not blocking the driveway. A Buchanan Sheriff's Department black-and-white. There was no sound, only that relentlessly whirling dome light. It lit up the street. Red light under dripping eaves, red light spidering up tree trunks and disappearing in the leaves. Nobody had come out to watch—none of the neighbors in their yards or standing in open doorways. Maybe they already know what's happening, Beth thought. Maybe they don't have to look.

The Yamaha's engine screamed; Beth clung desperately to Joey and the saddle as they roared down the Newcombs' driveway. Now Beth saw the man inside the cruiser, at least the shadow of his face as he turned to track their motion. The cop car had been silent, not even idling; Beth expected its siren to howl, motor gun, tires squeal, perhaps the beginning of a chase, dangerous on these steep wet streets. . . .

But the car remained silent, and Joey leaned into the curve as he pulled out of the driveway, came up short, and stopped with one foot on the road, engine idling—what was he *doing*? *Go!* Beth thought.

And then she understood: It was a dance between Joey and the cop.

Beth looked at the cop through his car window and knew from his joyless but placid expression that nothing more was going to happen: no chase, no trial, no jail.

Only this shadowy gaze . . . this *observation*.

We know you. We know what you're doing.

A raw shiver ran up her spine.

Arrest us! She aimed the thought at the cop car. *Wave your gun! Yell!*

But there was only a dreadful silence behind the idling of the motorcycle engine.

Then Joey twisted the throttle and the Yamaha roared downhill.

Crime and punishment in the new world.

Chapter
15
Meeting

Matt found Tom Kindle waiting in the empty hospital boardroom when he arrived. He had staked out a place by the window, lean and patient in his wheelchair.

"You're early," Kindle observed.

"So are you."

"Nurse wheeled me down before she went off shift. There's hardly any staff in this building anymore—you notice that, Matthew?"

"I've noticed."

"Gets to be like a ghost town at this hour. Kind of scary after the sun goes down. Makes you wonder what they're all doing with their time. Watching *Dallas* reruns and eating popcorn, I guess."

Matt wasn't in the mood. He took a notebook out of his briefcase and propped it on the podium, open to the page on which he had outlined every potential emergency and worst-case scenario he had been able to imagine (and there was no shortage) in the last month or so. He checked the clock: 7:30. Meeting was set for eight.

Kindle followed his look. "Almost time . . . assuming anybody shows up."

"Well, there's us," Matt said.

"Uh-huh. You know, I asked Nurse Jefferson how many people . . . you know, how many made the decision she did. She said, 'Almost everybody.' I said, 'Well, then, who *didn't?*' She said, 'About one in ten thousand.'"

"Really? How would Nurse Jefferson know?"

"Shit, Matthew, how do any of these people know the things they say? My theory is they're all hooked into the same library. ESP or something, but I'm only human—I have to guess. Last night I asked the janitor the same thing when he came down the hall. How many people turned down this wonderful offer of eternal life? He leaned on the waxer and said, 'Oh, about one in ten thousand.'"

"Tom, the night janitor on your floor is Eddy Lovejoy. He's mute and nearly deaf."

"Mm? Well, he isn't anymore."

They looked at each other.

Kindle said, "What do you really expect to accomplish here tonight? One in ten thousand—so we get maybe five people if everybody who ought to show up really does. Maybe six or seven if the notice got as far as Coos Bay or Pistol River. A pitiful handful, in other words. So what's the point?"

"The point," Matt said, "is that I mean to save Buchanan."

Kindle winced and shifted in his chair. "The world's been hijacked, Matthew. The whole fuckin' world. In the face of that, how do you propose to save one piddling little town?"

"I don't know," Matt said. "But I mean to do it."

• • •

Kindle's estimate had been pessimistic, but not by much. At fifteen minutes after the hour, eight people had shown up—six from Buchanan, two from outlying farms.

One in ten thousand? Was that really possible?

Matt supposed it might be. He was reminded that one in ten thousand was roughly the number of ALS cases in the general population—what people commonly called Lou Gehrig's Disease. He had heard of two such cases in all of Morgan County, which included Buchanan and three smaller towns.

If the numbers were correct, this turnout was a testimony to the effort Matt had expended, placing ads in the *Observer*, posting leaflets, even cadging a few minutes on the local radio news. The radio session had been especially difficult, since no one seemed to know a polite word to differentiate the humans in the audience from the recently immortal. "Shoot, Dr. Wheeler, we're *all* human," the station manager had insisted. Well, perhaps. Anyway, no one had made much mention of Contact even in the local news;

it was still too novel, too profound in its implications—or maybe they understood it collectively: ESP, as Kindle had said.

The radio news department settled on what Matt considered a cumbersome circumlocution: "Those unconvinced by the experience so many of us shared on the last Friday in August are invited to a meeting to be held in Room 106 at Buchanan Regional Hospital, the evening of September the 28th. For details, contact Dr. Matthew Wheeler," and his home and office phone numbers, followed by six seconds of dead air and a weather report.

He was grateful for the announcement, but the experience seemed to foreshadow a whole world of negotiations and misunderstandings—precisely what he hoped to anticipate and even forestall.

For the sake of Buchanan. For the sake, he supposed, of himself and Tom Kindle and these eight doubtful-looking souls waiting for him to speak.

■ ■ ■

He cleared his throat and introduced himself. He felt more than a little misplaced up here. He had attended how many meetings in his life—how many graduation exercises, board meetings, staff briefings? Too many. He had never liked any of them. Meetings, in Matt's opinion, were an excuse to drink coffee, accumulate career karma, and avoid the threat of real work. But here he was. He had even wheeled in the big silver coffee urn from the cafeteria, from which Tom Kindle was tapping a cup. Kindle glanced at him with an air of patient amusement—tilt on, Don Quixote.

He thanked everyone for coming.

"We're here to talk about the future," he said. "I think we share some common interests, and I think we're facing some common problems. Maybe if we get together now we can do something about that. But since there's not many of us present, maybe we should begin with introductions. Let's start with the front row. Thank you."

Matt jotted each name in his notebook as it was spoken:

Miriam Flett. Front row left. In her mid-sixties, Matt guessed, not infirm, but thin as a straw. She wore a silver stickpin in the shape of a cross, and she announced her name as if she expected an argument. She sat down immediately and without comment and folded her arms.

Bob Ganish. Two seats away from Miriam. A salesman, he said, at Highway Five Ford. A round man of middle age dressed as if he had just left a golf game. Were people still golfing, Matt wondered, or was it just that nobody cared anymore if you walked around in polyester slacks and a scuffed pair of putting shoes? "I agree we have a lot of problems, Dr. Wheeler, but

I don't know what we can do about it. But it's nice to know there are people left who still think the old way." Ganish sat down.

"I'm Beth Porter and this is Joey Commoner." No need to jot these names. Beth had dressed up tonight—wore a long-sleeved shirt to cover her tattoo. But Joey, who had also been Matt's patient more than once in the last fifteen years—who had been buying antibiotics on Matt's prescription since Beth dragged him into the office—sat with a grim expression, arms clasped together over a black T-shirt, sullen.

Clockwise from Beth and Joey: *Chuck Makepeace,* a sitting member of the City Council. That might be useful, Matt thought. Mid-thirties, three-piece suit, receding hairline, natty little wire-rimmed glasses. "If we do this again, Dr. Wheeler, we should elect a chairman and follow some rules of order—but maybe I'm getting ahead of myself."

"Excellent suggestion," Matt said. "But let's get to know each other first."

Tim Belanger, about Joey's age; blond, puppyish and eager to cooperate. "I work at City Hall, too. I'm a records clerk for Water and Power. Or I used to be. Hardly anybody shows up at the office anymore."

Abigail Cushman, who had driven in from her husband's farm out in Surrey Heights, "an hour in that old truck, but Buddy said take it. He doesn't give a damn, pardon me, *what* I do anymore." She wore a discount-house dress and sweater and thick glasses with masculine rims taped at one joint. Matt guessed she might be fifty years old, maybe older. "Buddy's looking after the kids. Our grandchildren, actually. Our daughter and son-in-law died last year, so we took the two boys. They're at home. They didn't want to come. I'm the only one who . . . I mean, they're not . . ." The words ran out. She paused and blinked at the room as if she'd forgotten what she was doing here. Bob Ganish coughed into his hand. "Anyway," she said. "Call me Abby." Abby sat down.

Paul Jacopetti, big, barrel-chested, sunburned, sixty-five, retired manager of a tool-and-die company in Corvallis, owned a hobby farm out along the Lake Roads. "Not sure if there's any point in being here," he said. "We can talk all we want, but it looks to me like the horse left the barn some time ago."

Tom Kindle introduced himself from his wheelchair, then turned to face the podium. "Mr. Jacopetti's got a point, Matthew. It's nice we're all here and everything, but what's the purpose? Therapy or strategy?"

"Strategy," Matt said. "Though a little therapy might be welcome." There were a few nervous smiles. He turned a page in his notebook. "The big problem ahead, it seems to me, is that you can't run a national economy when nobody's going to work. Everything seems all right so far. The grocery stores are open, the trucks are bringing in food, the water runs, and the lights are on. Good. But you've all noticed the changes. Mr. Belanger mentioned that people aren't showing up for work at City Hall. I guess nobody minds if the tax bills don't get out." Smiles—but only a few. Some of these people, like Mrs. Cushman, obviously hadn't thought this far ahead.

"But there are such things as essential services, and if those people stop working we could be in trouble. The hospital, for instance. There hasn't been much call for our work, admittedly, but even so, I can't maintain a twenty-four-hour emergency room all by myself. I'm not the only physician on call, but there are fewer every day. The administration tells me the hospital won't close entirely . . . at least not yet. It's the 'not yet' that worries me. I hear it a lot. People are vague about the future—maybe you've noticed. I don't think they know what's going to happen much better than we do. But they seem to expect something. Some kind of massive, sweeping change."

"Doesn't take a genius to figure that out," Jacopetti put in. "It's like I said—we *know* the barn's on fire."

"Not exactly," Abby Cushman said. "Could be a fire. Could be a flood or an earthquake. We don't know *what* the problem is . . . isn't that what you mean, Dr. Wheeler?"

"That's right. The best we can do is make some general plans. We're going to want to maintain as much of the quality of life in Buchanan as we can, and I think we'll have to be able to deal with a breakdown at the telephone company, say, or the interruption of food deliveries."

Makepeace, the City Hall functionary, was frowning. "How is that our responsibility? It doesn't follow. If these . . . other people . . . can't maintain basic services, won't they suffer right along with us?"

Tom Kindle raised his hand. "Use your imagination, Mr.—Makepeace, is it? It's not like everybody got converted to some new religion—though maybe they did that, too. Outside this room, people are physically different. They have things living inside them. Who *knows* what that means? Come next summer, they might all turn to stone, or live on air and sunshine, or move to Canada."

"And there are those things," Miriam Flett added. (Her voice, Matt thought, was as steely and rosinous as a violin note—and it commanded the same kind of attention.) "Those things on television, the Helpers, so-called, though they look like some kind of death robot to me. Probably one of them is coming to Buchanan."

"Lord, don't remind me," Abby Cushman said. "It makes me shudder to think of it. I got a phone call from my cousin Clifford in New York State. He said he saw one down on I-90, cruising toward Utica at about forty miles an hour. It stood a foot above the road, like an eight-foot-tall ace of spades, he said, and traffic parted like the Red Sea all around it."

"Tom's right," Matt said, trying to steer the conversation back on course. "Anything could happen, and I think we're obliged to do the most general kind of emergency planning. These are a few of the areas I'm concerned about."

The boardroom was equipped with a green chalkboard along the front wall. Tom scrawled out four categories:

Food
Medical Care
Water & Utilities
Communication

Everyone stared at the board for a long moment. It was Abby Cushman who broke the silence: "Holy God, Dr. Wheeler, is all that up to *us*?"

Jacopetti snorted. "That's nuts. There's ten of us in this room, Dr. Wheeler. Two of us, I would guess, over sixty. Three of us teenagers or not much older. None of us with much useful experience—though we do have a medical man. If all these things fail, I'd say it's game over. We couldn't truck food here from Portland—if there *was* food in Portland, which I don't guess there would be—or run the electric company, or pump water from the reservoir."

Kindle looked interested. "The numbers could be an advantage, though. Ten people can't run a town, but they can sure as hell run themselves. It's a survival problem, seems to me. If there's no electricity, we can operate generators, as long as the gasoline holds out—which would be a hell of a long time if we had free access to every gas station between here and Portland. Similarly water. We don't need every faucet in town running, only one or two."

"There might not even be ten of us," Bob Ganish said. "I've got family in Seattle. I guess they might be . . . you know, *changed*. But I still might try to get up there and see 'em. In the kind of emergency you're talking about, why stick around?"

"Why leave?" This was Tim Belanger, the City Hall clerk, frowning massively. "Things would be bad all over, wouldn't they?"

"We can assume that," Matt said. "But there's another point. We may be the only human beings in Buchanan, but there's the whole northwest to think about. If we have a plan in place, we might attract refugees from Portland or Astoria or even farther away. A small town is easier to manage than a city. We could turn Buchanan into a kind of safe haven."

"No room," Jacopetti said.

"Not if the original population is still here. But they might not be. That's one possibility, anyhow."

"Communications," Kindle said. "If we're a refugee camp, people have to know about us."

"No telephone," Makepeace mused, "no mail, no newspapers . . . this is hard to imagine. There's the local radio station, but I don't think we could run it by ourselves."

"Ham radio," Kindle said. "Shit—excuse me—any radio ham who didn't go over to the enemy must be laying eggs and hatching kittens. They love this emergency shit. Only there's nobody to talk to."

"We should look into that as soon as possible," Matt agreed. "Any hams present?"

No one spoke.

"Okay. I know we haven't elected a chairman, but does anybody object if I appoint Tom Kindle as our radio committee?" No objection. "Tom, you ought to be mobile by the end of the month. I suggest you price a decent ham radio rig—there's an electronics shop down by the marina, I recall. In the meantime, I can find you some books on the subject."

"Okay . . . but I'm not licensed, Matt."

"Do you suppose the FCC gives a damn right now?"

Kindle grinned. "I spose not."

Miriam Flett put up her hand: "Dr. Wheeler . . . are we expected to *pay* for this radio nonsense?"

"We should talk about funding. But I'm prepared to underwrite the Radio Committee for the time being."

Makepeace and Ganish both offered to chip in; Matt said he'd get back to them—no money was being spent until next week at the earliest.

"There's a fifth category," Jacopetti said. "One you neglected to write down."

Matt glanced at the chalkboard. "What would that be, Mr. Jacopetti?"

"Defense."

A chill seemed to settle in the room. Joey Commoner uttered a small, scornful laugh.

Kindle said, "We get the point, Mr. Jacopetti, but as you yourself said, we're kinda outnumbered. If this is the Alamo, we might as well pack it in."

Jacopetti folded his hands on his belly. "I agree. And I think it's the likeliest prospect. We don't fit into this new world of theirs. They'll get tired of us, and then they'll dispose of us."

"Not *my* kids," Abby Cushman said faintly. "They wouldn't do that to me . . . not my *grandchildren*."

Jacopetti gave her a stony look. "I wouldn't count on that. We have to be prepared—isn't that why we're here, Dr. Wheeler?"

"I don't think that's something we can prepare for, Mr. Jacopetti. And I don't think it's as likely as all that. No one's threatened us yet."

"*And no one will.*"

A new voice. Heads turned toward the doorway. A small presence there. It was Cindy Rhee.

• • •

Matt had the involuntary thought: *She ought to be dead by now.*

He was visited by the memory of Ellen Rhee wiping drool from her daughter's chin as Cindy's eyes roamed aimlessly and without focus.

That was before the intervention of the neocytes, this miracle cure. Now Cindy Rhee was walking—albeit stiffly—and talking, although her words were solemn and curiously deliberate.

"She's one of *them*," Miriam Flett announced. "She shouldn't be here."

The twelve-year-old focused her eyes on Miriam before Matt could frame an answer. "I won't stay if you don't want me to, Miss Flett. I came so that someone could speak for us." The collective, the inclusive, the universal *us*. She turned to Matt. "Dr. Wheeler, it's probably sensible, what you're doing here. But Mr. Jacopetti is wrong. We're not a threat to you."

"Cindy," Matt said, "are you speaking for everyone? All the Contactees?"

She remained in the doorway, a small silhouette. "Yes."

"How is that possible?"

She shrugged.

"Cindy, if you really know what's going to happen—next month, next year—I wish you'd tell us."

"I can't. It hasn't been decided yet, Dr. Wheeler."

Paul Jacopetti had turned a shade of brick red that caused Matt to speculate about hypertension. "Who is this kid? And how does she know my name?" To Cindy: "What were you doing, listening through the door?"

"She's a patient of mine," Matt said. "She—"

"They know *everything*," Miriam interrupted. "Haven't you figured that out? We don't have any secrets from them."

Jacopetti stood up. "I vote to have her removed. She's a spy, obviously."

"I'll go," Cindy Rhee said.

"No," Matt said. Lacking a gavel, he slapped shut his notebook. "I was about to declare a coffee break. Cindy, please stay until we reconvene. Twenty minutes."

■ ■ ■

He asked Cindy to sit in one of the boardroom chairs and pulled up a second chair in front of her. He felt he should take the opportunity to examine the child, though he couldn't say what moved him—sympathy, curiosity, dread. He took a penlight from his shirt pocket and shone it into her eyes.

The others had crowded around the coffee urn, talking in low voices and sparing an occasional glance at Matt and Cindy. He hoped he hadn't jeopardized his credibility by talking to the girl.

Tom Kindle sat apart, thoughtful in his wheelchair.

Cindy's pupils still seemed slow to contract, but their reaction was equivalent and otherwise normal. She tracked the penlight adequately when he moved it right to left, up and down.

He touched her forehead; the skin was cool.

"Thank you for being worried about me, Dr. Wheeler. I'm all right."

"I'm glad, Cindy. It's good to see you walking."

"But you think it's strange."

"I'm happy about it. But yes, it seems strange to me."

More than that. He wondered what kind of miracle it really was. He wondered what was inside her skull right now. Normal brain tissue, somehow regenerated? Or something else? Something fed by blood like dark molasses?

She seemed to sense the thought. "They had to work on me before Contact, Dr. Wheeler, because I was so sick. So I'm a little farther on than most people."

"That's why you came here?"

"Partly. Partly because even Mr. Jacopetti can't be too scared of a twelve-year-old." She suppressed a smile. The smile looked authentic. It was the way she had smiled last year, before the neuroblastoma put an end to all her smiling. "We aren't dangerous to you. It's important to understand that. You're right about the future. It might be difficult. But we're not the danger."

She was still woefully thin.

"You mean to help," Matt said. "I appreciate that. But it would be better if you didn't stay."

"I know. Thank you for the examination."

She stood up and seemed ready to leave, then frowned and tugged at his sleeve. "Dr. Wheeler . . ."

"Yes?"

"It's about your daughter. . . ."

He felt a deep interior chill. "Rachel? What about her?"

"You should talk to her. You haven't really talked to her since Contact. She misses you."

"How do you know that?"

It had become the great unanswerable question. Cindy just shrugged—sadly.

"Talk to Rachel, Dr. Wheeler."

■   ■   ■

There wasn't much more meeting. Chuck Makepeace said they should invest in a few copies of *Robert's Rules of Order* and elect a chairman at the next meeting. Matt agreed. Tim Belanger volunteered to take minutes next time. Abby Cushman said they would need a name—"You can't have us just be nameless."—and were there any suggestions? Abby herself thought "Committee of the Last True Human Beings" would be good.

"Too confrontational," Makepeace said. "That's not what we're about."

Jacopetti raised his hand. "Committee of Cockeyed Optimists. Council of Lost Causes."

Matt said he thought it could be the "Emergency Planning Committee" for the time being. Heads nodded, though Abby seemed disappointed.

It was past ten o'clock and people were eager to leave. Matt asked them to write their names, addresses, and phone numbers on a piece of paper, which he would photocopy and distribute to everyone on the list along with an announcement of the next get-together. Meeting adjourned. Beth and Joey Commoner were first out the door; Miriam Flett, last. Matt stood at the window watching cars pull out of the parking lot.

Tom Kindle wheeled himself to the door. "Care to push me as far as the elevator? Jeez, I hate this fuckin' chair."

"You'll be walking before long." Matt guided the chair down the semidarkened corridor. The walls were painted a shade of green that was supposed to be soothing but looked, under the ceiling fluorescents, unearthly. Kindle wouldn't be alone in this cavernous building—there was still a skeleton night staff on duty—but in some other sense he would be very alone, and Matt felt sorry for him.

"So," Kindle said, "are you going to take the girl's advice?"

"You heard that?"

"A little. None of my business, of course. Didn't know you had a daughter."

"I used to." He rang for the elevator and worked to keep the bitterness out of his voice. "I'm not sure I do anymore."

Chapter
16

The Battle
of U.S. 95

The problem, John Tyler thought, was that all the armies had gone home, all the factories had closed their doors, all the Congressional committees had adjourned forever—and where did that leave him?

Sidelined. Down, in other words. But not out.

Tyler lived alone in a two-story Georgian-style townhouse in Arlington, Virginia. He had equipped the spare bedroom with a formidable array of Nautilus exercise equipment, and in the days after his unproductive conversation with the Chief Executive he spent a great deal of time working out.

Tyler was a month away from his fifty-second birthday, and though he was in fairly good civilian trim, he wanted more: He wanted to be in fighting shape. At his age, it was a difficult proposition. Not that it couldn't be done. But he was paying for the effort. The token of exchange in this bargain was pain. First the obvious pain of a hard workout, the pain he took to a certain brink and backed away from. Then the stealthy pain that crept up in the night—the aching tendons, the protesting spine, the humiliating discomforts that sent him to the drugstore in search of Ben-Gay, Tylenol, something to help him sleep, something to help him move his bowels.

But there came a time when he was able to look at himself in the full-length bedroom mirror without flinching. Taut chest, lean belly tapering into the waistband of his Jockey shorts, firm legs. Gray stubble hair on his head and a down of gray hair on chest and limbs. It seemed to Tyler that he had created something good here, a reflection he could take some pride in. Appearances had always mattered to Tyler a great deal.

But the important thing was that he was fit for duty.

If anyone could be fit for the kind of duty he had in mind.

■ ■ ■

On the second Monday in October he took his old Army jacket out of mothballs, decided he liked the way it looked over a crisp white shirt and dress pants, and climbed into his car and headed for the Marine base at Quantico.

The Virginia countryside was deep in a sweet-tempered autumn. The sky was blue and the full blush of color was on the woods. The highway was mainly empty—as most highways were these days.

Tyler had given a great deal of thought to the crisis facing the country, and he rehearsed his logic as he drove. The problem, he thought once again, was that all the armies had gone home, and how do you engage an enemy without an army?

Guerrilla warfare was the obvious response to an occupying power of superior strength . . . but you still needed an infantry, a militia, a power base. "The revolutionary moves among the people like a fish in the sea." Mao Tse-tung. But "the people" had been coopted. The fish was beached. Tyler had seen videotape of African armies, Central American armies, Asian and European and even Israeli and American armies, rabble and trained troops alike, laying down their arms, bailing out of tanks, abandoning trenches and revetments like something from a hippie pipe dream of the sixties. It had happened from Ethiopia to Lebanon, from Turkestan to Latin America, and it had happened without exception.

But it seemed to Tyler that even this defeat could be used to his advantage. Weapons that were rusting in the field couldn't be turned on an insurgency. He could move among this pacified population, not like a fish in the sea, more like—say—a shark among the minnows or a whale among the krill.

But not by himself. One could be outnumbered. One ought not to be alone.

One in ten thousand, the President had told him.

Tyler didn't know if that was a reliable statistic. It surely wasn't an encouraging one. But the military had been a major employer prior to Contact, and even if the situation was as bleak as it seemed, he should be able to find one or two good men.

Maybe he'd waited too long. Maybe the plan he had devised wouldn't work . . . but that remained to be seen.

▪ ▪ ▪

Quantico was a disappointment.

Last month, the Marine Reservation had been a hive of activity. Local newscasts had shown an apparently endless relay of Hercules transport aircraft buzzing in and out, part of the post-Contact grain airlift to the famine zones of the world.

But that airlift was over now, and the huge USMC complex at Quantico appeared to be deserted. He drove among these brick buildings and overgrown parade fields honking his horn until he grew weary of the echoes rolling back.

He drove to the main gate, stopped his car, and opened the trunk. Sunlight warmed the skin of his neck and dappled the huge statue of the Iwo Jima flagraising. From the trunk, he unwound ten yards of bright orange rip-stop nylon on which he had painted, painstakingly, in letters of waterproof black acrylic, the words:

Any Member of the Armed Forces Remaining on Duty
Call Colonel John Tyler (202)212-5555
or Report to 731 Portage Street Arlington ASAP
God Bless the USA

He had sewn nylon cords into the fabric at several points, and he attached these to the fenceposts so that the banner hung suspended across the road.

The nylon drooped in the still air, but the message was easy to read.

▪ ▪ ▪

Over the course of a week and a half Tyler constructed similar banners and left them at smaller military installations from Baltimore down to Richmond. Every evening, he checked his answering machine for messages. To date: None.

On his trips, Tyler was able to monitor the evolution of the new world. Superficially, not much had changed. Traffic was substantially lighter, especially on the interstates. Tyler saw more people out walking than there used to be, and fewer at work. A lot of small businesses (muffler shops, hairstylists, bookstores) were closed or unattended. People were still running the food stores and shopping at the malls, but he wondered how much longer that would last. Come to that, he wondered how several hundred thousand military and government employees were surviving without paychecks.

The thought was intriguing enough that Tyler tried an experiment. He went into a suburban Arlington grocery store—not in his neighborhood—and filled a cart with canned goods and bottled water. When he came to the checkout he told the clerk, "I don't have any money. I used to work for HUD."

He expected security guards. Instead, the clerk—a chubby young redhead wearing a nametag that said "Sally"—smiled and waved him through.

So why was *anybody* paying? Tyler lingered by the door and took an eyeball survey of the tills. According to his count, it was roughly half and half—half paid, half didn't. Those who did seemed to be operating mainly by force of habit. Tyler guessed that paying for what you take was a reflex deeply entrenched in the American psyche—not an easy habit to break. It continued regardless, like the Major League playoffs. But he guessed the country was already well on the way to a moneyless economy.

Perfect communism, he thought, as practiced by perfect robots.

Tyler heard a voice inside him say, *You're surrounded by monsters.*

It was Sissy's voice. Sissy was an old, sad ghost. Tyler squared his shoulders and paid no attention. Sissy had been telling him he was surrounded by monsters since the day he was born.

■　■　■

Over the years, all his memories of Sissy had condensed into a single image. Here was Sissy as she appeared in his dreams: A middle-aged woman in a swaddling of canvas and polyester skirts, two sweaters buttoned over her pillowing breasts, gypsy-bright and red-faced, pushing a wire buggy full of old newspapers on a too-bright city sidewalk.

A bag lady, as they would say nowadays. She was his mother.

His father had been a salesman for a company that sold plastic novelty cups on which the name of a business could be printed in gold flash. The cup Tyler drank from for the first seven years of his life was inscribed with the legend FLETCHER'S TAXIDERMY, 33 EAST FITH ST, CINCINNATI. When Tyler learned to read—he taught himself to read at the age of four years—he discovered the word FIFTH had been misspelled. Which made him cry, for no good reason he could think of. By then, his father was long gone.

His mother (she demanded he call her Sissy) lived in an ancient three-story row house on a hilly street in an urban neighborhood declining toward slum status. She owned the house. Sometime in her younger days,

Sissy had inherited money from an aunt in Pittsburgh. Sissy had been young and childless and perhaps, Tyler thought, aware of her own impending dementia. She had bought the row house outright and put the remainder of the money in a trust, which issued her a monthly check.

Tyler's father had come and gone without gaining access to any of this money. Sissy, a cautious woman by nature, had remained tightfisted even as the world began to slip past comprehension.

Tyler wasn't sure when he figured out that Sissy was crazy. Probably some other child had been kind enough to let him know. *Hey, Tyler, your mother's dressed like Freddy the Freeloader! Hey, Tyler, your house smells like shit!*

He learned early on that the best response was a firm and uncompromising *Fuck you*. It got him beat up a lot. But in the long run, it also got him left alone. And it taught him a valuable lesson about people. You could be afraid of them or you could hate them; those were your choices. Anything else was a trap . . . a temptation to punishment.

He hated and feared Sissy, but she was also the exception to the rule. Although she was insane, Sissy was still his mother. She fed him, sporadically; she clothed him, eccentrically. She was supposed to care about him, and she was capable of hurting him with her indifference.

He could tolerate the indifference of anyone but Sissy.

That was why, when he went to school for the first time in his life—five days late and in the company of a truant officer—he was driven to tears when everyone laughed at his torn pants, his food-stained shirt.

Not because he cared what they thought. It was Sissy who had wounded him, Sissy who had sent him off so badly dressed.

Sissy, *why*?

Didn't she know any better?

Obviously, she didn't. Sissy had moved into a land where reason and custom had given way to bright strokes of invisible lightning, fearsome revelations too private to share. Sissy, the adult Tyler recognized, had been schizophrenic. Sissy had been defending her home by stockpiling it with garbage and rags, and it was a miracle she had dressed him at all.

Sissy had been dead now for many years. But she visited Tyler regularly and she wasn't shy about making her opinions known.

▪　▪　▪

The phone call came while he was watching television.

Tyler had installed a satellite dish on the roof and an illegal descrambler in his living room. The descrambler was a neat little sync regenerator based on a CMOS chip and a 3.58 MHz oscillator. He could decode anything, including C-SPAN, HBO, and military broadcasts—not that any of these were on the air anymore.

In fact, since mid-October, there had been only a couple of hours of national TV a day—skeleton CNN broadcasts, mostly coverage of the disarming of the world and the continuous slow unwinding of the octahedrons.

It was this last that interested Tyler. Today, another bright autumn morning, windows open and a breeze tangling the curtains, he sipped a diet soda and watched a videotape of a lone Helper, so-called, gliding along an empty highway near Atlanta.

He was fascinated by the look of it. Seven feet of matte-black formless menace. It was a "Helper" the way Stalin had been "Uncle Joe."

These curious items had been unwinding steadily from their octahedral bases in New York and Los Angeles, spreading out, forming a network across the country—the world—for purposes unannounced. You can call them Helpers, Tyler thought, but he recognized an occupation force when he saw one.

What would you need to take out one of these dreadnoughts?

Well, Tyler thought, let me see. . . .

And then, as if in answer, the telephone rang.

He stood up from the chair with his heart battering his ribs. Christ! How long since he'd heard that sound?

He had just about given up waiting.

He thumbed the mute button on the remote TV control and snatched up the telephone handset. "*Hello?*"

It'll be a wrong number, he thought. Some Contactee who dialed a 5 instead of a 6. Or did they still make such human errors?

"Colonel Tyler?" asked a male voice.

"Speaking," he managed.

"Saw your sign, sir. Down at Quantico." Pause. "One of the strings came loose, but I hooked it up again."

"I thank you for that," Tyler said. "Are you a Marine?"

Turned out he was, a fairly raw one: a weapons specialist, twenty-one years old. "Name's A.W. Murdoch."

"What's the A for?"

"Alphonse, I'm sorry to say."

"I'm sorry to hear it. I won't ask about the W. Do I understand you managed to turn down the invitation to Life Eternal?"

"Yes, sir."

"Well, then, we ought to get together."

"We will. Uh, Colonel Tyler . . . I take it you're thinking of offering some resistance here? Meaning no offense, I'm not in need of company for company's sake. I thought, from your sign, you'd probably want to kick a little ass?"

Eager young buck, Tyler thought. Well, so am I. Eager, at least. "I think that's a safe assumption. When can I see you?"

"You can see me right now if you step to the window, sir."

Tyler did so. He peered down from his second-story bay window into the sunny street. Parked there . . .

. . . parked on a quiet tree-lined Arlington avenue . . .

. . . was a camouflage-brown M998 Hummer, the one-and-three-quarter-ton vehicle that had replaced the Jeep of Tyler's youth, a sturdy and versatile machine . . .

. . . on the roof of which was mounted an M-109 TOW launcher, a tank killer par excellence, looking a little like a ray gun from an old science fiction movie . . .

. . . *or like an answer to a prayer*, Tyler thought . . .

. . . and grinning up from the interior of this vehicle was a lanky blond youth whose regulation haircut had grown a little shaggy but whose uniform remained relatively clean, holding in his right hand what appeared to be a cellular phone.

Obviously a smart-ass, Tyler thought, but a smart-ass bearing gifts.

Murdoch saluted, squinting into the sunlight.

"It appears we have a lot to talk about," Tyler said.

"I'll be right up, sir."

"No. I'll be right down."

▪ ▪ ▪

Tyler had learned how to establish a certain tone in male conversation, a certain rank. In the military, the rules of conduct were explicit. In civilian conversation the matter was more subtle; thus it was important to take command and do so quickly. It was the inability to take command that had frustrated him during his interview with the President, which was still a sore memory. He'd been off balance, at a disadvantage; taking a pistol to the White House was an impulse he should never have obeyed in the first place. It was hasty.

Here, the situation favored Tyler.

A.W. Murdoch was an active Marine Sergeant. John Tyler was a retired Army officer, technically a civilian, a superior officer by courtesy only. But it started well, Tyler thought, when Murdoch addressed him as "sir." Given that, Tyler thought, all else falls into place.

They sat in the front of the Hummer and swapped stories of the invasion as a prelude to more serious talk.

Murdoch was a California boy, the kind of adolescent drifter that state had so often produced, until he drifted into the Corps and discovered a purpose in life. That purpose was the maintenance of portable weaponry and the instruction of recruits in the use of same, and it was the only thing Murdoch seemed to care much about. When Contact emptied Quantico, Murdoch was devastated. He kept driving back to the base, he said, every few days, like an ant to an empty nest.

Then he saw John Tyler's sign and guessed there might be a future for him after all.

Tyler offered in exchange some of his own recent history. It was hard to explain the civilian work he'd done, since it crossed so many borders—Congress, the defense industry, banking. His job had been to know people, but not too well; to say things, but not too explicitly. In fact, that life was already beginning to feel vague and distant; the intricacies that had once intrigued and compelled him seemed as abstruse now as the mating dance of an extinct species.

He didn't say exactly this to Murdoch. He did make some mention of the revolt that had been derailed, at the last minute, by Contact. Murdoch was fascinated: he'd been aware of the high-level alert that August night, the furtive troop movements. "It was exciting," Murdoch said. "Like something out of the Civil War. Firing on Fort Sumter. I never did care for that windy old fart in the White House."

Bolstered by this, the Colonel described his last meeting with the Commander in Chief—a somewhat polished version.

Murdoch was wide-eyed. "You actually had a pistol on him?"

"Yes," Tyler said.

"You could have killed him."

He nodded.

"Why didn't you?"

"It wouldn't have helped. It might have attracted attention. Anyway, he was . . . too malleable. Too yielding. Do you understand, Mr. Murdoch?"

"I know what you mean. I meet people. People I used to know, even. They're real nice. *Too* nice. It's scary, but you can't hate 'em for it. Much less shoot 'em. Be like killing a rabbit with a pipe wrench."

Tyler nodded.

Murdoch extracted two cans of Coors from a cooler in the back of the vehicle. He offered one to Tyler, who popped the tab and listened to the hiss.

"No," Murdoch said, "*they're* not the enemy. Those things on the road, on the other hand . . ."

"Helpers," Colonel Tyler said.

"Uh-huh. Now, to me, *they* look like the enemy."

"I share your thought," Tyler said.

"You thought about what to do about it?"

"Obviously. But why don't you give me your perspective first."

"Well . . . there's all this technology lying around, but most of it you can't manage if you're just one person—or just two. Might be fun zooming over the treetops with an A-10 and twelve-hundred rounds of those depleted uranium-tipped slugs, say. But, shit, I'm no pilot. Sir, are you?"

"About a hundred hours in a Piper Cub."

"We couldn't even preflight an A-10. So we're looking at portable ground weapons. Not a tank or a self-propelled Howitzer or anything sluggish like that. I mean, we don't know for sure what we're up against. So, something *lean*. A Dragon, an AT-4. Okay, we can get lots of those. The whole world's an armory, right? And the doors are wide open. But for a first encounter, I'm thinking power and mobility. I'm thinking shoot and scoot."

"The Hummer," Tyler interpreted.

"The Hummer, and more specifically that TOW on the roof. The way I see it, we encounter a Helper on the open road, we can bust it and break away before their cavalry arrives."

Tyler sipped his beer and pretended to be thinking it over.

"Mr. Murdoch, we don't know what defenses those things might possess."

"I don't think we can find out except by shooting at 'em."

"Might be dangerous."

Murdoch heard something in Tyler's voice, some unsuccessfully suppressed note of mischief. He smiled. "Sir, it might indeed. It's a pretty day for shooting, though, isn't it?"

"Don't get ahead of yourself. You have to teach me how to operate this TOW." Tyler glanced up at a sky the color of blue chalk. "It's a pretty day for some live-fire exercises, too."

Murdoch wasn't pleased with this. "I'd hoped to operate the TOW myself—you know—when it comes time."

"Rank has its privileges, Mr. Murdoch. I expect we'll both get a chance."

"Yes, sir," Murdoch said.

■   ■   ■

They came to know each other that first week they were together on the live-fire range at Quantico, Murdoch teaching him the TOW and some smaller tank-killers. Tyler guessed you could say they were friends, the barrier of command fractured a little by their odd situation. Tyler shared some secrets, as friends do. But there were secrets he simply couldn't share, had never shared with anyone—such as the history of his madness.

"Madness," too strong a word, but Tyler used it to remind himself that it was not merely unhappiness, not merely self-pity, it was a darker and more powerful presence that from time to time settled upon him.

Ever since Sissy died.

These memories came back at night.

Key events during his twelfth year: He achieved a B+ average at school, scored well above the norm on a Stanford-Binet intelligence test administered by the school board, and fainted twice, once in gym, once in homeroom. The school nurse asked him what he usually ate for breakfast and dinner, and he answered, both times, "Frosted Flakes." He liked the picture of the tiger on the box. He did most of the shopping himself. He never bought vegetables because he wasn't sure how: you put them in these plastic bags, you weighed them . . . it was confusing; he worried he might spend more than the three or four dollars Sissy let him carry to the store.

As for canned vegetables—he had tried that once. Canned peas, which came out pale green and wrinkly, not much like the picture on the label. Sissy said they tasted like rat poison. Had he ever watched a poisoned rat die? Sissy had. Sissy described the event. "You want to do that to *me?*"

Tyler thought he'd better stick to Frosted Flakes.

The nurse and his homeroom teacher conferred, which led to a visit from a social worker, which led, after no little trauma, to Tyler's installation in a foster home and Sissy's forcible remittance to a white brick building out of town, where she died six months later of "an accident while bathing." Tyler had seen the guards who worked at this institution: They were barrel-chested, stupid, and permanently pissed off. Sissy used to spit at them. So Tyler was suspicious when they told him the "accident" part. But Sissy was dead—that was a fact.

He never found out what happened to the old row house or Sissy's remittance money. He didn't want to have anything to do with either one. He was *glad* Sissy was gone. Life was better without Sissy.

Still, when he overheard a social worker say the same thing—that he would be better off without Sissy—Tyler tried to kill the woman with the sharp end of a blue Bic pen.

He didn't do much more than scratch her face, though he privately hoped the ink had dyed the skin beneath the wound, a permanent tattoo, a reminder that such calculations were not hers to make.

The act propelled him out of his foster home and into a grim institution (perhaps not unlike the white brick building in which Sissy had died spitting at her captors) in which Tyler was kicked, assaulted, humiliated, sometimes brutalized, at best ignored. He was rescued from this limbo when a legal inquiry into Sissy's holdings discovered a living relative who was willing to take custody of the boy.

Tyler never actually met this man, who preferred to remain safely distant; he was a retired lawyer, Tyler understood, who paid his way into a military boarding school of some repute. The boy was bright; everyone admitted that. Sullen sometimes. Given to fantasy. A loner. But smart as a whip.

He enlisted in the Army with good prospects, earned his lieutenant's bars, earned a bachelor's degree at the government's expense, faced a bright future as a commissioned officer.

He did carry a few black marks on his record. During basic infantry training, he had come close to killing another man, a memory that still troubled him. It was an impulse. There was no other word to describe it. One moment he was practicing a takedown; the next he was strangling the man. It was nobody in particular. It happened to be a stringbean named Delgado, who was actually a friend of his, more or less. But that didn't matter. What mattered was the sudden and overwhelming need to *do harm*, to carve his name on a stranger's life as painfully as strangers had carved their names on his. Plus it gave him an erection.

Three other men had dragged him off Delgado, who gagged and vomited. No permanent damage had been done, however, and in view of Tyler's otherwise excellent record, the event was written off as an anomaly. It was a pattern he would come to recognize. The phrase *in light of this soldier's otherwise commendable performance* decorated a whole drawer of complaints. Not insubordination—never that. Drunkenness, fistfights, slovenly dress, once a speed run through Saigon with the military police behind him. But only at certain intervals, certain dark passages in his life, certain times when he heard Sissy's voice too often in his head—that is, only during his madnesses.

It had slowed his rise from the ranks. When you reach a certain point, Tyler discovered, your private life begins to matter. You start being seen at parties with embassy personnel, in a decorative role, offering dances to the wives of ambassadors and the daughters of diplomats; consorting with people who want you to be their little brother in uniform, an American Centurion with a cute little pixie wife and maybe a freckled three-year-old in military housing somewhere. They didn't want you trafficking, for instance, with Asian prostitutes, unless you were *very* discreet, and they didn't look kindly on the rumor that you'd been seen in a different red-light district altogether, where the traffic leaned toward young Asian boys.

It was only that his passions inclined to youth, a certain androgynous beauty he craved but couldn't define. He came to the Asian boys, Asian girls, telling himself it was simply a need to be satisfied, and he left hating them for their grace, their wantonness, their doe-eyed acquiescence.

He learned discretion. Discretion served him well for some years. Discretion did not fail him until his posting to West Germany, where his military career came to an end. He had found a whorehouse in Stuttgart, in a pretty little building next to a pretty little beer garden in a part of the city not much frequented by Americans; and he had selected a Turkish immigrant girl who claimed to be thirteen years old and by her looks might not have been lying; and he had been upstairs with her, the girl naked and mumbling "*Bitte, bitte,*" through a mouth filled with the Colonel's erect penis, while he held his service revolver to her head and stroked its trigger, gently, not even *near* the point of firing the weapon—when the house matron came through the door screaming at him.

Apparently it was her custom to keep an eye on her employees through a number of peepholes in the old plaster walls, and she had seen Tyler put his revolver to the girl's head—but it was really only a kind of play; was that so hard to understand?—and believed he was about to commit a murder.

Tyler was startled by the woman, and when he turned the revolver *did* go off—he shot the girl through her skinny left arm. It was a mistake.

An ambulance came, the police came, he was arrested. He was held for questioning by a red-faced man who told him, "This is not the Wild West! This is not where you shoot and fuck!"

He was never charged. But he was held for three days, and the incident was reported to his superiors; there was an investigation, some local scandal-mongering. People began to look at him differently. That was the hard part. People *knew*. They looked at him . . . well, the way people used to look at Sissy.

He resigned his commission. He had made enough friends to ease the transition into civilian life, but it was a difficult time. The Stuttgart incident seemed to be always at his heels, seemed to follow him like some odorous lost dog.

It fades, Sissy said. *Memory fades. Everyone forgets everything. That's the rule.*

But the nights were long. Some nights were too long, and on those nights he would drive his second car, an anonymous brown sedan, along dark city streets where the girls were usually black or Hispanic and very young, to cheap hotel rooms that stank of insecticide and perspiration, where he would sometimes, even after Stuttgart, play the Gun Game with them.

And in the aftermath, home before dawn, alone, he might toy with his service revolver, pick it up, put it down, put it to his temple, the touch of the steel a familiar sensation after all these years, the oily smell of it a comforting smell. Sissy always talked him out of pulling the trigger. The Sissy in his head. Sad ghost. *Don't kill yourself and be like me.*

And in time his daylight life grew bearable. He was trustworthy, he was discreet—he had learned all about discretion—and he was smart. He moved between the military, the defense contractors, and the congressional committees with a growing familiarity. His job was to say plainly what his employers could only hint at, and to hint at what his employers would publicly deny.

And his madnesses came and ebbed in their own slow, tidal rhythm; never predictable and impossible to resist. And the years passed.

Meeting A.W. Murdoch and wearing himself out on the firing range had postponed the madness for now. But it would come again, Tyler knew. It always came. And came again.

■   ■   ■

When he had learned the basics of the TOW, he drove with Murdoch to an empty stretch of U.S. 95 and parked in the breakdown lane under a stand of shade trees.

Yesterday Murdoch had roamed up and down this pike in a commandeered sports car making notes on the position of the Helpers. A stream of the devices had been flowing through Baltimore on 95 for some weeks now, always travelling at a steady forty miles per hour and at regular intervals. Some turned west on 70 or installed themselves in road towns like Columbia or Wheaton; most continued south on 95. One had taken up a position on the White House lawn.

Tyler himself hadn't seen one with his own eyes, only the TV pictures. It was worse close up, Murdoch told him. "They aren't just black, like painted black or anodized black. They don't shine in the sunlight at all. They're blacker than their own shadows. And when they move, Colonel, they don't tremble or bounce. They glide. You ever play a computer game, sir? You know how things move on a video screen? Like math. Like oiled perfection. That's how these things move." The idea of trying to stop one, Murdoch confessed, as much as it appealed to him, it also . . . well, it scared him a little.

"You can deal with it, though?"

"Oh, hell, yes. Sir, I'm *anxious* to deal with it."

So here they were, parked on a sunny stretch of road at the edge of a cow pasture where a few Holsteins grazed, or perhaps they were Guernseys, Tyler got those confused; a dairy breed, in any case. Crickets sang in the high grass and faint clouds dappled the horizon. The air was cool. November was only a day away.

"Any old minute now, sir," said Murdoch, who had calculated this somehow.

Tyler focused his attention on the highway where it crossed a low ridge a couple of thousand yards north. The Helper would be coming over that ridge. Well within range. But nothing moved there now, not even traffic. The roads were sparsely travelled these days.

Murdoch popped a can of Dr. Pepper, which made Tyler jump. "Christ's sake."

"Sorry, sir."

Tyler's mouth was dry. He envied Murdoch that can of pop fresh from the cooler. But he had to be ready to man the TOW. He guessed this was Murdoch's revenge for not being allowed first shot at a Helper. Tough luck, Tyler thought. I guess I can wait for a cold drink.

"Sir? I think you have a target, sir."

Tyler stood up on the shooting platform and manned the weapon.

The TOW was manufactured by Hughes, a company Tyler had done some business with. He had a lot of respect for the TOW. It was a wire-guided weapon, almost mind-numbingly complex, but reliable in service. It was designed to penetrate heavy armor plate and render even the best-protected tank functionally unserviceable, i.e., blow it the hell up.

He got his first good look at a Helper through the cross hairs of the 13x optical sight.

The Helper looked like a death-black ball and cone—the aliens seemed to love these Euclidian shapes—and it was travelling well below the speed limit along the slow curve of the road. The image rippled slightly in the heat rising from the asphalt.

The cattle shuffled and raised their heads as if they sensed this presence.

Tyler was suddenly nervous—suddenly this seemed like real combat—but he didn't let the anxiety affect his timing. He kept the Helper in his sights until it cleared the high spot in the road. He wanted this target clean.

"Sir," Murdoch said nervously. "We're a little exposed here."

"Keep your shirt on, Mr. Murdoch."

A long pause, then: "*Sir?*"

Tyler triggered the weapon.

The TOW performed a number of complex tasks between one eyeblink and the next. Tyler's finger on the firing button ignited a rocket motor, which popped the missile from its launch container. All the rocket fuel was used up before the missile left the tube, which was what protected Tyler, Murdoch, and the vehicle they were sitting in from the backwash. The sound of the launch was blisteringly loud. It was a sound Murdoch had compared to the hiss of Satan's own steam press.

When the missile was well clear, a sustainer motor ignited; the missile unfolded four wings and accelerated to 900 feet per second.

Tyler's eyes were on the Helper.

The TOW missile trailed two fine wires attached to the launcher. Tyler actually used the sight and a joystick to *drive the missile*, which never failed to astonish him, this video-game aspect of it. He steered the missile down a trajectory that seemed eternally long, but was not. He kept the cross hairs centered on the moving Helper. Picture-book launch.

The missile arrived in the vicinity of its target travelling at 200-plus miles per hour.

The warhead was fitted with a standoff probe that exploded fifteen inches from the target.

The main warhead detonated a fraction of a second later.

Hell of an explosion, Tyler thought, his ears ringing.

"Holy damn!" Murdoch whooped.

The cows and crickets had fallen silent.

▪ ▪ ▪

Tyler had once seen a movie called *War of the Worlds*, loosely based on the H. G. Wells novel.

Martians land in California and build monstrous killing machines.

Conventional weapons fail. At last, the Air Force drops a nuclear device.

Explosion. Mushroom cloud. Nervous observers wait for visibility to improve. The firestorm abates, the dust settles . . .

The Martian machine is still there.

Tyler leaned against the hot mass of the TOW launcher, scrutinizing the spot on the highway where the missile had detonated.

The smoke swirled up and away in a lazy easterly breeze. . . .

And nothing at all was left behind.

▪ ▪ ▪

Murdoch couldn't resist driving to the spot, though Tyler's instinct was to get away as quickly as possible.

He stopped and idled a few feet from the scorch marks.

Nothing remained of the Helper but a fine, sooty-black dust—a thick arc of it clean across the highway.

"Nice shot," Murdoch said.

"Thank you."

"Spose you're right, though, Colonel. Spose we ought to scoot."

"Commence scooting," Tyler said.

It was a small beginning. But it was also, Tyler thought, the first human victory after a long humiliation. He closed his eyes as Murdoch raced the Hummer into the cool October air. It had been a genuinely lovely autumn, Tyler thought. A beautiful fall.

After a time, the crickets started up again.

Chapter 17

Two Eagles

Northwest autumn weather moved in from the ocean on the third of October and settled over coastal Oregon like a contented guest. The sky darkened, the rain came in mists and drizzles, dusk began at lunch and lingered till dinnertime.

Matt was afraid this would go on through the winter, that they wouldn't see the sun again until April. He was happy to be proved wrong. Five days before Halloween, the clouds parted. One last bubble of warm air, drawn across the Pacific from Hawaii, paused above Buchanan. The dew dried on the pine needles and the grass wondered whether it ought to start growing again.

Over breakfast, Matt recalled what Cindy Rhee had told him.

Talk to your daughter.

The child was right, of course.

He had barely spoken to Rachel since Contact. He'd been busy—spending time at the hospital, trying to keep the ER functional, then organizing the Committee.

But even when he was alone with her in the long evenings, too silent, when the sun declined and the Artifact cast its bony light, or the rain talked to the roof . . . still, he couldn't bring himself to speak.

Not to say the important things.

He was too much aware of the change in her, of the neocytes, so-called, at work inside her skull.

Changing her. Carrying her away.

To speak of it would be to invite the grief, which he could not allow, because there had been too much grief in his life already. He couldn't afford more grief. He was tired of grief.

▪ ▪ ▪

But maybe the time had come.

He found her sitting at the kitchen table eating a bowl of cereal and reading a library book. The book was propped against the cornflake box and braced with her left hand. It was Dostoevsky's *The Idiot*, and it seemed to Matt she was turning the pages a trifle too quickly. Better not to dwell on that. Her hair was uncombed and she was wearing a blue nightgown. She looked at him as he entered the kitchen, a look both hopeful and wary.

He moved to the counter and started measuring out coffee. His hands were hardly shaking at all. "Busy today, Rache?"

"No," she said.

"Feel like a drive? I thought maybe we could ride out to Old Quarry Park. Last nice day of the year, maybe."

"We haven't been up there for a long time," Rachel said.

"In the mood for it?"

She nodded.

▪ ▪ ▪

Rachel understood that her father wanted to talk, wanted to make sense of what had happened; and she knew how hard it was for him.

She wanted to help but didn't know how.

He drove the long way up toward Old Quarry Park. As the road rose along the flank of Mt. Buchanan, she could see the town sparkling in its bay, polished bright as a jewel by all that rain. There was no plume of smoke from the Dunsmuir pulp and paper mill down south. There'd been no smoke from the mill for a couple of weeks now.

The car turned down a side road past the reservoir, and Rachel realized where this detour was taking them: "The Old House!"

Her father nodded.

They always called it the Old House. It was the house where Daddy had grown up. Back in the old days, before her mother died, they would go on this drive every once in a while . . . maybe twice a year, when Daddy was in the mood. They would drive past the Old House, and Daddy would talk about what Buchanan had been like long ago; and Rachel would picture him as a child, as strange as that seemed, her father as a ten-year-old in jeans and a grubby T-shirt, trekking through the power company clearcuts on his way to school, or carrying peanut butter sandwiches out to the bluffs on warm Saturdays like this.

The street where he had grown up was called Floral Drive, a grand name for ten 1950s box houses on a cul-de-sac with backyard views of the distant bay. Rachel recognized the Old House at once as Daddy slowed the car. There was nothing special about it. It had a shake roof and aluminum siding painted brown. The number 612 was marked on a gatepost with ornate brass numerals. Daddy didn't know who lived here now. Strangers. He hadn't lived in the house himself for more than twenty years.

There was no traffic; he stopped the car and let it idle.

"My grandfather died here," he said. He was looking at the house, not at Rachel. "I was ten. He lived with us for the last three weeks of his life. He died of a bone cancer just before Christmas. But he loved to talk, and he was fairly lucid those last three weeks. I sat in the bedroom with him so he'd have somebody to talk to. He was born one year before the century turned, if you can imagine such a thing. He was twenty during the labor troubles in 1919. He talked about that a lot. Seattle was the big IWW capital of the Northwest, but there was a lot of labor trouble in Buchanan, too. Buchanan was a logging town back then. Some bars, a hotel, City Hall, the harbor, loggers in on weekends to drink and carry on. The Wobblies were organizing at the Dunsmuir mill. In 1919 they called the big general strike up in Seattle. Buchanan had its own sympathy strike. Just like Seattle, the strike was put down with clubs and cops. Your great-grandfather—this was Willy, on the Hurst side of the family—he worked at Dunsmuir. He was part of the labor parade. Two hundred men marched into the City Hall Turnaround with red banners. The mayor in those days was Bill Gunderson, he was in the pocket of the Dunsmuir family—he called out a bunch of Army regulars and they advanced with fixed bayonets. Three people were killed before the fight was over. Everybody went home bloody. Willy said the big fight was over the IWW banner. Everybody was yelling, 'Protect the flag!' Two guys got hurt, one blinded, the banner went down, but Willy and another man grabbed it and carried it up the hill behind City Hall and planted it in the Civic Gardens—it stood there ten minutes before the troops fought through the crowd and pulled it down."

He turned to face Rachel. "That was his victory. That bloody flag. Ten minutes. He wanted me to know that before he died. He wanted me to know he wasn't just an old man sick in bed. He was Willy Hurst, and he had saved the flag from the soldiers."

"You never told me that before," Rachel said.

"It was the first time I really understood this town had a history . . . that *people* had histories. A town is a living thing, Rachel. It has memories."

"Yes," she said.

"I can't walk away from it. Not without trying to save it."

She nodded unhappily. "I know."

"That's how it is for me." He shifted gears and drove away from the Old House, back toward the road, toward Old Quarry Park. The morning sunlight was hot through the car windows. "Now you," he said. "I want to know how it is for you."

∎   ∎   ∎

Old Quarry Park was a wooded ridge running from the northern slope of Mt. Buchanan to the sea, a mile southwest of the abandoned mineral quarry that had given it its name. Hiking trails wound through the tall coastal firs, but the center of the park had been developed in the 1970s: There was a bandstand, a Little League diamond, a playground. Rachel had been taken to play here on summer weekends since she was three years old.

On one of those long-ago summer Saturdays, she had fallen and cut her forehead on the rim of the whirl-around. Matt had cleaned and bandaged the cut. She remembered his hands, huge and warm. Doctor hands. Their confident touch.

These memories had been coming back to her lately. It was part of the change.

He walked beside her from the parking lot through the trees to the picnic grounds. He was superimposed on her memory of him, an older version of himself. It seemed as if he had aged years in the last few weeks.

They sat at a wooden table at the western end of the picnic grounds where they could see through the trees to the ocean. The sun was bright and high. A couple of jays made a quarrelsome sound overhead, but the bees, a summer peril, had deserted the park altogether.

I want to know how it is for you. She was a dutiful daughter and she meant to give him an answer. But it wasn't easy.

There was so much to say.

"Daddy, you know what Contact was like. You must remember, even if you said no. That feeling of doors opening up . . . of a promise of something wonderful. Of being something that doesn't live and die but goes on, changing all the time but not stopping."

"I remember," he said. His face was drawn, expressionless, pale in the sunlight. "That didn't frighten you?"

"Not when I understood what it meant. It was hard at first being so . . . *transparent*. They talk to you, but they're talking to the inside of you. Your, I guess, soul. And your soul talks back. *That's* scary. You can't hold anything back, you can't hide anything. But then you understand they're not sitting in judgment, it's not St. Peter at the Pearly Gates. They're not even offering forgiveness, that's not their business—their business is understanding. And then you start to realize how *big* they are. Big with all the growing and learning they've done over the centuries. Like some kind of beautiful seashell that gets more complicated and more colorful the longer you look at it, every chamber with a smaller chamber on one side and a bigger chamber on the other, all echoes and alabaster. . . ."

Her eyes were closed, and she realized she'd drifted into rhapsody. This Contact memory was strong. But she wasn't accustomed to talking about it and she was probably scaring her father.

She glanced at him. His lips were drawn tight.

"I couldn't say no," she finished, inadequately.

"Even though it means giving up so much?"

"Giving *what* up?"

"Life. A normal life. A family. The way human beings have lived since they came out of the trees."

"But I haven't given that up. People used to say, is there marriage in heaven? Well, this isn't exactly heaven. But I think there will still be marriage. People are *people*, Daddy. They're each unique, they want different things from each other. They find partners. They fall in love. Maybe they don't get married at the First Baptist anymore. But we're not turning into loveless monsters."

"It's hard for me to know that."

Rachel said, "I don't know how to convince you."

"What troubles me is that there's a mechanism that's altering your brain. Physically changing it. Rachel, that's where love *is*. Loyalty, trust—even the way we perceive the truth. I tell myself this is all voluntary, you're not being deceived. But I've seen surgeons produce bliss with an electrode in the cerebral cortex."

"*Have* I changed?"

"Yes. You don't talk the same way. Aren't you aware of it?"

"I know about that. But *me*. Everything that makes me Rachel. Has *that* changed?"

He was silent for a long time. Finally he looked away from her, and the pain in his eyes was nearly unbearable. "I don't know, Rache. I honestly don't know."

She felt herself on the verge of tears. She didn't want to be understood.

She wanted to be held. She wanted him to wrap his arms around her, tell her it was okay, tell her he still loved her.

Voice trembling, indignant, she could only manage: "I'm *not* different."

Not inside, she meant. Not where it counted.

▪   ▪   ▪

On the day Rachel turned four years old, Matt had caught her drawing on the living room wall with her birthday crayons—big lime-green loops and whorls. The wall had been painted two weeks previously, and it must have looked to Rachel like a big blank sheet of paper.

Matt had paid for the painting the same week the car insurance came up for renewal. The household budget had bottomed out; Celeste was cooking Kraft Dinner instead of steak. Rachel's tricycle, which she had ignored since this morning, had pushed their VISA card to the credit limit.

He went a little crazy when he saw the wall.

He grabbed the crayon out of her clenched fist and pushed her back. "Bad," he said, "bad, Rachel, bad, *bad!*"

Her legs went out from under her. She sat down hard and her face clouded instantly.

Almost as immediately, Matt's remorse began to flush away the anger. Rachel stammered through tears: "I'm . . . *not* . . . bad!"

He thought it was a cogent moral point. He also thought he wanted to shoot himself.

He picked up his daughter and held her. "You're right, Rachel. You're *not* bad. But it was a bad thing to do. Even good people do bad things sometimes. That's what I meant to say. It's a bad thing to draw on the wall. But *you're* not bad."

It was the way she phrased her objection in Old Quarry Park that convinced Matt he still had a daughter—at least for the time being.

I'm NOT different.

He felt those old father tears well up.

"Ah, Rache," he said. "This is all . . . so confusing."

She came around the picnic table to him. He stood up and barked his knee on the pineboard tabletop. It was an awkward ballet, but the hug went on a long time.

▪   ▪   ▪

After a while, she went to a swing and asked him to push. A little bit of old times, Matt supposed. Maybe it was good for her to be ten years old for a few minutes. Maybe it was good for him.

He pushed her, she laughed, the sky was blue.

After that they walked the short trail that looped into the forest, but the track was muddy after all the rain. When they emerged into the sunlight, Rachel said, "We should have packed a lunch."

"I have a better idea. Lunch at Dos Aguilas."

"Really?"

"My treat." He added, "If it's open."

"I think it is," Rachel said . . . and he wondered how she knew.

■   ■   ■

Dos Aguilas was a Mexican restaurant at the bayshore. Matt recalled that Celeste had once classified it as a "linen-tablecloth" restaurant, as opposed to the plastic-booth kind at the malls. It had a cook, not a controlled-portion dispensing machine.

Arturo, the manager, had inherited the business from his father. The restaurant itself had been here since 1963. A landmark. It was still open for business. Empty, but open.

Arturo welcomed them in, and Matt nodded to him, but he understood by the glance that passed between Arturo and Rachel that they were of the same tribe now; Matt was the outsider here.

He chose a table by the window where they could watch the sunlit water lap the pier.

"It means 'Two Eagles,'" Matt said.

Rachel opened a menu over her cutlery. "What?"

"Dos Aguilas. It means 'Two Eagles.' The story is that a pair of harbor eagles have a nest near here. You can have dinner some nights and maybe see them circling over the crab boats, diving for fish."

"Really?" She gazed out across the water. "Did you ever see them?"

"Nope. Don't know anybody who ever did. The story's almost half a century old. But people still look."

Rachel nodded, smiling at the thought.

Arturo came to the table. He took their order and headed for the kitchen, disappearing into a foliage of decor: sombreros, pistol belts, pottery.

Matt said to his daughter, "You knew the restaurant would be open."

She nodded.

"You know things. Not just you. Other people, too." He told her about the figure Tom Kindle had been quoting, one in ten thousand. "Rachel, how would anyone know that?"

She looked thoughtful. "It's approximately the right number."

"Okay. But how do you *know*?"

"Oh, I just . . . shift gears."

"I'm sorry?"

"Well, that's what I call it. It has to do with making connections." A pause. "Daddy, do you want all the details of this?"

"Yes."

"Because it's strange."

"I kind of took that for granted, Rache."

She gave him a look: *Well, okay . . . if you insist.*

"It has to do with the neocytes," she said. "One of the things they are is a kind of connector. You can think of them as drawing invisible lines—between people, between people and the Artifact."

"Like telepathy?"

"In a way. But I think that gives the wrong impression. The lines they're drawing are *knowledge* lines. The Travellers think there should be as few barriers to knowledge as possible. People's lives are private, if they want them to be, but knowledge—knowledge is infinitely sharable."

"What kind of knowledge?"

"More or less any kind."

"Give me an example."

"Well . . . suppose I want to know how to get from here to Chicago. Used to be I'd have to look at a map. Now I can just remember it."

"Rachel, you've never been there."

"No, but I'm not remembering it from myself, I'm remembering it from somebody else. Anyone who's ever looked at a road map. It isn't *my* knowledge, but I can get to it if I need it."

"That's all there is to it? *Remembering*?"

"That's hardly all there is to it, but that's what it feels like. I suppose it's more like data sharing or something computery like that. But it feels like remembering. You have to actually *do* it, I mean there's a mental effort involved—like thinking really hard. *Shifting gears.* But then you just . . . remember."

"What if it's something complicated? Quantum theory, say. Neurosurgery."

She frowned, and Matt wondered if she was *shifting gears* right now, as they spoke.

"You can do that," she said, "but it has to be orderly. In the Traveller world, knowledge is infinitely available but functionally hierarchic. You have to take the logical steps. What's the good of knowing, for instance, that you can derive classical probability from the squared modulus of the quantum complex amplitude, if you don't know what a *modulus* is, in physical terms, or an *amplitude*? The knowledge is available, but if you want to understand it you still have to eat it one bite at a time. Like this salad. Thank you, Arturo."

"My.pleasure. Get you something to drink?"

"A Coke," Rachel said.

"For you, sir?"

"Anything." His mouth was dry.

■ ■ ■

Rachel said, "I didn't mean to be scary."

"No. You took me by surprise, that's all."

"I surprise myself sometimes."

The meal passed in awkward silence. Matt noticed Rachel glancing off across the water—checking for eagles. Once you started, it was hard to stop.

"You still look sad," she said when Arturo had brought his coffee.

"Do I?"

"You were happy for a little while. Because we talked. But only for a while. Because of what's happening."

"Because it's stealing you, Rachel. You're right, I'm happy we talked. But it doesn't change anything, does it? You're going somewhere I can't follow."

"Doesn't that happen anyway? If I'd gone off to college, or—"

"It's hardly the same. I know you're not a teenager forever. You go to college, maybe you get married, you have a career, things are different. Of course. But, my God, this is something else entirely. You go to college, I can phone you on weekends. Next year—can you guarantee we'll even be able to talk to each other?"

She looked away.

"So what do we have?" Matt asked. "A few months?"

She pondered the question. Her eyes strayed to the harbor, the calm water there. "Maybe a few months. Maybe less."

"You *are* going away."

"Yes."

"All of you?"

"Yes."

"Where? When?"

"It's not—it isn't altogether clear."

He balled his napkin and threw it on his plate.

She said, "Daddy, it works both ways. You made a choice, too. I'm entitled to a little resentment."

"Oh?"

"Because you're going to die. And I'm not. And it didn't have to be that way."

▪   ▪   ▪

He followed the bay road toward home.

"You know I mean to save this town," Matt told his daughter.

"I've heard you say so."

"You don't think it's possible?"

"I'm . . . not sure."

"Rachel, listen to me. If you know anything about the future, anything at all about what might happen to this town—to the planet—I need you to tell me. Because we can't plan for what we can't imagine."

She was silent for a long time in the passenger seat. Then she said: "Things will go on as they are now. At least for a little while. Maybe into the winter. After that . . . people will start to disappear."

"Disappear?"

"Give up the physical body. Oh, Daddy, I know how horrible that must sound! But it isn't. It really isn't."

"If you say so, Rachel. What happens to these people?"

"They move to the Artifact, at least temporarily."

"Why temporarily?"

"Because we'll have a place of our own before long."

"What are you saying—a *human* Artifact?"

"That kind of environment, yes."

"For what purpose—to leave the planet?"

"Maybe. Daddy, these decisions haven't been taken yet. But the planet is a serious consideration. We've left a terrible mark on it. The Travellers have already started cleaning it up. Erasing some of the changes we made. Taking some of the CO_2 out of the air. . . ."

"They can do that?"

"Yes."

"So people disappear," Matt said. "So Buchanan is empty."

"We don't *all* disappear. Or at least, not all at once. In the short run . . . What would you call a day like today? Indian summer? Last nice day of the year. Last chance to get in a ballgame, maybe, or go to the park. Well, I think the next four or five months are going to be Indian summer for a lot of us. Our last chance to wear skin and walk around on the earth."

"Last chance before winter," Matt said.

"Last chance before something *better*. But even if you were moving from a log cabin into the Taj Mahal, you'd still want to look around the old place before you locked the door." Her eyes were vague, unfocused. Her voiced seemed faint. "It's the cradle of mankind. Not always easy, leaving the cradle."

Curious, Matt thought, how a sunny day could feel so cold.

■　■　■

After dinner, she curled up in the easy chair with Dostoevsky in her lap.

"How come you still need to read that?" Matt asked. "How come you can't just remember it?"

"I'm not that good yet."

"So the library's not defunct."

"Not yet."

"But the time is coming."

"Yes." She looked up. He was wearing his jacket; the evening had turned cooler. "Are you going out?"

"Just for a drive."

"Want company?"

"Thank you, Rache. No. Not this time."

■　■　■

He drove down to the parking lot where the summer ferry took tourists over to Crab Pot Island, a dot of National Park greenery in the embrace of the bay. The parking lot was low to the water, and Matt parked facing west, where the sky was still gaudy with sunset, although the light had begun to fade.

He used to come here in the bad time after Celeste died. When you wanted privacy and you lived with a daughter, you found your own retreats. A parking lot was one place where you could sit by yourself in an automobile and be left in peace. People assumed you were waiting for someone. They didn't look closely. A person could be alone with his grief . . . could even weep, if he did so discreetly, if he forestalled the kind of helpless sobbing that would attract a stranger's attention.

He was past that now. But he wanted the solitude.

It was that time of evening when the streetlights flicker on and everything solid seems hollow and flat; when dark thoughts come easily and are harder to ignore.

He wondered what he was trying so hard to save.

What was he sorry to lose, in this new world they were making? War was finished, after all. Disease, apparently, was a thing of the past. Starvation was history. Lies were becoming impractical.

He had never loved war, disease, starvation, or deceit.

So what was it?

What had he loved so much that he turned down the offer of eternal life?

Something evanescent.

Something fragile.

A family. Rachel's childhood. Celeste.

The possibility of a human future.

All these things were illusions. He thought of Willy's IWW banner, an old rag invested with glory by his stubborn defiance. Or the eagles of Dos Aguilas, a beautiful lie.

The sky above the bay was empty.

But the eagles flew, Matt thought. They flew when we believed in them.

Willy flew, those ten minutes on the hillside.

I will save this town, Matt thought.

See if I don't.

And if I can't save the town . . . if it comes to that . . . then, by God, I will save some part of it.

Someone.

Chapter
18

Annie
and Bobby

On the Saturday Matt took his daughter to Old Quarry Park, Annie Gates drove south for an hour on the coast highway.

She had made this drive one weekend out of two—sometimes Saturday, sometimes Sunday—for ten years now.

She had never spoken of it, even to Matt.

She was going to visit Bobby.

∎   ∎   ╱ ∎

Bobby lived in a room in the east wing of a long, low building in a pine grove near the sea. His window overlooked a broad green lawn and a portion of the lot where Annie parked her car. Of course, Bobby seldom looked out the window. But maybe that had changed. Maybe he was beginning to appreciate the view. Annie hoped so.

The sign at the front door of the building said:

WELLBORNE CARE COMMUNITY
Where Caring Is Commonplace

Commonplace but very expensive. Since Bobby moved in, Annie had been paying Wellborne the equivalent of a Park Avenue monthly rental. She had cut a great many corners. The furniture in her apartment was fifteen years old. Her salad and tuna diet was not for cosmetic purposes. She rarely bought a hardcover book, which had been the most difficult economy of all.

Worth it, of course, to know that Bobby was decently looked after.

She checked in at the desk—Wellborne was still fully staffed, the effects of Contact slow to take hold among its patients—and walked down the east corridor to Bobby's room, 114.

She'd noticed an improvement on her last visit. Usually Bobby retreated into a fetal curl when he saw her coming. Last time she visited, he had unbent and regarded her with a solemn expression on his face . . . an expression, however, that Annie could not decipher. Nor could Bobby explain it. He never spoke to her. He spoke to the staff sometimes, simple food and bathroom words. But never to Annie.

Today . . . her hopes were high.

She crossed her fingers and said a silent, wordless prayer before she knocked and opened the door.

■   ■   ■

"Annie!" he said.

Her heart did a startled double-beat. How long since she'd heard his voice?

Almost thirty years, she thought. She remembered quite distinctly, too distinctly, the last words Bobby had spoken to her.

Annie, don't.

He had been nine years old; she had been ten.

Annie, he had said. *Please don't.*

He looked good today. He was dressed in clean blue jeans and a white cotton T-shirt. The T-shirt said "I LOVE WELLBORNE," except that "love" was a heart shape. He was still way too skinny. For the last couple of years, Bobby had been a problem eater. Just before Contact, he had bottomed out at 102 pounds. The staff doctor had called to discuss intravenous feeding as an option.

Now he was eating again, and although she could see the staves of his chest through the T-shirt, she could tell he was gaining weight.

His face was terribly thin. His smile was skeletal. But it was a smile, and that was miracle enough. His eyes, deep in their sockets, twinkled at her.

"Hi, Bobby," she managed through the lump in her throat.

He climbed off the bed where he had been sitting cross-legged watching baseball on TV. "They said I could go out today. Annie! Go for a walk with me?"

"Sure, Bobby," she said.

▪ ▪ ▪

He looked painfully fragile as he hobbled down the front steps onto the lawn, but Annie supposed it really was all right for him to be outside. The medical staff at Wellborne knew what they were doing. And of course, since Contact, Bobby was immortal. Like everyone else. But it was hard to convince herself of that.

He walked like an old man. He was thirty-four years old. He talked like a nine-year-old, which was how old he had been when the accident happened.

Annie walked with him across the sunny lawn.

She ventured a question: "Bobby, do you like it here?"

"It's not bad," he said. "The food is all right."

"You want to stay?"

He shrugged. She recognized the gesture, a particular Bobby-shrug. The shrug meant: Don't know. Don't want to talk about it.

"Nice day," she said, helplessly. After all these mute years! Discussing the weather!

Bobby just grinned.

She said, "What have you been doing?"

"Watching TV," he said. "Remembering."

"Remembering?"

"I remember a lot. Since *they* came." He touched his head—the side of it that was not quite symmetrical—and pointed to the sky: the Travellers. "Annie . . . guess what I remember?"

She cringed at the thought of what he might remember.

"I remember *lawn tag*!" And he tapped her on the shoulder and went hobbling away.

She pretended to chase, smiling to herself. All that last summer, they had played lawn tag through the long evenings. Daddy was the town doctor in Bruce, a little Canadian prairie town, a one-road grain town; of all the lawns in Bruce, the Gates's lawn was the biggest.

Lawn tag was a simpleminded chase: under the privet hedge, past the willow tree, mustn't stray beyond the border of the sidewalk, around back, past the doghouse. Annie, a year older, could have caught Bobby anytime. But she liked the sound of his laughter when he dodged her hand. Some evenings she tagged him once, twice, played hard to get, then let him win. Some evenings she let him win from the start.

Now . . . she could scarcely believe he was running again. The sunlight was radiant on the big Wellborne lawn; the air was silky cool. He moved in a slip-jointed lope, his jeans threatening to fall off his bony hips. It would have been easy to catch him.

She pretended to chase. Bobby looked back and laughed out loud. Annie savored the sound.

▪ ▪ ▪

Sometimes, of course, he made her mad.

The hardest part of Contact had been facing this memory. But it was a memory that had to be faced: Most of Annie had said yes to the Travellers, but this memory part of her had said *Annie doesn't deserve to live.*

She was ten. Only ten. A child. Impulsive. Wasn't every child?

Bobby and Annie were playing on the roof of the house on the hottest day of summer.

It was easy to get onto the roof. Bring the ladder from the old bunk beds in the basement, step onto the tiny balcony outside Annie's room, up to the steep and baking slope of the shingles. You could lie there and see all the way out past the water tower, past the highway, past the granaries, past yellow quilts of wheat to the horizon.

Bobby was scared of the roof. Annie always helped him up, helped him down. But she sometimes took a shameful pleasure in his fear. Bobby, the younger, often got more attention than he deserved. Bobby was the baby of the family. Annie was expected to help with the dishes. Bobby never did.

Today—well, it was hot. Prairie-summer-itchy-sunburn-tight-clothes hot. Bobby had been whining about it. So she went up on the roof by herself, hoping he wouldn't follow.

Of course, he did.

He pulled himself over the eavestrough and scuttled up the shingles behind her, clinging to her foot until he could safely lie down. Stay still, silly, and you won't slip. But that's not what Annie said.

If you get scared, she said, *your hands get all sweaty.*

Bobby's frown deepened.

And if your hands get sweaty . . . you might slip.

He looked at her aghast across a space of cedar shakes and hot air. *Annie, don't.*

It's a lo-o-ong way down, Bobby.

Panicking a little, he grabbed her left foot with both hands.

Hey, let go, no fair!

But he hugged it tighter. She was wearing shorts and no shoes. In the hot air, his fingers felt sticky as tar . . . his touch was an intolerable itch.

Bobby! Let go of me!

The Harvest ▪ 167

She kicked her ankle out to shake him loose.

Annie, he said, *don't.*

Now *she* was starting to get scared. Her gaze drifted down from the blue deeps of the sky, across those farms, grain elevators, houses, streets, to the rain gutter and the paved walk down below. Mama had put the garbage out. The garbage cans shivered in the rising heat.

She thought of Bobby tumbling down there and carrying her with him.

She shook her foot again, harder.

One hand came loose. Bobby scrabbled against the shingled roof.

She kicked again.

Annie. Please don't.

It was peculiar, it was maddening, how calm his voice still sounded.

Annie kicked to pry him loose, felt his hand separate from her ankle. She had turned her head away and when she looked back she caught the briefest glimpse of him as he disappeared over the edge, an expression of vast surprise on his face.

She scrambled down the bunk-bed ladder and looked over the edge of the balcony and saw Bobby on the paved walk beside the garbage cans. She looked for a long time, unable to make sense of what she saw. His head was broken open and some of what was inside had come out.

▪ ▪ ▪

When Bobby left the hospital, he was back in diapers. Mama had to change him all the time.

Once, she shook a soiled cotton diaper in Annie's face. "This is your fault," Mama said.

Bobby's head was curiously flat on one side and he didn't talk, but whenever he saw Annie coming he curled away from her and closed his eyes.

▪ ▪ ▪

Mama died a couple of years after that.

Annie had hoped to win back her father's affection with a medical degree; but he died, too, while she was away at school.

She finished her degree anyhow. Bobby was institutionalized, and the estate was paying for everything, but that money wouldn't last forever, and she would need a good income—a doctor's income—to keep Bobby cared for.

Her residency was the hardest part. The sight of a head wound still made her dizzy.

When she took up the partnership with Matt Wheeler, he talked about his wife Celeste and how he had lost her. Annie never talked about Bobby. Bobby was a secret. It kept them apart, but Annie understood that this was what they both needed: something more than friendship, something less than love. Matt was guilty about loving someone after Celeste. And Annie . . . Annie wasn't convinced she *deserved* to be loved.

The Travellers had stirred up these memories, but the Travellers had offered something in return: objectivity, as cool and cleansing as mountain water. The ability to forgive herself.

Annie forgave Annie, a quarter-century down the line.

But it wasn't her own forgiveness she really craved.

▪   ▪   ▪

Bobby tired himself out playing lawn tag, so they retreated to the shade of the patio at Wellborne. Annie brought out two glasses of lemonade from the staff cafeteria. The lemonade was tart and perfect. They sat on the steps, drinking it.

"We're going on a trip," Bobby said.

She thought he meant the Wellborne patients. "That's nice," she said. "To the seashore, Bobby?"

"No, I mean—*us*. We're *all* going on a trip."

"Oh. *That* trip. Yes."

"Are you excited, Annie?"

"It's not for some time yet, Bobby. A few months, anyhow."

"They have to build the spaceship."

"Yes."

He shook his head. "I have a lot of growing up to do."

"There's no rush."

"I got kind of . . . left behind."

She wanted to say, "I'm sorry!"—but couldn't find her voice.

"I'm getting stronger," Bobby said. "Annie—look what I can do!"

A wooden railing ran all around the patio of the Wellborne building. Before she could say anything, Bobby had boosted himself onto the banister. He was clinging to the narrow timber with hands and feet . . . then he stood up, like a tightrope walker, balancing himself.

His hips stuck out in bony ridges from the loose jeans. His arms, thrown out for balance, were fragile as twigs.

A brisk wind could knock him down from there. She felt a surge of panic. "Bobby, stop it!"

"No, Annie, *look!*" He took two tentative steps. Proud of his balance. Proud of his new life.

"Bobby, you'll hurt yourself!"

"No, I—"

But she was up without thinking about it, running to him, grabbing him around his painfully thin waist and lifting him down. He was lighter than she expected. He was as light as a nine-year-old.

"Annie, Annie, it's okay!"

Bobby wrapped his skinny arms around her and pressed his misshapen head against her cheek.

"I know why you're crying," he whispered.

Did he? Oh, God!

"That was all a long time ago," Bobby said. "We were kids. It doesn't matter anymore."

And Annie cried in her brother's arms as if she had tapped a reservoir of tears, a well of sorrow ancient and eager for the light.

Part
Three

Indian
Summer

Chapter 19
CQ

Tom Kindle decided he would stay in Buchanan until the end of the World Series. After that . . . well, the horizon had an alluring look, these rainy autumn days.

Matt Wheeler didn't appear to approve of the idea.

Kindle walked with him through the empty hallways of the regional hospital. Some of the overhead fluorescents had burned out; some flickered like candles in a cold wind. The building was increasingly spooky, in Kindle's opinion. Nobody but Matt came around anymore.

"I'd be happier if you stayed," Matt said.

Kindle didn't answer. He was concentrating on the pleasure of locomotion. Christ in a basket, it was good to get out of that wheelchair! It was good to be walking under his own steam.

It hurt like hell, but it was good anyway.

Monday he'd made it halfway to the maternity wing and back; today, all the way to Maternity and far beyond, as far as the fabled corridors of Physiotherapy, where empty sitz baths gleamed like strange idols in dim green rooms.

He stumbled once. Matt took his arm. "Don't overdo it."

"No pain, no gain."

"It was a bad break. At your age, you don't heal as fast as you used to."

"Thank you, Dr. Kildare."

"You want me to lie?"

"Every once in a while it might be nice."

A pause. Matt said, "You're serious about leaving Buchanan?"

"Yes." Kindle gritted his teeth and closed his eyes. "Okay, *now* we turn around."

They shuffled back through ancient odors of ether and antiseptic. Kindle wore his old jeans and a cotton workshirt. The doctor wore his hospital gown over a similar outfit. We don't look all that different, Kindle thought. He caught their reflection in a rainy corridor window. Not doctor and patient. Just two guys who ought to shave more often. Two guys with similar worry lines. Different pain.

Matt said, "You have somewhere in particular to go?"

"It's a big country . . . I haven't seen it all."

In fact, he was thinking about the Wind River Range, the Tetons, that area. He hadn't seen Wyoming for about twenty-five years.

"What about the Committee?"

"I never signed on to salvage Buchanan. I barely lived here, you know, before Contact. The Committee'll get on without me."

"You said you'd do radio."

"Yeah, yeah, I'll do radio. I'm not leaving yet."

"There's a meeting at the end of the week."

"Right, I'll be there."

"I want you to talk to me before you leave," Matt said. "Maybe I can change your mind."

Kindle promised he would, though it rubbed him the wrong way. No strings attached, damn it. He'd leave when he felt like it. Stay or go as the spirit moved him.

It was how he'd lived his life. Why change now?

Matt left him alone in his room. Kindle checked the TV, but there was nothing but fuzz. All they showed on TV anymore was a couple of hours of news per day. Plus the Major League playoffs.

■ ■ ■

The first-of-November Committee meeting was brief and morose. Five people showed up in addition to Kindle and Matt Wheeler. Joey Commoner and Beth Porter were two of them. Abby Cushman, the somewhat ditzy farm lady, failed to appear. Paul Jacopetti unfortunately did. The pessimistic ex–tool-and-die maker issued his usual evil-minded prophecies, including a prediction that the Helper recently arrived at the City Hall Turnaround would murder them all while they slept. Poison gas, maybe. Matt seemed too dazed to refute this paranoia, and Kindle listened with disgust.

After that they held their first election. Matt stood for chairman. His single opponent was—inevitably—Paul Jacopetti, who didn't think Matt should run unopposed, "although of course this whole exercise is futile." There was a show of hands and Matt took the vote six to one. ("Figures," Jacopetti said.)

Old business. Kindle promised he would drive down to Causgrove Electronics the next day and look for a ham set.

"A lot of those stores are closed," Matt reminded him. "Call first. Or call the owner and see if he'll let you in."

"Or I could jimmy the lock."

Matt shot him a disapproving look. "I don't think it's come to that."

Maybe, Kindle thought. Or maybe not.

▪   ▪   ▪

But he did as Matt asked: phoned the store, no answer, phoned three Causgroves out of the book until he found the one who owned the shop.

"You're right, Mr. Kindle, the front door's locked. Locked it myself. Force of habit, I guess. But the back is open. You can get in that way."

"You want to meet me there?"

"For what purpose?"

"Well, I can write you a check. Unless you want cash."

"Please, don't bother. Just go ahead and take what you need."

"I'm sorry? What?"

"We had a reasonable stock last time I looked. I presume you can find the stockroom, or just root around the displays. If we have what you want, take it."

"Pardon me. You said—take it?"

"Yes, sir."

"Just—*take* it?"

"Yes."

"Just like that?"

"Yes. I'm happy to see the goods serving a purpose. I thought they'd all turned into scrap metal. Please, take whatever you want. But it's nice of you to have called, Mr. Kindle."

The connection broke at the other end. Kindle stared at the phone for a while.

▪   ▪   ▪

His first experience with a motor vehicle since the accident wasn't his pickup truck, which had been towed or trashed, but a car Matt Wheeler left for him in the hospital lot: a little blue Japanese device. Kindle was long-legged, and the act of climbing inside this automobile left him feeling like he'd been folded into a mailbox. His knees bumped the wheel until he figured out how to lever back the seat. Everything was digital. The dashboard looked like a cockpit display.

But it was transportation, what the hell. Maybe, when his leg didn't hurt so damn much, he would take himself to a car dealership. Maybe the price of a new car had dropped since Contact. Maybe to zero. He wondered what it would be like to drive one of those bullet-shaped vans he used to see on the road. It would be nice to have an enclosed space to keep a few things out of the rain.

This morning, a Tuesday morning, the roads were wet and empty. The rain fell in mists; the windshield fogged until he figured out how to run the heater.

Driving west from the hospital, Kindle was impressed with the stillness of the town. It was as if some languorous, fatal calm had settled over Buchanan. He counted the cars he passed—eight altogether, their brake lights making comet-tails on the slick asphalt. No pedestrians. Most of the shops were dark.

It resembled a ghost town, Kindle thought, but no one had really left. What *were* all those people doing?

He parked in a no-stopping zone. Anarchist outlaws of the world, unite. He extracted himself from the car, moaning when his bad knee knocked against the steering column.

Causgrove had been correct: The front door of the shop was locked, but the door facing the service alley opened at the turn of a knob.

Kindle switched on lights as he entered the building. He realized as soon as he found the dimly daylit front room that shopping was going to be harder than he'd expected. The racks were full of indistinguishable black boxes with endless, cryptic numeric displays. Some of these items were marine radios, some were ham rigs, some served no obvious purpose. "Should have studied up on this," Kindle said aloud.

"You just have to know what you're looking for."

He was startled by the voice, and he turned thoughtlessly on the axis of his left foot. A flare of pain sizzled up the leg. "Ouch, goddamn it!" He steadied himself on a steel rack. "*Who's there?*"

It was Joey Commoner.

■   ■   ■

Joey came out of the shadows behind the cash counter. He looked like a hood, Kindle thought, but not a dangerous one. The kind of suburban white kid who dresses like a drug dealer but doesn't know any. He stood with his hands in the pockets of his leather jacket and an unreadable expression on his face.

"Knew you'd show up," Joey said.

"You were waiting for me?"

"What you said at the meeting last night . . ."

"What about it?"

"Figured you wouldn't know what you wanted."

Kindle glanced again at the relentless racks. Kid had a point. "So are you here to help or did you just want the fun of watching?"

"You need a transceiver," Joey said.

"Show me one."

Joey pushed away from the counter and sauntered over to a wall display. Yet more big black boxes. Some of them had microphones attached. Joey said, "How much are you planning to spend?"

"Do you see anybody behind the register?"

"We're ripping this off?"

"Not exactly. I talked to the owner. He says we're welcome to take anything we want."

"What, for free?"

"No money down, no monthly payments."

"Shit," Joey said. "That's weird. I knew these people weren't human." He turned his attention to the stock. "So we want the best, right?" He put his hand on a huge rig. There was a Japanese brand name on the face of it, next to more knobs and technical graffiti than Kindle cared to look at. "This is a three-hundred-watt transceiver. They come more powerful, but I don't think we need it."

"You know ham stuff? How come you didn't say anything at the meeting? Save me the trouble?"

"I don't know much. Mainly theory. I know how radio works. I never got a license or anything."

"One up on me."

"Uh-huh. Probably we could use an ARRL Manual, too. . . ."

"Which?"

"The book on the rack over there? Looks like a phone book?"

Kindle considered his leg. The ache, which never ceased, was cranking up toward real pain. "Tell you what . . . I'll carry the book if you carry that machine."

"It's a transceiver. Or you can call it a rig."

"All right, Christ, it's a transceiver. Can you carry the fuckin' trans-ceiver?"

Joey smiled. "Should have brought your wheelchair."

"Smart-ass."

■ ■ ■

Joey rooted in the stockroom for a boxed unit with a manual, then loaded it into the trunk of Kindle's car. "I appreciate the help," Kindle said.

"You're not done yet."

"No?"

"Think about it. You want to be a radio station. So you need more than a box. You need—"

"An antenna." It *was* obvious. He felt a little stupid. "Well, shit." He squinted at the kid. "You know about antennas?"

"Could figure it out."

"They stock 'em here?"

Joey nodded. "But we should come back with a truck or some-thing. We're talking about maybe a big beam antenna. You got a three-hundred-watt transceiver, so you want a big antenna and a big tower to do it justice."

"Why don't I just go home and let you take care of it?"

Joey backed up. "I didn't volunteer for this."

"No, hey, I didn't mean it that way—"

"I mean, fuck you if you want me to do your job. . . ."

"No—"

"Just wanted to *help*."

"So *help*." Kindle slammed the trunk shut. "Let's not stand here in the pissin' rain. We'll come back with a truck. But maybe tomorrow, all right? My leg hurts."

Joey gazed at him. "You broke it?"

"Yeah."

"How?"

"Fell down a mountain."

"Uh-huh," Joey said. "You look too old to climb a mountain."

Kindle sighed and took a pen and notepad from his shirt pocket. "Write down your phone number. I'll call you about the antenna."

"Told you I'm not doing your work for you."

"You don't have to work, goddamn it, you only have to *point*."

"I just like the electronics."

But Joey wrote his number down.

• • •

There was a baseball game on TV that night. There had been a long hiatus after Contact, then the season had picked up where it left off. The World Series would run into cold weather, but with all these domed stadiums Kindle supposed that wasn't a problem.

He had watched all these games. Everything else on TV since Contact had been bizarre and kind of frightening, even such laudable events as the relief flights to the Third World. The food flights had been good, but they had also been operated with scary precision. There was something unnerving about all those military planes in V formation, even if their cargo bays were filled with wheat.

Now the relief flights appeared to have stopped; the implication was that the refugee populations of the world had found some new way to get along . . . or had "discorporated," a word Kindle remembered from his youth. Feeding the poor had been a stopgap effort, a bridge to that great unspoken mysterious millennium Kindle felt bearing down on him like a runaway locomotive.

But baseball went on. The NBA hadn't started a new season, football was finished, but a decision had been made in some telepathic congress: The World Series would be played out come hell or high water.

Maybe in Spain it was soccer, or in Russia it was hockey or chess or whatever the hell they played over there, but games still mattered. According to Matt, there were still Little League games being played in Buchanan, even some pick-up football on the high school field. Whatever it was people were turning into, they still liked to get out on the turf and chase a ball.

He hadn't followed baseball since the 1978 World Series, the last time he'd owned a TV. The Yankees took the Dodgers that year, as Kindle recalled. Things had changed since then. He didn't recognize names. Everybody looked too young. But he had watched the season progress on his hospital Sony, and he was determined to see the end of it.

Tonight it was an AL game, Detroit at New York. He thought Detroit looked good for the Series. He thought it would be a Detroit/Chicago Series, and his money was on Detroit.

The Tigers would take the Cubs, and then Kindle would pack up his possessions and move on.

■   ■   ■

He spent that night at the hospital, but he wasn't sick enough to stay longer and he didn't intend to. It was a charmless place at best. At the same time, it seemed pointless to move back to his cabin. He could get all the isolation he wanted much closer to town.

In the morning he phoned the local realty office. No one answered, but Kindle was ready for that. He knew a guy who worked there, or used to, a guy named Ira who sometimes hired his boat for fishing trips. Kindle reached him at home. Ira's voice had the detached, bemused quality Kindle had come to expect from a Contactee. Kindle identified himself and came to the point: "Just a question, Ira, seeing as you're in the business: Are houses free?"

"What do you mean . . . you want to buy a house?"

"Nope. I just want one. Yesterday I wanted a radio rig and I got one for free. Can I have a house?"

There was a pause. "Well." Thoughtful. "I know of some empty properties. If you move in, I don't suppose anybody will mind."

"You're shittin' me!" Kindle couldn't contain himself.

"Beg pardon?"

"Christ, you're *serious*! I can move into any fuckin' house?"

"Any empty one, I suppose."

He recalled Joey Commoner's remark about an antenna. "I want a house on a hill. No obstructions. Nice view all around."

"Ocean view?"

"Doesn't matter."

"I can give you a few addresses. . . ."

Kindle fumbled for his pen.

■   ■   ■

He spent the next day looking at properties. By mid-afternoon he'd picked one out: A two-bedroom frame house in Delmar Estates, a mildly upscale part of town, overlooking Buchanan and a northerly piece of the bay. The house was empty and unfurnished.

He moved in his single piece of property—the radio transceiver, still boxed. He put it in the middle of the living room floor.

The house had an empty-house smell. He guessed the broadloom had been cleaned before the property went on the market. Maybe the walls had been painted. He breathed in, breathed out.

He had never lived in such a place and never really wanted to . . . but he guessed a month or so here might be tolerable. Although, at the moment, there was nothing to sit on but the floor.

He drove to the Sears at the nearest mall and found the doors standing open but no one on duty at the cashiers' stations. What else? He realized with some startlement that he could equip the house with any furniture he happened to like, price being no object. He'd always kind of admired these imitation-leather sofas, for instance. He tried one out, right there in the deserted Home Furnishings department. It was like sitting on a stuffed lizard. Sumptuous but probably sticky in hot weather.

But this was all academic—there was no way he could transport any of this stuff, not at the moment, not without grinding his bad leg down to bloody splinters. He sighed and moved on to the patio furniture. Two folding chairs and a chaise longue, just about his speed. He tucked them under his arm and carried them to the car.

He went back for fresh clothes—a pair of jeans and an armload of cotton T-shirts and underwear.

It had been a long day and he was beginning to tire, but he made a second stop at the A&P, where he picked up canned food, cold cuts, a couple of loaves of bread. The house was equipped with a refrigerator and stove . . . but hang on, was the electricity working? It hadn't occurred to him to check the lights. He supposed he could phone the power company. If the *phone* was connected. If there *was* a phone. Okay, one more stop, back to the mall to pick up a touchtone telephone.

It was nearly dusk by the time he arrived back at the house.

Electricity, it turned out, wasn't a problem. The refrigerator was humming vigorously. He switched on the kitchen lights and began putting away the food.

He noticed the wire shelves in the refrigerator were barely cool, and he frowned and checked the freezer. No frost. Not even a trace. Was that significant? Maybe it was a frost-free unit; Kindle had heard of such appliances, though he had never owned one.

But the refrigerator was humming like a son of a bitch. When he was here earlier . . . had he noticed that sound?

Maybe not.

Maybe, this afternoon, the electricity *hadn't* been turned on.

He plugged in the phone and called Ira.

"Ira, I found a place."

"I know," Ira said cheerfully. "Up on Delmar. I was the listed agent on that property, by the way. Good view. I hope you'll be happy there."

"Pardon me, Ira, but how the fuck do you know where I picked to live?"

There was a pause. "The neighbors saw you leave some belongings. We assumed you were moving in."

"What, you talked to the neighbors?"

"Well. In a way."

By voodoo telegraph, in other words. "So tell me . . . did the neighbors also talk to the power company?"

"Well, Tom. Everybody more or less talks to everybody."

"Well, Ira, doesn't that more or less scare the shit out of you?"

"No. But I apologize if we alarmed you."

"Think nothing of it." He put the phone down in a hurry.

Unfolded a chair and sat in it.

He'd forgotten to pick up a TV set. Was there a game on tonight? He couldn't remember.

Kindle went to the kitchen, where the light was brighter, and unpacked the transceiver. Ungainly object. He tried to read the manual, but it was written in some language only theoretically English. "Do not allow to contact with moisture or heavily wet." Words to live by.

He guessed Joey Commoner would be able to figure it out.

■   ■   ■

November was rainy; he postponed the chore of erecting an antenna. The ache in his leg retreated some. He began stocking up on groceries, beginning to suspect that Matt's fears about the food supply were well-founded. The staples were still being trucked in, but luxury items had begun to disappear from the shelves. He stockpiled some of those, too. He felt like making a trophy list. Successfully hunted down in Buchanan, Oregon: Last bag of Oreos. Last bottle of gourmet popcorn.

He ferried down some items from his cabin, mainly tools and books. *The Decline and Fall of the Roman Empire* had been sitting where he left it last August and was a little musty, since he'd left the windows open, but still readable. A trudge through Gibbon might not be too bad, given all this rainy cool weather. Then on to *Madame Bovary*.

The Tigers took the American League pennant late that month.

He called Joey when the skies cleared for a couple of days.

"Been waiting to hear from you," Joey complained. "I got a lot of tower parts from Radio Shack. And a beam antenna from Causgrove's. But you weren't at the hospital."

Kindle gave the kid his new address. "You can transport all that?"

"Took a van out of the lot at Harbor Ford."

Must do that myself one of these days, Kindle thought. "Are we talking hard physical labor here?"

"Some," Joey said.

"Bring beer," Kindle said.

"You got it."

■   ■   ■

Kindle had worked erecting TV towers back in the sixties, and he remembered enough of that experience to temper Joey's recklessness. He used a power drill with a masonry bit to anchor the antenna base in a concrete trailer pad in front of the house. He guyed the tower as it went up, extra guys on the first ten feet so Joey wouldn't come plummeting down. Probably Matt Wheeler would resent being called in on another broken leg. Would resent it even worse if he lost one of his one in ten thousand—even if it was Joey Commoner.

They had the tower stabilized and the antenna installed by dusk. Joey did all the climbing, in deference to Kindle's leg, a nice thought, or his age, which was insulting; he was careful not to ask.

Joey stood back from his work. "This ought to give us good access to the twenty-meter band, which I guess would be the busiest band under the circumstances, though who knows?"

"I sure as hell don't."

Joey had taken off his shirt during the final guying of the tower. As they entered the house, Kindle read the tattoo on his right bicep. Neat blue letters.

WORTHLESS, it said.

"You believe that?" Kindle asked.

Joey shrugged his shirt back on and began fiddling with the back of the transceiver. Kindle cracked a beer, waiting for an answer that didn't come. This would have been a good time to order in a pizza, he thought, except nobody delivered anymore. He wondered who in Buchanan had eaten the last delivery pizza.

He persisted, "It just seems like a strange thing to write on yourself."

Joey put his head up from behind the transceiver. "Since when do you give a shit?"

"Don't get hostile." Anyway, Kindle's attention had refocused on the dinner problem. "Maybe I could cook us up some hamburgers on that Jenn-Air in the kitchen. . . ."

"Cook whatever you want. Fuck!" Joey had jammed a screwdriver into the palm of his hand. He added some other words.

"Shouldn't have written, 'worthless,'" Kindle said. "Should have written, 'Bad tempered little SOB.'"

"Fuck off," Joey said.

"I thought you *liked* to do electronics."

Joey stood up. What was that on his shirt—a skull? Skull and roses? "It's too many words."

"Eh?"

"'Bad-tempered little SOB.' Would have hurt too much."

"Kid has a sense of humor," Kindle said.

■　■　■

He cooked up hamburgers the way he liked them, with a startling amount of chili worked into the ground beef, an acquired taste, perhaps, but Joey just ladled on the ketchup and forged ahead. Kindle asked, "When do we power up?"

"I guess after we eat."

"Might not be anything to hear."

Joey shrugged. He had absolutely mastered that gesture, Kindle thought. He had a vocabulary of shrugs.

Kindle said, "If it's one in ten thousand, how many of those are hams or have the sense to rig up a radio? I read a statistic in one of those library books. Maybe one out of six hundred adult Americans has a valid amateur license. So what does that come to after Contact? Fifty people in the continental U.S.?"

"How should I know?"

"Well, we *don't* know. But it can't be very many. And how many of those are on the air?"

"More at night," Joey said. "Reception's supposed to be better at night."

"Even so. Some of them are bound to be out of range or at the wrong angle to the antenna or some damn thing. Some of them maybe tried and gave up. We might not hear a blessed word."

"Might not," Joey said.

"What, you don't give a shit?"

Joey seemed to ponder the question. "I want to work the transceiver," he said finally. "You need somebody to talk to."

"So as far as you're concerned, this isn't about saving the world."

"Is that what *you* think?"

"No," he admitted. "It's maybe what Matt Wheeler thinks."

"Stupid idea," Joey said.

"Is it?"

"Everybody's gone already. I mean they're still here, but they're gone. Some of us just got left behind. We can't do anything about it."

"Help ourselves, maybe."

"If we were that smart, we would have gone to heaven like everybody else. There's a reason we got left here. All the important people are gone, and we're still here because basically . . . because we're . . ."

"What?"

Joey smiled. "Worthless."

■   ■   ■

Joey switched on the radio, but the twenty-meter band was empty. All that static gave Kindle a chilly feeling. Little crackles of who knows what—interstellar radiation, cosmic noise, like rain on a rooftop, faint as memory. It was like listening to the restless sleep of the world.

It wasn't just Buchanan that had gone strange, it was the entire planet. You could know that—he had known it for months—and still not feel it. But he felt it now, listening to the radio hiss like waves on an empty beach.

This was the silence of Detroit and Chicago, the silence of Washington, the silence of Ceylon and Baghdad and Peking and London.

We must have been the most talkative species for light-years around, Kindle thought, but tonight the Earth was as still as an empty church.

He heard what he thought was a snatch of voices amidst the static . . . but when Joey tuned back, there was nothing.

"Try putting out a call," Kindle suggested.

Joey took up the microphone. He cleared his throat. "Calling CQ," he said, then covered the mike with his hand. "I feel like an asshole!"

"I expect everybody does the first time. Carry on."

"Calling CQ. This is—" He covered the microphone again. "We don't have a call number."

"Just say your name, for Christ's sake! Say we're in Oregon."

"CQ, this is Joseph Commoner in Buchanan, Oregon, calling CQ." Joseph?

"CQ, if anybody can hear me, calling CQ."

■   ■   ■

Kindle sat through a couple of hours of this, then told Joey he was going to bed. "When you get tired you can crash on the chaise longue if you want to."

Not that Joey showed any sign of wanting to sleep. He continued to patrol the twenty-meter band with an obsessive glaze in his eyes.

Kindle brushed his teeth and stretched out on a mattress he had ferried here from the mall. He closed his eyes and listened to the sound of Joey calling CQ in the next room.

He thought about the antenna, about Joey's radio waves zooming off into the dark night. Seek you, seek you.

Just the idea of it gave him the lonely shivers.

▪   ▪   ▪

Kindle got up at dawn. Joey, curled on the lawn recliner in the living room, slept till noon. When he woke he came into the kitchen looking smug.

"Any luck last night?" Kindle asked.

"I talked to a couple of people," Joey said, and checked out Kindle's reaction with a sideways glance.

"No shit?" Kindle said. "Who?"

"A guy, a ham, in Toronto. That's in Canada, right?"

"Last time I looked at a map it was. What's happening in Toronto?"

"He says the situation is about the same as here. We're supposed to talk again tonight. Ask him yourself. And another guy, down in Georgia."

"Southerner, huh?"

"Well, he's travelling around," Joey said. "He's an Army Colonel. Name of Tyler."

▪   ▪   ▪

Some nights later, Kindle watched the final game of the World Series on his color TV.

It was a Tigers/Cubs series, as he'd predicted. The game was broadcast without narrative, which gave it an eerie atmosphere. The only sound was the crack of the bat, the murmur (not a roar) of a sparse crowd.

All these games had been close. Pitchers' games, Kindle thought. Scientific. Mistakes were few and counted for much: If a breaking ball stayed up and over the plate, it was bound for glory.

Detroit took the game 2–1 in the eleventh inning, winning the series.

Last at bat for the Boys of Summer.

The final score rode up the screen . . . then, suddenly, there was static.

Nothing on TV tonight, Kindle thought.

Nothing on TV tonight ever again.

He phoned Matt Wheeler and told him he'd stay till Christmas.

Chapter 20

Christmas

Matt Wheeler saw less of his daughter Rachel as winter settled in. She was out of the house much of the time. She seldom told him where she was going or where she slept at night. Matt seldom asked.

They talked occasionally. He appreciated the effort she made, but increasingly it was dialogue across an invisible wall.

"Daddy," she told him, "you have to talk to the Helper."

He thought: Talk to it? What—that statue?

The Helper had stood in the City Hall Turnaround like a piece of grim abstract sculpture for weeks now. It neither moved nor spoke.

"If you talk to it," Rachel said, "it'll talk back."

"That's . . . difficult to believe."

"You have to talk to it," Rachel said. "It can tell you things I can't, and it'll be here when I'm gone. That's what it's for."

•   •   •

The rain was nearly constant now. On the day he closed the hospital, the second of December, Matt posted a sign at the Emergency entrance. His name and phone number were written in red letters under a waterproof plastic sheath. The number would reach him at home or in his car, as long as the telephone and local cellular system survived. He was considering the possibility of fitting a mobile medical unit in a hospital ambulance, or trying to locate the hospital's own rural treatment unit, abandoned somewhere after

Contact. But there didn't seem to be a pressing need. The hospital's facilities were intact if he should need them . . . though he could foresee a time when the town would exhaust its supply of drugs, of sterile needles—of doctors, perhaps.

On his way home, thinking about what Rachel had said, he stopped at the City Hall Turnaround.

The center of this traffic circle had been developed as a park, planted with grass and equipped with a water fountain and a plaque commemorating the town's incorporation. Much of Willy's IWW battle had been fought on this circle of alkaline soil.

The Helper stood here. It had floated into town along the coast highway, made a right turn where the highway crossed Marine, glided past Matt's office in the Marshall Building and across the railway overpass, and stationed itself on the Turnaround green.

Matt walked toward it through the rain. The rain was cold; he shivered under the wet bulk of his overcoat.

He stopped a short but wary distance from the Helper. He was intimidated by its size—it stood at least seven feet tall—and by its glossless black surface, somehow untouched by the rain.

They called it a Helper. The name, he thought, was grotesque but appropriate. It suggested a blunt, totalitarian benevolence—a meaningless gesture from a humorless tyrant.

Talk to it?

Not possible.

He stood in the park a while longer, listening to the rain as it fell on the grass and watching the clouds roll down from the slope of Mt. Buchanan. Then he turned and walked back to the car.

■   ■   ■

Hard times coming. Rachel repeated the warning a few days later. "The Travellers are doing things to the planet," she said, and Matt experienced a tremor of fear that stitched into the deepest part of him. It wasn't what she said—though that was frightening enough—but how she said it: blandly, if not happily.

They were sitting in the living room looking past the blank TV set, through the window to a faraway ridge of wet Douglas firs in their dark-green winter coats. It was another rainy December morning.

Matt cleared his throat and asked what "doing something to the planet" might entail.

"Fixing it," Rachel said. "Restoring it. Reversing all the changes. What we did over the last century or so—what *people* did—was to set forces in motion we couldn't control. Global warming, for instance. The Travellers are taking some of the CO_2 out of the atmosphere and trying to bind it into the ocean." She turned to face him. "It was worse than we suspected. If the Travellers hadn't come . . . it would have been awfully hard for all of us, next century, or the century after that."

"They care what happens to the Earth?"

"They care because *we* care."

"Even if you're leaving?"

"It's where we were born," Rachel said. "It's our planet. And it won't be entirely empty."

"Restoring the balance," Matt said. "That doesn't sound so bad."

"No. But in the short term . . . Daddy, I can't explain all the things they're doing, but in the short term, it could mean some chaotic weather, at the very least. Storms. Bad storms."

He nodded, grateful for this nugget of hard information. "When?"

"I don't know . . . maybe soon. Late winter, early spring."

"There'll be some warning?"

"Of course. That's what the Helpers are for . . . one of the things they're for." Her expression now was not bland at all; she regarded him with a desperate unhappiness. "Daddy, you *must* talk to the Helper."

▪   ▪   ▪

It had been agreed at the November Committee meeting that they would gather to celebrate Christmas Eve at Tom Kindle's new house in Delmar Estates. Guests were welcome, even Contactees, especially family, and Matt asked Rachel to come along—but she declined.

He drove to the party through a chill, heavy rain that threatened to turn into hail, along streets grown ragged with winter potholes. He wondered whether he might be the only one lunatic enough to brave the weather. Some party. But there were other cars parked at the house; and Kindle welcomed him inside, took his coat, told him that, in fact, all ten members of the Committee had shown up, but nobody else: "Just us human beings. Which is probably just as well. Come on in, Matt. Everybody else got here early 'cause of the weather, I guess. Abby's been here since two this afternoon, puttin' up these goddamn Christmas decorations, plus that little plastic tree in the corner. Had me hangin' bulbs and lights on it."

"Looks good, Tom."

"Looks like a fuckin' department store, but there was no stopping her."

Matt remembered the way Buchanan used to dress itself up for Christmas—tinsel across the avenues, pine boughs on the lamp standards.

"The punch is over there," Kindle said, "but go easy for a while, we got a turkey in the oven and some radio calls coming in from the east—I don't want anybody throwing up on the microphone."

▪   ▪   ▪

Dinner was festive. Even Paul Jacopetti seemed to have mellowed for the occasion. Matt sat between Chuck Makepeace, who was promoting the idea of a New Year's reconnaissance trip to the waterworks and the power company, and Abby Cushman, who had taken most of the dinner chores on herself and was away from the table between courses.

Matt noted the way she fluttered over Tom Kindle, served him generously, asked his opinion of the gravy, the dressing, the plum pudding. ("Looks real good to me," Kindle said. "Real good, Abby.") She was married, Matt reminded himself, and had a couple of grandchildren living with her—but they were like Rachel, lost to Contact. It was no wonder she had adopted the Committee, and Tom Kindle in particular.

He gave a brief, sober thought to Annie Gates. He hadn't spoken to her for months. He hadn't wanted to say all the necessary things. All the things that amounted to: *Goodbye, good luck, I loved you in my own fucked-up way but now you're not human anymore.* Surely silence was better than that.

Abby recruited Paul Jacopetti, Bob Ganish, and a reluctant Beth Porter to deal with the dinner dishes. Everybody else adjourned to the living room; Joey Commoner began warming up the transceiver, scouting for stray voices prior to the east-west hookup scheduled for 8:00 Pacific time.

Kindle took Matt aside. "That Abby . . . she's a pain in the butt. She's been over three times this week. Stops to *chat.* I don't know *how* to chat. She brings food. Matthew, she *bakes.*"

"She seems nice enough," Matt said.

"Hell, she *is* nice. If she wasn't nice it wouldn't be a problem. She talks about her family—she doesn't see 'em much anymore. She's having a hard time and she needs somebody she can latch onto. And, you know, I'm only human. It's been a while since I had a woman around, barring some Saturday nights in town, and even that's all finished since Contact. So I think yeah, okay, Abby's nice . . . but it's not fair to her."

"Why not?"

"Because I'll leave. The only advantage to getting old is that you learn this shit about yourself. I was married once—little Coast Salish girl up in Canada. Lasted about six months. She went back to the reserve, I came back

192 • Robert Charles Wilson

across the border. And that was pretty much the endurance record for Tom Kindle. Maybe I won't leave this month, maybe not next month, but I'll leave. And Abby's been left too much just now."

"Maybe you should tell her that."

"Good advice. Maybe I should just club her down with a stick—it'd be kinder."

"Or don't leave. That's the other choice."

"Uh-huh."

"The thing is, you're useful around here."

"Right. About as useful as half a crutch. Speaking of which, I'm still limping. Is that normal?"

"You'll limp a while longer. But don't put down your own contribution. You're like an anchor at the Committee meetings. The radio's been a morale booster, too."

"Mostly Joey's work."

"And Joey, come to that. He's turning into a human being. You treat him with a certain amount of respect. That's a new thing for him."

"You ever see that tattoo on his shoulder?"

Matt nodded.

"'Worthless,'" Kindle said. "You suppose he believes that?"

He thought about it. He didn't know Joey Commoner particularly well. Joey must have been eighteen years old when he had that word dyed into his skin, and it was precisely the kind of thing a pissed-off eighteen-year-old might do. It might mean nothing.

Still, if he had to render an opinion—"I think he might believe it, yes."

Kindle shook his head.

"Shit," he said finally. "I didn't sign on to be anybody's husband . . . and I sure as hell didn't sign on to be a goddamn *parent*."

■ ■ ■

Come eight o'clock, Joey established contact with the community of survivors in Toronto. The weather was bad and the signal was poor; voices faded in ghostly fashion. But the contact across all that distance was heartening. Everybody gathered around the microphone and sang "Adeste Fidelis"—they had rehearsed this—and the Canadians sang "Silent Night" through the static. It was snowing there, the Canadian radioman said. The streets were knee-deep and the municipal plows weren't out this year; the survivors were partying in a downtown hotel: "Lots of rooms and an emergency generator in the basement. We're cozy."

The Canadian chorus was bigger than Buchanan's: perhaps eighty people, almost as large as the nearly one hundred in the Boston community Joey had contacted a few days ago. Which meant, Matt knew, there must be more such groups, but only a few of them had thought to attempt radio communication.

Toronto said "Merry Christmas" and signed off. Joey tried for Boston and a third contact in Duluth, but the weather wasn't cooperating—"The skip isn't in," Joey said.

"We could phone 'em," Kindle said. "Guy in Boston gave me his telephone number." But the long-distance exchanges were unreliable these days and, anyway, a phone call wasn't the same as radio contact; they could wait until tomorrow to pass on Christmas sentiments.

"Telephone service won't last the winter," Jacopetti predicted. "Wires go down. Relay towers. I doubt anybody'll fix 'em."

Joey went on DXing. Kindle said Joey had twice made brief contacts with other continents—a ham in Costa Rica, and on one memorable clear night a voice speaking what Joey said was Russian but might have been Polish or Ukrainian . . . the signal faded before he could respond.

Beth Porter, in a gesture that took Matt by surprise, had brought along a VCR and two tapes from the big video store on Ocean Avenue: *White Christmas* and *It's a Wonderful Life*. "Because I used to watch those movies every year. You know, I just thought it would be nice."

Joey took time away from the radio to hook up the tape machine. Kindle freshened the punch and Miriam Flett, in another surprise move, volunteered to make popcorn.

Somewhere between Bing Crosby and Jimmy Stewart, Matt thought: My God, there are only ten of us. But this might work. This might still work. This might still be a town.

■   ■   ■

Sometime after midnight, the rain turned to sleet and the roads began to ice. *It's a Wonderful Life* cranked to an end, and in the silence that followed, without warning, Paul Jacopetti began to weep—racking sobs that shook his large body like seizures. Beth retrieved her videotape: "Jeez, I'm sorry, maybe that was the wrong thing to show."

"It was fine," Matt told her. "Don't apologize."

But the party was over. Kindle offered bedroll space to anyone who wanted to stay the night. Tim Belanger had confined his drinking to Diet Pepsi and offered a drive to those who hadn't; he left with Bob Ganish and the still-teary Paul Jacopetti.

Joey was still working the transceiver. Beth told him a couple of times she wanted to go home, she was tired, the streets weren't getting any safer. "Just wait," Joey said, turning the dial with a relentlessness that looked nearly compulsive to Matt.

Kindle said Beth could take one of the spare rooms, if she didn't mind sleeping on the floor, but she shook her head and pursed her lips: "I want to go *home*."

"I can drop you off," Matt said. "If it's okay with Joey?"

Joey shrugged, his back turned. Another voice crackled from the radio speaker: ". . . *read you, Joseph . . . signal's faint*. . . ."

"It's that Colonel Tyler," Kindle said. "I swear, that son of a bitch never sleeps."

"Tyler," Matt said. "He's the guy down south?"

"He moves around. Loner type." Kindle escorted Matt to the door, out of Joey's earshot. "You should talk to him some night when the signal's less feeble. Joey thinks the guy is hot shit."

"You don't?"

"Well . . . it's too soon to be choosy about the friends we make, right? But Tyler's full of all kinds of ideas. He says we should form a defense committee or something. Says he's seen some mayhem out on the road. A lot of peculiar people turned down Contact, he says. He keeps talking about some big project out in Colorado he's heard about. . . . Matt, he claims the aliens are building a spaceship out there. Is that possible?"

"I guess it's possible. I suspended judgment last August. You don't believe him?"

"Oh, I believe him, I guess." Kindle rubbed his chin. "I believe him, all right. I just don't, you know, *trust* him."

"He's in no position to do us harm."

"Not at the moment," Kindle said.

■ ■ ■

Beth huddled into the passenger seat. Matt asked her to fasten her seat belt. The roads were slick with sheet ice, and it was easy to imagine his little import sliding into a ditch.

Beth strapped herself in and gazed through the window at dark suburban houses.

He signalled a left turn on Marina, crossing town to Beth's house, but she touched his arm: "No, keep going . . . I don't live there anymore."

He frowned but crossed the intersection. "Moved out from your family?"

"It never was much of a family, Dr. Wheeler. Mainly just my dad, and he's—you know. Changed."

"I guess it's hard to talk to him."

"It used to be hard. Now he *wants* to talk—but it's worse, in a way. I think part of the deal is that if you want to live forever you have to understand what a shit you were in real life. He figures he kicked me around too much, and he doesn't know what to do about it. He wants to apologize or make it better somehow."

"You don't want that?"

She shook her head fiercely. "I'm not ready for that. Christ, no. It's hard even being around him since he changed. He even looks different now. You remember how big he used to be? Now he's almost skinny. None of his clothes fit. He looks—" She chose a word. "*Empty.*"

She used the nail of her right index finger to draw an oval in the fog on the passenger window. She gave it eyes, eyelashes, a pursed mouth. A self-portrait, Matt thought. "So I'm staying at the Crown Motel. The one by the waterfront, past the ferry dock."

Matt turned right at the next intersection, toward a blankness of fog and rain, the ocean. "You could have done better than a motel. Look at Tom Kindle."

"The room is big enough. It has a kitchenette, so I can cook. I get along."

The rain turned icy again, clattering against the roof of the car. Matt eased past the sign that said CROWN MOTOR INN, the car fishtailing on a slick of ice. He realized he hadn't seen a single other vehicle during this drive from Tom Kindle's house—no traffic of any kind.

A light was burning in Beth's room. She left it on, she said, so she could find the door at night. "It gets lonely in this big parking lot." She cocked her head at him. "You want to see the place?"

"The roads aren't getting any better, Beth."

"You could walk me to the door, at least."

He agreed . . . though it seemed somehow careless to leave the dry enclosure of the car.

Beth had appropriated a ground-floor room. The number on the door was 112. The door wasn't locked. It opened into yellow light. "Just take a look," Beth said. "Tell me it's a nice place. God, it would be nice to have somebody tell me that."

He stepped inside. The room was hot; the thermostat was turned up. She had decorated this ordinary suite with cheap art prints—pastel watercolors, kittens and farmhouses. A quilt, obviously homemade, had been thrown across the bed. She followed his look. "It's the only thing I took with me when I left home. I slept under this quilt since I was little. My grandmother made it." She sat on the bed and stroked the quilt with one hand. "Do I have to call you Dr. Wheeler? Everybody at the party called you Matt."

"You can call me Matt."

"Matt . . . you can stay here tonight if you want."

Some part of him had expected the offer. Some part of him was surprised, even shocked.

"Because of the weather," Beth said. "The weather being so shitty and all." She began unbuttoning her shirt. "I hardly see Joey anymore. He just plays with that fucking radio over at Kindle's. It wouldn't be so bad—I mean, Joey's hardly a prize—but he was the only person who ever . . . I mean, he used to say I was pretty." She paused to gauge his reaction. "Nobody else ever said that."

She slid out of the shirt. Her skin was perfect, blemishless, flushed pink. Her breasts were small, the nipples almost childlike. There was a line of freckles across her breastbone. Why couldn't he say anything? He felt as if his mouth had been disconnected from his body. He was mute.

WORTHLESS, said the small blue letters on her shoulder.

"I'm twenty years old," Beth said. "I guess you've seen me naked since I was ten. You never said if you thought I was pretty. I guess doctors don't say things like that. Matt. Matthew. Matt—do you think I'm pretty?"

"Beth, I can't stay here."

She unzipped her jeans and stepped out of them, then sat back on the bed. She frowned. Then she folded her hands in her lap in a gesture that was oddly shy. "I don't know why I do this shit." She looked imploringly at him. "It's hard being alone all the time. The town is empty. It's not just that no one comes out on the street—I think people are actually *missing*. And I don't know what happened to them. And I lie here and I think about that and it's just so fucking scary. Sad and scary. And I would like not to be alone. But you can't stay?"

"I'm sorry."

"Is it as easy as that?"

"It's not easy."

It wasn't. She was twenty years younger than Matt . . . but he wasn't old, and she wasn't a child, and the sight of her was deeply arousing. He hadn't shared his bed with anyone since that August night with Annie Gates. And Beth was right about the town, Matt thought: It *was* empty, and it *was* scary, and the touch of another human being would be a powerful magic on a bitter winter night.

But she was vulnerable and too needy, and it was an act that might have unforeseen consequences.

She managed a small, embarrassed smile. "Telling the truth?" She looked him over, perhaps noticed the obvious bulge in his blue jeans. "I guess you're telling the truth. You want to stay but you think if you stay it might be . . . dangerous? Can I use that word?"

He managed a nod.

"Hey," she said. "I'm *dangerous*." She stretched out across the bed in a motion that was both sensual and weary. "Maybe I had too much to drink. . . ."

"Maybe we all did."

"Or maybe I'm a round-heeled little cunt. As my daddy used to say."

■   ■   ■

He drove home on ice, through ice, a night all ice and darkness.

The house was dark when he arrived. The baseboard heaters stuttered and creaked. Rachel wasn't home.

He hoped she was sleeping in a warm place this Christmas Eve.

But it wasn't Christmas Eve anymore, Matt realized; it had been December 25 since midnight, since before he left the party. It was Christmas morning.

■   ■   ■

By Christmas noon, most of the ice had melted from the streets.

Matt drove to the City Hall Turnaround and confronted the Helper a second time.

He wore his winter coat and a scarf Celeste had knitted for him in a time so remote it seemed like prehistory. Blades of grass, stiff with frost, crackled under his feet.

He stood close to the Helper—close enough to touch it. Rachel had said the thing could speak; but where was its mouth? Could it see him? Did it have eyes? Did it know he was here?

He supposed it did.

He began by cursing it. He called it a fucking intruder, a monster, a stony heartless motherfucking monument to all the needless cruelty that had been visited on the Earth.

He had to restrain himself from striking it, because he sensed its invulnerability, knew how easy it would be to beat his hands bloody on that unyielding surface.

He cursed it until there was nothing left in him but speechless hatred. The silence, after that, was almost shocking.

He waited until his voice came back—he had worn it raw.

"Tell me," he whispered. "Tell me what you know. Tell me what we have to do to survive."

He took a quick step backward—surprised in spite of himself—when the Helper opened its eyes, or what seemed to be eyes, twin patches of sleeker blackness on the black orb of its head, weirdly mobile, like two slick dots of oil.

And it spoke—a voice deeply resonant, somehow artificial, completely terrifying.

"This is not a safe place any longer," it said.

Chapter
21

Skin

It was good, at first, cruising through these southern towns, drowsy little November towns in Virginia, North Carolina, parts of Kentucky and Tennessee.

The towns were much alike. Each had its church, its central school, its highway mall—and each town had its Helper, nested at the center of it like a worm burrowed into an apple.

John Tyler personally destroyed several of these devices, and his friend A.W. Murdoch dispatched more. Murdoch was a surer hand at the TOW, much as Tyler disliked to admit it. We each have our talents, he told himself, and Murdoch was an excellent shooter.

At first they took elaborate precautions. Tyler thought the M998 was too obvious a vehicle; to conceal it, they navigated the highways in a stolen eighteen-wheel A&P truck with the Hummer and its TOW platform parked in the rear.

Murdoch argued that this was a simpleminded piece of sleight-of-hand, not likely to fool anyone. The Artifact was probably as effective a surveillance tool as the average military satellite, and the Contactees were an unlimited source of information on the ground. "Sir," Murdoch said, "if they want to get us, face it, they can get us—we're mostly counting on their pacifism."

Tyler yielded to the argument. After a week or so they abandoned the container truck and simply drove the Hummer from place to place, along highways and secondary roads that were generally empty, following a route Tyler hoped would seem random but that tended to the south. Tyler had not been warned about the weather, but he had already noticed an odd restlessness of wind and rain; he thought they'd be safer wintering below the snowbelt.

All this, plus his friendship with Murdoch, served to keep despair comfortably distant. At least for a time.

▪ ▪ ▪

Tyler's first warning that things had changed came in a little Georgia town called Loftus.

They had driven through dozens of towns like it. These little towns seemed emptier as the days passed, Tyler thought. One seldom saw the populace; either they had gone elsewhere or were locked indoors. Only a few lights came on at night. It was disturbing. It was even, if you let yourself dwell on it, frightening; but at the same time it made travelling easier. They spent nights in deserted motels; they drove freely in the daylight.

They arrived in Loftus at noon. These buildings, the three-story hotel and restaurant, the barber shop bedecked with Wildroot Cream Oil stickers, had probably not changed in any important way since the Korean War. There was a Helper, of course. It stood on a traffic island where the highway passed between a hardware store and a yellow-brick Kresge's. Murdoch fired the TOW and Tyler watched what he had come to think of as the customary fireworks: an explosion that shattered windows on all sides and left the road littered with glass and black dust.

Murdoch drove on through Loftus in moody silence. Murdoch had been moody since they left D.C., but hadn't wanted to talk about it. Tyler mentioned that they would need to locate another source of missiles before too long: the munitions they had carried from Virginia were about to run out.

"If there's any point to it," Murdoch said. "We're pissing in the ocean, if you ask me."

Tyler gave him a hard look. Murdoch's uniform was ragged, oil-spotted, and torn from working on the Hummer. He wore a jacket he had stolen from a retail shop in an empty mall. His hair was long and matted.

"There's more of these Helpers than we can ever hope to shoot," Murdoch added, "and I don't see any evidence we're doing any real harm—and shit, Colonel, maybe that's as it should be."

"I don't understand," Tyler said.

"Don't you? Are you sure? After Contact, I figured everybody was turned into zombies, it was like a horror movie, *Invasion of the Body Snatchers*. . . . I just wanted to kick some ass. Show somebody the human race wasn't that easy to knock over. You know what I mean?"

"Certainly."

"But it isn't like that. Fuck, I knew all along it wasn't like that." Murdoch kept one hand on the wheel and used the other to unscrew the lid from the coffee thermos. "Didn't want to admit it." He took a long swallow. "But maybe they aren't getting such a bad shake—all those zombies. Life eternal. Not such a shitty deal."

"Christ, Murdoch," Tyler said. "After all our work, you can't tell me you believe that."

"Don't you? I mean, down where it counts? When they came to you that night, didn't some part of you want to go along? Even if you said no, some part of you thought, shit, I don't want to live and die and never understand what it's all about. . . . Wasn't it like that?"

"Stupid question."

"Seriously." He startled Tyler by stopping the vehicle, standing on the brake until they were poised motionless on the white line of this country road. "Cutting all the crap," Murdoch said.

Tyler just stared.

"What do you think we'd find," Murdoch pressed, "if we turned around and drove back into that little pissant town?"

"Some evidence of our ability to harass an enemy. Were you asleep when you fired that TOW?"

"So we knocked down one of their ducks. I'm sorry, Colonel, but big fucking deal. How long till they send another Helper? They can have another unit there in a couple of days. Probably hours. They're that efficient. The more I think about this, the more pointless it seems. The only reason we get away with it is that they don't care. We're like fleas on an elephant. Too insignificant even to scratch."

He jerked the Hummer into a U-turn. Tyler said, "You really mean to go back there?"

"We need supplies. We should have stopped before we fired that missile. Plus I'd like to see just how long it really does take to repair the kind of damage we've been doing. Think of it as target assessment." He gave Tyler another long look. "If you don't mind, Colonel."

Tyler minded a great deal, but he didn't say so. It might be dangerous to linger at the site of an attack, but it might be more dangerous still to override Murdoch when the younger man was in this hostile mood.

Everything since Contact had become a matter of balances, Tyler thought. One thing weighed against another. What was buoyant might suddenly sink; what fell might rise.

■ ■ ■

They parked the Hummer out of sight—Tyler's precaution—in the service bay of an Exxon station. Because Murdoch intended to stay the night in this village, they located two adjoining rooms in the brick hotel overlooking the remains of the Helper. The hotel was empty. The afternoon sky was dark and the corridors rattled with the sound of distant thunder.

Murdoch left to scrounge for food. Tyler stayed in his room, dwelling on the problem of the younger man's doubts.

Maybe he should have seen this coming. Murdoch had been a technician in his old life, more loyal to the weapons he maintained than to the abstractions they served—the country, the Corps, the national defense. It was a thin reed to cling to, and lately Murdoch had grown sullen. The decline had been gradual but marked.

Maybe it was predictable. All the standards had fallen, Tyler thought. There was no propriety anymore, no decency. The norms had become fluid.

It was a frightening thought. Tyler had spent a lifetime negotiating the borderline between sanity and compulsion, and he had learned what Sissy in her madness had forgotten: *Appearances matter.* In the question of sanity, you were allowed to pretend. You were *supposed* to pretend. *Everyone* pretended. We prove we're sane by pretending to be sane. To fail at the pretense, or not to bother, was the *definition* of insanity.

But now . . . it was as if gravity had failed, as if every solid thing had come unhooked from the earth. In an empty world, who was to judge? Where were the boundaries to separate one thought from another? What impulse might surface unobserved? How to distinguish the daylight from the dark?

We're naked in this place, Tyler thought, and God help us for that.

He dozed for a time on the hotel bedspread and woke with a skull-splitting headache.

Murdoch came in the door with bags of canned food and bottled water. He dumped these on the bureau and took a towel from the bathroom—he was wet, his hair streaming water; it had begun to rain.

"It's funny," Murdoch said. "Most of the towns we've been through, you see at least a couple of people. This place—I'd swear it's deserted. Didn't see a living soul out there. For a while I thought I heard music. But I couldn't track it down—not in this weather."

Murdoch toweled his hair vigorously. The window was open a notch, and the room smelled moist and cool.

Murdoch gave him an odd, cautious look. "By the way, Colonel, have you seen the Helper?"

Tyler came alert. "What about it?"

"Well, it's doing something," Murdoch said.

"We destroyed it—what could it be *doing*?"

"Well, sir, it's more or less putting itself back together."

• • •

A.W. Murdoch followed Tyler down to the lobby, where the Colonel stood rigidly at the shattered front window and stared across the road at the remains of the Helper . . . at all that black, sooty dust that had begun to move as if stirred by an imperceptible wind, to heap itself into a crude, wet mound where the Helper had been.

Murdoch hadn't been too surprised to see the Helper putting itself together. All the Traveller technology seemed to use subordinate but independent parts—the octahedrons, which were part of the Artifact; the Helpers, which were smaller fractions of the octahedrons . . . and all this impact dust, which was just the smaller constituents of the Helper, he guessed, mobile and smart enough to crawl back into the original order.

Or the microbes that had infected everybody, come to that. Murdoch supposed *those* were machines, too, tiny but intelligent. There must be some irreducible level—a disorganization from which a Helper, for instance, couldn't recover—but they hadn't achieved that with a simple TOW.

Murdoch thought, It's like punching mud. We should have known.

But Tyler hadn't known, and Tyler was plainly horrified. He stood at the frame of the broken window shaking his head. Murdoch approached the older man cautiously. "Colonel?"

"Is it a threat?" Tyler said. "Are we in danger from it? Maybe we ought to move on."

"I don't imagine so. I don't think we really damaged it. I doubt we even annoyed it. If these things carried a grudge, we'd be dead by now." He felt a little guilty for breaking this news to Tyler in such an abrupt way; he felt he should make up for it. "Sir, we might as well go upstairs. You're getting all wet. Cook us some food up there. I got some Coors from the grocery."

When Tyler decided to leave D.C., they had assembled a kit that included a hot plate, pots and pans, plastic cutlery. Upstairs, Murdoch plugged in the hot plate and started frying eggs. The hotel room filled with the smell of hot butter.

Tyler cracked open a beer and stared out the window. His manner, Murdoch thought, was frankly a little crazed.

Murdoch had decided weeks ago that Colonel Tyler might not be firing on all cylinders, but so what? Who was? Maybe all the sane people accepted that nighttime offer last August; maybe only a pair of lunatics would be driving around the country taking shots at these machines, like two kids soaping windows on Halloween.

He came to understand that Tyler lived in a world of orders given, rules obeyed, limits respected—a world as fragile as the egg Murdoch had just cracked and as hard to repair. Naturally, Tyler was finding it hard to adjust.

"My father only gave me one piece of advice in his life," Murdoch said, "and that was to play the hand they deal you. I think he got it from a song. Or Dear Abby. But you can't argue with it, right? Colonel, we got a shitty hand here. But we're not dead yet."

Tyler looked away from the window. "You never talked about your father much, Mr. Murdoch."

"Not much to say."

"What did he do for a living?"

"Raised sinsemilla up in Mendocino County." To Tyler's uncomprehending look Murdoch added: "He grew marijuana."

"Christ. Really?"

"Honest to God."

"He was a drug dealer?"

"Well—more like a bootlegger. That was the spirit of the enterprise."

Tyler absorbed this information. "He must have hated it when you joined the Marines."

"I can't say it pleased him. But he told me it was my life, I should make my own mistakes. When I got on the bus at Ukiah, he said, 'Try not to shoot anybody!'"

And I never really did, Murdoch thought—unless you count the Helpers. Even then, he hadn't done them much harm, apparently.

Tyler shook his head. "It's always a surprise. People's families."

"You don't talk about your own family much."

"No," Tyler said. "I don't."

Murdoch let it drop.

He served the eggs; but Tyler put his plate aside. "Sir," Murdoch said, "speaking frankly, are you all right?"

The Colonel, who had been sitting stoop-shouldered in the chair by the window, drew himself up, almost into a sitting brace, his chin tucked, frowning, as if the question had stung him. "Of course I am."

And they ate in silence and listened to the hiss of the rain on the window.

▪ ▪ ▪

Murdoch told the Colonel he thought they should stay in Loftus until the cold rain passed, and Tyler had surprised him by agreeing. It seemed to

Murdoch that the Colonel had grown both very unhappy and very agreeable recently.

Privately, Murdoch was curious about this little town. There were some questions that had piqued his interest during this shooting-gallery trek across the South, and he hoped to find some answers here.

For instance, exactly what *was* happening to the people in these little road towns? Where were they going? They weren't on the highway, for sure; the highways were deserted. But so—increasingly often—were the towns.

Tyler disliked these questions and refused to discuss them, but Murdoch was simply curious.

In the morning he left the morose Colonel and wandered out into the street.

The rain had eased, but the sky was dark and restless with cloud. While he was asleep, the Helper had achieved a blurry approximation of itself. Minute grains of black dust moved over its surface, giving it the look of something swarmed by insects. It was as strange as anything Murdoch had recently seen, but he was growing accustomed to miracles . . . he watched for a moment, then shrugged and turned away from all these shattered storefront windows.

Yesterday there had been music. He'd heard it while he was scrounging for food at a grocery store a couple of blocks from here. The music had come very faintly through the rain, and Murdoch guessed it might have been imaginary, the kind of thing you hear when you're alone in a strange place in a storm . . . but he remembered it as music, faint but unmistakable.

Today, he stood still and listened.

There was a faraway bark of a dog. A few wind sounds. The grit under his shoes as he shifted back and forth.

No music.

Spooky.

He turned a corner away from the main street. He had decided that today he would find somebody—a human being or a Contactee, it didn't matter. Murdoch just wanted to look at a new face, ask some questions. The name of this little street, posted on a rusty sign at the intersection, was ELM. Every one of these towns had an Elm, or an Oak, or maybe a Peach or a Magnolia as they pressed on into Georgia. What better place to find out what had happened to everybody? Everybody lived on Elm. He decided to knock on the door of the first house he came to.

The first house on Elm was a little bungalow with a tiny front yard. It had a wooden porch, and on the banister, five terracotta pots of dead flowers. Murdoch stepped up onto the sagging porch and nudged aside a child's red wagon. He pushed the doorbell and listened as the buzzer rang inside.

Nothing stirred.

He opened the screen and knocked at the door. The sound of his knock seemed to make the silence heavier.

"Hey!" he said. "Hey, anybody in there?"

This was a strange thing to be doing, and he was suddenly aware of himself—a lonely figure, thin in his ragged uniform, his hair grown long and his stubble unshaven. Christ, he thought, I must look like a scarecrow. What if somebody *did* open the door? One look at me and they'd close it in a hurry.

But no one answered his knock.

He tried the knob. The door was locked.

He looked up and down the street. He'd never broken into a house before. Well, fuck it, he said to himself. I'm coming in there. Heads up, you ghosts.

He put his shoulder against the door and pushed. The door was old, and wood rot had gotten into the framing of it. The latch sheered out of the molding with a creak and a snap. Murdoch peered into the inner darkness.

Who had lived here? Somebody with kids, judging by that wagon. The room inside, now dimly visible in the watery daylight, was dusty but reasonably tidy. A brick-red sofa stood against one wall. Above it hung a framed oil color of a woodland sunset. There was a TV set, a stereo, an empty fish tank. Some kids' toys were scattered on the floor.

Also on the floor . . .

Murdoch stared at it a long time before he recognized it for what it was: A human skin.

▪ ▪ ▪

After he vomited over the porch railing, Murdoch selected a long willow branch from among the windfall on the neighbors' lawn. He was reassured somewhat by the weight of the stick in his hand. He was otherwise unarmed—but what was there to shoot at?

All up and down this rainy street, nothing moved.

Murdoch clutched the stick and forced himself to climb the three steps up to the porch, to cross the intervening space to the door, open it, step once again into that terrifying dimness.

The skin lay at his feet. It hadn't moved.

But it was definitely a skin. Fragile, empty—almost transparent. But human, Murdoch thought. Its shape was difficult to discern; it was folded into itself, accordioned together; but one arm projected, a fragile white papyrus, with a hand like an empty glove and five delicate, pale fingers.

It reminded Murdoch of a discarded skin of a spider he had once found in an empty locker—spider-shaped, but so delicate that a breath would carry it away.

He lowered the willow branch until it was almost touching the empty human skin, then pulled it back, revulsion winning out over curiosity.

He stepped over the hideous thing and deeper into the house.

The house was a bungalow with only a few rooms: this living room, the kitchen, two bedrooms, a bath. Murdoch investigated them all, flicking on lights where the daylight didn't reach.

He found two more skins: one in the kitchen; one—smaller, which made it somehow more horrible—in the child's bedroom.

Leaving that room, he felt dizzy; and realized he'd been holding his breath as if something in the house might infect him . . . might suck away his substance, might drain him as thoroughly as these people had been drained of themselves.

He hurried to the door, but stopped there.

He turned back. He took a firm grip on the willow stick and held it with its narrow end pointed at the first of the skins.

The urge to poke at the thing was as strong as the urge to turn and run. There was something childish about this, Murdoch thought. He was like a little child poking at a rattlesnake's shed skin. He dreaded it . . . but he couldn't help wondering about it. Would it crumble or would it fold? If it broke at his touch, would it make a sound? Would it move in leathery fashion, like parchment, or would it rattle like sun-bleached cellophane?

He touched the skin with his stick.

In fact, it made only the faintest noise as he turned it . . . a whisper of membranous surfaces, like the murmur of leaves in an autumn tree, or the turning of a page in an old dry book.

Murdoch thought he might vomit again. He turned and stumbled to the porch railing.

That was when he saw the girl.

■   ■   ■

"You don't look so good," she said.

Murdoch didn't think he could stand much more startlement. One more shock and his ventricles might explode. He looked up from the railing with a terrible, emasculating dread.

But it was only a girl, standing on the sidewalk with a frown of concern.

A local girl, judging by her accent. She wore a too-big man's windbreaker over a yellow T-shirt. Her blue jeans were tight, and she had sneakers on her feet. Murdoch pegged her at about eighteen, but she might have been younger or older. Her head was cocked and she was studying him with patient sympathy.

"You found those skins in the house, huh? First time you seen one?"

She was pretty in a stringy-haired kind of way. Her face was a perfect oval and her eyes were intelligent.

Murdoch tried to reassemble some masculine composure. "First time," he admitted. "Christ! You've seen them before?"

"Yup."

"Scary as hell."

She shrugged.

The nausea had passed. Murdoch straightened and unclamped his hands from the railing. "You, uh, live here?"

"No—not *this* house. This's where the Bogens used to live." She pointed: "I used to live a couple doors down. But I moved out of there. Guess where I live now!"

He felt like saying: Girl, there are three dead people in this building— nothing left but their *packaging*. Under the circumstances, maybe a guessing game kind of verged on bad taste.

But here was a new face, which was what he'd set out to find, and he didn't want to chase her away. "I can't guess."

"The Roxy," she said.

The Roxy? A theater? Did this town have a Roxy Theater? Was there an old trestle town like this that didn't?

"I turned the manager's office into kind of an apartment," she said. "And I taught myself how to run the movies."

He said, "You were running a movie last night? Last night when it was raining?"

She brightened. "How'd you know?"

"Heard the music."

"It was *42nd Street*. There was an old-movie festival playing when Contact came. Those are the only films I can find. I got *42nd Street* and *Golddiggers of 1934* and *The Maltese Falcon*. I don't play 'em much. It's pretty hard work by yourself. And if you see 'em too often, what's the point? But on a cold night like that . . ."

"I understand," Murdoch said.

"Already, I could sing that *42nd Street* song in my sleep."

"Uh-huh. Hey, what's your name?"

"Soo," she said. "Two ohs. It's not short for anything. Soo Constantine."

"I'm A.W. Murdoch."

"What's the A for, A.W.?"

"Abel," he lied.

"Mmm . . . I like A.W. better."

"So do I. Soo, tell me—are there more of those, uh, those—"

"Skins?"

"Are there more of those *skins* around?"

"Most every house," she said. "If you look. I hope you're not planning to look."

"No, I just . . . well, Christ, it took me by surprise. I mean, is everybody in town like that?"

"Nearly. 'Cept me."

"Well, what happened to them? Do you know?"

"They left, A.W.," she said flatly. "They went away. But not their skins. They just used up their bodies and they left their skins behind."

■   ■   ■

"A radio," Colonel Tyler said. "Maybe that's something we ought to have."

Murdoch, cooking dinner over the hot plate, wondered what this might portend. "Sir, a radio?"

"To contact other people. Other human beings."

Tyler sat in the hotel chair where Murdoch had left him this morning. He hadn't shaved, which for the Colonel was a serious omission. Murdoch had pegged Tyler for the kind of man who'd shave in a hurricane and stock the storm cellar with Aqua Velva.

"I think we need that contact, don't you, Mr. Murdoch?"

"Sir, how many of those Coors have you been into?"

Tyler looked at the can in his hand, then set it aside. "What are you suggesting?"

"Nothing."

"I'm not drunk."

"No, sir."

"Maybe you should have a drink yourself."

"Later, sir, thanks." Murdoch served out equal portions of canned corned beef hash. Tyler liked canned corned beef hash, but Murdoch thought it resembled dog food too closely. It was like ladling out hot Alpo. "Shitty weather, sir." The rain had returned with a vengeance; there was occasional sheet lightning and a muted, continuous thunder.

Tyler accepted his bowl of hash and held it in his lap. "We're nothing without a community, Mr. Murdoch."

"No, sir."

"A community defines the perimeters of behavior the way a border defines the perimeters of a nation."

"Mm-hm." Alpo or not, Murdoch was hungry tonight. He sat opposite the Colonel and gazed past him at the window. Nighttime now. Night came early these days.

Tyler was frowning. "*Skins*, you say."

"Yes, sir."

Murdoch had told the Colonel about the skins he'd found. He'd kept quiet about Soo Constantine, however. Murdoch couldn't explain his reticence even to himself, but it seemed better that way. Soo was a new and particular discovery. His own.

"Just their vacant . . . their empty . . ."

"Skins, sir, yes."

"Horrible."

Murdoch nodded.

"What do you suppose happened to their *insides*, Mr. Murdoch?"

"I think—" Soo had told him this. Best be cautious. "It's possible they just kind of faded. Disappeared from the inside out. Didn't you get that hint in Contact, sir? That it would be possible to leave the body behind?"

"I never thought—not like a lizard shedding its scales, no. I wouldn't have expected anything that repellent." The Colonel took a halfhearted spoonful of the hash. "And the Helper?"

"Nearly assembled."

"I would prefer not to linger in this town, Mr. Murdoch."

"Sir, the weather—"

"You were never scared of rain before we came to Loftus."

"It's a cold, dirty rain. Some of these mountain roads could wash out."

"We can deal with that."

"Yes, sir. I'd just prefer to deal with it when it isn't storming."

Tyler showed him a baleful look. "Something in this town attracts you?"

"Shit, no, sir." But Murdoch felt himself begin to sweat.

"Community," Tyler said. "A human presence."

"Sir?" *Was the son of a bitch psychic?*

"We need a radio for the sake of community, Mr. Murdoch. Maybe we can be more effective in numbers than we are individually. Between the two of us, frankly, there isn't much in the way of discipline. We say the words, but it's reflex. You don't respect me as a superior officer."

Murdoch was startled. "That isn't—"

"It's not your fault. On the road, we're simply two men. All the structure has fallen away. I should have understood that when I talked to the President.

He was in Lafayette Park, Mr. Murdoch, with his shirt undone at the collar. The center cannot hold—isn't that what the poet said? Mere anarchy is loosed upon the world. Anarchy is without structure; it flows like water. Mr. Murdoch, do you suppose we've lost structure entirely? Has it gone that far?"

"I—wouldn't know."

"If there were more of us," Tyler said.

"Yes, sir."

"It's as if we left our own skins behind. Our skins of propriety. Our skins of good conduct. Suddenly we're raw; our nerves are exposed. We're naked. With the right provocation, we could say or do anything."

"Yes, sir," Murdoch said, realizing as he spoke that his friendship with Colonel Tyler had also peeled away; that the skin of amicability had been shed in this room and the thing beneath exposed: a queasy mutual fear.

∎ ∎ ∎

After dinner, he left the Colonel and hurried into the dark street. He was meeting Soo at the Roxy, and he was already late, according to the digital watch on his wrist. Since Contact, Murdoch had kept two watches, one on his wrist, one in his pocket, so when he replaced the battery in one watch he could set it by the other.

The Roxy was easy to find. It was one more peeling Main Street movie theater, its blank marquee shedding rainwater in cold sheets. Murdoch hurried past the empty ticket box, inside to the lobby where Soo had turned on the lights.

She was waiting for him, still wearing her yellow T-shirt, one hand cocked on her hip, standing in the doorway of the auditorium. Murdoch looked at her and felt weak all over.

Probably it was only the effect of a long separation from female company. What it felt like was high-octane, knee-buckling, adolescent lust. She was a compact package of curves and smiles and he wanted to pick her up in his arms and feel her weight. *Soo,* he thought. Some kind of weird southern name for a young girl. He said it twice to himself. Lord, Murdoch thought, take pity on a soldier.

"You shaved," she said.

He nodded, blushing.

"There's no more candy at the popcorn stand," she said. "But I got some Cokes in a cooler. The movie's ready to go. It's *42nd Street.* We can watch it from the projection room. Come on, A.W.!"

Speechless, he followed her upstairs.

■ ■ ■

Between reels she talked about herself; while Murdoch, listening, writhed in a fever of hormonal suspense.

He watched the words come out of her mouth—the way her lips moved when she talked.

"I wasn't born here. I was born in a town two counties east. Town of Tucum Wash, if you *call* it a town, really a gas station and a post office. They bused us thirty-five miles to school every day. Well, I hated that place. It's a common story, I guess. Everybody hates their hometown—especially if they come from a little wide-place-in-the-road like Tucum Wash. So when I graduated high school I came here looking for work. To Loftus, yeah, I see you smiling. Bright lights, big city, right? I guess you must have seen all kinds of places. But I'll tell you, A.W., I never wanted much more than Loftus. Loftus isn't bad. I worked at the K mart checkout and two nights a week at the Sandwich Castle in the mall. It's actually an okay kind of life. I kept myself in TV dinners and I had some fun. Had a boyfriend. Dean Earl was his name. Oh, he's gone—you don't have to look so long in the face. Dean didn't mean that much to me. Except every Friday night or sometimes Saturday we'd come here to the Roxy. I love movies. I won't watch 'em on video. Like watching a postage stamp. Plus it don't smell right. You know what I mean? You ever smell a theater? People think, oh, popcorn, but it isn't the popcorn. In summer it's that air-conditioning down the back of your neck, smells like cold metal, and the smell of sweaty people comin' in with their jackets over their shoulders and mopping their faces with handkerchiefs, waitin' for that chill to shiver up their spine. And when everybody's cool, the lights go off and the movie starts. Course I can't make it be like that. But when folks started leaving, you know, *leaving*, I couldn't help but think of the Roxy and how nice it would be to come here all by myself. And I did. Maybe you think I'm crazy. But it's nice here. It's not the same, but it reminds me of the old days. Well, maybe I *am* crazy. A.W., let me work this machine! Your hands are cold. You're still wet from the rain, aren't you? Shivering like a pup. You want dry clothes? You know, I thought you might get wet. I picked up some clothes at the K mart after we met this morning. Clothes about your size. Bet that A.W. comes out in the rain, I thought. He looks like he'd come out in the rain. Take that shirt off. *Your* shirt! Well—mine, too, if you like."

■ ■ ■

Later, Murdoch felt obliged to tell her about himself.

They shared a mattress on the floor of what used to be the office of the manager of the Roxy Theater. She was naked in the faint light, sitting cross-legged in a curl of woolen blankets. Murdoch was full of quiet wonder at the sight of her. Five minutes ago, they'd been joined in a passion so intense that Murdoch thought they might penetrate each other's skins, occupy each other's space. Now she was sitting apart from him, a little aloof, but smiling, in a blur of light from a high window where the rain washed the dusty glass. It was after midnight by the watch on Murdoch's wrist.

He felt a need to justify himself.

So he told her about growing up in Ukiah, leaving home, enlisting, discovering his aptitude for machines. How he had learned the tolerances and mannerisms of small arms, their maintenance and renewal, their weaknesses and strengths. A weapon was a complex environment in which a small event—the squeezing of a trigger, say—led to vastly larger consequences: the discharge of a bullet, the death of a man, the winning or the losing of a war. But only if everything was in balance; only if the weapon was correctly toleranced, unworn, clean and dry here, oiled there. It captured his imagination. In a world Murdoch often found confusing, here was a map he knew how to read.

Soo listened attentively but began to frown, and he hurried to change the subject: "Then came Contact, you know, and then I met Colonel Tyler and we started this little cross-country turkey shoot."

"Turkey shoot?"

"Well, you saw the Helper—what happened to it."

"Uh-huh. Big mess, frankly. Took out the window at the five-and-dime and the rain came in and ruint the magazine rack. You guys do that a lot?"

He wasn't sure whether he ought to boast or confess. "Maybe twenty times, twenty different towns since October."

"Isn't it dangerous?"

"The Helpers don't fight back." They don't have to, Murdoch thought.

"I mean, dangerous for regular people. Like civilians."

"We haven't killed anybody so far."

She nibbled her thumb. "I don't want to hurt your feelings, A.W., but it seems kind of pointless. Like, the Helper's almost back together again."

"We only just found out they can do that. But is it sensible, you mean? Soo, I don't know. Colonel Tyler thinks so."

The taste of her skin, her lips, was still in his mouth. Murdoch thought: We smell like each other.

"Going to do it some more?"

"The TOW shoots?" He shrugged. "Maybe I won't. Colonel Tyler . . . I can't speak for him. Sometimes I think . . ."

"What?"

"He's maybe not the world's most stable individual."

"You didn't look that stable yourself, this morning." Her smile was mischievous.

He shook his head at the memory. "Well, Christ . . . *skins!*"

"Come on . . . it's not so terrible."

He looked at her sidelong. "You said those people, what, faded away?"

"Kind of. You know, A.W., it was something they decided to do. It's how they wanted it. Maybe in some other town more people stayed in their flesh. Around here—I guess it sounds stupid, but there isn't that much to *do*. You remember Contact? Travellers said in time people might not want the flesh? Well, that's all this is. Mrs. Corvallis, she used to run the hair salon, she rented me a basement room—I watched her go. We were friends. I sat with her a lot. Toward the end she was just—I don't know how to describe it—very pale. You could tell she was going. She was like china. Like porcelain. Almost shiny, light as a bag of feathers. The Travellers were holding her together until the end. A.W., you know what they call *neocytes?*"

He nodded. He'd heard the word from a medic at Quantico, shortly after Contact.

"Well, the neocytes kept her together. Until she was living mainly on the other side, hardly here at all. Then one morning I knocked on her door and nobody answered and when I went in her skin was there, all empty. It wasn't so bad. She was happy about it."

But Murdoch couldn't suppress a shudder. "It was her choice—you honestly think so?"

"I know it."

"Horrible," Murdoch said.

"A.W., what's the alternative? When you die, you know, you leave your skin behind, too . . . and considerably more than that. It gets buried in the ground and rots. This was cleaner—and it wasn't death." She was still smiling, but gently, almost absently. "What was Contact like for you?"

"Same as for everybody," he murmured—softly, because a terrible suspicion had touched him and lingered a moment before he could dismiss it.

"No," she said, "for *you*. I really want to know."

"The Travellers came that night in August and they made an offer. What else is there to say?"

"You turned them down."

"Obviously."

"Any particular reason?"

"I think—no, it's stupid."

She focused her large eyes on him. "Tell me, A.W."

"When we moved from L.A. up to Mendocino County, I used to follow my father around those woods. Big Pacific woods. I was nine or ten years old and it scared the shit out of me—redwoods, helicopters, but not just that: it was the *bigness* of everything. I got lost once. Only for maybe half an hour. I sat under a tree until my old man found me. But I couldn't help thinking about the woods rolling on for miles all the way to the sea, the sea big enough to cover up every place I'd ever lived and everyone I knew, and a sky big enough to drown the sea—shit. Does this make any sense?"

Soo nodded gravely.

Murdoch was embarrassed, but he went on talking almost in spite of himself. "I don't think I trusted anything after that unless I could hold it in my hand or take it apart. Contact sounded real good, you know, in its own way. I'm not ashamed to admit that. But it was like being out in those woods again. Everything was so—" There wasn't a word for this feeling. "*Big.*"

"So you said no."

Murdoch nodded.

"A.W.—did you ever regret it?"

"You mean, would I do it the same way over again? I don't know." He thought of the skins. "It *still* scares the shit out of me, frankly."

"Maybe if there was somebody with you."

He looked at Soo a long time in the dim light. "But that's not possible."

"I think it might be."

"They said—the Travellers said—Soo, the neocytes aren't inside me anymore."

"A.W., if you want a second chance, I think it could be arranged."

He backed away across the sheets. "How would you know that? I mean, how would you know?"

She looked deeply worried. "Is it possible to fall in love with someone in less than a day? It wouldn't surprise me. Because I think I did. Stupid me." She sighed. "No, they aren't inside you. But they can be if you want them. It would be as easy as a touch, A.W. A kiss. If you want them. It's not too late."

Murdoch couldn't think clearly. He grabbed his pants and pulled them on, backed against a wall and stared at her. He summoned words and the words spilled out: "*I thought you were human!*"

"Oh, God. I *am*! I just wanted to stay this way a while longer. It's a *choice*, A.W., it really is. I *like* my skin. There's skin in the new life, too, I mean it's not just angels floatin' around heaven, but . . . I wanted to have my Earth skin and be in Loftus a while longer." She hung her head. She looked weirdly penitent, like a little girl caught stealing cookies. "I should have told you!"

He thought of what he'd seen this morning, dry parchment in the shape of an arm, a hand, fingertips. He looked at Soo. This skin he'd just touched. He imagined it empty and dropping like isinglass, perhaps blowing down the street in a strong wind.

God help me, Murdoch thought, *I held her in my arms!* And all along . . .

. . . all along, she had been one of *them* . . .

. . . one of *them*, under her skin. . . .

"A.W.," she said, "*please* don't leave. Please! I'll explain."

The monster wanted to explain.

Murdoch shook his head and ran for the door. He left most of his uniform behind. He didn't want his uniform. There were other clothes. He wanted this cold rain to wash him. He wanted it to wash him clean.

▪ ▪ ▪

John Tyler placed his service revolver on the desk opposite the bed where he could see it. He was reassured by the sight of the weapon. It was substantial and weighty. It was like an investment, Tyler thought, something withheld until its value increased.

He was thinking about loyalty.

Loyalty was the fundamental thing, Tyler thought. Loyalty was normalcy reduced to its essentials. Loyalty allowed no room to maneuver. Loyalty was precise.

He had begun to entertain doubts about Murdoch's loyalty.

Tyler was sitting at the rainswept window watching the dark main street of Loftus when Murdoch came stumbling back to the hotel.

Murdoch was a ludicrous sight, naked above the waist and barefoot, mincing over patches of broken glass in the midnight rain.

It might have been funny, except for its implications about what Murdoch had said and refrained from saying . . . implications about this town and about Murdoch's loyalty to Tyler.

He listened through the wall as Murdoch let himself into the adjoining room. There wasn't much to hear. The shower ran for a long time before the room grew quiet again.

Tyler eased back into his chair.

He had been without sleep for two days, and he hadn't left this room since Murdoch took him down to see the Helper rebuilding itself. This was his madness come back again, Tyler recognized, but he had forgotten that madness was also clarity; madness was the ability to see things as they really were, to make decisions he might not otherwise be capable of making.

He could even admit that this might be a form of Sissy's madness, a madness he had inherited. Sissy had heard voices. Tonight Tyler heard a crowded confusion of voices hovering on the edge of intelligibility; and if he listened closely he thought the sound might resolve into words, the same words, perhaps, that had frightened and exalted his mother. But Tyler wasn't interested in voices. They were what the doctors called an *epiphenomenon*, a secondary symptom, like the curious sterility of the yellow light radiating from the room's electric bulbs, or the sour odor of stale tobacco smoke that had begun to seep from every surface. Perhaps Sissy could be deceived by such trivia; Tyler was different.

What interested him was the clarity, the speed of his thoughts. He was able to see the threads of significance that bound one event to another in a complex web of meaning.

It was both hideous and quite beautiful.

Colonel Tyler examined it, turned it this way and that in his mind, this glittering web, as the hours marched toward daylight.

The rain had been falling now for forty-eight hours.

■   ■   ■

Murdoch knocked on his door early the next morning.

Tyler rose and walked to the door and opened it just as Murdoch was preparing to knock a second time.

"Sir," Murdoch said, "I've reconsidered, and I think you were right. I think we should pull out of this town."

Tyler surveyed the younger man. "You look shitty, Mr. Murdoch. You look like you haven't slept."

Murdoch blinked. "No offense, sir, but you're no bed of roses yourself."

"It's still raining," Tyler said, savoring this.

"Sir, yes it is, but—"

"You made a convincing case about navigating these mountain roads in the rain."

"Well, as you yourself said, sir, we shouldn't be scared by a little rain. I think—"

"No. You were eloquent on the subject. We have to be careful. We can't phone 911 if we slide off a mountainside. It's a new world, Mr. Murdoch."

"Yes, sir, " Murdoch said miserably. "But—"

"We can afford to stay another day."

Murdoch seemed to surrender; he bowed his head. "Yes, sir."

"Or longer."

"*Sir?*"

"Depending on the weather."

■　　■　　■

Tyler was buoyed by this small victory, and in the afternoon he felt well enough to brave the rain. He ducked across the street to a clothing store, found a yellow rain slicker, and wore it for protection as he explored the immediate neighborhood of the hotel.

The town was small and might not contain what he was looking for . . . but then again, it might.

He stalked the rain-washed streets of Loftus with his gaze aimed at each shingled roof he passed. He was scouting for an antenna.

Some of these houses were equipped with ancient rooftop television antennas; some had satellite dishes mounted on their lawns like enormous mushrooms. Most, Tyler presumed, were wired for cable. But it wasn't a TV antenna he was hunting for. Tyler walked on, a strange figure in his yellow raincoat, the only color and motion in these gray and empty streets.

By five o'clock, the light had nearly failed. Tyler was preparing to turn back when he looked east on one of these narrow residential streets and saw a tower silhouetted against the blue-black sky—a radio tower with a beam antenna mounted on it.

Smiling to himself, Tyler hurried down the block to the pertinent house and kicked open the front door. The lights blazed on at the touch of a switch. It was amazing, he thought, and maybe it was more than amazing, that the power hadn't failed. In every one of these whistlestop towns they'd passed through, the wall plates continued to offer 120 volts of AC as reliably as ever—maybe *more* reliably. It was a mystery . . . but Tyler set it it aside for later pondering.

Inside the house, he found two of the skins Murdoch had talked about. He regarded these relics with a faint distaste, probing them with his shoe. The skins were dry and snaky and he understood Murdoch's alarm.

But they were harmless dead things, too, and Tyler was able to ignore them.

In the basement he found what he'd been looking for: a small room decorated with QSO cards and antique code keys, and on a knotty pine desk, a Kenwood radio transceiver of recent vintage.

Tyler switched on the machine to make sure it worked. The faceplate lit up; static whispered from the speaker.

Who might be out there? Out there even now, Tyler thought, voices buried in this whisper of noise.

Maybe no one, Tyler thought. Or maybe a population of survivors. One in ten thousand Americans was still a large group of people. Such a population would know nothing about him. None of them would know about Stuttgart or any other of his long nights; none of them would know he had held a gun on the President. Among such people, he would have essentially *no past*. He could be a new thing; he could be what he looked like in a mirror.

He tuned the radio with scrupulous care. He was disappointed by its silence, but he persisted for hours, until long after dark, until he heard the faint sound of Joey Commoner talking to Boston, Massachusetts.

■   ■   ■

When Tyler analyzed the events that followed, his verdict was: *I shouldn't have played with the pistol.* It was the pistol that made things go bad.

When he came back to the hotel he found Murdoch frying hamburgers on the hot plate. Tyler wasn't hungry; his headache had gotten worse. After dinner, Murdoch hauled a case of beer into the room. Tyler matched him bottle for bottle. It was a stupid thing to do, under the circumstances. The alcohol affected his judgment.

He talked long and volubly and perhaps not too coherently about the large things on his mind: about loyalty and sanity. "In the end," he told Murdoch, "it comes down to obedience. Obedience and sanity are the same word—wouldn't you agree, Mr. Murdoch?"

Murdoch—who had been nervous to begin with and seemed no better for his massive intake of Coors—looked at Tyler wearily. "Tell the truth, sir, I have no idea what you're talking about."

"That's a hell of an admission."

"Is it? What's *that* supposed to mean?" Now Murdoch was angry. "It's an insult, right? Jesus. I swear I don't understand you. Half the time you come on like a good old Army boy, half the time you sound like some faggot college professor. I don't even know why we do this military routine. Aye sir, Colonel sir. Just because you're walking around like you have a ramrod up your ass. Salute me, I'm wonderful. Well, fuck it. It's not just stupid, John, it's not even sane."

Tyler was stung by the extremity of this.

"Epictetus," he said.

Murdoch, exasperated: "*What?*"

"The *Discourses*. 'Why, then, do you walk as if you had swallowed a ramrod?' Epictetus. He was a Stoic. An educated Roman slave. You shouldn't insult me, Mr. Murdoch."

"All I meant—"

But Tyler's attention had strayed to the pistol on the side table. Spontaneously, in a motion that seemed to belong to his hands alone, he picked the weapon up.

Murdoch's eyes widened.

It was an old-fashioned revolver. Tyler opened it to show Murdoch the chamber. "Empty," he said. Then he took a single bullet from the tabletop, displayed it between his right thumb and forefinger, and placed it in the pistol.

Or pretended to. In fact, he palmed the bullet . . . but Murdoch didn't see.

"One round," Tyler said.

He spun the chamber without looking at it.

He raised the pistol to his own head. The act was familiar, but he had never performed it in the presence of another man. It made him feel strange, dizzy, not altogether connected to Murdoch or this room or the exterior world in general.

He looked steadily at Murdoch as he pulled the trigger. *Click!*

He spun the chamber again.

"That's the advantage I have over you, you lame little fuck. That I'm capable of this."

Perhaps Murdoch, the weapons specialist, was visualizing the internal working of the pistol, the firing pin as it came down on empty air—or not.

Click!

"I can do this without flinching. Now. Can you?"

Murdoch huddled away from the barrel of the pistol. He looked pinned in his chair by an invisible wind. His Adam's apple bobbed in his throat, a motion Tyler watched with fascination. It looked like there was something inside him trying to get out, something more substantial than a word.

"Christ," Murdoch said in a strangled voice, "please, Christ Jesus, don't!"

"*This* is why you call me sir. You understand?"

"Yes! Yes, *sir!*"

"I doubt it."

Click!

"Christ, Christ, put the gun away, Jesus, don't do this to me!"

Murdoch was rigid with terror. His hands were clamped on the arms of the chair. In the sterile light of the hotel room, Murdoch's wristwatch was clearly visible. Tyler watched the numerals blink. He counted thirty seconds, then he lowered the pistol.

He looked at Murdoch and smiled. "We'll leave in the morning," he said.

Murdoch opened his mouth but no sound came out.

Tyler put the pistol back on the table. "Maybe you should get your things together, Mr. Murdoch."

Murdoch blinked until he realized he had been excused, the ordeal was over. Then he stood up on shaky legs, walked to the door, turned, and took a last bewildered look at Tyler before he left and closed the door behind him.

Tyler's headache was much worse.

Later, it occurred to him to look for the bullet he'd palmed; but it wasn't beside the chair, nor in his pocket, nor on the tabletop. Finally he opened the pistol and found the bullet resting in the chamber—exactly where he had led Murdoch to believe it was. Which worried him a little. It was a strange sort of mistake to have made.

■   ■   ■

Murdoch lay awake for what remained of the night with the door of his hotel room locked and chained—eyes open, because when he closed them he saw the barrel of Tyler's service revolver pointed at him.

Or Soo Constantine, pale and naked in a darkened room.

Or an empty human skin littering the doorway of an old house.

Dear God, he thought, what if Tyler had shot him? He wouldn't be a skin. He'd be a corpse. A messier object, as Soo had pointed out.

She'd talked about the missing people as if they had really gone somewhere. Had they? True, the Travellers had promised that. The memory of Contact was vague in Murdoch's mind, a dream that paled by daylight. But he remembered the promise of a new kind of life, both physical and bodiless . . . an idea that had made sense, somehow, in the intensity of Contact.

It's not too late, Soo had said.

And why did the words linger on?

Was he actually *tempted* by the offer? Was such a thing possible?

But that's terrible, Murdoch thought: I don't want to be an empty skin on some empty street, like a bottle somebody drained and threw away.

It's something they choose.

No. Bullshit, Murdoch thought.

But she hadn't seemed like a liar.

He tried to imagine himself travelling on with Tyler, watching the old man sink into outright lunacy, firing missiles at something, anything—trying to make sense of the world by dismantling it.

Christ, Murdoch thought miserably, I don't even know where I am! I couldn't find this town on a map. Loftus? Where *is* it?

I'm lost, Murdoch thought.

Rain tapped on the window.

He tossed and slept a little in the last hour before dawn.

■   ■   ■

Tyler woke regretting the incident of the night before and tried to act as if it hadn't happened. He knocked on Murdoch's door and asked for some help loading up the Hummer. Murdoch nodded—both of them a little sheepish, Tyler thought, in the sober light of morning—and began to assemble the cooking gear.

They carried their personal items to the street, around the corner to the Exxon station where the Hummer was parked under cover. Tyler arranged the baggage in the rear of the vehicle and made sure everything was strapped down. Murdoch, looking baleful and confused, watched from a few feet away.

Then Tyler took the passenger seat and waited for Murdoch to climb in behind the wheel. It was a conciliatory gesture, giving Murdoch the reins, a small apology for the night before.

But Murdoch didn't move. "Sir," he said, "I think I left something in the room."

Tyler took a pair of sunglasses from his breast pocket and polished them on a handkerchief. "What sort of thing, Sergeant?"

"Compass," Murdoch mumbled.

"Isn't that with the mess kit? I thought I saw it there."

"Sir, I don't think so." He made no move to look.

The air in the garage was thick. It smelled of gasoline and old solvents. This is a dark place, Tyler thought, an oppressive place.

"It was a cheap compass," he said. "We can find one like it anywhere."

"It's easier if I just go back, sir."

"Back to the hotel room?"

"Yes, sir."

Tyler understood the lie and the significance of the lie. It made him feel enormously sad—this shabby little betrayal.

"Well," Tyler said. "You'd better hurry, then, Sergeant."

Embarrassingly, Murdoch couldn't hide his relief. "Yes, sir."

"I'll be waiting."

"Yes, sir."

Colonel Tyler watched his young blond-haired friend leave the Exxon garage. Murdoch was haloed for a moment in the morning light—the rain had finally stopped—then he turned into the shadow of a taller building and was gone.

▪   ▪   ▪

Soo was in the manager's office of the Roxy, only just awake, wearing a gray sweatshirt that reached nearly to her knees. She looked up as Murdoch came through the door.

The room was different in the morning light, Murdoch thought. Sunlight came through the small, high window. The floorboards were lustrous and ancient. The mattress looked disheveled, as if the girl hadn't slept much herself.

"Soo—" he began.

"You don't have to explain, A.W. I understand." She stood up. "I know why you're here. It's okay."

He was as scared as he had ever been. More frightened than when Tyler was pointing his pistol at him. The impulse that had brought him here seemed reckless, foolish.

She moved closer.

"I don't know," he said, "I mean I'm still not sure if I—"

"It doesn't hurt or anything."

That's what they tell you about vaccinations, Murdoch thought. About dentists.

"It's just life." She touched him. She put her hands on his shoulders and tilted up her head. "A new kind of life."

And Murdoch closed his eyes and kissed her.

▪   ▪   ▪

He guessed the neocytes entered his body at that moment. There was no sensation, nothing more ominous than the touch of her lips. It reassured him that she still smelled like Soo, still tasted like Soo. The fear began to subside.

She stepped back and smiled at him. "Now we can be together, A.W. Together as long as we want."

He was about to frame a reply when three things happened almost simultaneously:

The door flew open, striking Murdoch across the ribs and throwing him aside. . . .

And John Tyler strode into the room, his pistol at arm's length. . . .

And there was a sound like the snapping of an immense tree limb, as Tyler's weapon kicked and Soo Constantine's head shuddered in an explosion of blood and tissue.

▪   ▪   ▪

Tyler put three more shots into the girl's prostrate body. Bang, bang, bang. He felt the recoil in his arm and shoulder. It felt good.

He had drawn the obvious inference from Murdoch's silences and night visits, his hysteria and his quicksilver urges to leave or stay. But look, Tyler wanted to say, consider this evidence: She can die after all. She can die as dead as any human being.

Her blood was dark, viscous, and strange, and the sight of the body mesmerized him for a time.

Then he turned and looked for Murdoch; but Murdoch had slipped out the open door.

Not good.

Tyler hurried down to the lobby and into the street.

Murdoch was a block away, frantically rattling the doors of parked cars. Murdoch had forsaken him for the girl. Murdoch himself might be infected; there had been hints, a word or two Tyler had heard through the door. *Now we can be together.*

Tyler sighted down the barrel of the pistol. Sunlight gleamed on the fenders and windows of these parked cars; Tyler moved to shade his eyes.

Murdoch caught sight of him and ducked away. The pistol bucked and the shot went wide; Tyler saw it kick dust from the brick facing of a muffler shop. Murdoch crouched and hurried on to the next car, an old Ford; Tyler walked out into the street quickly but calmly and assumed a shooter's stance.

He had begun to squeeze the trigger when the door of the Ford popped open and Murdoch ducked for the interior.

Tyler cursed but followed the motion. The pistol kicked again in his hand.

He saw Murdoch lurch as if he'd been hit—a gout of blood came from the left leg or thigh—then the car door slammed and the engine turned over twice, rattled on the edge of a stall, finally began to roar. Murdoch threw it into gear and Tyler watched helplessly as the vehicle screamed away from the curb. The Ford made a drunken swerve; its rear fender caught a lamp standard on the left side of the street, then it straightened and accelerated west.

Tyler turned and ran back to the Hummer . . . but the Exxon station was three blocks away; precious time was lost.

He drove west on the highway for an hour without sighting the Ford. Murdoch might have followed one of these dirt side roads, Tyler thought, or hidden the car in a barn, in back of a billboard, even along some back street in Loftus.

But I hurt him, Tyler thought with some satisfaction. In a place without doctors, without medical care, maybe that was enough.

It was a question of principle, Tyler thought. Murdoch had forsaken his humanity. And Tyler was better off without him. Murdoch had seen too many of his lapses. Murdoch had seen him shoot the girl. It was precisely the kind of baggage Tyler wished to leave behind.

He pulled over to the side of the road well beyond the limits of Loftus, in a patch of cool November sunlight, and listened to the silence. It was the new silence of his aloneness in this increasingly empty world. Murdoch was gone. That second voice, second self, was gone. There was only Tyler now, Tyler talking to Tyler; or those other voices, the Sissy voices, whispering from the trees, the earth, the air.

▪ ▪ ▪

Murdoch's wound was more serious than the Colonel had guessed.

The bullet entered his hip, shattered a wedge of bone, and opened a raw round exit wound. Blood instantly soaked the seat of the Ford. The pain was blinding; but Murdoch was sustained by the vivid memory of Soo Constantine dead under the barrel of Tyler's gun.

He drove two blocks at high speed, turned right, and rolled into the first empty garage he spotted.

The car wouldn't be invisible here, but it might be inconspicuous in the shadows. Murdoch didn't have a choice. It was stop now or pass out on the street. The car came up the driveway too fast; he fumbled his right foot ineffectually between the gas and the brake pedal; the Ford coasted into the garage and collided with a stack of pineboard shelves. Murdoch fell against the steering wheel as a pair of garden shears dented the hood of the car and a can of Varsol cracked the windshield.

He managed to turn off the engine before he slipped into unconsciousness, curled in the hot salt smell of his own blood.

▪ ▪ ▪

The Helper responded promptly to the distress of a soul in transition.

The transition had hardly begun; but the neocytes in Murdoch's body broadcast the terrible news of the organism's impending death.

Moments after Tyler ran west in the M998, bouncing over buckled tarmac and hunting vainly for Murdoch's Ford, the reconstructed Helper moved from its place in the center of Loftus and glided to the garage where Murdoch was dying.

It came up swiftly along the driver's side of the car and stopped there. The only sound was the drip of dilute Prestone from the Ford's cracked radiator.

The Helper was many awarenesses, some of them human. One of them was Soo Constantine, who had recently been killed by Colonel John Tyler. Her distress was its distress.

The Helper looked at Murdoch's bloody organism with pity and grief.

If he died—and he was nearly dead now—Murdoch would be dead forever. There hadn't been time to engineer a transition, to grow a second Murdoch for the Murdoch-essence to inhabit. There was only this fragile plasmic Murdoch with a scant few neocytes inside him. The neocytes had only reproduced a few tens of tens of times. They had not mapped or expanded Murdoch in any significant way.

But Murdoch had made his choice. This was an involuntary death, which the Travellers found abhorrent.

The Helper made an arm and reached out to the window of the car. The window glass shattered and fell away in a fine gray powder. The arm extended further, reached inside the car to Murdoch and touched his damaged body.

Mass surged inward from the body of the Helper, which was proportionately diminished. Multiple millions of its subunits anticipated new tasks—sealing broken blood vessels, containing and fostering the spark of plasmic life.

Soon Murdoch was covered in what appeared to be a featureless black cocoon.

The cocoon was motionless; Murdoch was motionless inside it. Prompt and feverish activity had begun, but it was internal and below the threshold of perception. Superficially, nothing changed.

Days and nights passed. The sky outside the open garage roiled with clouds.

Periodically, that December, there was lightning.

▪ ▪ ▪

Murdoch woke in January.

The Helper had retreated; he was alone in the car. He opened the door and staggered out into dim daylight.

The sky was gray and threatening. The weather was bleak and dangerous everywhere that winter; he had been warned about storms.

The neocytes were still at work inside him. Murdoch could have chosen to move directly into his new life, his virtual life; but he wasn't finished with the flesh . . . Tyler's gunshot had interrupted him.

There were things he wanted to see.

He couldn't say precisely what things—literally *could not say*, to himself or to anyone else. In the aftermath of his injury, he had very nearly died; the flow of blood to the brain had been interrupted for too long. The neocytes were reconstructing that tissue, but much of their work was conjectural and slow, elaborating the holon of Murdoch's self from its fragmented parts. He was himself, but he was inarticulate and he didn't trust himself to drive; too much neuromuscular memory remained unreconstructed.

Mute, he walked in the direction of the setting sun.

■   ■   ■

He walked for weeks.

His legs were unnaturally strong and his stamina seemed unlimited. The weather was only a minor hindrance, and his wordless contact with the Artifact helped him anticipate and avoid the worst winds and lightnings. He sheltered in abandoned buildings, storm cellars, gullies.

Some nights he slept in the rain. His body had been changed on the inside; extremes of hot and cold no longer bothered him. He seldom ate. He didn't need to, though he drank copiously when there was water.

He crossed the Mississippi at Cairo and passed into the prairies, where the storms were often fierce. One night, crouched in a pipe section where a four-lane bypass had been abandoned in mid-construction, he watched a blizzard unroll from the western horizon like a flat white wall. The wind made a sound like freight trains passing through the sky. After midnight, when the snow had almost blocked the pipe at each end, a wild fox—drenched and miserable—crept inside with him. The fox was terrified of Murdoch but more terrified of the blizzard. Murdoch strengthened his tegument and let the fox chew harmlessly on a finger until the animal was exhausted and no longer afraid of him. Then he cradled the fox against the warmth of his body until both of them were asleep.

In the morning it was gone, but Murdoch was startled and pleased that he had remembered the name of the animal during the night. *Fox:* the animal was a *fox*. He said it out loud. "Fox!"

It made his throat hurt. He didn't care. The pleasure of speech was almost unbearable.

"Fox!"

He walked west and north along a road shrouded in glittering blue-white snow.

"Fox!" he exclaimed from time to time, and the word fell away across the empty winter farmland. "Fox, fox, *fox!*"

▪ ▪ ▪

Late that winter, Murdoch passed through Kansas and crossed the state border into Colorado, where he glimpsed for the first time the thing he had come all this distance to see: the Home he had heard about from the Travellers.

This was what had drawn him, this was his reason for clinging to the flesh. Some stubborn fraction of A.W. Murdoch had wanted to see this miracle with his own eyes.

From a great distance it looked like a mountain, a curvature of blue and white nearly lost in the haze of the horizon.

It was Murdoch's good fortune that the skies had cleared in the eastern lee of the Rockies. With a little more luck, the weather would hold until he was closer. But distances were hard to calculate with such an object. How many more miles to go? How far to the horizon, and how far beyond that?

He walked a day and a night and another day and another night.

Words returned to him piecemeal as the days passed and his neural tissue was restored. The effect was sometimes comic, as when Murdoch would suddenly halt along the verge of an empty road, point his index finger, and announce to the heedless air some newly acquired noun—"*Window!*" or "*Fence!*"

Proper names were more elusive. He could barely pronounce his own. "Murdoch," he said, but it sounded clumsy and grotesque. Nor could he remember the name of the girl he had met in Loftus, though the memory was vivid and he often felt her silent presence. Maddeningly, the name lingered on his tongue but couldn't be coaxed from his mouth. "Suh-suh-suh . . . " He worked at it, day after day, until his jaw was sore.

Home stood on the horizon, closer now. It drew the eye irresistibly, a miraculous blue pearl capped with white. The white was snow. Like a mountain, Home rose more than 50,000 feet into the rarified air, up where it was always cold, where the snow never melted.

The Travellers had explained to him, wordlessly but vividly, how the creation of Home had begun. Months ago, on the eve of Contact, a single microscopic neocyte—a kind of seed—had come to rest on this plain of dry, rolling land where Colorado met Wyoming. Instantly, the Traveller organism had begun to reproduce itself. One made two, two made four, four made eight—in less than an hour, a million; two million; four million. The organisms grew themselves from the constituent parts of soil, sand, water, air, and light. When their numbers were large enough—uncountably, inconceivably large—they organized themselves into machines, into devices as big as cities.

Home required immense tonnages of raw matter. The building machines began by digging into the earth, cratering the prairie and displacing the antelope herds. But that was only a modest first step. As Murdoch approached, he felt a series of rhythmic tremors. Under the imponderable substance of Home, he knew, a conduit had been opened into the magma of the earth itself.

The days remained clear, but a cold wind blew steadily from the west. Murdoch felt weaker, the farther he walked.

He understood that he couldn't get as close to Home as he might have liked. It wasn't a healthy environment. The wind, curling around a sphere more than thirty miles in circumference, created a turbulence that could sweep him off his feet. Deadly gases vented from the magma tap, and the heat at the cratered base was well beyond human tolerance.

But he could get a little closer than this.

"Suh," he pronounced. "Suh—suh—"

It wasn't good enough.

■　■　■

The snow came back that night.

It was a hard, granular snow, difficult to walk through. Murdoch slept in an empty Best Western motel, in a hallway away from windows that had been broken by the winter storms, and walked on in the morning. His compass—he had pocketed it in Loftus—and his road map kept him aimed in the right direction.

But Home was hidden by the weather.

The weather settled in and showed no inclination to change. He walked for three days blindly . . . walked until he was forced to stop by a violent tremor and a wind so sulfurous and hot that it melted the snow on the ground.

Murdoch felt himself growing lighter. When he was finished here, there was no reason to cling to the flesh; he understood that. But he worried that the process might be happening too quickly, that he would be gone before the weather cleared.

He curled under a tarpaulin in the rear of a gas station . . . drifting in and out of sleep, listening to the hard snow sift across the roof, the gas pumps, the empty road.

▪   ▪   ▪

Time passed. He couldn't have guessed at day or month; knew only that it was after midnight when the snow stopped.

He woke to a blanketing silence, stood up stiffly, and hurried outside.

The clouds had passed on. There were stars—vivid prairie stars—and a few, faint streaks of cirrus.

And Home.

Murdoch caught his breath.

It was a wall that dominated the sky. Perspective made it seem truncated, a looming dome about to tumble over and crush him. A crescent of snow at its apex reflected the starlight, but most of that part of the sphere was a occluded by its nearer slope. The lower section of Home wasn't solid; it was a gridwork, a lace of bone-white struts and spars, as fine, from Murdoch's vantage, as spider silk; but each one must be immense, he thought, columns as wide as towns, as long as highways.

It was illuminated from within by the light—many miles away—of the magma tap, and by the luminescence of the earth's own toxic gases, pearlous and strange.

Periodically, balls of blue lightning seemed to flow and stutter along the countless struts and spars of the structure. And there was a sound—a distant, continuous thunder that had been obscured by the snow, but echoed now, in the cold night air, across the plain.

A wind blew, and Murdoch anchored himself between the pillars of the gas pumps.

Here was the strangest and most beautiful thing he had ever seen. He felt both fragile and grateful; he had been lifted up, exposed to the elements, abandoned to this vision. His uniform was a rag. He felt his own tenuous existence flickering inside it. This was the moment he had saved himself for.

He opened his mouth to make some exclamation, to vent his human awe. But what came out was: "Suh—suh—Soo!"

He felt her presence.

He felt it so strongly that he looked left, looked right. He was alone, of course. She was with him, but not here; with him in the new life.

He was rising now. He was lighter than air.

Murdoch gazed at the Home growing out of the plain, at its astonishing size and its interior lights and its reflection on the snowy plain.

"Soo," he said faintly, proudly.
And she reached for him.

▪   ▪   ▪

The wind took what was left of Murdoch, took his rags and his skin and carried them away, up beyond the snowbound Colorado flatlands, up and away from the mountains.

Chapter 22

Flesh

On a windy afternoon late in January, Tom Kindle found a human skin snagged on the leafless azalea bush outside his front door.

The skin had been carried some distance by the wind. It was tattered and incomplete, bleached by the weather to so colorless a shade that Kindle thought for a moment it was some old ghost that had fetched up on his doorstep.

Kindle studied the object for a time, then ducked back into the warmth of the house and telephoned Matt Wheeler.

■   ■   ■

Matt drove the short distance to Delmar Estates with his black bag on the car seat beside him. Not that this was a doctor's job, if he had understood Tom Kindle correctly. A coroner's, perhaps.

He examined the skin where it was trapped in the naked branches of the azalea, his expression fixed but emotionless. Then he looked at Kindle. "Do you have a pair of tongs?"

"Pardon me?"

"Kitchen tongs. Barbecue tongs."

"Well . . . I think Abby brought over a pair. Hang on." He disappeared into the house and returned with a pair of kitchen tongs. The handles were cartoon-blue plastic; the business end, stainless steel. Matt used them to lift the tattered skin away from the spindly bush and carry it into the garage, out of the reach of the wind.

He laid out the tissue with some care across the gasoline-stained concrete floor, unfolding it meticulously, layer by layer, until it resembled a nearly transparent pair of body tights torn beyond any utility. One leg ended in frayed nothingness at the knee. One arm was missing entirely. The head—there was very little of the head.

Kindle stood well back. "I wonder who the hell it is? I mean—*is* it somebody, like a corpse? Or just a *piece* of somebody?"

Matt crouched over the object. It didn't frighten or disgust him—he had encountered worse things as an intern. But he was careful not to touch it with his naked hands. "This is the first one I've seen."

"First?" Kindle cocked his head. "There are others?"

"You should have come to the meeting Sunday night. Bob Ganish found a couple of them in his neighbor's house. Paul Jacopetti says the farms out in his area are all empty—except for these."

"Jesus, Matthew! Empty *skins*?"

He nodded.

"What about the people *inside*?"

"Gone."

"Gone where?"

Matt shrugged.

"So," Kindle said, "does *everybody* end up like this?"

"I think so. Eventually. Except us, of course. Abby said she's worried about her husband, her grandchildren. She says they're getting . . . well, thinner. Paler."

"Jesus," Kindle repeated. "What about—"

He checked himself. But the question was obvious. *What about Rachel?*

Matt couldn't bring himself to form an answer, not even to himself.

Kindle looked back at the fragile envelope arrayed on the floor of the garage. "Matthew, is there something—I mean, what should I do with it?"

"Put it outside. Let it blow away. It won't last long. A few days in the sun and it'll turn to dust."

"Not much to leave behind," Kindle said.

"What is?"

• • •

He drove home to Rachel.

She had arrived at the house this morning and hinted that it might be her last visit. Matt made the obvious connection between this and the discovery of the skins throughout Buchanan. But it was an impossible thought, a thought he must not allow himself. The image of a dry shell of Rachel, of his daughter, abandoned to the wind, lonely and empty in the cold rain—dear God, not *this*.

He told her what the call from Tom Kindle had been about. He described the skin, described it clinically, made himself the Doctor Machine, because this was his last defense, his only defense. And when the telling was done, he shook his head, dazed at his own story. "It isn't human, Rachel. I know what you've said. But this isn't—it isn't something human beings do."

He expected an argument. She only nodded. "Maybe you're right."

She was pale, somehow ethereal; she moved with a certain new lightness—and these observations, too, Matt didn't care to mark or consider.

"Maybe too much has changed. Maybe the word 'human' doesn't apply anymore." Her voice was solemn. "I don't feel different—not *basically* different. The basic part of me is still Rachel Wheeler. But there's more now. More layers. More ways of seeing things. If I leave this behind—" Gesturing at herself, her body. "Am I Rachel? Am I human? I don't know."

She might have been confessing to some disease, some terrible wasting illness.

She seemed to feel the thought. Lately she had seemed able to interpret the smallest nuance of his expression, although he was laboring to conceal his grief.

"Daddy, I'm not sorry. About any of it. You're a doctor—you know how many lives were saved. Even at the local hospital, how many terminal cancers were cured? How much heart disease? And in the world, my God, all the starvation, the malnutrition, the crippled lives—"

But Matt could not dispel the memory of the skin that had fetched up, a pathetic and unassailable statement of grim fact, on Tom Kindle's leafless azalea bush. "Rachel, is this *better*?"

"Yes." Firmly. "We couldn't have gone on, you know, the way we were. The planet wouldn't support us. We were damaging it beyond recognition, beyond its ability to recover. Something had to change, something *human* had to change. Do you know who said yes to Contact? Who accepted the offer of eternal life? Almost everybody. Everybody—including dictators, pickpockets, child molesters, murderers . . . people who killed people for their wristwatches, killed them for their tennis shoes. People who tortured children to death in front of their parents. But it was immortality with a price. They had to understand what it means to hurt someone, to damage someone. And if that didn't work, if they could witness human pain and understand it intimately and *still not care*, or worse, enjoy it—that meant they were flawed, broken, not complete. So they had to be repaired."

"They can't choose to commit violence?"

"Anyone can choose anything. But only if they understand what they're choosing and why."

"Rachel . . . it sounds like compulsion."

"Daddy, you've told me since I was a baby that there's no good reason for all the wars, all the bullying, all the hurt in the world."

It was what one told a child. And, pressed, he would have admitted to believing it himself. But the fact was—as Scott Fitzgerald had written, if Matt remembered his American Literature correctly—the fundamental decencies were parceled out unequally at birth. "There's no excuse for it. But people don't seem to know that."

"Now they do."

"You can't change human nature, Rachel—not without taking away the thing that makes people human."

"Then we're *not* human. In a way, that was always the point. Humanity was reaching its limits, facing problems we couldn't even begin to solve in the usual human way—global problems, planetary problems. And the main victim of our inadequacy was *us*! Our *children*! They were already dying by the millions in Africa, and we were too human to do anything about it!"

Matt bowed his head. This was true, of course. The Contactees had done a better job. At least in the short term. "But what were they saved for, if their humanity wasn't saved?"

"But it wasn't *lost*, either, just outgrown. Do you know what we're building? Has anyone told you? A spaceship. An Artifact of our own. A human one. Daddy, do you know what's inside it? The Earth is inside it. Not literally, of course. But a model of it. *All* of it, every leaf of every tree, every mountaintop. . . ."

A memory of this was mingled with his own fading memory of Contact. "You mean a simulation. Like a computer program." Or a paperweight, he thought: the Earth, in a globe of water, with snowflakes.

"More than a simulation. It's a place, as real as this place, except that it doesn't occupy a physical space. It's alive in a very real way. It has winds. It has seasons. We're human enough to need that—not just immortality, but a place to live."

"Even if it's an illusion?"

"Is it? Is an idea an illusion? Is the value of pi a hallucination, just because you can't touch it?"

"Rachel, it's not really the Earth."

"No one pretends it is. No matter where we stand, we'll know that. Because there will always be a door, not a physical door, but a sort of direction, a way to turn, and through the door is always the bigger world, all our knowledge and the knowledge we inherited from the Travellers—the *epistemos*, people are calling it; the idea-world."

"We might have done it by ourselves," Matt said. "Given time. If we'd survived a couple of centuries without vaporizing ourselves, without poisoning the planet, we might have moved into space. Maybe it seems trivial, but we walked on the moon without anyone's help. Given time, maybe we could have met the Travellers on their own terms."

Rachel's eyes widened. "What a terrible thought!"

"Is it?"

She frowned. "Daddy . . . I know more human history than I used to. It's an ugly parade. Infanticide, bloody warfare, human sacrifice—those are the *norm*. They're not exceptional at all. And modern history is no better. When I was in school, we studied Roman history and we pretended to be horrified by it. The Romans left unwanted children to die by the side of the road, did you know that? How horrible. Well, it *is* horrible . . . but compared to what? The century of Auschwitz, of Hiroshima and the Khmer Rouge? Going into space wouldn't have civilized us. We'd have had our robots disemboweling Moslems on the surface of Mars. You *know* we would."

"Is that how the Travellers saw it?"

"Yes. And it terrified them. There's no monopoly on power or knowledge. Given time, given our own survival, maybe we *could* have stopped them . . . destroyed them before they got close enough for Contact."

"And that's why all this is happening? Not because they're doing us a favor. It's self-defense."

"In part. But they didn't have to go to all this trouble. They had the means to exterminate us. That would have worked, too."

The coldness of the statement made him feel both frightened and ashamed.

He took a long look at Rachel: who used to be his daughter, who used to be a human being.

"There wasn't just brutality, Rachel. People lived lives—small, useful lives. Sometimes helped one another. Often loved one another. There was beauty. Sometimes there was even decency."

Her expression softened. "Daddy, I know. *They* know. The Travellers know that about us." She paused. "That's why they *couldn't* exterminate us."

"Only change us."

"Yes. Change us."

A silence filled the room.

• • •

Rachel left the house before midnight, after her father had fallen asleep on the sofa.

She had wanted a better goodbye, but she supposed there was no way to say what she meant—no words to encompass her grief and fear.

She loved her father enormously and hated the idea of abandoning him to an empty planet . . . abandoning him to die.

A cold rain had begun to fall and the wind in the street was sharp and gusty. Rachel adjusted herself so that the temperature ceased to be unpleasant. Then she paused—alone among dark houses—and listened to the trees talk their sibilant winter language.

The wind lifted her hair and waved it behind her like a sad flag. Overhead, high above the streetlights, midnight clouds tumbled and dipped.

It was a stormy night, and there was worse to come. Although it was winter in the northern hemisphere, temperature gradients in the tropical oceans had risen dramatically; winds in the upper atmosphere had shifted. North and east of Hawaii, a low-pressure cell, a vast and powerful weather-engine, had begun to churn above the turbulent ocean. A typhoon—unheard of, this time of year. But all things were new.

Her father would learn about the storm soon enough, because he had begun to talk to the Helper.

Still, Rachel thought, he was so *fragile.* . . .

She wondered why he had resisted the offer of immortality—why *anybody* had. But she didn't submit the question to the Greater World, where there might have been an answer; she didn't want to dwell on it more tonight.

There was not much left of her time on the cradle Earth, and Rachel wanted to make the most of these hours.

Not everyone relished the flesh. Many had already abandoned it— whole towns, in some cases, some as large as Buchanan. Buchanan itself was largely empty and would be emptier by the day. But some chose to linger . . . a leavetaking made strange by personal transformation, in some cases, like the group hidden in the basement of the high school, some forty strong, who had elected to share each other's memories in every detail. They were there still, cross-legged on the floor and welded at the fingertips; motionless, enraptured, waiting to surrender their joined flesh in a single communal act.

Others—mainly but not exclusively the young—just wanted to play a little longer on the surface of the Earth . . . stay up past bedtime, do what had been forbidden.

Rachel encapsulated her grief and set it aside. She focused all her attention on this January night—the bite of rain on her exposed skin, trickle and drip of water in storm drains, creak of tree limb, rush of wind.

She hiked through the maze of tract housing that had overgrown the northern foothills of Mt. Buchanan. Rainwater streamed off the shingles of silent houses, empty houses where abandoned human skins were crumbling to dust. She paused at every high cul-de-sac that allowed a view. The rain obscured much, but there were still a few lights in Buchanan itself, lonely and far and fog-obscured. And she could sense as much as see the ocean, feel its enormous mass troubled by the climatic adjustments the Travellers had begun to perform.

She was wet to the skin. Her clothes were sodden and heavy. But none of that mattered. It was a cold rain, Rachel knew, but the touch of it was soothing, like the rain that carries away the heat of a summer day.

She walked toward Old Quarry Park, where sleepless others had gathered by unspoken mutual consent to share the pleasure of the night.

It was a long walk, nearly two hours by foot from her father's house, but Rachel finished it without weariness. She was lighter and stronger than she had ever been before. A year ago, a hike this long in this weather would have left her exhausted and ill. Tonight there was no fatigue at all; only a growing excitement, a first tremulous presentiment of joy.

She followed an empty access lane into the deep green darkness of the park.

But it was not a complete darkness even in the rain, even at two o'clock on a January morning. A faint light radiated from the low wrack of clouds. Douglas firs tossed in ponderous slow motion, like the masts of ancient sailing ships. The rain was everywhere, a silvery presence on lips and skin.

Figures moved in the dim light.

Not human, Daddy had insisted, and Rachel supposed that was especially true here. In the human history of Buchanan, there had never been such a gathering on such a raw January night. Before Contact, no one had come to smell the wet winter earth and walk among the mossy winter trees; no one had come for the caress of flesh against flesh—at least not in the cold, not fearlessly, not openly. It wasn't human.

But it seemed very human to Rachel, who had recently been studying the Travellers. The Travellers in their organic form had been almost incomprehensibly strange. She had seen them in borrowed and ancient memories: porous antlery creatures like mobile sponges, slow in the thick atmosphere of their chilly moon. Like humans, their bodies had been cellular in structure, but there the resemblance ended. The Travellers were uninucleate and genetically haploid, more like algae than animals. A mature

Traveller was a colony of secondary systems—as if human beings were assembled from cultivated crops of livers, hearts, lungs, brains. The parts reproduced independently of the whole. For the Travellers, "sex" was a series of protracted, continuous events . . . they spoke of karyogamy the way people talked about middle age.

Human sex had seemed to the Travellers equally strange: a grotesquely foreshortened reproductive whirlwind, allied to something like a repeatable religious trance.

But they understood pleasure. Rachel remembered some of their slow, protracted pleasures. She remembered a glade of crystalline fans, warmed by pale sunlight and enriched by volcanic vents of gaseous water, where an ancient Traveller whose name was a shape had come to bask and root. She remembered the pleasure of hyphae uncoiled in a solitary erotic flowering. The pleasure of germinal sterigmata scattered in glittering clouds to the tidal wind.

Rachel left her soaking-wet clothes at the entrance to the park. Bodies moved along the grassy green, or timidly, like fawns, among the trees. The emerald light made these people seem golden and diffuse.

Rachel opened an eye to the Greater World and saw them, not just as surfaces, but as lives; as shapes of lives, complex and many-colored. She longed for their touch.

She found a man whose life-shape was a pleasing, temperate complexity—his name was Simon Ackroyd, and he had once been the Rector of the Episcopal Church, but he was something else now, a creature as fresh on the Earth as herself.

Infinitely light, lightly wedded to her skin, Rachel touched and joined his rain-wet flesh in the shadows of the great trees, in the cold air after January midnight on the surface of the cradle Earth.

■ ■ ■

The rain stopped falling sometime after dawn. Matt woke from a fitful sleep on the living room sofa and noted the absence of his daughter and the silence of the rain.

At noon, Tom Kindle and Chuck Makepeace arrived in Chuck's Nissan. Committee business: The three of them drove to the municipal reservoir at the northeastern end of town.

Next to the stone slope of the reservoir was a white limestone building, the filtration plant, a WPA project as old as the Roosevelt administration. Set in a wide, rolling lawn, it looked to Matt like the temple of some serene religion.

The three men sat in the car gazing at the building from the gravel parking lot, Kindle taking long pulls on a can of Coke. Together they were the Public Works Subcommittee, and their job was to report on the condition of water and power resources inside the county line. Starting here. But none of them seemed to want to move from the car just yet.

All three had recently been spooked. Kindle had found the human skin snagged on his azalea bush just yesterday. Makepeace had discovered a similar relic in a neighbor's house. And Matt was still troubled by Rachel's visit last night . . . worried that he might not see her again; or that, if he did, she might be changed beyond recognition.

But these were common fears and none of the men spoke about them.

Last night's rain had left a high, cool overcast. The filtration plant, with its whitewashed steel doors, waited with infinite patience in the green.

Kindle said, "You ever see *The Time Machine?*"

"No," Makepeace said.

"In the movie, the time machine gets carried off into this building where the Time Traveller can't find it. Morlocks are in there. Nasty, ugly people. Big old building."

"You have a point?" Makepeace asked.

"Looked like *this* building." Kindle tipped back his Coke. "Funny how they used to build public works in the old days. Like you ought to wear a toga to go inside."

"You guys are pretty thoroughly out to lunch," Makepeace said. "I hope you're aware of that."

Chuck Makepeace, former City Councilman, former junior member of the town's second most prestigious law firm, was still wearing three-piece suits. To Matt this seemed deeply neurotic, like formalwear on a lifeboat, but he kept his opinion to himself.

"I was inside there once," Matt said. "School trip. About twenty-five years ago."

"Oh?" Kindle said. "What's it like?"

"There's a double row of filtration tanks and a walkway in between. I remember a lot of big-diameter pipes and valves."

"You know how any of it works?"

"Nope."

Makepeace laughed. "It points up the stupidity of this whole expedition. We don't know what to look for and we won't know what it means when we see it."

"Not necessarily," Kindle said. "If we go in there and everything's humming along, we tell the folks they can use the kitchen faucet a while longer. On the other hand, if the floor's under water and the pipes are broken, we can all put a bucket on the roof and pray for rain."

"Let's get it over with, then . . . if you're finished with that soda."

Kindle drained the can and tossed the empty into the backseat.

"Hey," Makepeace said, "don't litter my car!"

"You can get a new car," Kindle said.

■　■　■

Kindle had brought a big iron crowbar with him. The filtration plant was liable to be locked and nobody knew where the maintenance people had gone, much less their keys. But when Matt approached the windowless steel door he found it standing ajar.

Inside was darkness.

No one wanted to reach out and yank the door wide. Certainly Matt didn't. He heard the muted thump of machinery inside, like a massive heartbeat.

Kindle said, "Did it always sound like that?"

"Maybe," Matt said. "I was ten years old when I came here last. It could have changed."

Privately, he thought: No, it wasn't like that. It had been quiet. This was a high reservoir; the tanks were gravity filters.

"Sounds like Morlocks to me," Kindle said.

"Jesus!" Makepeace said. "Open the damn door!"

Matt tugged it wide. Moist air gusted out.

There was no light in the great windowless space inside. Once there had been banks of lamps suspended from the ceiling. No more.

"Got a flashlight in the car," Makepeace said.

"Get it," Kindle said.

Makepeace ran for the cherry-red Nissan while Matt and Kindle took a tentative step through the doorway. Neither of them spoke until Makepeace arrived with the flashlight.

The beam probed the farther darkness—once systematically, once wildly.

The filtration plant didn't look the way it had looked during Matt's fifth-grade field trip. What had once been copper pipe was now a tangle of fibrous tubing, columns thick and knotted as mangrove roots sweating condensation into the warm interior air. Much of the floor was occupied by a black dome, a pulsating hemisphere attached by ropy ventricles to the looming black filtration tanks.

From this dome came the building's heartbeat—periodic kettledrum throbs, like a distant organic thunder.

And the room *smelled* strange. Maybe that was the worst of it, Matt thought. It was not a bad smell, but it was wholly alien—as penetrating as nutmeg and as rich as garden loam.

Silently, the three men backed out into the cold January noon.

■   ■   ■

Chuck Makepeace drove the coast road back into Buchanan, not talking much, his hands clenched on the steering wheel. The road had grown potholes over the winter; the little Nissan bucked and jumped.

"All I want to know," Kindle said, "is what's it *doing* there?"

"My guess?" Matt said. "It's filtering and pumping water. That's all. There aren't enough people to maintain essential services, so the Travellers grew a machine to do it. If we check out the power company we'll probably find something similar operating the local grid—all the way back to the power plant."

"Why would they be so interested in keeping Buchanan going?"

"I don't suppose it's only us. If they're running utilities in Buchanan, they must be doing the same for every other city." Hoover Dam, Grand Coulee Dam, all the nuclear plants, all our little engineering miracles: He imagined tangled black machines operating the massive turbines. No one had put these devices there; they had just grown, like weeds.

"Matthew, do you suppose all our water flows through that thing?"

"It appears to."

"Well, Jesus—I *drank* that water!"

"I don't think they mean to poison us. They could have killed us a long time ago if they'd wanted to."

Exterminated was the word Rachel had used.

They could have *exterminated* us.

"But it's control," Kindle said. "That much is obvious. If they can turn off the lights and shut off the water, they can tell us what to do. . . . We depend on them."

"Do we? You can dig a well. Nobody's stopping you."

"We could dig wells and press lamp oil, but we aren't going to, 'cause the faucets still work and the lights are still on. So why do *you* guess they did it? Civic spirit?"

"Maybe," Matt said. "Maybe because it's easy for them, so why not? You remember Contact. I don't like the fact that they're here, and I don't like what they've done, but I don't think they did it because they hate us."

"You believe that?"

He shrugged. "That's what it felt like."

"Sure it did. But only a really lousy lie is gonna *feel like* a lie. The best lies feel like God's own truth. That's the point. And anyway . . ."

Matt looked at the older man. "Anyway what?"

"Even if they're Jesus and Buddha in one happy package . . . who says I *want* 'em working for me? I mean, how does this go? We get water because the Travellers favored us with a big ugly pump? If it's a dry spell, do we pray for rain? And if we do, do they send some along?" He shook his head. "I don't happen to believe in God, Matthew, but if I did, I think I'd prefer the one that works in mysterious ways His miracles to perform. Pray for rain, in other words, but keep the tanning butter handy. It's more human."

"We'll get rain enough to suit," Chuck Makepeace said, running a red light at the vacant intersection of Commercial and Marine. "I understand there's a mother-bitch of a winter storm on the way."

Kindle gave him a sharp look. "How would you know that?"

■   ■   ■

It turned out Chuck Makepeace had heard the news the same way Matt had: through the agency of the Helper.

Twice since Christmas, Matt had gone to stand before that motionless obsidian giant. He had asked it questions: about the Travellers, Rachel's transformation, the future of Buchanan.

The Helper had answered concisely in a sedate baritone of neutral accent. Beyond that, it had no discernible personality. It spoke to Matt in colloquial English, but he didn't doubt that it would answer an Iranian in Farsi or a Brazilian in Portuguese.

It was Rachel who had first hinted to Matt about the weather, but the Helper elaborated that warning, described the new and fiercer storms spinning to life in the altered waters of the tropical seas. Matt had withheld that warning from the last meeting of the Emergency Planning Committee— there had been too much new business and the threat was safely distant—but he had planned to bring it up tonight.

But Chuck Makepeace knew as much about the weather as Matt . . . because Makepeace had talked to the Helper, too.

Matt arrived at the hospital boardroom unshaven and somewhat lightheaded, five minutes late. He had skipped dinner. Maybe lunch, too; he couldn't recall. He missed a lot of meals these days. Time seemed to slip past; his attention often wandered.

He had hoped to chair a fairly sedate meeting and introduce the storm-warning during New Business. At this point, the best and simplest strategy was to secure a shelter—maybe the basement of the hospital—and stock it with water, food, Coleman lanterns. It was an important job, but not a difficult or costly one.

But the news had arrived before him. Chuck Makepeace had heard it, and so had Bob Ganish and Abby Cushman. All three had been urged by Contactee friends or family to talk to the Helper. All three had done so. And all three had received the same warning: strange and powerful weather moving eastward from the far Pacific.

The news had spread by telephone the day before the meeting, had spread even farther in the crowd around the coffee machine before the Emergency Planning Committee was gaveled to order. Matt arrived in time to hear Tom Kindle wonder whether he was the only human being in Buchanan who wasn't having long conversations with that damn robot up at the City Hall Turnaround.

"By no means," Paul Jacopetti said. "I haven't talked to it either. Wouldn't. Not on a bet. I'm with you there, Mr. Kindle."

"That's a consolation," Kindle said.

Matt called the meeting to order. Nine people took seats and gazed at him. There was no use postponing this; he upturned the agenda and asked for debate or resolutions on the subject of the weather emergency.

Abby Cushman expressed her astonishment: "The Travellers are going to a lot of trouble to help us—as Mr. Makepeace mentioned, they're keeping our water and electricity on line—so why would they create a storm that might *kill* us? I don't understand!"

"I don't think it'll kill us," Kindle said. "Not if we're careful. As for the logic of it—Abby, by any calculation, they're a superior species. More powerful than us, at least. I knew a guy in Florida one time, ran a hospital for injured birds. He had a wild heron with a broken beak, and he worked real hard on it, taped the injury, fed the bird by hand until it was strong enough to go free. Finally he released it with a metal tab on its leg for some kind of wildlife census. Three months later, he gets back the banged-up tab with a nasty letter from the FAA: Apparently the bird got sucked into the intake of an Alitalia 747."

Abby looked dismal. "I *still* don't understand."

"Well—the heron got some nice treatment. But that bird shouldn't have jumped to any conclusions about how safe it is to deal with another species. The fact that we're getting free electricity doesn't mean the jets aren't rolling out onto the tarmac all the same."

"That's macabre and terrible," Miriam Flett announced.

Kindle regarded her mildly. "Do you disagree, ma'am?"

She thought about it. "No."

Matt proposed a shelter to be provided in the hospital basement and asked for volunteers for a Storm Precautions Subcommittee, then suggested the whole subject be tabled until there was more substantial information: "We have other business pending, after all."

Agreed, with random grumbling. Matt consulted the minutes. "Okay . . . is there a weekly report from the Radio Subcommittee?"

Joey Commoner stood up.

▪ ▪ ▪

"Radio report," Joey said.

He cleared his throat. If Matt's memory served, this was the first time Joey had spoken at a Committee meeting. Joey had dressed up for the occasion: there was nothing on his T-shirt more offensive than a tennis-shoe ad.

"This week we logged thirteen calls. Most of those were Mr. Avery Price from the Boston group or Mr. Gardner Deutsch of Toronto. Plus a few from Colonel John Tyler and some one-time contacts like a woman in Ohio and someone in Costa Rica who I didn't understand.

"Mr. Price says Boston is leaving town in a convoy, and Toronto is also going to leave tomorrow morning according to plan so the two groups can meet in Pennsylvania and travel together. He says—"

Matt banged the gavel. "Joey, *what are you talking about*? Boston is leaving Boston?" Damn it, this might be important.

Joey glared at him. "It's all written down. I'd like to just read it."

"Well—carry on. I suppose we can reserve questions until later."

Joey cleared his throat again. "The Boston and Toronto people are going to an area along the fortieth parallel, probably in Ohio, which their Helpers say will be safe from storms and where they can establish a town and a radio beacon for people to follow. They say this will attract survivors from all over the continent and they'd like us to join them as soon as we can, because there are about enough people in North America to make one good-sized town. They're carrying mobile radio equipment and they want us to let them know as soon as possible when we're going to join them.

"Also, Colonel Tyler is travelling toward the northwest looking for survivors and he'll be passing through Buchanan in a couple of months, or he can rendezvous with us on the road if we decide to join the Boston-Toronto convoy.

"End of report."

Pandemonium.

■   ■   ■

Several people wanted to pack up and leave immediately. Bob Ganish, the ex–car dealer, spoke for the group: "We can *beat* the damn storm, get across the mountains before it finds us. No offense, people, but I like the idea of seeing some new faces."

Abby raised her hand. "There are things here we'd all hate to leave . . . but maybe it's better if we do. Should we put this to a vote?"

Matt argued that they should stay in Buchanan at least for the time being—wait until the Boston group had a more solid plan, have somebody besides Joey talk to them. Weather the storm, *then* think about moving. It wasn't the kind of decision that could be made impulsively.

Privately, the idea terrified him. He didn't want to abandon Buchanan. Christ, not yet!

It was too soon to give up Buchanan. Everything was still intact, still functional, only a little tattered.

There's hope, he wanted to say. *We can salvage something. It's not over yet.*

Kindle moved to postpone debate until more facts came in—"This is the first I've heard of it, and I'm half the damn Radio Subcommittee." With a long sideways look at Joey Commoner.

The motion passed five to two.

Matt listened numbly through three more subcommittee reports and adjourned the meeting at midnight.

■   ■   ■

He wanted only to go to bed, to sleep, to table for a few hours all his own private debates.

But Annie Gates was waiting when he pulled into his driveway.

She must have walked here, Matt thought; her own car was nowhere in sight. None of these people seemed to drive anymore. He saw them walking sometimes, a curious light stride, not quite human, as Rachel might have admitted.

The sight of Annie filled him with fear.

He had avoided her for months, avoided her because she was one more component in a problem he couldn't solve . . . and because he had slept with her when she was human, loved her when she was human, an equation he didn't care to balance.

But now she scared him, because she was waiting on his doorstep under the hospitality light, dressed too lightly for the cold night air, looking at him with a terrible sympathy, terrible because it was authentic, because she was waiting to speak.

"Rachel's gone Home," Annie said. "Matt, she's not here anymore. She wants me to tell you that." Annie's voice was solemn and very sad. "She says she misses you. She says she loves you, and she's sorry she didn't say goodbye."

Annie was not human, but Matt put his head against her pale shoulder and wept.

Chapter 23

View from a Height

It was the winter the oceans bloomed with strange life.

The Travellers, perceiving the thermal imbalance of the planet and the human desire to restore it, dispatched seed organisms into the Earth's restless hydrosphere.

The organisms multiplied in the shallow surface waters. Like the phytoplankton they resembled, the new organisms fed on mineral material from the upwelling ocean currents, fed on sunlight, but fed also on the water itself, assembling themselves from atoms of hydrogen and oxygen. The ocean was food, and the Traveller organisms increased their tonnage by the minute.

As they multiplied, they began to avoid the coastal waters rich in natural diatoms. Their role in the oceanic ecology was temporary and there must always be enough phytoplankton to feed the krill. They confined their bloom to less nutrient-rich waters far from land.

They grew so numerous that autumn that in places they covered the surface water in crystalline slicks hundreds of miles in diameter, their opalescent coats bouncing rainbows from the swell.

Then they began their significant work: They began to devour atmospheric carbon and bind it to themselves, as the phytoplankton do, but more efficiently—voraciously.

The oceans combed the air of CO_2.

∎   ∎   ∎

The population of the Earth plummeted daily.

In the Greater World, a few acts remained *malum in se* but none were *malum prohibitum*. The inhibitions of a thousand generations had been swept away by Contact. The last devotees of the flesh celebrated their bodies even as their bodies grew pale and light.

They danced to silent music in abandoned mosques, made love in infinite variation in the shadows of cathedrals. They laughed and embraced and surrendered their bodies by the light of Arab sunsets, Oriental noons, African dawns.

Daily, they vanished into the Greater World; and their abandoned skins, like phantom armies, roamed the streets of Djakarta, Beijing, Reykjavik, Capetown, until they crumbled to dust and the dust was borne off by the rising wind.

▪ ▪ ▪

Matt Wheeler picked up a school notebook at Delisle's Stationery— where Miriam Flett used to buy Glu-Stiks and paper cutters before the *Observer* ceased publication in October—and began a private journal.

> According to Rachel, everyone started fresh at Contact. Basically, they entered a new state of being. It's not the Last Judgment—no sins are punished. It's not the Judeo-Christian paradise at all. More like the ancient Greek idea of the Golden Age, when men were so pious they socialized with the gods.
>
> "Everything is forgiven," Rachel said. "Nothing is forgotten."
>
> I try to believe this. It sounds noble. But what does it really mean? It's hard to imagine guys who wore Cartier watches joined in spiritual union with Third World sharecroppers. Or, much worse, men who battered their infant children to death allowed to live forever. Nirvana for mass murderers. Terrorists surviving their victims by a millennium or more.
>
> Unless they've changed, it isn't just. And if they've changed so radically—it isn't human.
>
> Rachel admitted as much. The human baggage is too unsavory to carry into a new life.
>
> She claimed the real punishment for such people is to understand what they were—to truly understand it.
>
> I suppose this is possible, though it beggars comprehension. For her sake, of course, I want it to be true.

He chewed on the end of his pencil and decided he might as well ask the big questions: There was nothing to be lost by honesty, not at this late hour.

But what about those of us who stayed behind? What made it possible or necessary for us to turn down immortality? Why are we here?

None of us seems extraordinary in any outward particular. The opposite, if anything.

What is it we have?

What is it we lack?

The next morning, Beth Porter phoned and said she wanted to be a nurse and would Matt be willing to help her?

He asked her to repeat the question. He hadn't slept much the night before . . . these days, his eating and sleeping habits didn't encourage a lucid state of mind. He'd lost fifteen pounds since November. His reflection in mirrors took him by surprise: Who was this skinny, hollow-eyed man?

"I think you should teach me how to be a nurse," Beth said. "I've been thinking about this. You're the only doctor in town, right? So maybe you need an assistant. At least somebody who knows what to do in an emergency. This storm that's coming, for instance. Say a lot of people get hurt. Maybe I could at least put on a bandage or stop some bleeding."

He closed his eyes. "Beth . . . I appreciate what you're saying, but—"

"This is not a come-on. Jesus, I hope you don't think that." Pause. "I'm serious. Maybe I can save somebody's life somewhere down the road."

"Beth—"

"I mean, I feel so useless just sitting here in this room all by myself."

He sighed. "Do you know CPR?"

"I've seen it on TV. But I don't know how to do it, no."

"You should."

■　　■　　■

Joey Commoner used the handicam he'd stolen from the Newcomb house to videotape Buchanan.

Joey had heard all this talk about the weather. If half the talk was true, there might not be much left of Buchanan in a month or so. He didn't love this ugly little bay town, but he liked the idea of saving it on videotape while it was still intact. Joey Commoner, the town's last historian.

So he drove up and down the main streets and some distance into the suburbs, guiding his motorcycle with one hand and running the camcorder with the other. He drove slowly in order to capture all the detail.

The images he played back on his basement VCR were unnerving and strange: empty streets bouncing when the Yamaha bumped over buckled asphalt; empty storefronts, empty sidewalks, empty buildings in whitewashed ranks all the way to the Marina and the cold winter sea. Empty *everything*.

It made him feel peculiarly alone. It was the feeling you might get, Joey thought, if you were locked inside some big mall at night with the mannequins and the mice.

It made him want to ride over to Tom Kindle's place and work the radio. But that was probably a bad idea; since the big cities began their migration, Joey had been edged off the radio by Kindle and Bob Ganish and that asshole Chuck Makepeace. Gimme the microphone, this is *important*. Well, fuck it. He was tired of the radio. He had better things to do than DXing foreigners who couldn't even speak English.

He videotaped some important personal places. His basement. His street. The street where Beth Porter used to live. The motel she'd moved into.

Hidden behind a highway abutment where she couldn't see him, he videotaped Beth climbing into a white Volkswagen and driving north.

Beth didn't have a driver's license. She had only started driving since Contact, and it was funny how she drove, a clumsy jerk-and-stop. He wondered where she was going.

Where was there to go?

He watched the car bump out of sight.

She might be shopping. Idly curious, or so he told himself, Joey waited a prudent few minutes and then followed on his Yamaha. He checked the empty mall lots along the highway for her car, but it wasn't there.

Visiting somebody?

So who was to visit?

Slow suspicions formed in Joey's mind.

Not that he cared what she did. He hadn't seen her much lately. He wasn't sure what Beth meant to him or used to mean to him. A few good Friday nights.

But he remembered the way she used to undress for him, shy and bold at the same time. He remembered her shrugging out of an old sleeveless T-shirt in a dark room, unbuttoning her pants with one hand while she watched him watch. The memory provoked a knot of tension in his belly. Not desire. More like fear.

He rode past Kindle's house, past Bob Ganish's ugly little ranch house. No Volkswagen.

Then he drove past the hillside house where Matt Wheeler lived.

Her car was in the driveway.

Joey parked his motorcycle in a garage half a block away. He approached the house along a line of hedges and used the camcorder's zoom to spy on the doctor's house. But the blinds had all been pulled.

He waited about two hours until Beth came out again, looking somewhat pink in the cheeks.

He taped her climbing into the car and bump-jerking away from the curb.

Bitch, Joey thought.

■ ■ ■

Among the last things Tom Kindle moved down from his mountain cabin was his Remington hunting rifle, old but sturdy.

He hadn't used it much in the last few years. Hunting in the coast forests wasn't what it used to be; too many hobby shooters had moved into what had once been some pretty secluded territory. Every autumn, the woods grew a new crop of chubby CPAs in orange flak jackets. It made for a dangerous situation, in Kindle's opinion. He didn't relish getting shot by somebody who carried his ammunition in a nylon fanny pack.

But this talk of storms and travel made him nervous, too. So he brought down the Remington and picked up some shells and took some practice shots at the knotholes of a long-dead slippery elm back of his house.

The crack of the gunshots echoed a long time in the still air; the bullets struck the decayed tree with a different and softer sound, like a mallet head hitting a fence post.

Kindle found his aim was reasonably accurate even after too many lax years. But the rifle kicked harder than he remembered. Of course it wasn't the rifle that had changed: He was getting old. There was no denying the fact. He bruised too easily, went to bed too early, and pissed too often. Old.

For shooting, he wore the corrective lenses he'd had made up a couple of years ago. Kindle was mildly myopic, which affected his aim, but the condition didn't seem to have worsened—which was good, because where were the opticians since Contact? Gone to heaven, every one.

He sighted on a circle where the bark had dropped from the tree. Squeezed off a shot and missed by what appeared to be a good half foot.

"Damn," he said, and massaged his shoulder.

He could have gone inside, where Chuck Makepeace was talking by radio to Avery Price, the Boston guy, but Kindle distrusted this business about Ohio. It was where everybody wanted to go, a new Promised Land, a Place Prepared; worse, it was where the Helpers wanted them all to go. Boston and Toronto were both travelling with Helper guides, and probably so were a bunch of small towns like Buchanan.

At least they called it *guiding*. Another word for it was *herding*. All the wild human beings were being assembled in one place—and Kindle guessed there were other such places on other continents, little reservations, little corrals. Barns. Pens.

He didn't like that idea at all.

No doubt, he thought, the promises were true. Everybody would be defended against the weather; the land would be fertile and the skies would be blue. They would all be well cared for.

Like cattle.

Cattle were well cared for.

Cattle were also slaughtered.

He put three more shots into the bole of the tree and then stopped because his right shoulder felt damn near dislocated.

The sky was a high, luminous blue brushed with cloud. The air smelled of brine. There had been ground fogs every morning for the last week. Sunsets had been wide and vivid.

If old bones tell the weather, Kindle thought, then something big was indeed about to break. The last few days he had been sleeping restlessly. This morning, he had woken up at dawn in a cold sweat. His body felt tight, as if it was braced for something.

He turned and squinted across the bay. The water was choppy, whitecaps feathering in a stiff breeze.

The ocean, Kindle thought.

Dear God, what mischief had been committed out there?

■   ■   ■

Storms were already raking the east coast as the President of the United States prepared to leave the White House.

He was alone in the building. The First Lady had abandoned her skin many weeks before. Elizabeth had been captivated by the Greater World and had wanted to explore it in greater detail, an impulse William understood; in any case, she had never liked bad weather. It frightened her.

William, on the other hand, had been a devotee of thunder, a relisher of storms.

It was not entirely his aim to relish the weather that had already begun to wreak so much destruction. There were still many mortal human beings on the surface of the Earth . . . and many of them would die, despite the best efforts of the Helpers. But it was the paradox of the senses that they did not make such distinctions. A stormy sky made his skin tingle, his pulse quicken, no matter what the circumstances.

Fundamentally, though, it wasn't the storms William wanted to see; it was the country—the nation he had once governed, if "govern" was a meaningful verb.

That was why he had clung to the flesh even after Elizabeth went Home. (Besides, she was not really absent, merely less accessible.)

Only a small minority of Contactees had retained their corporate bodies, and many of those, like William, had changed or were changing themselves in some critical way.

After all: it wouldn't do to go tramping across the landscape in an old man's cumbersome shell.

Therefore William went to bed for a week; and while he slept the neocytes altered certain genetic instructions and ran his cell division at a feverish pace. He radiated heat, and when he woke he was many pounds lighter than he had been. He was also younger.

He peered at himself in a full-length mirror and saw a face he hadn't seen since the year the Allies marched into Berlin.

What age would he have guessed this boy to be? Twelve? Thirteen?

Anticipating the change, William had obtained some clothes to fit before he went to sleep. He dressed himself in blue jeans and a T-shirt and fresh running shoes. The shoes were a little loose; he'd had to guess at the size. But how glorious.

He felt newly minted. He felt like a bright penny.

He felt restless and hungry. The White House seemed suddenly bigger and more ridiculous than ever, and he couldn't wait to get away from its stifling frills and history. He thought of all those miles of America opening out from his doorstep, a continent like a long empty beach.

William laughed a high child's laugh and ran down the steps of the Main Portico.

The sky that day was heavy and fat with clouds.

▪   ▪   ▪

By January, the albedo of the planet had risen considerably.

Traveller-engineered phytoplankton laced the surface waters of the tropics. Like crystals of fine glass, they bounced sunlight back into the sky.

Above these vast reflective ocean plains, domes of moisture-laden air punched into the troposphere. Convection clouds the shape of fists rose and flared into cirrostratus.

From orbit, the tropics resembled a fractal image, a fury of greater and lesser whorls. The air above the sea was knotted with hurricane crowns.

Individual pressure cells broke loose and travelled with the prevailing currents like tall ships of wind, wound tighter as they penetrated the cooler latitudes.

Some rode the monsoon drift into India and Asia.

Some rode the equatorial currents to Australia or Africa.

Some followed the Gulf Stream across the East Indies into the Gulf of Mexico.

A few rode the Kuroshio Current to Japan and then veered eastward, gaining new strength over the phytoplankton-heated North Pacific, and turned at last like lazy giants toward the coast of North America.

Chapter 24

Hard Rain

The storm, once a comfortably distant threat, seemed to hurry closer as the days passed.

Matt organized the men into a work crew, nailing plywood sheets over accessible windows on the first floor of the hospital and crossing the plate glass with duct tape. The hospital was a relatively new building, constructed under a strict State building code for regional emergency centers. Essentially, it was a three-story reinforced-concrete bunker. It stood on high ground in a neighborhood of middle-income residences and tall conifers. The basement contained a records room, generator room, laundry room, heating and plumbing, and a kitchen and staff cafeteria.

Matt chose the cafeteria to serve as shelter. It was a cheerless cinderblock box painted salmon pink, but it was spacious and well away from any exterior walls. Tables were shoved up against the service line to make room for mattresses and bedding. By the first Thursday in March the storm was still a day or two away, according to the Helper, but the shelter was as complete as Matt could make it, and people had already begun to truck in their valuables, protecting photographs, souvenirs, memories against the wind.

Abby Cushman served as coordinator, keeping in close touch with all nine members of the Emergency Planning Committee and relaying Helper updates. She conferred with Matt by telephone and they chose Friday at 6:00 P.M. as the hour when everyone should be in the hospital basement, doors closed, exits bolted.

"Incidentally," Abby said, "I heard about Rachel. I'm terribly sorry, Matt."

Matt accepted her condolences. Abby had recently lost her husband and two grandchildren to what Rachel had called the Greater World. For a moment, an unspoken understanding flowed between them. Then Matt was hailed by Bob Ganish, who had run out of duct tape; Abby said, "Tomorrow at six—and everybody better be there!"

■   ■   ■

The storm was preceded by strange gusts of warm air, flurries of rain, a racing overcast.

Matt had expected something sudden, a burst of weather as quick and violent as a spring thunderstorm. Tom Kindle, ferrying canned food down to the hospital kitchen, told him it wouldn't be that way. A typhoon—which was what this was, if not something even more powerful, still nameless—wasn't a localized event. It was a vortex of air, miles wide, slow at the edges, more intense as you moved toward the eye . . . or as the eye moved toward *you*. It would not come all at once; but it would come quickly, insidiously.

Friday afternoon, Matt packed up a few things at the house—the family album Rachel had cherished, Celeste's letters, a change of clothes. It wasn't much, but the act of selection was both agonizing and more difficult than he had anticipated. By the time he had the trunk full and his car on the road, his watch said 4:45.

The wind plucked at the car like a playful hand as he drove to the hospital. High clouds tumbled inland from the ocean, and the bay was so white with froth it seemed to be boiling. The roads were already littered with twigs and branches.

He parked close to the Emergency entrance but was drenched before he could dash inside with his two cartons of worldly goods. The rain was cold and the wind so intense he had to put his shoulder against the door to close it again.

The basement cafeteria, by contrast, was warm and noisy. He felt unreasonably cheered by the sight of other people, by the babble of their voices. Abby's deadline was only a quarter of an hour away. If we're all here, Matt thought, we can nail plywood over the last door and hunker down for the night. He looked for Abby Cushman, meaning to propose a final head count and a battening of the hatches—but Abby was on the phone.

It took him a second to work out the implication.

She waved him over. "It's Miriam Flett. Miriam won't leave her house—it's too stormy to drive, she says. She thinks she'll be safe where she is."

Matt checked his watch again. "How about if we send someone to pick her up? Would she be willing to go with an escort?"

"Matt, do we have time? It's getting bad awfully fast."

"Ask her if she's willing."

Abby took her hand away from the receiver. "Miriam? Miriam, how about if we *send* somebody? Somebody to drive? Because we're not sure your house is safe enough. No. But it's not just the wind, Miriam. There's the storm surge to worry about. Flooding, yes. You might be too close to the water. I know, but . . . yes, dear, but . . . but if we send someone, how would *that* be?"

Five-fifty, according to his Timex.

Abby covered the receiver again. "She's willing to go, but she wants to know who to expect."

"Tell her I'll be there in ten minutes."

"Matthew? Are you sure?"

He shrugged. "I'm already wet."

"Well—you be careful. We can't afford to lose the town doctor."

"Tell Miriam to make sure she's packed."

"All right. We won't barricade the door until you're back."

"No. But do it if you have to."

▪   ▪   ▪

Ordinarily it would have been a five-minute drive from the hospital to Miriam's bungalow on Bellfountain Avenue. Allowing for the weather, Matt had estimated twice that. Outside, he wondered whether he should have doubled it again.

Coming around Commercial, he managed to stop just short of a toppled Douglas fir. The tree was a giant, old growth left to mature next to a grocery store parking lot; its trunk obstructed the road as neatly as a fence. It would mean a detour, but not a long one: another block south and left to the highway. He backed up, sweating despite the cold.

The fallen tree made the storm seem suddenly real, an immediate danger. For Matt, a kind of emotional electricity always accompanied even a modest summer cloudburst. He used to love the sight of a storm coming in around the crest of Mt. Buchanan, the thunder rolling up the slopes. Grotesque as it seemed, maybe he had been getting the same kind of pleasure from this storm.

But the fallen tree had cut his euphoria as neatly as it divided the road. This wasn't a cloudburst or an out-of-season thunderstorm. This was something immensely more powerful, an engine wound on a column of air as tall as a mountain. It had the power to lift, to compel, to move, slash, shatter; to destroy. It could pick up his car and spin it like a top—probably would, if not now, then in an hour or two hours. It had already toppled this ancient fir, and the storm had not even begun. This was only its curtain-opener, its prelude.

He circled down to Marina with his high beams on. The storm had blotted up all but the last trickle of daylight; streetlights cast a feeble iridescence into the gloom. Every house he passed was dark. The Contactees had turned out the lights before they left, a universal primness as alien as their means of departure.

Coming toward the highway along a familiar residential road, he was startled to see a house with windows blazing yellow light . . . even more startled when he recognized it as the house where Jim and Lillian Bix had lived for the last ten years.

He looked at his watch, fretted a moment, then pulled over to the curb.

The house wasn't fortified against the storm. The windows weren't taped or shuttered. Matt hoped the building was simply unoccupied, the lights left burning for no good reason—but then he saw a shadow against the downstairs curtains, a motion there and gone again.

He sighed and climbed out of the car. He was instantly wet, wetter than before, the rain drilling through his topcoat. He ran to the shelter of the porch, knocked once, waited, and knocked again.

Jim Bix opened the door.

Matt recognized him immediately, although his friend had changed.

The last time he had seen Jim Bix was when they argued over Lillian's pregnancy, Jim insisting she didn't need prenatal medical care: the Travellers would protect her. And Jim had cut his hand, and the blood had been viscous and very dark.

Now Jim stood in the doorway, haphazardly dressed, as tall and ugly as he had ever been . . . but thinner and inhumanly pale. His skin, Matt thought, didn't look like skin at all; it looked like some much finer membrane, a transparent sheath drawn over bones as delicate as seashells. His eyes, in their china hollows, were like dusty blue marbles, as if the color of the irises had bled into the whites. The pupils, fixed and small, were the bottomless black of night shadows.

Matt thought of the empty skin he had inspected at Tom Kindle's house. It looked like his old friend wasn't far from that condition.

"Thank you for stopping," Jim said. His voice was a husky whisper. "But it's not necessary, Matt. We're fine. You should get under shelter."

He said, somewhat breathlessly, "So should you."

"Really—we're fine."

"Is Lillian here?"

Jim hesitated, still blocking the doorway.

Matt called out, "Lillian? Are you all right?"

No answer—or if there was, it was masked by the roar of the wind along the overflowing eaves.

Lillian would have been three months from her due date by now. "The baby," Matt said. "Is that why you're still here when everyone else is gone? Jim, for Christ's sake, is it the baby?"

The thing that had been Jim Bix peered frowning at him but failed to answer. Frustrated, frightened, Matt pushed past him into the house.

Jim fell away instantly from the pressure, and Matt sensed his lightness, the terrible lack of solid weight behind his ribs.

"Lillian?"

"Matt," Jim said. "It would be better if you left. Will you leave?"

"I want to see her."

"She doesn't need medical care."

"So you say. I haven't examined her since Contact."

"Matt—" His friend looked at him mournfully. "You're right. It was the baby that kept us here. Lillian wanted to finish the pregnancy. But the storm—it would be awkward to linger past tonight. This is a private moment, Matt. Please leave."

"What do you mean, finish the pregnancy? You mean she's *having the baby*?"

"Not exactly. We—"

"*Where is she?*"

"Matt, don't force this on yourself."

The front door was still open. Distantly, from somewhere down the street, came the sharp sound of a window shattered by the wind.

He felt driven by the need to see Lillian and speak to her; or, if not, to know what had overtaken her, know precisely what maze of transformation she had stumbled into. Maybe he wasn't being reasonable. He didn't care. She was his patient.

"Lillian?" He stepped into the kitchen; it was empty. "Lillian!" Shouting up the stairs.

Jim, too fragile to stop this, stood aside and gazed at him with a vast sadness in his cavernous eyes. "Matt," he said finally. "Matt, please stop. She's in the bedroom off the hallway."

He hurried there and threw open the door.

Lillian was naked on the bed.

Her ribs were stark against her papery flesh, and her eyes were as strange as her husband's, though browner. She raised her head to look at him and seemed unsurprised by his entrance.

Her legs were spread. There was no blood, but Matt recognized with horror that she had delivered . . . *something.*

It resembled a shriveled homunculus—a monkey fetus, perhaps, as preserved on the shelf of some medieval apothecary. It was quite dry, quite motionless.

His horror was overtaken by an immense, weary sorrow. He looked at Lillian. Her face was bland. She had wanted a baby very badly. "Lillian," he whispered. "Dear God."

"Matt," she said calmly. "You don't understand. This is not the baby. You must understand that. This is only an end product. The baby is with us! He's been with us for some months now. A boy. He's alive, Matt, *do you understand me?*" She tapped her head. "Alive here." And spread her arms. "Here." The Greater World.

She smiled a bloodless, paper-thin smile. "We named him Matthew."

■　　■　　■

He arrived at Miriam Flett's small house grateful for the anesthetizing noise of the storm. The roar of the wind had become so intense it was hard to think. Which was good. He didn't want to think.

Miriam met him at the door, a small woman, her spine curved with what Matt diagnosed as a mild osteoporosis. Her expression was grim. "You're late."

"I had some trouble on the way over."

"You look sick, Dr. Wheeler. Are you sick?"

"Miriam, I may very well be, but we don't have time to worry about it. We have to get you to shelter."

"I told Abby on the phone—I *have* shelter."

It was an invitation to argue that Matt did not accept. "Are these your bags?" Two pale gray Tourister cases.

"Yes," she admitted. He picked them up. "Well," she said. "All right. But they're heavy. Be careful."

He carried them to the trunk of the car, came back to help her into a bright yellow raincoat. He took her arm, but she resisted. "My journals!"

"What?" The door was open and the wind was shrieking.

"My *journals!*"

"Miriam, we don't have time!"

"We *would* have had time if you hadn't been *late!*" She stamped her foot. "I won't leave without my journals!"

Have mercy, Matt thought. How many minutes back to the hospital? And what were his chances, in that time, of staying on the road? "Damn it, we simply can't—"

"*There's no call for profanity!*" Shouting to make herself heard.

He closed his eyes. "Where are they?"

"What?"

"The *journals!* Where *are they?*"

She took him to the kitchen, where it was marginally quieter, and pointed to three shelves of bound notebooks so full of newspaper clippings they were bent as round as bread loaves.

Matt gathered up an armful.

"No!" Miriam shrieked. "They'll get wet!"

"I can carry them to the car. I can't make it stop raining."

"Don't be testy! Here." She shrugged out of her raincoat and draped it over the journals.

"Miriam—you'll be soaked to the bone."

"I'll dry out," she said.

He took her to the car, helped her inside, and piled the journals at her feet. She slammed the door to keep the rain away from the books, narrowly missing the fingers of Matt's left hand.

He climbed in behind the wheel and advised her to fasten her seat belt. The engine stuttered a little when he cranked it, as if some moisture had crept in where it didn't belong.

He said as they pulled away from the curb, "Have you talked to Abby? She must be worried."

The wipers, on double-speed, did very little to improve visibility. The road in front of him was a liquid blur.

"I would have liked to talk to Abby," Miriam said, "but the phone stopped working twenty minutes ago. Dr. Wheeler, may I ask *why* you were so late?"

"Believe me, Miriam, it isn't something you want to know."

She examined him over the rims of her eyeglasses and rendered a judgment: "Maybe you're right."

▪   ▪   ▪

He took a different route back to the hospital, longer but higher; he was afraid of flooding down by the marina. The road rose along the foothills of Mt. Buchanan and Matt was forced to crawl along in the breakdown lane, away from the winds that had begun to sweep up the hillside with devastating force. Many of the houses he passed were already windowless and the road surface was littered with broken glass. Debris rolled past the car at a constant rate—loose garbage bins, cardboard boxes, green matter.

At the apex of the drive, where the road began a descent into the hospital district, the battering rain suddenly eased. Matt spared a glance to the west. The clouds, skimming overhead at a dizzying speed, had briefly lifted. He could see the water of the bay driven up beyond the marina and nearly to Commercial Street, the hulls of overturned pleasure boats bobbing level with the roofs of warehouses and restaurants. The bay itself was a furious caldron, though calmer than the sea beyond, where waves the size of houses battered the stony southern tip of Crab Pot Island. The last daylight came from the west—seemed to come from the storm itself, a strange, weak radiance.

He turned his attention back to the road and swerved to avoid a cartwheeling tree limb. The wind made his steering awkward; it was like driving into a tide of molasses.

"Dear God," Miriam said suddenly. "Look at that."

And he looked again, reluctantly, toward the west.

Offshore, the racing overcast had begun to dimple.

Black clouds grew lazy tails, which spiraled toward the sea.

Where they touched, white foam erupted.

Waterspouts, Matt thought. He counted five of them. It was fascinating, almost hypnotic, how they moved. There was something awful about their twisting, like the lash of a cat's tail, plucking the water here and there, then lifting and falling again. Moving in the dim light. Moving toward shore.

A sudden curtain of rain obscured the view.

"Maybe you had better drive a little more quickly," Miriam said.

■　　■　　■

Everything would have been all right, Abby Cushman thought, except for the ventilator ducts.

The storm was way too big, and coming way too fast, and Matt Wheeler was still out there somewhere, hadn't even arrived at Miriam Flett's house when the phones went dead . . . and then the lights in the basement cafeteria began to dim, and Tom Kindle ambled away to some other corner of the building to start up a generator, leaving Abby alone with six more or less terrified people in the flickering dark . . . and all this would have been endurable, except for what she had begun to think of as the God Damn Noise.

She had no idea how the hospital was ventilated. She knew only that several pressed-tin ducts ran along the ceiling above the fluorescent fixtures, and that the wind had somehow penetrated these conduits. Worse, the wind had begun to play them like a pipe organ. Not any ordinary pipe organ, Abby thought, but a pipe organ for mastodons and great whales; a pipe organ that produced sounds too fundamental for the human ear, perceptible only, like fear, in the hollow of the stomach.

The God Damn Noise had begun a little after six o'clock. It was innocuous at first, almost a whisper; then above that, as the velocity of the wind increased, came an intermittent keening note—eerie, but bearable.

Then the whisper rose to shouting volume, the sound of a bathroom shower running full tilt. And other noises began to creep in along the columns of hammered tin, in particular a low wail that made Abby think, uncomfortably, of a crying child; and periodic creaks and pops, as of sheet metal stressed beyond its tolerance.

She endured that . . . though it made her feel absurd, serving Oreos and lukewarm coffee to six individuals huddled knees-to-chest on hospital mattresses on a cold linoleum floor. Pollyanna in a pantsuit. She felt like a jennyass, frankly.

But then Bob Ganish began to complain of claustrophobia: It was *too close* in here, he insisted, especially with the fluorescents out and the damn battery lanterns casting such a dreadful low light—seemed like the *air* had gone bad. So Abby had to sit with him and share her cookies and change the subject. Hey, what was the best sale he ever made down there at Highway Five Ford? The drop-dead pinnacle of his sales career? And Bob smiled nervously and launched into a description of the near-criminal flogging of a used 1990 Pinto. The monologue lasted twenty minutes, by Abby's watch, including details on the financing. All the while the ducts screaming and Abby beginning to feel that Ganish's hysteria, by some reverse osmosis, was draining into *her.*

Okay, all that, and Dr. Wheeler still out in the storm. . . .

But then the wind made a sound that was, in Abby's imagination, precisely the sound the last *T. Rex* might have made, dying in a pool of hot Cretaceous mud . . .

(—her grandson Cory had been a dinosaur buff—)

. . . and to top it all off, *that* was the moment Paul Jacopetti picked to have his goddamn *heart attack.*

■   ■   ■

Abby was startled by the sudden commotion of voices. She turned away from Bob Ganish, spilling her coffee onto his pant leg. ("Ouch, Abby, hey!")

Jacopetti lay face-up on his mattress, his hands clutched over his chest. His face was pale, and he was breathing rapidly, wheezing.

Worse, everyone seemed to expect Abby to do something about it.

She hurried to Jacopetti's mattress and crouched over him. "Paul? What is it?"

"I'm having a fucking heart attack," he gasped, "what does it look like!"

Her first impulse—she was instantly ashamed of it—was to slap him. Tell him: *Not now! This isn't the time or the place, you idiot. Have your heart attack later.*

Instead she asked, not too intelligently, "Does your chest hurt?"

"*Yes*, it hurts. Hurts like a son of a bitch." He closed his eyes and grimaced.

Abby looked up. Everyone had gathered in a circle around the mattress, their attention on Jacopetti, or worse, on her. The ventilator ducts screamed. Abby heard the sound of a window breaking, perhaps up on the second floor, a nerve-wrenching sound conducted directly into her eardrums.

She said, half to herself, "I don't know what to do." Then, as the last buckles of restraint broke loose, louder: "I don't know what to do! Stop *staring* at me!"

She felt a hand on her shoulder, gently pulling her aside—Beth Porter's hand.

Abby bit her lip but retreated from the mattress.

Dazed, she watched Beth kneeling over Paul Jacopetti.

"Mr. Jacopetti?" Beth said. "Mr. Jacopetti, can you hear me?"

He opened his eyes. "You . . . what do *you* want?"

"Mr. Jacopetti, you have to tell me what's wrong."

Perhaps the pain had gotten worse—Jacopetti seemed suddenly more malleable. "Chest hurts."

"Show me where," Beth said.

Jacopetti raised his right hand and drew a circle on his shirt above the breastbone.

"There in the center?"

Nod.

"How about your arm? Does your arm hurt at all?"

"No."

"How about your breathing?"

"Tight."

Gently, Beth levered back the man's head so his chin jutted up. "Mr. Jacopetti, I know this is a personal question, but are those false teeth?"

"Dentures," he managed. "Why?"

"Can you take them out? In case you fall asleep or anything. It's safer. Or I can take them out for you."

Jacopetti pried out his teeth. Abby had always been a little frightened of this man—his barrel-shaped body, his booming voice, his invincible cynicism. But Jacopetti without his teeth looked altogether less threatening. His cheeks seemed to collapse inward, giving him an old man's gummy frown.

Jacopetti looked up at his audience. "Thuck you," he said. "Thuck *all* oth you."

"We could use some more light," Beth said hurriedly. "Maybe if everybody would just sit back down?"

They did, though Abby stayed close, mad at herself for failing this test. If it hadn't been for the noise . . .

"Mr. Jacopetti," Beth said, "are you nauseated?"

Nod.

"Feel like you might throw up?"

"Maybe."

"Could somebody fetch a towel just in case?"

Chuck Makepeace dashed for the bathroom.

"Mr. Jacopetti, listen to me. . . . Did you ever have this pain before?"

"Not as bad."

"But you've had it before?"

Nod.

"Seen a doctor about it?"

"No."

"It always went away?"

Nod.

"Okay," Beth said. "That's good. I think what you have isn't a bad heart attack. I think it's angina. It'll probably pass if you lie still."

Joey Commoner, leaning against the wall with a strained expression, said: "How would *you* know?"

"Hush," Abby told him, and got a sullen glare in exchange.

Bob Ganish, his claustrophobia forgotten—misplaced along with his common sense, Abby thought—offered: "This man should be in a hospital."

Jacopetti: "I *am* in a hothpital, you *athhole!*"

Ganish reddened. "I mean, he needs proper medical attention."

Abby took the salesman aside a second time. "I know he does, Bob, but our proper medical attention seems to be lost in the storm. Let's sit down, shall we?" She looked at her watch. Seven-forty-five. How much worse could this weather get? Much worse, she supposed. The eye, the Helper had told her, would probably pass directly over Buchanan, possibly around midnight. And that was only half the storm.

"I wish," she muttered, "somebody would turn off this goddamned *noise*."

•   •   •

Matt felt as if he had fallen into some peculiar time warp: The smaller the distance between himself and his destination, the more slowly he was forced to proceed.

The enemy wasn't so much wind—though that was bad enough—nor even Miriam Flett's relentless backseat driving. The enemy was visibility. More precisely, invisibility.

All traces of daylight had passed. The rain was continuous and dense as fog. It carried with it tiny particles of salt and something else, a crystalline dust, some sort of sea life, Matt presumed. The effect of this was to obscure his vision so completely that he turned onto Campbell Road, the direct route to the hospital, without any certainty that he had chosen the right intersection. There were no landmarks, nothing perceptible beyond five or six feet from the car even in the high beams. He drove hugging the right side of the road, scanning for the sign that marked the entrance to the hospital, then worrying that he'd passed it—maybe it was set too far back from the tarmac.

A particularly strong wind rocked the car up on its right-hand wheels; Miriam sucked in her breath. "I should have stayed home!"

"Home might be underwater by now," Matt said. "Try not to worry, Miriam. We don't have far to go, and we'll be safe at the hospital."

"Can you guarantee that?"

"Stake my life on it."

"Not funny, Dr. Wheeler."

"Not meant to be." Desperate, he took the next available right. It *looked* like the entrance to the hospital—the shrub on the corner seemed familiar.

But it wasn't the hospital. He identified, on close approach, an unfamiliar yellow speed bump, a parking lot that curved the wrong way; finally, the broken window of the local 7-Eleven.

Miriam's hands were clenched together in her lap, arthritic knuckles knotted together. She said, "Are we stopping for snacks?"

It wasn't the hospital, but it was at least a landmark. Matt tried to recall the relationship of the 7-Eleven to Buchanan General. He'd driven this route at least twice a week for years, but when he tried to map it in his head . . . was the 7-Eleven *before* the hospital? Certainly. Close to it? He thought so. But how many yards exactly? Was there another store en route, possibly a camera store? He seldom stopped at any of these shops; they were vague in his mind.

He navigated turtle-fashion back to Campbell Road and crawled onward.

Miriam gasped as a yard-long tree limb came whirling out of the darkness and struck the rear left window. The glass starred but didn't shatter. Miriam whispered something inaudible. Matt clenched his teeth and drove.

He slowed where the curb yielded to a driveway on the right. He exchanged a glance with Miriam, then turned the wheel. This might be the hospital. It probably was. Better be.

The access lane seemed to crawl on forever in front of the car. Matt began to entertain the possibility that he had driven from the 7-Eleven into a horizonless limbo of rain and wind, all landmarks erased. He fought the temptation to check his watch every thirty seconds, try to calculate his progress. He was suddenly aware of the pungent smell of the sealed automobile, his own sweat mingled with the lighter, sourer odor of Miriam and the reek of wet upholstery and wet clothing.

He was grateful when a brick wall loomed up in the twin circles of his headlights—even more grateful when he recognized it as the east wall of Buchanan General.

He pulled abreast of the Emergency entrance. "Thank God," Miriam said.

Matt switched off the engine but left the lights on. "I'll come around to your side. Wait for me. We'll go in together." He didn't say it, but he was afraid Miriam was light enough that the wind might simply sweep her away.

She nodded.

The door was wrenched out of his hand as soon as he opened it. The wind, Matt thought, had made everything dangerous, even an ordinary act like opening a car door. The door banged against its stops and bounced back, whacking his hip. Matt stepped aside and pushed it closed, sparing Miriam more than a momentary blast of salty rain.

He fumbled around the hood of the car with his hands braced against the cold metal. The wind was nearly strong enough to lift him up—certainly strong enough to knock his feet out from under him if he took a miscalculated step. The combination of wind and rain was blinding. With his eyes pressed tight in the darkness, every surface of his body awash, it was as if the world had been reduced to some few essential elements: the wind, the automobile, the wet concrete under his feet. Variables in a complex equation.

He groped along Miriam's side of the car until he found the door handle. Then he steadied himself, took as deep a breath as the wind allowed, and opened the door. Instantly, the door kited into its stops; but this time Matt was ready for it; he wedged his body against the door frame and held it fully open.

He held out his hand to Miriam, but she drew away.

Matt leaned into the meager shelter of the car, where he could see Miriam—blurrily—in the faint illumination of the map light. "*What's wrong?*"

She hissed back: "*My journals!*"

Christ in a red wagon, Matt thought.

"*Dr. Wheeler! You can leave what's in the trunk! But I want my journals!*"

The journals were bundled at her feet, still wrapped in her yellow raincoat. Matt leaned over her, conscious of the wet woolen odor of her skirt—it smelled like a wet dog. He tied the arms of the raincoat together to make a sort of bag for the journals, a tedious process that left him plenty of time to reflect on the absurdity of his position, standing ass to the wind in the midst of the most powerful typhoon to approach the Oregon coast since the ice age. The rain was sluicing into the car now, soaking Miriam, but Matt had ceased to care: Let her get wet, she deserved to get wet. He couldn't shake the memory of those funnel clouds snakedancing toward shore; couldn't shake a suspicion that one of them might reach down and fold him into the dark wing of the sky.

When the journals were bundled together, he stood and offered Miriam his right hand. This time she took it, moaning as she stepped out of the car. As soon as she was standing he put his right arm around her waist and tugged her, half-lifted her, in the direction of the Emergency door. Only these few steps, Matt told himself. One two three.

But the hospital door resisted when he tried to pull it open. The wind? No—not just the wind.

He banged a fist against it. The door was quarter-inch-thick wire-mesh glass. Inside there was a dim light, perhaps motion . . . but he couldn't see much through the blur of rain.

Feeling panic like a third presence, something large perhaps just over his shoulder, Matt pulled the wide handle of the door a third time . . . and this time it opened outward.

He hurried Miriam inside. She stumbled a few steps, then righted herself and took the package of journals from Matt. "Thank you," she said breathlessly, not looking at him, brushing water from the raincoat bundle. "That was . . . harrowing."

Tom Kindle pulled the door closed behind them.

Kindle held a hammer in his hand. A sheet of plywood and two pine planks were leaning against one wall.

Matt sat down on the tiled floor, panting. Water ran off him in all directions. He looked at Kindle. "You were about to board up that door."

"Yup."

"You couldn't have waited?"

"It didn't seem wise."

"Kind of a vote of confidence, isn't it?"

Kindle smiled. "Welcome back anyway."

▪　▪　▪

Abby Cushman met him where the stairs opened into the hospital basement. She briefed him on Paul Jacopetti's medical crisis and added, "He's resting easier now, though the pain hasn't entirely gone away."

"I'll look at him. But I need to change into dry clothes first. Do me a favor—make sure Miriam gets dried off, too. Maybe you can find some fresh clothes to fit her."

"All right." But Abby hesitated. "Matt—I should tell you, I nearly fell apart when Paul got sick. It was a little embarrassing. Well—more than a little."

"Abby, you've done fine. Without you, we wouldn't all be here. You can't handle every crisis that comes along—nobody could."

"But I could have done better. Matt, I don't know anything at all about first aid! The most I ever did at home was spray Bactine on scraped knees. Maybe sometime you could give us a short course?"

"I will. Should have done it months ago."

"We've all been busy. But speaking of first aid, Beth was a wonder! She didn't do anything in particular—mainly convinced Mr. Jacopetti to take his dentures out. But she calmed him right down, and it looked like she knew what she was doing. You have a student there!"

"I taught her CPR. Gave her a first-aid manual to read at home."

"Well, she's a quick study, anyhow. Bright young woman."

"When she wants to be," Matt said.

▪　▪　▪

In clean, dry denim—and despite the shriek of the ventilator ducts, which Abby had warned him about—Matt felt 100 percent better.

It was his experience that bad weather tended to shrink a room. The basement cafeteria, a cavernously large space, had contracted to circles of light around the battery lanterns. It wasn't just a room anymore. It was a huddling place, a dry cave.

He spoke to Paul Jacopetti and read his blood pressure, which was slightly but not dangerously elevated.

"Doc," Jacopetti said.

Matt unwound the sphygmomanometer cuff from Jacopetti's pale arm. It was always the difficult ones who called you "Doc."

"Yes, Mr. Jacopetti?"

"Can I put my thucking teece back?"

"Certainly. Beth was worried you might pass out. But that doesn't seem likely at this point."

And Matt looked away politely while Jacopetti slipped his dentures into his mouth.

"Everybody says angina," Jacopetti said. "It's not a heart attack, it's angina. Okay, good, but how is that better? It feels like a fucking heart attack."

"They're not necessarily different. Angina pectoris is the pain you feel when your heart's not getting enough blood through the coronary arteries. The heart works harder to compensate, and it simply gets tired—the way any muscle hurts if you overwork it. It's a symptom of coronary disease, but in your case the heart itself seems to be basically sound. We can treat the angina with drugs called beta blockers, which help the muscle ease up a little bit."

Jacopetti was frowning, trying to digest this information. "How long do I take these drugs?"

Probably the rest of your life, Matt thought. If we can find a supply. And keep them from going bad. It was one of those facts of life he still hadn't grown accustomed to: no new pharmaceuticals. No more free pencils or coffee mugs from drug companies promoting Tofranil or Prozac. No more Tofranil. No more Prozac. No more insulin, come to that, or penicillin, or measles vaccine . . . not unless he could locate every ounce of every significant drug and store it somehow, refrigerate it, prolong its active life.

Must get this advice to the Boston and Toronto people, Matt thought. Should have done it sooner.

Christ, everything had gotten away from him these last few months. He had been blinkered by his fear for Rachel, transfixed by her slow evolution. But Rachel was gone. It was past time to pick up the fragments of his life, including his work.

"You'll probably be on medication for some time," Matt said, "but I can't tell you for sure until we do a more thorough workup. Not until the storm passes, obviously."

"If it ever does," Jacopetti said. "In the meantime . . . it still hurts."

"I'll go up to the pharmacy and find you something. Lie still while you're waiting, all right? Don't exert yourself."

"I'm not going fucking dancing," Jacopetti said.

■ ■ ■

Matt checked in with Abby before venturing upstairs.

She might have fumbled the Jacopetti crisis, but she was doing a fine job as den mother. She had helped Miriam Flett into a dry outfit and settled her onto a mattress with coffee and Oreos. Now Abby was contemplating the possibility of a hot communal meal—"Maybe a little later, if Tom gets his generator working and we can run the microwave. I think that would cheer people up, don't you? It's hard enough just keeping track of everybody. Some of us want to move into the hallway—it's quieter there and closer to the bathroom. Would that be all right?"

"I don't see why not."

"People are scattering all over. I don't know where Beth got to. Or Joey, for that matter. Is the whole basement safe?"

"Oh, probably. But we should encourage people to stay together. And I don't want anyone running around upstairs."

"Upstairs is dangerous?"

"It could be. If not now, later."

"But you're going up there."

"Only for a moment, Abby."

"Matt, you look terribly tired. Maybe you should lie down for a while."

"Soon. I just have to pick up some pills for Mr. Jacopetti."

"Poor man. Sick on a night like this. Matt, I had the most terrible thought about him." She lowered her voice. "I thought he was having a heart attack because it was the best possible way to annoy *me*. For maybe three seconds, I really thought that! Should I be ashamed of myself?"

"Abby, if I'd been here, I might have had the same suspicion."

She looked pleased and grateful. "Really?"

"Really."

"Check in when you come back downstairs?"

He promised he would.

At that moment, the thunder began.

■ ■ ■

The storm was complex, peculiar—a whole inventory of storms, Matt thought, one layer upon another.

The stairs ran upward through a cinderblock stairwell at the southwestern corner of the hospital. The ground-floor fire exit had been boarded over, but there hadn't been time to seal the second- and third-story windows. One had broken. A trickle of rainwater ran down the stairs between Matt's feet.

The thunder, a sudden new presence, was continuous. It had taken Matt a moment to identify it as thunder, not the approach of some mechanical leviathan from the west. With the thunder, lightning. The lightning lit the stairwell from above with a diffuse reddish-purple glow. It flickered but was never wholly absent.

Matt supposed Abby was right, he *was* tired, mortally tired—too tired, at any rate, to be frightened of this new evolution of the storm. It wasn't even a hurricane, it was something larger, still nameless. Peak winds in a hurricane were what, 200 miles per hour? Maximum. And in this tsunami of wind currently breaking against the flank of the Coast Range? Three hundred miles per hour around the eye wall? More? And how powerful was that? Powerful enough to level Buchanan, Matt supposed. And drown half of it in the storm surge.

As he climbed from the hospital basement to the ground floor, he listened to the wind gusting through the upper reaches of the hospital, slamming doors and rattling gurney carts down vacant corridors. And he listened for the voice of the storm itself, a tympani growl, alive, organic, pervasive.

It was out there devouring his town. Uprooting it and devouring it.

He thought of Jim and Lillian Bix, wholly changed and wholly alien, inhabiting their paper-thin bodies only long enough to consummate some process he didn't understand or wish to understand, the translation of Lillian's unborn child and the delivery, incidental and trivial, of its derelict hulk. He supposed Jim and Lillian had abandoned their own skins by now. Their skins, like so many others, must have been carried up by the typhoon wind, perhaps to the high atmosphere, somewhere peaceful above the rain.

Matt shook away these troubling thoughts and concentrated on the task at hand.

Pharmaceuticals were stored at various key points around the hospital so that each floor had an accessible supply. These caches were locked—the drugs stored there included narcotics—but Matt had been carrying a key and a duplicate since September. He followed the corridor from the stairwell and cursed himself for not having had the wits to bring a flashlight. Kindle had hooked up a gasoline generator in the basement, but it was only feeding the emergency lights, incandescent bulbs at ten-yard intervals.

The drug cupboard, a room approximately large enough for one person to stand in without touching the shelves, was dark as night. Inside, Matt stood blinking, hoping his eyes would adjust, boxes and labels would reveal themselves in the faint glow leaking from the corridor. They didn't.

He stepped back into the hallway, pondering the problem. He could go back for a flashlight, but there was an element of time here. He didn't trust that elevating rumble of thunder, the new intensity of the storm.

He hurried to the nursing station down the corridor. For years, Hazel Kirkwood had been the clerical day nurse on this station. She had her own desk at the rear, away from the busy corridor. Nurse Kirkwood, Matt recalled, had been notorious for her ten-minute breaks every hour, when she would duck outside—or into the stairwell, furtively, in bad weather—to indulge a cigarette habit.

He rummaged in Nurse Kirkwood's desk drawers. He found an abundant supply of Bic pens, paperclips, and knobby pink erasers; a stapler and a pocket calculator and a single, lonely, plastic-wrapped tampon . . . and lastly, at the back of the bottommost drawer, a package of filter Kents with a matchbook tucked into the cellophane.

He took the matchbook into the supply cupboard. One match to home in on the propranolol for Paul Jacopetti. Another match to empty a cardboard box of tongue depressors; a third match as he filled the box with anything nonperishable he hadn't already crammed into his Gladstone bag: antibiotics, painkillers, a bag of sterile cotton. All the while berating himself for not having done this before the storm.

A last match to double-check his work . . . then he turned and found Joey Commoner blocking the doorway.

■   ■   ■

He was too weary to interpret this—Joey's presence merely baffled him—until he saw the knife.

It wasn't a big knife, but it caught the faint light from the hallway; the blade glittered as it trembled in Joey's hand.

Joey said, "I want you to stay the hell away from her."

His voice was shrill and barely controlled, and it occurred to Matt that, whatever else might be troubling him, Joey was also very frightened of the storm. "You shouldn't be up here. It's dangerous up here."

"I don't want you near her," Joey said.

"Can't we talk about this later?" There was a guncrack of thunder above the general dull roar. "We could end up with a wall on top of us."

"Fine," Joey said. "Just tell me you'll stay away from her and we can go downstairs."

Matt was suddenly, deeply tired of all this. The storm, Miriam, Jacopetti, Joey. It was all a single phenomenon, and it was too much; it made him weary. He dropped the pharmaceuticals and stepped forward.

Joey thrust the knife wildly. The blade nipped his forearm, slicing his shirt, digging into the skin beneath—a vivid, immediate pain.

Matt stepped back and came up against a shelf. The walls were mercilessly close, there wasn't room to swing his arms, and Joey was poised at the entrance like a snake.

But Matt's resentment was irresistible. It propelled him forward. The situation was childish, inappropriate, a frustration not to be borne. He kept his eye on Joey's knife hand and thought about getting inside the periphery of it, knocking Joey out of the way. In the corridor he would have room to maneuver.

He took a second step forward. Joey shrieked, *"Don't make me do this!"* and slashed the air. The knifepoint missed, but narrowly. "Just say you'll stay away from her! That's all you have to do! That's—"

He didn't finish his sentence. There was suddenly a taller silhouette behind him—Tom Kindle.

Kindle twisted Joey's arm up behind his back until Joey yelped and opened his hand.

Matt came out of the supply cupboard and backed away from the two men.

Kindle pushed Joey against the wall of the corridor and let him go. Joey spun around. Slowly, Kindle moved away, hands spread. Then he bent and picked up the knife. Peered at it.

"Swiss Army knife," Kindle said. "Real good, Joey. After you kill him, you can trim his nails."

"Fuck," Joey said, rubbing his abused arm, "I didn't come up here to kill anybody."

Matt clamped his hand over the cut on his forearm. It was superficial but messy. He'd left a trail of blood spots on the green linoleum floor.

Kindle shook his head. "You came a little too close, in that case. Stupid thing to do. Wave a knife at somebody! There's only ten of us in town, Joey, is that too many for you?"

No answer.

"Is there some *reason* you came up here?"

Joey nodded. "He fucked Beth."

Kindle did a small double take. Then he pocketed the knife.

"Matt? Any truth to the charge?"

"I taught her CPR," Matt said. "She's been getting first-aid training."

"That's not what I hear," Joey said.

"What do you hear?"

"I hear the doctor's fucking her."

"Who told you that?"

Self-righteously: "Beth did."

There was a momentary silence . . . if you could call it silence, Matt thought, with the wind banging the walls.

Kindle said, "Joey . . . a woman might say a thing and not mean it. Especially if she thought she was being neglected. A woman might think, What would piss off Joey the most? What could I say to really aggravate this asshole who hasn't even asked me the time of day since Christmas?"

Joey seemed to ponder the idea. Maybe, Matt thought, on some level, he was flattered by it.

"I just wanted to warn him. . . ."

"Warn him *what*? That you'll kill him if he hangs around your ex-girlfriend?"

"Fuck you," Joey said mildly.

"Fuck me because I don't want the town doctor knifed by a jealous asshole? Christ's sake, Joey, how is it even your *business* what Beth gets up to? She's not your wife, and even if she was, adultery's not a capital crime. You were pissed off and you wanted to wave that knife and make yourself feel better. But that's so stupid—in the situation we're in, that's absolutely *suicidally* stupid. And that surprises me, frankly, 'cause you're not as stupid as people think." Joey looked up, wary of a trap, not sure whether he'd been insulted. Kindle went on: "I know what people say. What they *used* to say. Nobody held Joey Commoner in high esteem. But that's changed a little, maybe you noticed. You set up the radio—"

"That shithead Makepeace took it over," Joey said. "I don't get close to it anymore."

"Point is, it wouldn't be there without you. Who found Boston on the twenty-meter band? Who found Toronto? Shit, Joey, you're the only individual in town who can read a circuit diagram. You *know* that. So why do a stupid thing like this? Come up here wavin' a little red pocketknife just because some girl tickled your nuts?"

"You don't understand," Joey said, but there was a note of conciliation in it, a hint of regret.

"Maybe," Kindle said, "if the doctor agrees—and it's his call, he's the one who got cut—*maybe* we can not mention this incident downstairs. Not ruin your reputation for being smart."

Joey said nothing. Waited, his eyes averted.

Matt said, "I guess I can go along with that."

Joey looked at him expressionlessly.

"Get on downstairs," Kindle said, "and consider yourself lucky."

Matt watched him amble down the corridor to the stairwell. The door opened and closed inaudibly, the sound of it buried under the noise of the storm.

Kindle turned to Matt. "Some medical advice from a civilian? You ought to bind that cut."

He bandaged it quickly and rolled his sleeve down to cover the evidence. "Since you're here, maybe you can help me carry some pharmaceuticals."

"Sure enough," Kindle said. "I brought a flashlight, by the way. Abby mentioned you'd gone up without one."

"Thanks. And thank you for what you did with Joey."

"I didn't do anything except derail him. I've been worried he'd do some shit like this. When Joey gets mad . . . he gets mad all over. You know what I mean?"

"He said he didn't come up here to kill me. But it might have happened."

"It's not just temper. It's like some old hurt he never paid back. There's a button in Joey that shouldn't get pushed."

"You did a good job turning him around."

"Yeah, for now, but in the long run . . ." Kindle looked unhappy. "People are such shits, Matthew."

"They can be."

"Joey sure as hell can be. You're still shaking."

"It's been a long night."

"Damn noise," Kindle said. They had been shouting to make themselves heard. His voice was raw. "Matthew . . . a little more friendly advice? You have to watch out for yourself."

"I think we all do."

"Sure we do." Kindle, looking vaguely embarrassed, gathered a carton of pharmaceuticals from the shelf. "So what do you think, are we gonna live through the night?"

The roar of the storm had increased a notch. It sounded like some disaster more tangible than wind: trucks colliding, trains derailing in the dark.

"Probably," Matt said. "But we should get downstairs and stay there."

"Come morning," Kindle said, "there won't be much left of this town."

■ ■ ■

Matt gave Abby some of the sterile cotton, which she wadded into her ears: "It *does* help. Though it makes conversation difficult. But no one's talking much anyhow. Matt? Did you hurt your arm?"

The bandage had seeped a little. "Cut myself on some glass. Nothing serious."

"Get some rest. If you can!"

He promised he would. He medicated Paul Jacopetti, then found a mattress for himself and stretched out on it. Everybody had moved into the hallway where it was quieter. Beth and Joey were three mattresses apart, glaring at each other from time to time. Tom Kindle wadded towels under the stairway door where some rainwater had begun to trickle through. Everyone else was simply waiting.

Waiting for the storm to peak, Matt thought, or for the ceiling to drop. Whichever came first. And because there was nothing to see of the storm, the temptation was to listen to it . . . try to decipher every rumble that penetrated the basement.

After a time, Abby consulted Tom Kindle, and the two of them managed to tap enough generator power to run a microwave oven—suddenly Abby was distributing cafeteria trays of steaming instant dinner. She'd been right, Matt thought, about the restorative power of hot food. It was an act of defiance: We may be huddled like rats in a hole, but we don't have to *eat* like rats.

Dinner ended with a crash that seemed to shake the concrete under their feet.

"Jesus," Chuck Makepeace said. "We must have lost part of the building."

Kindle, who was collecting empty trays, said, "Maybe. More likely something hit us. One of those big trees at the west end of the parking lot, maybe."

Jacopetti, pain-free but still pale, was impressed by the idea. "What would it take to pick up one of those trees and fling it that distance? What's a tree like that weigh? Eight, nine hundred pounds?"

"I never weighed one," Kindle said.

"Pick it up like a stick," Jacopetti marvelled. "Pick it up and throw it!"

Matt checked his watch. Ten forty-five.

▪ ▪ ▪

Eleven fifteen: Beth Porter said she thought she smelled smoke . . . maybe coming down through the ventilators? Kindle said he didn't think it was likely, but for safety's sake he was going to shut off the generator. "Get those battery lamps going. Eye of the storm should be overhead soon."

The hallway seemed colder without the overhead light. Maybe it *was* colder. Hadn't been that warm to begin with, Matt thought. He helped Abby distribute blankets.

Another huge crash shook the hallway, and another directly after it. Christ, Matt thought, what must it be like out there? He tried to picture an exterior world so transformed that Douglas firs flew through the air like javelins.

At half past eleven there was a new and even louder crash, a rending roar that shook the foundation—the vibration seeming to come from beneath, up through the concrete, through the bedrock.

"Lost part of the building for sure," Jacopetti said. "Maybe a whole floor."

"You may be right," Kindle said. He added into Matt's ear, as nearly a whisper as conditions permitted, "I hope you didn't go to too much trouble to *cure* this man."

Abby said, "I think I might scream." She sat down, pale in the lantern light. "Fair warning, people."

We must be near the eye wall, Matt thought. A wall of wind harder than brick, wind become a substance: solid, deadly.

He thought of that wind sheering at the broken stump of the hospital and prying at what was beneath—rooting for these few human lives like a terrier digging up a nest of field mice.

The foundation shook again. Matt looked at his watch. Perversely, the battery had chosen this moment to die. The display was blank; when he tapped it, the watch said 13:91. "Abby? Do you have the time?"

It was twelve twenty-five when the wind suddenly paused.

■   ■   ■

The freight-train roar faded gradually.

The air stirred. Dust rose from the floor of the hallway and danced in the lantern light.

"Eye of the storm," Kindle said. "The building is *exhaling*."

"My ears popped," Abby said.

Matt thought of gradients of air pressure steep as a mountain, the engine of the storm.

"Worse," Bob Ganish said. "My nose is bleeding."

There was a dreamlike quality to the stillness. Matt had heard that in the eye of a hurricane you could look up and see stars—it was that clear. He tried to imagine Buchanan, or the ruins of Buchanan, enclosed in a perfect rotating column of cloud . . . the moon shining on a landscape of wet rubble.

Warmth, what remained of it, seemed to drain from the basement. Matt wrapped his blanket around himself and saw others doing likewise.

Abby appeared hypnotized by the calm. "It'll come again, won't it? Just as hard. Maybe harder. And all at once. Like a fist. Isn't that true?"

Kindle moved onto Abby's mattress and put an arm around her. "True, but then we're through the worst of it. After that, Abby, it's only a question of waiting."

Bob Ganish said, "I need some cotton for this nosebleed. I'm a bloody mess here."

Matt attended to it. In the dim light, the blood on Ganish's shirt looked dark. Shiny rust. He worked mechanically, still thinking about moonlight.

"Oh," Abby said sadly. "I can hear it . . . it's coming back."

Matt breathed shallowly, listening. She was right. Here it came. That freight-train roar. It was advancing across the water, onto the land, marching uphill to Buchanan General. Impossible not to think of it as a living thing. Vast and ponderous and stupid and malicious. Leviathan.

"Best sit down, Matthew," Kindle said.

My God, he marvelled. Listen to it come.

■   ■   ■

The Helper—anchored to the high ground where City Hall recently stood—had witnessed the destruction of the town.

It assembled vision from disparate wavelengths, peering deeply into the storm. It saw what no mortal human could have seen.

It saw the storm advance. It saw the ocean flood the lower reaches of the town; it saw tornadoes dipping from the dark shelf of the clouds.

It stood in the calm center of the eye, seeing what Matt Wheeler had only imagined: moonlight shimmering on splintered tree stumps, loose bricks, battered truck bodies, fractured bridge abutments, fragments of drywall, road tar, torn shingles, torrents of rainwater, while the microscopic shells of Traveller phytoplankton hovered in the still air, a silver mist.

Then the eye wall approached once more from the west, eclipsing the moon—a black horn of wind.

The Helper saw Buchanan General Hospital as the eye wall devoured it.

The storm had already sheered away the hospital's roof and much of its third floor. This new impact was more than the weakened structure could withstand.

Chunks of concrete whirled upward, trailing rust-red structural rods like severed arteries. Pieces of the hospital joined fragments of other buildings in a stew of airborne debris. Lab coats tangled with tree limbs, bedsheets embraced splintered glass.

There were human beings in the hollow under the ruins of the building. But not even the Helper's powerful eyes could see into the earth.

▪   ▪   ▪

The building came down in a noise of wind and destruction so intense that Matt didn't register it as a sound. He was simply battered by it. It knocked him down.

He saw Abby screaming but he couldn't hear her.

The others shrank into their mattresses, making themselves small.

The cafeteria ceiling collapsed. Fractured concrete poured through, the remains of the west wall of the building. Matt saw this clearly from the hallway through the open cafeteria doors. The doors were open because the storm wind, rushing through the lapsed ceiling, forced them open.

If we had been in there, Matt thought, if we had stayed in the cafeteria—

A gap had been opened to the tortured sky. The wind penetrated the hallway in a single terrible thrust. Tim Belanger took the brunt of the assault. He had laid out his mattress by the entrance to the cafeteria, a mistake. The wind—heavy with dust, wet, almost tarry—cracked his head against the wall and tossed him aside.

The wind picked up the battery lanterns and threw them down the corridor. Tom Kindle managed to snag one, but the rest winked out as they struck the stairwell door. Kindle waved the single lantern, beckoning with it, shouting something inaudible.

Matt fought his way upwind to Tim Belanger. The City Hall clerk was unconscious. Matt took a breath full of grit and dirty rain and began dragging Belanger away from the cafeteria, toward the faint beacon of Kindle's lamp.

Breathing was the hard part. Everything would be okay, Matt thought, if only he could extract enough oxygen from the moist sludge that had replaced the air. Every breath filled his mouth with grit and drove a dagger into his lungs. He fell into a rhythm of inhaling, hawking, spitting, exhaling. The dead weight of Belanger became an intolerable burden, and several times Matt considered leaving him behind. It would be the wise thing to do, he decided. Save yourself. Maybe Belanger was already dead. But his hands wouldn't let go of the injured man's arm. Traitorous hands.

He bumped into Abby Cushman, who gestured left: a doorway. Matt pulled Belanger over the threshold. Kindle was braced against the wall, holding his lantern into the corridor; he saw Belanger and said, "That's it! Matthew, help me close this door."

They wrestled it shut. Kindle hawked and spat a black wad onto the floor. "Grab that two-by-four, we'll nail this thing shut. Then see how people are doing." Kindle took a hammer from his carpenter's belt. He drove nails into the framing of the door while Matt braced the two-by-four and struggled to clear his throat.

This was some kind of furnace or plumbing room, from what Matt could see—concrete floor, exposed pipes, a huge water heater. The air in the room was dense with suspended particles, but it was relatively still. Eventually some of this garbage would settle out; in the meantime—"Any of you having trouble breathing, try wrapping a cloth over your nose and mouth."

Jacopetti, weakly: "This isn't the linen cupboard."

"A hank of shirt or something. For those who feel they need it."

With the door barred, Matt set about investigating injuries. He took the lantern from Kindle and called Beth to help. Tim Belanger first: the City Hall clerk beginning to recover from a bad blow to the head. His hair was sticky with blood, but the injury didn't appear to be severe—as far as Matt could tell under these primitive circumstances.

Miriam Flett was having trouble catching her breath, but so were they all. He encouraged her to spit if she needed to: "We're not being formal tonight, Miriam."

She managed, "I can *see* that." She held a ragged plastic shopping bag clutched in her left hand—the journals.

Jacopetti had suffered some recurrence of his angina, but it wasn't crippling—"That's normal, right, Doc? I mean if a fucking building falls on you?"

"I think we're all doing pretty well."

"We don't have blankets," Abby said mournfully. She coughed, gagged, coughed again. "We don't have *anything*."

"There's water in that tank at the back," Kindle said. "I checked this place before the storm. Maintenance guys used to come down here for their breaks. We got a card table around the corner and a coin machine full of candy bars."

"Do we have any change?" Abby asked.

"No," Kindle said. "But I got this hammer."

▪   ▪   ▪

The wind howled on. But the storm was breaking, Matt thought. That was the basic fact. They had come through the worst, and now the storm was wearing itself out on the heel of the continent. Morning would come in a few hours.

Overhead, the wind still gnawed the raw ruin of the building; but the wind had begun to ease.

Tom Kindle joined Matt, sat down wearily with his arms on his knees. Kindle had been a great strength, but he was starting to show his fatigue. His face was caked with dust; his hair was a gray-black tangle.

"If the hospital's gone," Kindle said, "there can't be much left of Buchanan."

"I guess not," Matt said.

"Knowing the sentiments of people, once this storm clears, we'll probably be heading east."

"Probably."

"Pity about the town being gone."

Was it gone? Matt had avoided the thought. But it must be. What could stand up to the wind? Commercial Street: gone. City Hall: gone. The marina: washed out to sea.

Dos Aguilas: gone. Old Quarry Park, a wilderness of mud and fallen trees.

And his house, the house where he had raised his daughter, the house where Celeste had died. Gone.

But—

"That isn't the town," Matt said. The thought came to him as he spoke it, rising out of his fatigue and his sorrow. "The people in this room are the town. We're the town."

"Then maybe the town survived after all," Kindle said.

Maybe it did, Matt thought. Maybe the town would live to see morning.

Part
Four

The
Harvest

Chapter
25

Traveller

The boy had come a long way.

He had the skinny body of a twelve-year-old, toughened by his time on the road. His eyes were blue, his hair a dusty brown. He wore jeans, a plain white T-shirt loose at the waist, and a fresh pair of high-top sneakers.

He liked the sneakers. Laced tight, they braced his ankles. They felt good on his feet, a second skin.

He rode an expensive Nakamura mountain bike he had found in a store window in Wichita. The bike had grown dusty as he pedaled north on 15, crossing the border from Utah into Idaho. Last night, camped at an Exxon station, the boy had cleaned the bike with a damp rag. He had oiled the freewheel and the brake calipers, the cables and derailleurs. He had tightened the chain and the crank arm and adjusted the bearings. This morning, the small Nak ran like a dream.

The air was cool. The sky was a hard, glassy blue—the color of a marble he had once owned.

The boy wheeled through sagebrush plains where Interstate 84 followed the Snake River, humming to himself, as absentminded as a bird. He liked the way the wind tossed his hair and snapped his T-shirt behind him like a flag.

In eighty days, he had seen a great deal of the country. He had crossed the Mississippi at Cairo, rolled through Arkansas into Texas, and sheltered for three weeks in the empty city of Dallas while storms raged overhead. He had skirted the Mexican border at El Paso and headed north along the Rio Grande, then west again on I-40 across the Continental Divide.

He had pedaled through the immense deserts of the southwest, landscapes as large and strange as the moon. A cloudburst caught him in Arizona, filling the arroyos, spiking the arid hills with lightning and drenching him before he could find shelter. But he was never ill; he was never tired.

Now he was looking forward to the Salmon River Mountains, some of the most impassable territory in the continental United States—a wilderness of larch and hemlock, cedar and spruce.

At noon, he stopped at a nameless little farm town for lunch. He broke into a gas station cooler and pulled out two bottles of Grape Crush, drank one immediately and saved the second for later. In some towns, like this one, the electricity was still working—the soda was cool, if not icy. In the Handi-Mart next door he found TV dinners still preserved in a working freezer. That was unusual. The freezers didn't always last without maintenance, even if the electricity was on. The TV dinners were past their best-by date, but only a little. The boy opened one and heated it in the store's microwave oven. It tasted okay. He drank the second bottle of Grape Crush. It turned his lips purple.

The boy carried some items in a bag attached to the rear of the bike. After lunch, he opened the bag and took out a hat—a khaki bush hat from a hunting-and-fishing store back east. It didn't fit too well, but it kept the afternoon sun off his face and neck.

He climbed onto his bike and pedaled down the white line, the precise meridian of the empty road. The wheel bearings sang a high, keen note into the silence.

He passed irrigation farms, big Ore-Ida potato plantations gone brown in the absence of humanity, then more sage prairie as he followed the Snake westward.

Near dusk, as he was thinking about breaking camp, the boy came around a slow curve into another tiny road town where a number of trucks and campers had parked in a string. He saw the motion of people among the vehicles.

The boy realized he knew a few things about who these people were and where they were going.

Their presence was troubling. It demanded a decision.

Paths diverged here. One way: the Salmon River Mountains, a last dalliance before he went Home. The other way: a less certain future.

It was perhaps not an accident that he had come across these people.

The boy stood with his bike between his legs, frowning at the choice.

Then he sighed and walked his bicycle to the nearest camper.

▪ ▪ ▪

The camper was a dusty Travelaire. The rear door was open and an elderly woman sat in the doorway with a book across her knees. She wore a baggy cotton print dress and a blue quilt jacket over it. Her hair was gray and sparse. She was reading by the light of the low sun, squinting at the ricepaper pages of a King James Bible.

She looked up at the tick of the Nakamura's oiled bearings. The boy stopped a yard away. He stood beside his bicycle gazing at her.

She gazed back.

"Hello," she said at last.

Cautiously, the boy said, "Hi."

She set the book aside. "I haven't seen *you* before."

"I was riding this way. From the east."

"Are you alone?"

He nodded.

"No mother? No father?"

"They're dead."

"Oh. Well, that's too bad."

"It was a long time ago."

"Are you going somewhere?"

"Nowhere in particular."

"Are you hungry?"

It had been hours since lunch. He nodded.

"I have some food," the woman said. "Fresh eggs and cured beef. And a little stove to cook it over. Would you care to join me?"

"All right," the boy said.

He followed her into the camper. There was a propane stove inside. She lit it and put a skillet over the flame. The camper began to warm up. The day had been sunny and fairly nice, but nights were cold this time of year. The boy looked forward to sleeping inside.

He looked around the camper while she cooked. There wasn't much to see. A few books, including the dog-eared Bible. A stack of scrapbooks that must have soaked up water at some time in the past—the covers were round, the pages wrinkled. Some clothes, unwashed. He sat at a small table, the folding kind.

Eggs sizzled in the skillet. The woman hummed a tune. The boy recognized it. It was an old song. "Unforgettable." Nat King Cole made that one famous.

Long time ago.

He waited while she said grace, then tucked into a plate of scrambled eggs. "Here's the salt," the woman said. "Here's pepper. I'm boiling water for coffee. Do you drink coffee?"

He nodded, mouth full.

"I suppose I'll have to introduce you around." She picked at her own eggs. "We're a travelling group. We're going east. There are other people east. We're from Oregon. The coast. There was a terrible storm, and then—oh, but it's a long story. You can hear it all later. Tell me, are you tired?"

"A little."

"You must have come a long way on that bicycle."

He nodded.

"Yes," she said, "I'll introduce you tonight. There's a meeting. Sort of a town meeting. If you call us a town. We can leave early if you like, but I think people will want to know you're here. . . . My Lord, I don't even know your name! Pardon my manners. I'm Miriam. Miriam Flett. And you are—?"

"William," he said.

"William—?"

"Just William."

"Misplaced your last name?"

He shrugged.

"Well. I'm pleased to meet you anyway, William. And I'm sure everyone else will be, too." She took a delicate bite of eggs, eating slowly, old-lady style. "It won't be troublesome," she said. "There are only ten of us. Well, eleven, including that Colonel Tyler."

Chapter 26

Election

Beth Porter shook the boy's hand and gazed a moment at his wide blue eyes.

They were strange eyes for a kid that age, Beth thought. Too . . . something. Calm? Calm but observant.

But he seemed like a nice-enough kid. People seemed to enjoy seeing a new face. Everybody shook William's hand and made welcome noises at him. Even Colonel Tyler bent and ruffled the boy's hair—though William's smile at that moment looked suddenly less genuine. And that was odd, too, Beth thought.

Then Matt Wheeler called the meeting to order.

They had gathered in the living room of a little wood-frame house next to a gas station. The house was dusty and stale from being closed up so long, but cozy enough on a chilly spring night. Matt had brought in ten folding chairs from his camper. Tom Kindle had plugged in an electric heater, which was minimal help, but what really mattered, Beth thought, was that they had come over the Cascades into the Land of the Functioning Wall Sockets. She guessed it was some Helper voodoo that kept the electricity working in all these derelict towns . . . as in Buchanan before the storm trashed everything. She didn't care. Lights that didn't need batteries: heaven. Hot water: bliss.

This very afternoon they had broken into the house and taken turns under a working shower. Beth recalled that first amazing flourish of steamy water on the skin of her back. It was like the caress of some fiery angel. She'd been savoring the memory for hours.

She settled into a folding chair next to Abby Cushman, a row behind Joey. Up front, with the room's two sixty-watt floor lamps making him look pale and skinny, Matt Wheeler zipped through some old business, chiefly the news that Joey had scavenged a portable ham rig in Twin Falls, plus a quick unanimous "aye" on the proposition to continue east first thing tomorrow.

Then it was time for the *serious* vote of the evening . . . the one Beth had been dreading.

Matt looked tired when he announced it. "Last week we resolved to open the position of Chairman to an election. We can start with nominations—anyone?"

Joey jumped up, almost knocked his chair into Beth's knees. "I nominate Colonel John Tyler!"

"Seconded," Jacopetti said.

Well—*that* was quick, Beth thought.

Abby Cushman, looking a little startled, put her hand up. "Matt, you've been doing a fine job. Can't we just carry on? I nominate you."

Now it was Miriam who seconded. Another surprise.

"Two candidates," Matt said. "Anyone else?"

Jacopetti said, "Isn't two enough? Why don't we *all* run?"

No more.

"Okay," Matt said. "Do we need debate on this? I think everyone knows where the Colonel and I stand."

Conceded.

"We'll vote by show of hands. Colonel Tyler and I will abstain—and maybe our new resident should, too, at least until he's more familiar with current events."

Miriam smiled. "I'm sure that's all right with William."

"Good. Show of hands for Colonel Tyler?"

Beth looked around hastily. Joey's hand shot up, of course. Jacopetti's, in a gesture that was somehow smug.

Two, Beth thought.

Two out of nine.

Bob Ganish offered a plump hand.

Three.

There was a long, tense moment.

Nothing.

"Hands for yours truly?"

Abby's, at once, and Tom Kindle's; then Miriam's hand went up.

Three versus three, Beth thought.

Abby said, "In the event of a tie?"

"Ordinarily," Matt said, "the Chair would cast the deciding

vote . . . but that's hardly fair, since both Colonel Tyler and I agreed to abstain. There's probably something in the *Rules of Order*. Maybe it would be simpler just to try it again—we had a lot of abstentions. Maybe some of those folks will change their minds."

Meaning me. Beth found herself blushing. Me and Chuck Makepeace and Tim Belanger.

Makepeace she couldn't predict. As for Belanger . . . Matt had saved the guy's life, dragging him down a hospital corridor during the storm. But Belanger had been pretty close to Tyler ever since the Colonel arrived. And this was only a chairmanship vote, after all, not a test of loyalty . . . or at least that was all it *seemed* to be.

Makepeace, Belanger . . .

And me, Beth thought. Please God, don't let it come down to me.

"Hands for Colonel Tyler?"

The same three: Joey, Jacopetti, Bob Ganish . . . and now, *uh-oh*, Beth thought, a fourth—Chuck Makepeace had slid into the Tyler camp.

"Could still be a tie," Abby commented.

"No cheerleading," Matt said. "For yours truly?"

Miriam, Abby, Tom Kindle.

Beth folded her hands in her lap and stared at them.

When she looked up, Belanger had raised his hand for Matt.

Four to four.

Jacopetti turned to her. "Time to shit or get off the pot, m'dear."

She thought about Matt: weary, unhappy at the front of the room.

She thought about Colonel Tyler. The way he shook her hand one time. The way he smiled.

She couldn't bring herself to look at either candidate. Or at Joey. Or Jacopetti, the toothless SOB. *"Tyler,"* she said, a whisper.

Jacopetti: "Pardon me?"

She gave him a hateful stare. "Colonel Tyler!"

There was a silence in the room.

Joey turned, offered an evil grin.

Matt cleared his throat. "Colonel?"

Tyler stood up, immaculate in his uniform. "Yes, Dr. Wheeler?"

"I believe this is your gavel now."

▪ ▪ ▪

Beth remembered when Colonel Tyler came to town.

It was in that desperate time when the storm had passed, when Beth had climbed out of the rubble into a world of no landmarks—a world of everything flat and broken, where you might find a bedframe nestled in the hollow shell of a Volkswagen, or a pleasure boat riding on a sea of windfall pines.

After a few days, Beth had been assigned to the food search. With Abby Cushman and Bob Ganish, she had hiked south on the highway—which was not even a road anymore, barely a trail among the scattered detritus of ruined buildings—to the place where the big A&P had stood. Just finding it was an act of archaeology. Beth had always navigated by the man-made markers, road signs and intersections and malls. Now there was nothing except the curve of the bay, the cryptic angle of Mt. Buchanan above a plain of homogeneous junk.

The storm had left chalk-blue skies and a chill wind behind it. Beth was cold in a ragged sweater, soon dirty from prying up soggy drywall and ancient lathing, hunting for canned food, which they loaded into big double-ply garbage bags for the trip back into town. She felt like something medieval. A ragged, scrounging peasant.

Mid-afternoon, her nose running from the chill, she stood up straight to ease the ache in her back; and that was when she saw him.

Colonel John Tyler.

She knew immediately who that distant figure was. Joey had talked to him on the radio. More recently, Chuck Makepeace had announced that the Colonel was on his way to Buchanan. But that was before the storm. Beth thought the storm must have changed everything—all plans had been erased.

But Colonel Tyler had arrived as promised.

He was on foot. He was a little dusty. But he came along the ruin of the highway with his head high, face clean-shaven, his Army jacket threadbare but neat, and Beth felt a voiceless rush of pleasure at the sight of him—ghost of a world that had seemed so lost.

She didn't tell the others. Let them scrounge in the ruins while Beth watched this man come closer. She wished her face was less dirty, her hair not so tangled.

Then Abby straightened and caught sight of him.

"Well, gosh," she said.

Bob Ganish stood with a green garbage bag in one hand, mouth open and his belly spilling over his belt. Some welcoming committee, Beth thought. A middle-aged lady, a grimy ex–car dealer. Me.

Tyler smiled as he approached. You could see his age. He wasn't young. But he was in good shape. His gray hair was cut close to his skull. He looked like he wasn't tired. He looked like he could walk forever.

Beth, suddenly embarrassed, plucked at the hem of her ratty sweater.

Ganish stepped forward and introduced himself. Colonel Tyler shook hands solemnly. "We talked once on the radio," he said: a resonant, calm voice. "Nice to meet you in person." And Abby. "Heard a lot about you, Mrs. Cushman."

Smiles and breathless welcome-stranger bullshit. Then they introduced Beth.

Colonel Tyler shook her hand.

His hand was big and warm. Her own hand was cold from the weather, raw from the work. She was grateful for the touch. She thought his hand was one of the most interesting things she had ever seen—a big man's hand, creased and hard, but gentle.

"Prettiest face I've encountered in a long time," Tyler said, "if you don't mind me saying so, Miss Porter."

"Beth," she managed.

"Beth."

She liked the way it sounded when he said it.

Then they all hiked back into town, Tyler sharing the weight of the canned food, and he talked a little about how bad the roads had been, "but it's a different story over the mountains," and how they would have to take their time, plan for the journey east, and so on and so forth, Beth not speaking or really listening much; and then all the others had to meet Tyler, show him the shelter they'd made of the intact corner of the hospital basement; and Joey was beside himself, glowing whenever Tyler talked to him, which was often, since Tyler and Joey had become good radio buddies. Then there was planning to do, Tyler conferring with Matt and Tom Kindle mainly, and the days had run in a busy torrent ever since.

But she remembered the touch of his hand.

Prettiest face I've seen in a long time.

Beth had passed her twenty-first birthday on the road out of Oregon. She didn't mention it; no one knew. But it got her thinking. Maybe she'd been acting like a teenager well past her due date—riding around on Joey's motorcycle committing penny-ante vandalism. But she was twenty-one years old; she was a woman; maybe not the world's most attractive or well-bred specimen, but the only woman under forty among the local survivors. A fact that made Joey paranoid (not that he had any *right* to be) and everyone else a little nervous. Chuck Makepeace had made a couple of very tentative passes; so, even more tentatively, had Tim Belanger.

But they didn't attract her.

Who did?

Well . . . Joey had, once, but that was over. An aspect of her life she didn't much care to recall.

Matt Wheeler attracted her.

Colonel Tyler attracted her.

None of this was very surprising. What was new was the idea that *she* might attract *them*. And maybe (and here was the *real* novelty), *maybe not just because she was the only game in town*.

Since Matt, since her experience with Jacopetti in the hospital basement, Beth had been exploring a new idea—the idea that she might have some work of her own to do in this new world.

Something more significant than clerking at a 7-Eleven.

A new world, new work, a new Beth Porter coming up through the rubble.

Which reminded her of the tattoo on her shoulder.

WORTHLESS.

It had seemed like a good idea at the time.

Maybe it had been.

Maybe it had been true.

Maybe it wasn't anymore.

■　■　■

She would have to explain to Matt about the vote. Not something she looked forward to.

For now, she watched Colonel Tyler at the front of the room. He smiled, thanked Matt for everything he'd done, thanked everybody for demonstrating their confidence in a relative newcomer. He said he took the chairmanship seriously and he'd do his best to live up to their expectations.

Then he looked at his watch. "It's late and I guess we all want to get some sleep before we move on in the morning. So just a little bit of business here. Some people have been complaining about the weekly meetings. We see each other every day, maybe there's no reason to have a formal assembly so often when there's no special business pending. Seems reasonable. I think we can safely schedule full Committee meetings at a rate of once a month, and I'll ask your consent for that—unless there's any objections?"

No objections, though Matt was frowning massively.

"Okay," Tyler said. "Some picayune items . . . I've posted a watch tonight, and I think we should make that a permanent fixture. Joseph and Tim volunteered for duty. They can be our regular standing guard as far as I'm concerned—until they get tired of it, and unless anybody has a reason why not."

Kindle said, "We're talking *armed* guards here?"

"Handguns," Tyler said.

Abby: "Is that necessary, Colonel?"

Tyler smiled his gentle smile. "I hope it isn't, Mrs. Cushman. I trust it won't be. But we'd be stupid to take an unnecessary risk. There's always the possibility of wild animals, if nothing else. I won't ask a man to sit alone all night without some form of protection."

("Holy crow," Kindle said softly.)

And more such items, none offered for a vote, but the Colonel pausing briefly for "objections," which never came. It was businesslike, Beth thought. A little dizzying, however.

There was something about the radio: Makepeace and Joey were a joint committee and controlled access. Communication with Helpers—there was a Helper in every one of these microscopic towns—would be strictly through a designated representative: Tim Belanger. "Helper communication should be kept to a minimum, in my opinion, since we've all suffered at the hands of the Travellers, and I'm not sure we should place absolute trust in their emissaries, though I'll be the first to admit they've been useful from time to time."

Finally a motion to adjourn. Hands shot up.

Kindle whistled appreciatively from the back row. "Fast work, Colonel."

Tyler looked mildly irritated. "You can voice your dissent at any time, Mr. Kindle. That's what this forum is all about. However, we're adjourned."

"We sure are," Kindle said.

■　■　■

Matt had picked up some material for Beth at a local lending library—a Red Cross first-aid handbook with a chapter on traumatic injuries, which he had annotated in the margin where it was out of date. In a couple of weeks, he wanted her familiar with the use of a hypodermic needle and a range of common antibiotics. The problems they were most likely to be looking at, aside from Jacopetti's coronary trouble and Miriam's geriatric complaints, were injuries and bad food. He had scheduled a session with her tonight.

But the meeting had run late . . . she might not show up.

Might not want to, Matt thought. It was cold in his RV. A lot of people were sleeping indoors tonight. Kindle had been warning people about turning on long-disused oil furnaces ever since they passed that burned-out section of Twin Falls, and gas furnaces weren't working anymore, anywhere, for no known reason. But the Travellers had been scrupulous about electricity. Kindle had hooked up expensive space heaters, the kind with gravity switches to turn off the juice if somebody knocked the thing over. Heat a room, let people camp in it. It was reasonably safe and it took the chill off some arthritic bones, including Miriam's.

But Matt preferred his camper. He had converted the RV into a combination of home and consulting office. It provided a little continuity in a world that had turned so many things so completely upside-down.

He picked up another library book, a Raymond Chandler mystery, its urban setting so distant in time and circumstance that it felt like science fiction. And he switched on a battery light and settled down.

The wind came briskly along the dry margins of the Snake River and rocked the RV on its old, loose shocks. Matt found his attention drifting: from the book to Tyler, the election, the boy who had wandered into camp this afternoon. . . .

He was yawning when Beth knocked.

She let herself in. Matt checked his watch. "Beth, it's late—"

"I know. Everybody's asleep." She hesitated. "I came to explain."

About the election, she obviously meant. *Explain*, Matt noted. Not *apologize*. "It's all right," he said.

"No." She frowned. "It's not all right. I don't want to leave it hanging. Matt, it's not that I don't trust you or you haven't done a good job. Everybody knows you have. But when you were standing up there, it just seemed like . . . you just looked so fucking *tired*."

Had he? Well, maybe. *Was* he tired?

More than he dared admit.

She said, "It might have been the wrong thing to do."

"You did what seemed right at the time. That's all anybody can ask."

"It just seemed like you didn't really want the job."

"I didn't."

"But you don't want Colonel Tyler to have it."

"Well—no."

"He doesn't seem like a bad person."

"That's not the issue. He didn't just take over the Committee, Beth, he bulldozed it. Ten minutes of Colonel Tyler, and what do we have? Restricted access to Helpers. Restricted access to the radio. The camp under an armed guard."

Beth looked uneasy. "You make it sound sinister."

"It *is* sinister."

"I think he's just used to the military way of doing things."

Colonel Tyler, by his own testimony, had left the military almost fifteen years ago. It wasn't force of habit that had put him in charge tonight. It was careful planning, Matt thought, and a couple of partisan malcontents: Paul Jacopetti and Joey Commoner.

And something else. Matt sensed in the Colonel a certain restlessness, an impatience that always seemed about to break out into violence. Catch him in a quiet moment and you'd find Tyler tapping his foot to some inner rhythm, his eyes fixed and absent and his big hands closed into fists.

But he couldn't say this to Beth without sounding paranoid or petty. Anyway, her vote hadn't mattered any more than Chuck Makepeace's vote, or Bob Ganish's. It was only bad timing that made it seem that way.

She had done what she thought was the right thing, and in the end maybe her call was as good as his.

She said, "I guess I should leave."

"Only if you want to."

Tentatively: "You're not angry?"

"No." He realized he wasn't.

She sat beside him. Relieved, weary, she put her head against him.

He stroked her long hair and listened to the night wind tugging at the corners of the RV. He would never get used to these inland plains. He missed the sea.

He thought about Beth—all the aspects of Beth Porter. The neglected, sullen Beth: the Beth who had tattooed WORTHLESS on her shoulder, who had baited Joey Commoner until Joey felt compelled to pull a knife.

And this other Beth. Beth treating Jacopetti's anxiety with the anodyne of her own calm. Beth studying anatomy textbooks with the dedication of a monk.

Something clean and strong rising out of all the garbage in her life.

"Joey's standing watch," she said. "He has a campfire on the highway facing west."

"Did he see you come?"

"No. Anyway, I'm tired of worrying about Joey. He's acting like an asshole."

"Maybe a dangerous one."

"Joey and his pocketknife? I doubt it."

"After what you said that night . . ."

"I shouldn't have. I know. But he doesn't own me. He never did."

"We're a fragile community. I don't want to create one more problem."

"Then should I leave?" Challenging him.

"Beth—you know you don't have to."

"I want to stay a while longer."

"Then stay."

A cold night. A little warmth.

Chapter
27

Destinations

The caravan of ten dusty RVs and trailers, led by Colonel Tyler in a four-wheel-drive Ford pickup, turned south on Interstate 84 toward Utah.

Tyler drove with the windows rolled down, admitting a breeze so dry it made his lips bleed. He drove at a cautious, steady pace. Sometimes he felt fettered by the train of ponderous vehicles behind him. But it was a privilege, he thought, to blaze the trail. To see the way ahead.

The highway seemed wider for being empty. Periodically he passed an abandoned truck or car, and it was nice to know that in an emergency the Committee could siphon gas from one of these. But no emergency arose. Most of the roadside gas stations had functional pumps, and Joey Commoner and Bob Ganish had been scrupulous about keeping the convoy's engines in decent repair.

Tyler led them across the Great Basin into Utah, joined what had once been a populous stretch of I-15 north of Brigham City, then veered east on I-80 where the towns grew sparse again.

Tyler read the road maps with great care. He was worried about crossing the Rockies. I-80 skirted much of the mountains, followed the Union Pacific route through the Red Desert in Wyoming, but late or early storms had been known to strand unwary travellers.

He called a halt at a town named Emory and pressed on in the morning. The sky when he started his engine was bright with herringbone clouds.

The road climbed and subsided and began to climb again.

He felt better when the road wound away from civilization. Those empty towns were oppressive. Mountain and desert were simply eternal. Granite and sagebrush and cheat grass: invulnerable to all the discord that had dropped like bad magic out of a starry sky.

He was alone in the cab of the pickup truck, although Sissy kept him company.

▪ ▪ ▪

Sissy had been keeping him sporadic company since that town in Georgia—Loftus.

She spoke to him, a voice out of the wind, but he didn't actually see her until one afternoon in rural Texas while he was driving the Hummer west. It seemed appropriate that Sissy should appear in the desert. The desert was a place of mirages, dust-devils, chromium-blue lakes shimmering where the highway touched the horizon. Sissy had seemed exactly that tenuous, sitting next to him where A.W. Murdoch used to be. She was a translucent, desert-dry Sissy—dressed as inappropriately as ever in cotton and nylon and polyester of all colors, clothes so brittle with old dirt that any motion emitted a greasy rustle and exuded an odor too stale to be offensive. It was the smell, Tyler thought, of something dead that had dried a long time in the sunlight.

The radio was good, Sissy told him, good to be talking to those people, smart, but be careful, she said: stay away from the crowds, all those East Coast city survivors, clever and dangerous in some way she never explained. Talk to that Joseph, Sissy said. He admires you.

Sissy was an illusion. Tyler knew that. Of course he did. You'd have to be crazy to believe she was really sitting there, some kind of ghost.

She was, as the psychologists would no doubt say, a private revenant, a fragment of *himself*. She was Tyler giving Tyler Tyler's advice.

But in another way she really *was* Sissy: Sissy cut loose from memory. His memory had lost its grip on Sissy the way a child might lose its grip on a balloon; and like a balloon she had risen up, had floated out of his head and come to rest in the passenger seat beside him.

Sissy advised him to drive to Oregon, hike down from the coastal mountains to Buchanan, assume a leadership position among these ragged refugees.

Lead them east, Sissy said.

To the gathering place of the survivors, a new home in the valley of the Ohio River, a sheltered place—or so Tyler told them, and it had even seemed true for a while.

But Sissy—always a repository of unpleasant surprises—had been coy about their destination.

Tyler led his caravan up a road walled with granite, threading a path around fallen rock. Whenever he turned his head to the right he found Sissy gazing at him. Today she was bright as the sun, her plump cheeks a blazing white, difficult to look at.

Those people back east, Sissy said. *They surrounded themselves with Helpers. They talk to Helpers.*

"True," Tyler said.

Helpers are the voice of that thing in the sky . . .

"I know," Tyler said, weary of these cryptic pronouncements. Sissy's eyes, volatile and relentless, demanded answers he was helpless to produce.

. . . and of the dead.

"Dead *what?*"

The skinless living.

The Contactees, Tyler interpreted. Contactees who had died might be able to speak through the Helpers.

The dead might talk to the living.

Tyler said, "The danger . . ."

They'll talk about you, John. That girl you killed in Loftus. Maybe it will be Murdoch talking. Maybe Murdoch crossed over, too. And who else might talk? They might talk about Stuttgart. They might remember every sin you ever committed.

This was a new and unwelcome idea.

People will know what you are.

Peevishly: "I'm no worse than the rest."

They'll know about Loftus. They'll call you killer.

Would they? Extraordinary circumstances, Tyler thought. Alien possession. The girl had been . . . not human.

Anyway, he told himself, I'm a man of some stature. A man who served his country, a man who made a place for himself in the business world. A man who had once been a familiar presence in the Capitol Building, a man accustomed to lunching with Defense Department functionaries or the members of oversight committees. Above certain kinds of innuendo.

That's a joke, Sissy said. *Another Washington crook. What's the difference?*

Tyler worked at remembering that period of his life. It had been structured, formal, complex. In those days he had known how to seal off this Sissy part of himself. Compartment A: The presentable Colonel Tyler. Compartment B: Certain phantoms. Certain urges.

But with Contact, the borders had grown tenuous. Like a naval vessel, he thought. Bulkheads breached. Flooding in the engine room. Fire in the hold.

The sad fact was, he talked to this ghost because he had no choice.

Pay attention, Sissy scolded him.

To . . . ?

The danger! You can't risk being exposed.

But even Colonel Tyler had dreamed of that green valley in Ohio. A gathering place, a new life—safety.

A *trap*, Sissy said.

"But if not there," Tyler said aloud, "if that's not where we're going . . ."

But when he turned to pose the question, Sissy had vanished.

■ ■ ■

They came across a fallen telephone pole blocking the highway. Tyler called a halt, then enlisted Joey Commoner and Chuck Makepeace to work a chain around the pole and hook it to the rear of the pickup.

Tyler revved the Ford's heavy-duty engine, inching forward against the drag. The pole gave a moan of stressed timber and then began to shift.

Tyler took careful note of the people who had climbed out of their campers and RVs to drink bottled soda and watch the show.

Kindle and Wheeler stood together, both poker-faced. Wheeler in particular seemed to be working to disguise some emotion. His resentment, Tyler supposed, at being elbowed out of the leadership position.

Among the rest Tyler identified idle curiosity, some cautious frowns from the likes of Abby Cushman and Miriam Flett, frank idolatry from Joey Commoner.

He turned away to measure his progress, and when he looked again he was surprised to see Sissy among the crowd—a more ethereal presence.

A dry wind came rivering down this pass, but Sissy's long, tangled hair hung limply over her shoulders; her layered clothes stirred not at all.

She extended her hand over the head of the new boy, William.

This one, Sissy said. Her lips moved soundlessly, but Tyler heard the words as if they were his own. *Watch out for this one.*

He drove until sunset.

■ ■ ■

"A lot of settlers came through here," Kindle said. "Mormons, especially, but also people on the Oregon Trail, the California Trail. You can still find their wagon tracks on the scrub prairie about forty miles north."

Matt walked with his friend along the highway away from camp.

They had stopped for the night along a stretch of high Wyoming rock desert that seemed to Matt infinitely dry, silent, and immense. Dinner was over now and the watch fires had been lit.

"Matthew," Kindle had said, "let's walk a bit. Get the kinks out." And Matt understood that the older man had something difficult to tell him.

Neither moon nor Artifact had risen and the stars were bright in a cold sky. When he spoke, Kindle's voice seemed to hover in the air.

"It was called the South Pass," Kindle said. "You followed the North Platte to the Sweetwater, Sweetwater to Pacific Creek, Sandy Creek, the Green River Crossing. The Overland Stage Route came through that way. Pony Express."

Scuff of shoes on empty road. Matt said, "Sounds like you know the territory."

"Lived two years up in the Wind River Range. Did a lot of hiking through Whiskey Mountain and Popo Agie. Beautiful country."

"You miss it?"

"Been thinkin' about it a lot."

They approached the small fire where Joey Commoner was keeping watch. Joey stood up at the sound of footsteps, turned to face them with his hand hovering at the pistol Colonel Tyler had supplied him.

"Halt," Joey said, his voice cracking.

Kindle yawned and regarded the boy. "Joey, if you ever aim a loaded pistol in my direction I'll feed it to you—fair warning."

"The Colonel doesn't like people outside camp perimeter at night."

"I don't suppose he does. I don't suppose he likes my shirttail untucked, either, but he'll have to put up with it, won't he?"

"You go on report if you're out of bounds."

"Fine," Kindle said. "Maybe later the Colonel can slap my wrist."

"You're such a shithead," Joey said.

Kindle looked at him a long moment—sadly, Matt thought. Then they walked on, past the fire, past Joey.

Matt tried to imagine crossing this blank immensity in a covered wagon. No highways, no gas stations, no motels. No Helpers. The stars sharp as needles.

"Matthew . . . can you believe this bullshit? Pass a checkpoint before we can take a walk?"

He shrugged. "Joey's just—"

"Joey isn't 'just' anything. Joey's following orders and loving every minute of it. We're not living in a town anymore, we're living in a barracks. That's why—"

Kindle hesitated.

Matt said, "Why what?"

"That's why I'm leaving."

No. "You can't."

Kindle was a shadow in the starlight, large and gray. "Matthew—"

"Christ, Tom, I know what's going on as well as you do. Tyler did his little putsch, and now we have to live with it. It's painful. But we're still moving. Heading for a place where Tyler will be one small frog in a big pond. They're holding real elections in Ohio. According to the radio—"

"When's the last time you *heard* the radio? The Colonel's got it locked up."

"Beside the point. In Ohio, the Colonel won't matter."

"Don't underestimate the man."

"The bottom line," Matt said, "is that we're more likely to get there if you're with us."

"The bottom line is that *it's not my job*." Kindle selected a pebble and threw it into the darkness, an invisible trajectory. "Anyway—I never wanted to live in Ohio. Tell you a story. Once upon a time I hiked along the Titcomb Valley, that's up in the Wind River Range. I was thirty-three years of age, and I thought that was pretty damn old. East side of the valley is Fremont Peak. North is Mount Sacajawea. At the head of the valley is Gannett Peak, highest in Wyoming. All well above the timberline. Glaciers on those mountains like blue rivers of ice. So pretty it hurts. I camped there a night. When I left, I promised myself I'd come back, one way or another, before I died. See all this a second time. I never got around to it."

"Tom—"

"I know you don't understand this, Matthew. You're happy with people. Happiest when you're helping them. That's admirable. I can't do it, however. I'd be happy by myself in the Winds. Or the Tetons, or the Beartooths."

Matt tried to imagine this wiry, strong, aging man alone in the wilderness. "Break a leg out there," he said, "no one comes to help."

"I don't relish the idea of dying alone. Who the hell does? But what choice is there? Don't we *all* die alone?" He shrugged. "Used to be Shoshone and Arapahoe through there. Might still be people around."

Matt said, "In Ohio—"

"In Ohio there's nothing *but* people. People and Helpers. Which is another question. Seems to me there's only two ways it can go, Matt. Maybe the Travellers move on and leave us alone—no Helpers, no electricity unless we make it ourselves. And pretty soon the planet is repopulated and we're back in the same bind. Or else they build us a private Eden, which is pretty much what they promised. A safe place, a protected place, easy food and probably some kind of population control. And maybe that's okay, too. But think about it. Everything the Travellers are capable of, doesn't that qualify them as gods? I think it does—by the standards humanity's used for thousands of years. But do you want to *live* with a god? A real one, I mean, one who appears in the sky every night? God who makes the rain fall, god who makes the crops grow, god who cures the sick child? What would we be after ten years of that—or a thousand years? Maybe about as human as those people who dropped their skins. Maybe less."

"It might not be that way."

"Uh-huh. But it might."

Matt was tired again. It was as if he had made some silent bargain, traded sorrow for fatigue. Ever since Rachel left, he had been empty of grief but full of this daily exhaustion.

He wondered whether Kindle was right, whether they were headed toward a kind of domestication. He wondered what dark marvels the Earth might harbor in a hundred years or a thousand. Two species of humanity, perhaps: the wild and the tame.

He said, "Have you talked to Abby about leaving?"

"Have I told her, you mean? No. I thought I'd speak to her closer to the event. Say I'm going, then go. No time to blame herself."

"She will, though."

"Maybe."

"It won't be good for her."

"She's survived worse. Hell, I don't mean all that much to Abby Cushman. Target of opportunity. If she were fifteen years younger I'd say you and her might hit it off. You both need somebody to doctor. Kindred souls. But she'll be happy in Ohio."

"Easy as that?"

"Not easy at all, Matthew. Abby's been generous. You've been generous."

"It's been paid back often enough."

Kindle looked at the stars, scratched himself. "We should maybe get back before Joey starts layin' eggs." They began to walk. "I'll ride as far as Laramie," Kindle said. "Turn back from there."

"It'll be hard," Matt said. "One less voice against the Colonel."

"Told you," Kindle said. "It's not my job."

Unspoken, in a glance from Kindle to Matt, in the darkness far from the firelight: *It's your job now.*

■　■　■

The next day dawned clear and cool. Engines revved in morning light, RVs threw long shadows over the scrub.

Colonel Tyler, leading the caravan as it wound through long miles of Wyoming prairie, was first to catch sight of the miraculous new thing:

It was a dusty blue dome on the horizon, too perfectly symmetrical to be a product of nature; capped with white, like a mountain.

Something artificial. Something large beyond comprehension. A work of engineering that beggared any solely human effort.

Calm and pretty in the dry blue distance.

It's that spaceship, Sissy told him. *To take the dead away.*

He recalled the idea, dimly, from Contact, from rumors he had heard on the radio: a vast thing nearly alive that harbored emigrant souls, and a miniature of the Earth inside it; Elysian fields, a world without evil.

Her voice was like a sizzle in his ears:

We must see it more closely. We must abide here for a time.

Even Sissy was excited.

Chapter
28

Earthbound

Rosa Perry Connor had always dreamed of flying.

She had grown up earthbound. Chained to a suburban Southern California tract development, restless by nature, Rosa spent her childhood summers exploring concrete storm drains, half-made houses, and the neighborhood's few surviving orange groves. A reader, she devoured stacks of Little Golden Books, then the Bobbsey Twins, finally her older brother's collection of How and Why Wonder Books, wherein she discovered a volume devoted to Airplanes—which ignited her long romance with the idea of flight.

The Orange County air was full of a number of things, mainly petrochemicals, but including passenger jets, helicopters, and military aircraft. Whenever one of these machines passed overhead, Rosa would come to a stop. She would stand at attention, head craned upward, one hand raised, as if in salute, to shade the sun from her eyes. "F-104," she would announce, or, "Looks like a DC-8." She became a student of silhouettes, a connoisseur of contrails. Always meticulous, she taught herself the history of flight from Montgolfier to the Atlas rocket.

Her obsession baffled her friends. Her parents were barely aware of it. Her father designed circuits for an electronics firm. Her mother played bridge with women whose suntans had acquired the quality of aged leather and whose jaw muscles stood out like taut little ropes when they laughed. Rosa imagined herself in a Fokker, strafing her parents' barbecues and garden parties. No more fat men in business suits exhaling sour whiskey clouds, no more creased women in pastel shorts drinking martinis. She would rise above all this.

Her parents hated flying.

They had family back east—Grandma Perry in Wisconsin, Grandma Hagstrom in Florida. Sometimes Rosa's parents took her visiting. By car. Across the desert. Across the farmland. Earthbound. Wheeling through an interstate hell of Stuckeys, Bide-a-Wees, and souvenir shops. Instead of *above* these dreadful things!

Rosa, from the age of seven to the age of seventeen, begged her parents to fly, at least once, one summer. Leave the car at home, she pleaded. The car was hot, crowded, and took forever. An airplane would save *days* of travel. An airplane would turn torture into ecstasy.

"But if we drive," Rosa's mother said with maddening patience, "we can see the country."

Ye gods, Rosa wanted to scream, we've *seen* the country! Every inch of every road was tattooed indelibly into their brains! What could be *left* to see? One more plastic teepee? One more jackalope postcard?

Meanwhile, she made plans. She would go to college. She would study . . . well, whatever was useful to a pilot. Mathematics, aerodynamics. Her eyes were good. She would take a job in civilian aeronautics. Somehow, she would find her way into a cockpit.

And then—ten days before her eighteenth birthday—her parents announced yet another trip to Florida. "But this time we're flying."

It was the best present ever, and it almost made up for all those miles on the road.

Rosa waited with itchy impatience for the appointed day. The trip to Los Angeles International was novelty enough. From the waiting room at the gate she was able to study in gratifying detail the silvery bodies of Vanguards, Convairs, 707s. They were cumbersome on the ground; out of their element, like beached whales. The distant runways turned them into sleek sky-things through the redeeming magic of speed and altitude. Watching, Rosa trembled with excitement.

The boarding call startled her. After an eternity of waiting, it seemed almost—too soon.

Their plane was a new Douglas DC-8 Super 61, a stretched version of the standard DC-8. Rosa had picked out, had insisted upon, a window seat, and she watched with honed attention as the luggage was loaded from a cart, thumping into an invisible space under the passenger compartment; listened with keen ears to the final latching of the door, revving of engines, rumble of wheels as the taxiing began.

She was able to see the runway before the plane turned for takeoff. The runway was long and empty, a strange road for this massive machine. The stewardess demonstrated oxygen masks and advised passengers that their seat cushions could be used for flotation. Rosa watched and listened with a sense of unreality. Flotation? She was interested in flying, not floating.

Then the engines whined to a higher pitch. The sound invaded every part of the plane: the bulkhead, the window, her seat, herself. A brake was released and the aircraft began to roll.

To *accelerate*. She had not been prepared for this brutal burst of speed. From below, every takeoff had seemed graceful. Elegant. From inside, it was patently an act of force. The wings, which had seemed so solid, bounced and wobbled against the air. The fuselage rattled as if its rivets were about to pop.

And Rosa began to entertain her first doubt.

Was this *practical*? Would all this machinery really work? Could this fragile bus possibly sustain itself a mile from the surface of the earth?

She believed in flight. She was not sure she believed in the invulnerability of engine parts manufactured by sweaty men in a Pratt & Whitney factory.

But then the wheels lifted from the runway . . .

. . . *and she was flying*.

The DC-8 rose with the prompt efficiency of an elevator. The ground simply dropped away at an angle that seemed to Rosa precipitously steep. . . . She couldn't help imagining the DC-8 as if on a hill, stalling and rolling backward.

Her hands began to sweat. She wiped them on her skirt.

There was a knot of excitement in her stomach. *I'm flying*, she told herself. *This is the real thing; I am true-to-God FLYING*. She gazed at Los Angeles below her, its gridwork vanishing into a gray diffusion of smog. The aircraft tilted and seemed to rotate around the point of the wing as it banked over the Pacific. Rosa's parents read magazines. Incredible, she thought. Her mother read *Redbook*. Her father read *Time*. As if they were in some dentist's waiting room! Not a metal cylinder high above the ocean!

The airplane circled as it rose until it was high and heading east.

A stewardess offered soft drinks. Rosa said, "No, thank you." The knot of excitement in her stomach had become . . . something else.

She felt flushed and hot and unwell. Her eyes crept to the window and back again. If she didn't look at the window, she wouldn't see the ground. Wouldn't be reminded of their astonishing height. Of the distance the plane would fall, if it fell.

But I'm FLYING!

But she *wasn't*. She was just sitting here, strapped in. Helpless! In a metal box, suspended above the San Gabriel Mountains by the clumsy rotation of a few greasy turbofans.

It might be flying . . . but it felt more like *risking her life.*

The aircraft lurched in a pocket of air, and Rosa gasped and tightened her grip on the armrest.

Her mother glanced over. "Are you all right, dear? You look pale."

"I think—" She swallowed hard. She couldn't decide what was worse: the fear, the humiliation, or the disappointment. A dreadful lump had formed in her throat. "How long is the flight?"

"Five hours. More or less."

Five *hours?* Could these engines really operate for *five hours?* Full of volatile jet fuel? Revolving at God-knows-what velocity? Bearings hot as griddles? Metal fatigue tearing at the fuselage?

She glimpsed mountains down below. Clouds. And an impossible volume of empty air.

"Rosa?" Her mother again. "Dear, what's the matter?"

"God's sake," she heard her father say. "Give her the goddamn paper bag. That's what it's there for."

■　　■　　■

She traded in her return ticket and rode a bus back to California.

The trip was long, uncomfortable, and depressing. Every inch of highway under the wheels was a confession of failure. She spoke to no one. She focused her eyes on the horizon, the uneasy intersection of Earth and sky.

Home, she registered at UCLA. Midway through the fall semester she met a B.A. student named Vincent Connor who drove all thoughts of flight and recrimination from her mind. Vince was a farmboy, gauche and handsome. He came from Wyoming, his daddy was a sheep rancher there, but to Rosa's glazed and grateful eye he was something out of the Broadway musical *Oklahoma!:* a sweet, big-boned blond man in a checkerboard cotton shirt. At any moment, Rosa thought, he might break into song.

She married him in the spring and became Rosa Perry Connor. Five of his cousins, brave about airplanes, flew in from Wyoming with his widowed father. The church was full. Her twin nieces, four years old, her brother's girls, carried Rosa's train. After the reception Vince began their honeymoon drive to San Francisco; they spent a night at a motel on Highway One where the sea fog came winding through the pines. They made love for the first time as man and wife, which seemed to inject a new vigor into the act. Rosa called him Cowboy, and he grinned.

After that—

Years later, she would wonder at how fast the time had passed. Vince took a series of jobs, one of them with her father's electronics firm in Orange County. Briefly, Rosa was thrust into the garden-party and country-club circle she had despised as a girl. She wasn't good at it. Vince was worse. He didn't know how to dress. At parties, he told coarse jokes or refused to say anything at all. "He has 'Wyoming' stamped on his forehead," a friend told Rosa, "and it's fucking *indelible.*" Vince had dreams of opening his own business, but he couldn't manage to save any money. He began to drink too much. So did Rosa. Her garden parties became haphazard affairs, at which she was liable to sit cross-legged on the patio steps indulging her old Fokker fantasy. Watch out, girls, it's the Red Baroness. Airsick bags provided for your comfort on the seatback.

When his father died, Vincent drove her across the desert to Wyoming, which Rosa regarded as a hostile alien planet. To her horror, Vince had decided to take over the family ranch.

"You'll get used to it," he told her, not much interested in her objections. "It's not so bad here."

But it was. It was a huge, lonely land full of bellicose men and submissive women. Rosa did nothing but cook meals, keep house, and watch TV. Vince wasn't keen on children, he said, and neither was Rosa—she thought about a pregnancy just to relieve the boredom, but never seriously enough to skip her pills. And yet, Rosa thought, for all the tedium, my God, how the years flew! Crackling cold winters, muddy springs, summers so dry her small garden plots inevitably failed before autumn. Seasons and seasons of network television. She drove into Cheyenne with Vince sometimes, but good lord, Chey*enne*? The last refuge of the bolo tie?

Her life became eventless, as smooth as the eastern horizon, and worse . . . somehow, her life *passed.* It eroded. She grew old. Yes, old. She was forty in Wyoming, and how had *that* happened? Then forty-five. Then, oh, Christ, fifty. Fifty years old on a sheep ranch in Wyoming!

She was fifty-one when the Artifact appeared in the sky like an ivory moon.

Rosa wasn't frightened of it, not even in the beginning. Vince thought it portended the end of the world. Maybe it did. Nevertheless, Rosa liked it. She liked its glide, smooth and effortless in the dark. It was flight as she had once imagined flight to be.

And didn't that stir some old memories?

She was more earthbound now than ever, of course, chained to this vast acreage of prairie. Chained to Vince. And she had put on weight over the years, a considerable poundage: her girlish walk had become a waddle. The revenge of gravity, Rosa thought. What was weight but the measure of her bondage to the Earth?

Then, the next summer, like everyone else, she came down with Contact flu . . . and woke to the realization that her life had been only a prologue.

Vince submitted to Contact just as readily, which surprised her. Vince had seemed satisfied with his life in Wyoming. The ranch had prospered under his supervision, and he seemed happy enough. Vince, after all, had never wanted to fly.

But Vince was suddenly eager for the Golden Age to commence, happy to drop his stolid Marlboro Man exterior and plunge into the fluid deeps of the Greater World.

After Contact she felt closer to Vince but at the same time more distant. She was able to appreciate the shape of his life, the spikes of pride and canyons of ambition that had driven him to California and back. There was even a broad, pastel bump of affection that comprised his feelings for Rosa, a pleasant discovery.

But she could see, too, that their connection had been arbitrary and accidental. Their love had peaked in a motel on Highway One, and what persisted was fondness, at best; boredom, at worst.

She wasn't surprised when Vince abandoned his skin. Winter was setting in, and Vince had never relished the bitter storms and cold Canadian air that came rolling each year from the north.

Rosa, however, had conceived a different plan for herself.

She had in mind a certain transformation, a dramatic farewell to the planet that had borne her.

It would take time. It would mean staying on the Earth longer than most. Therefore she began as soon as Vince was gone—his skin a delicate memory, carried off on a brisk autumn wind.

She retired to the bedroom of the ranch house, to the old double bed she had shared with him for so many years.

Then Rosa took off her clothes and looked at herself for the last time in the vanity mirror. She saw a bulging gray-haired woman whose expression was no longer perennially sad. Then she stretched out on the bed.

The neocytes in her body dimmed her awareness to make the time pass more speedily. Rosa was suddenly dreamy and afloat.

She weighed 237 pounds that day, a significant mass—enough for the neocytes to work with. Adipose tissue began to change its structure. Rosa's pores exuded a gray fibrous substance. Within days, it covered her body. Her physical functions dropped to negligible levels. After a week, Rosa ceased to breathe; her heart ceased beating.

Inside her hardened chrysalis, she began to change.

▪ ▪ ▪

The pale cocoon lay motionless on the bed all that winter.

Around it, the world evolved. The winter storms that year were particularly fierce. Not the hurricanes that had wreaked so much damage on the coast, but snowstorms that froze the water in the pipes and beveled the house with glittering blue dunes. The wind in January was so violent it broke a downstairs window. Rosa's bedroom turned cold and a fine lace of frost formed on the mirror; but Rosa was protected from the cold and the wind.

Vince, before he left, had torn down his fences and put the sheep out on the grazing land to fend for themselves. But the sheep were stupid and most of them died that terrible winter.

Not very many miles from the ranch, south past the Colorado border, Traveller organisms had begun to construct the new Artifact. If Rosa had stood at her ice-clad window she would have seen it grow; would have felt the tremors in the bedrock as the Earth's magma was tapped and channeled; would have seen a ghostly luminescence on starry winter nights.

That spring, as the snow melted and the ground softened, she would have seen Home dominate the southern horizon, a new mountain . . . would have seen it as A.W. Murdoch had seen it on the day he abandoned the flesh.

But Rosa Perry Connor slept on.

▪ ▪ ▪

The days were warming when Rosa finally began to stir. The nights were cold, but the snow was long past.

Each day, she quickened a little inside her chrysalis.

Awareness grew. She felt the process reaching its consummation; felt her new self struggling against confinement.

In a matter of days she would burst free.

Rosa felt the Greater World, too, all the new complexity of it since so many souls had gone over.

But she was not the only one left on the Earth. There had been other transformations.

Many, in fact, on every continent: New creatures half-human or ex-human or subtly post-human.

Like the man, Rosa thought as she rose toward dim consciousness . . . the boy . . . the old man who had *become* a boy . . .

. . . who was aware of *her*, too . . .

. . . who, in fact, was very close. . . .

Clamoring for her attention through the medium of the Greater World. . . .

Rosa, he said . . .

. . . while she struggled up from a winter's hibernation. . . .

Rosa, we're very close. . . .

I hear you, boy, she thought. But I'm sleepy. What is it you want?

Rosa, the boy said. *We're very close. Rosa, hurry. Rosa, finish what you have to finish, because we're close now, and you might be in danger.*

Chapter
29

I Know What
You Are

The caravan pulled into an empty truckstop on I-80.

Home, a mountainous three-quarters disc above the southeastern prairie, turned a deep royal blue as the sun dropped below the horizon. A faint last light played about its apex and gave the high frost a reddish glow.

We shouldn't linger here, William thought. Home was nearly finished, and soon—within a very few days—it would cast loose from the Earth. No doubt it would be a spectacular sight, but also a dangerous one to any unreconstructed humans in the area. The creation of Home had opened a deep wound in the mantle of the planet. When Home rose toward orbit, the wound would bleed magma; the bedrock would tremble and quake.

William knew all this through the agency of the Greater World, but he didn't speak of it.

It wasn't clear whether he should.

He walked a distance from Miriam's camper, across the still-hot tarmac of the parking lot to an abandoned Honda, and sat on the dusty hood. He wore a sky-blue T-shirt, too big, and a pair of jeans unravelling at the knees, and when he closed his eyes he felt the gentle touch of the cooling air on his young skin.

Debate was raging through the Greater World. As the human polis expanded to completion, it had begun to take over certain tasks from the Travellers—chiefly, the management of the Earth. It was an onerous burden.

The Travellers had approached the Earth like a benevolent but clumsy giant. For all their wisdom, they hadn't foreseen a ratio of resistance as high as one in ten thousand. They had underestimated the stubbornness of humanity, William thought, no doubt an easy mistake to make. Their own transition from a biological/planetary species to a virtual/interstellar *epistemos* had been self-generated and nearly unanimous.

But the question remained: How should the human collectivity, the Greater World, relate to this stubborn minority?

Leave them, one faction asserted. *They've chosen their independence and we ought to respect it. Let them find their own destiny.* The destiny of the polis was among the stars; the Earth could fend for itself.

It's inhumane to abandon them, other voices argued. *They're free to choose for themselves, but what about their children? If the human birthright is among the stars, how can we condemn another generation to death?*

No resolution had emerged.

William's problem was a miniature of the larger debate. He knew what Colonel Tyler was; he understood the threat Colonel Tyler posed . . . but should he intervene?

For the sake of his last sojourn on Earth he had elected to become a child again. He had put a great many memories behind him, stored them temporarily elsewhere, because he wanted this unmediated experience—not just to *feel like* a twelve-year-old but to *be* one. And so the Presidency had vanished into the misty past; the Greater World became a presence vaguely perceived.

Now this crisis had forced him out of his *ekstasis* and troubled him with doubt.

He supposed it wasn't coincidence that had led him back to Colonel Tyler. Some unperceived connection had been forged as long ago as that day in Washington when he sat in the park with Colonel Tyler's pistol at his throat. The boy had pedaled aimlessly across America; the man inside had maneuvered him into meeting this sad expedition. It wasn't clear what events might unfold, but he felt a role for himself in their unfolding.

And a scant half mile down the road was the Connor farmhouse, another dilemma. (*Rosa*, he broadcast silently. *Rosa, hurry!*)

He heard Miriam come up behind him. Her footsteps dragged on the gritty parking lot. *She's tired*, William thought. Miriam had demonstrated an enormous strength for her age—she insisted on driving her own camper. William recognized and appreciated her resilience. But she tired easily and was often short of breath.

She stood beside him, looking at Home where it dominated the horizon.

"In its own way," Miriam said, "it's beautiful."

It was. Like a vast canyon wall at sunset, Home was every shade of blue, from the palest pastel at its summit to the indigo shadows at its base. A few tenuous clouds had formed along its western slope.

"You look sad," Miriam said.

"I was thinking," William told her.

"About what?"

He shrugged. "Things."

There was a distant clatter of broken glass, the sound of Colonel Tyler breaking into the truckstop restaurant.

"William," Miriam said. Her voice was solemn. "I wasn't sure whether I ought to mention this. But perhaps the time has come. William, you don't have to lie to me anymore. It's not necessary to pretend. You see, I know what you are." She regarded him loftily. "You're one of *them*."

▪   ▪   ▪

Miriam had doubted him from the beginning.

Why not? Doubt had been her constant companion for months. Since Contact, all her certainties had melted away.

Miriam had said a resounding *No!* to the offer of immortality, but she had seen certain things that long-ago August night—had glimpsed certain immensities that shook her to the roots.

She went back to the Red Letter Bible her father had given her and read it from Genesis 1:1 to Revelation 22:21. The Bible had always been a cornerstone for Miriam. Not because it explained everything, as the TV evangelists alleged. The opposite. She trusted the Bible because it was *mysterious*. Like life, it was dense and contradictory and resisted interpretation. Rightly so, Miriam thought. How authentic could a book of wisdom be if you understood it at a glance? Wisdom didn't work like that. Wisdom was a mountain; you *climbed* it, short of breath, dizzy, unsure of yourself even as you approached the summit.

But after Contact—

Here is a solemn blasphemy, Miriam thought, but after Contact the Holy Bible had seemed almost *provincial*.

All that earthly preoccupation with slaves and kings, shepherds and patriarchs.

For one unforgettable moment last August, Miriam had beheld in her mind's eye the universe itself—indescribably ancient, large beyond comprehension, and as full of worlds as the sea was full of water.

Where was God in that immensity?

Perhaps everywhere, Miriam thought. Perhaps nowhere. It was a question the Travellers had refrained from answering. Increasingly, Miriam doubted her own access to the answer.

No, she told them. *I don't want your immortality.* She would be immortal at the Throne of God. It was enough.

But the world had never looked the same since.

By the time William came cycling from the east with his wide eyes and half-a-name, Miriam had grown accustomed to doubt; she knew at once he wasn't a normal sort of youngster.

For one thing, she *liked* him. During her years as a secretary at the elementary school, Miriam had not much cared for children. They were messy, impudent, and vulgar. *The children of this world are in their generation wiser than the children of light.* Luke 12:19. But Miriam guessed the children of Galilee seldom addressed their elders as "fuckhead."

Neither did William. William was different, and Miriam suspected he had once been much older. She told him so now.

He sat thoughtfully on the hood of the empty car, his heels tapping the grill. "I didn't lie to you."

"But you're not what you appear to be."

"I *am* what I appear to be. But I'm something else, too."

"Older."

"Among other things."

"You're not human."

He shrugged.

"You don't want the others to know?"

He shrugged again.

Miriam shifted her weight. Her feet were tired from standing for so long. "I won't tell them," she said. "I don't think you're anything to be afraid of."

William's smile was tentative.

She said, "But will you do me a favor?"

"What?"

"Talk to me. Tell me about—" She couldn't find a word for it.

He said, "The Greater World?"

"Yes." He was perceptive. She added, almost shamed by the admission, "I'm curious. . . ."

"All right," William said.

"But first we should go eat dinner." She hugged herself and shivered. "It gets so cold these nights. I'm cold to the bone."

■   ■   ■

The Colonel had organized dinner in the truckstop cafeteria. Abby Cushman had uncovered a cache of canned chili, and she warmed it in a big steel pot over the restaurant stove. It tasted like tin and vinegar, William thought. But any kind of hot food was a pleasure nowadays.

The group had divided into clusters. William watched Matt Wheeler and Tom Kindle, conspicuously silent, sharing some private uneasiness.

He watched John Tyler conferring with his cadre: Joey Commoner, Paul Jacopetti, Bob Ganish. There was some troubled conversation there—hushed and indecipherable.

Beth Porter stood with a bowl in her hand, glancing nervously between the two groups.

William didn't like the sour atmosphere of the room. The sooner we move on, he thought, the better. He thought about Miriam (who was silently spooning a bowl of soup: the chili, she said, was indigestible)—Miriam, who had guessed his secret.

He thought about Rosa Perry Connor struggling out of her confinement a scant half-mile away.

He thought about Home.

▪ ▪ ▪

Back at the camper, he did his best to answer Miriam's questions.

She wanted more than he could give. She wanted a tour of the architecture of the universe. He was hobbled by words. But he did his best—tried to translate into simple English his own new grasp of time and space.

We live in a well of time, William told her. Call up your most primitive memory, a cradle memory, something from your childhood. Now think of all the hours that have passed since then, all the ticks of all the clocks in all those years. An *ocean* of time. Double that amount, he said, and double it again, and multiply it by a hundred and a hundred more, and still, Miriam, still you haven't scratched the surface of the past. Multiply it by a number so large the zeroes would run off a page and you *might* reach as far back as the Jurassic or the Precambrian, when the Earth was a planet inhabited by monsters; but only an eyeblink in its history. Multiply again and again and eventually you reach the dawn of life, and again, the planet's molten origins, again and again, the formation of the sun. And multiply again: the elements that would form the sun and all its planets are forged in the unimaginable furnace of a supernova. And *still* you haven't removed more than a grain of sand from Time Itself.

"Lonesome," Miriam whispered.

And space, William said, was a mystery, infinite but bounded. The galaxy was a mote among billions of galaxies; the sun, a star among billions of stars; this moment, the axis of a wheel as big as the sky. . . .

"It's too much. William! How can you stand it?" Her voice was faint and sad. "So lonesome," she repeated.

But out of all that blind tangle of particles and forces had come life itself. It was a miracle that impressed even the Travellers. Consciousness unfolding from a cocoon of stars and time. Pearls of awareness growing in the dark. "Miriam, how can it be lonely?" He couldn't disguise the awe in his voice. "We were implicit in the universe from the moment it began. We're the product of natural law. Every pondering creature in the deeps of the sky. We're the universe gazing back at itself. That's the mystery and the consolation. Every one of us is an eye of God."

▪ ▪ ▪

She woke three hours after midnight, turned in her bed, and saw William in his sleeping bag with his arms cradled behind his head and his eyes still open in the faint light.

The curse of age was the elusiveness of sleep. An older person, Miriam thought, gets too familiar with the dim hours of the night. But William, the boy-man, was also awake.

Both of us restless, Miriam thought. The aged and the ageless.

"William" she whispered.

He was silent but seemed attentive.

"There is something I wonder about," she said. "I've been thinking about us. Us on this trip. And those in Ohio or other parts of the world—who said no. Who didn't want that immortality. That . . . Greater World. Do *you* think about it?"

His voice small in the darkness: "Yes."

"Do you think about *why?*"

"Sometimes."

"Why some of us chose to stay in our mortal bodies?"

Nod.

"William, is there an answer to the question?"

"Lots of answers." He paused as if to assemble his words. "As many answers as there are people. Sometimes it was religious faith. Though not as often as you might think. People say they believe this or that. But on the deepest level, where the Travellers spoke, words are only words. People call themselves Christians or Moslems, but only a vanishing few held those beliefs so deeply that they turned down immortality."

"Am I one of those?"

He nodded again.

At least, Miriam thought, I *used* to be. "And the others?"

"Some are so independent they don't mind dying for it."

Tom Kindle, she thought.

"And some people *want* to die. They might not admit it, they might even fear it, but in the deepest part of themselves they long for it."

Who was that, Miriam wondered. Bob Ganish, the fat used-car dealer? Maybe. Paul Jacopetti, the retired tool-and-die maker? Scared of death but secretly wanting it? Perhaps.

"Some are convinced they don't deserve immortality. The belief in their own shamefulness has gnawed down to the bone."

Joey, Miriam thought.

"Or some combination of these."

Beth.

"Perhaps," Miriam said, thinking of Colonel Tyler, whom she had distrusted from the day she set eyes on him, "perhaps some of them are simply evil."

"Perhaps," William agreed. "But some evil people laid down that part of themselves as gratefully as they might have given up a tumor. Others didn't. Others . . . Miriam, this is hard to accept, but some people are born so hollow at the heart of themselves that there's nothing there to say *yes* or *no*. They invent themselves out of whatever scrap comes to hand. But at the center—they're empty."

"Colonel Tyler," Miriam said.

William was silent.

But she recognized the description at once. John Tyler, hollow to the core; she could practically hear the wind whistle in his bones.

"But there are people like Dr. Wheeler—or that Abby Cushman. They don't seem exceptional."

The prairie wind rattled a window. William hesitated a long while.

Then he said, "Miriam, did you ever read Yeats?"

"Who is Yates?"

"A poet."

She had never read any poetry but the Psalms, and she told him so.

"Yeats wrote a line," William said, "which always stuck in my memory. *Man is in love*, he said, *and loves what vanishes*. I don't think it's true—not the way the poet meant it. Not of most people. But it may have been true of Yeats. And I think it's true of a certain few others. Some few people are in love with what dies, Miriam, and they love it so much they can't bear to leave it behind."

What a difficult kind of love that must be, Miriam thought.

▪ ▪ ▪

By some miracle of Traveller intervention, there was water pressure in the restrooms of the truckstop restaurant. A pleasure—Miriam despised chemical toilets.

At dawn, the new Artifact a crescent of pearl and pink on the horizon, Miriam hurried from her camper into the cold green-tiled ladies' room with the Bible clasped in her hand.

She opened it at random and began to read.

Lo, I am with you always, even unto the end of the world. Matthew 28:20.

There was blood in the toilet again this morning.

I am dying, Miriam thought.

Chapter
30
Fireworks

Matt woke to a knock at the door of his camper: Tom Kindle in ancient jeans, a cotton shirt, high-top sneakers, and a Cincinnati Reds baseball cap. He was carrying a rifle.

"Looks like you're loaded for bear."

"Rifle's for you," Kindle said. "Kind of a gift."

"Don't you need it?"

"I can pick up a fresh one plus ammunition in Laramie. Matthew, you might not like it, but you're on some dangerous turf these days. You're liable to need this."

Matt took the rifle in his hands. He didn't come from a hunting family, and he'd never done military duty. It was the first time he'd held a rifle. It was heavier than it looked. Old. The stock was burnished where it had been handled over the years. The metal parts had been recently oiled.

He didn't like the sad weight of it, any more than he liked the sad weight of Kindle's leaving.

He gave it back. "Not my kind of weapon."

"Matthew—"

"I mean it."

"Don't be stupid."

"Don't be stubborn."

"Shit," Kindle said, but he took back the rifle in his left hand and looked more comfortable with it there.

"Talked to Abby yet?"

"I'm about to. Not looking forward to it."

"You could change your mind."

Kindle shrugged. "I doubt it."

He put out his hand; Matt shook it.

"Take care of yourself, old man."

"Watch your back, Dr. Kildare."

■   ■   ■

"We thought you should know," the radio said, "all our Helpers have gone silent."

It was not a routine call, coming at this hour of the morning, and Tyler listened with a rising interest.

He and Joey had set up the receiver in a seedy staff lounge at the back of the truckstop cafeteria. Tyler had made the room his command quarters, and he was alone in it.

As alone as he ever got, these days.

He held the microphone in his right hand and thumbed the talk button. "Say again, Ohio?"

The transceiver was hooked to a mobile antenna and plugged into a wall socket. Since they came over the Coast Range, they'd been doing radio wherever they found live AC. Joey wanted to rig a ham unit to run off a car battery—it was easy, he claimed, and would be more convenient. But Tyler had discouraged him. Tyler didn't much care for the radio anymore. He had begun to see it as a liability.

"Helpers have fallen silent," the Ohio man said. Ohio ran a twenty-four-hour radio watch, and this was their morning shift, a guy named Carlos with a faint Hispanic accent. "Wondered if you had the same experience."

"We're not currently near a Helper, Ohio."

"Theory here is that the Travellers are fixing to move on. Maybe the Contactees take over, maybe not. Could be we'll see the Artifact move out of orbit soon. End of an era, huh? If that's true." The man seemed to want to *chat*.

Sissy appeared in a corner of the room, faintly luminous and anxious to speak.

"All the Helpers are silent?" Tyler wanted to nail down this new fact.

"Every one," Carlos said. "They don't talk anymore. Or move or nothing."

Tyler thought about it. He turned it over in his head, wanting to make sense of it.

He glanced out the greasy window at the curvature of the new Artifact, still earthbound—the human Artifact, a spaceship the size of a mountain.

"Ohio," he said. "Your signal is weak."

"Sorry, Colonel . . . weather problem there?"

The sky was baby-blanket blue. Windless. "Got a front moving in," Tyler said.

"You in any danger, Colonel?"

"Not that serious. We might be out of touch for a while, though."

"Sorry to hear it. Look for you later?"

"Indeed. Thanks, Ohio."

Sissy beamed approval.

Now, Tyler instructed himself, now *think*.

If the Travellers leave . . . If the Helpers fall silent . . .

Then we'll be safe. All our secrets safe.

Sissy's voice was faint but strident, like the buzz of a high-tension wire.

It might not work that way, Tyler thought. We don't know.

Therefore wait. Wait and see.

Wait here?

Yes.

How long?

Until it's over. Until the Travellers are gone, dead are gone, altogether empty skies.

People don't want to stay here, Tyler thought. They want Ohio.

Make up something. Tell them Ohio told you to wait. Bad weather. Like you said. Bad weather along the Platte, say. Dam washed out, say.

Sissy possessed a wonderful imagination.

It might work, Tyler agreed. But not if they can talk to Ohio, or Ohio talk to us. The radio—

You're not stupid, Sissy said. *You can fix the radio.*

▪ ▪ ▪

Tyler closed the dusty horizontal blinds and jammed a chair back under the knob of the door.

It was still early morning, not much activity yet among the people Tyler had come to think of, pleased with his own sense of humor, as the Unhappy Campers. Joey was walking a perimeter, exactly the kind of idiotic task Joey adored. Jacopetti slept until noon if no one bothered him. No one else was likely to knock in the next few minutes.

He lifted Joey's toolbox onto the trestle table where the radio was. He unplugged the transceiver and worked out the sheet-metal screws that held the cover in place.

He used two alligator clips and a stout piece of wire to make a jumper cable. Then he hooked one clip to the 120-volt primary of the transformer and the other clip to the positive rail of the DC supply. For insurance, he added a bare wire across the internal fuse.

Put the lid back on, Sissy reminded him, *before you plug it in.*

Tyler did so. He threw the power switch to the *on* position, for good measure.

Then he hunkered down and pushed the plug into the wall socket.

There was a half second of silence. Then the big transceiver made a sound like a gunshot and jumped a quarter-inch off the surface of the table. It belched a spark as bright as a camera flash and sizzled with high-voltage overload.

The ceiling light flickered and faded altogether as the building's circuit breakers cut in.

Now hurry, Tyler thought. He unplugged the unit, then cracked the blinds to admit just enough light to work by. When he pried up the lid, the transceiver gushed sour smoke into his face. Tyler ignored the stench and hurried to disguise his handiwork. He pulled out what was left of the jumper, the alligator clips, the wire across the fuse. Then he jammed the lid back on and began to drive home the screws one by one.

The sound of Tim Belanger's voice came faintly through the window, something about the *lights* going off, anybody know where the *fuse box* was?

Eight screws, four to a side. Tyler drove the fifth, the sixth, the seventh, sweating.

Footsteps sounded in the hallway.

He fumbled the last sheet-metal screw into its hole. The screwdriver didn't want to find the slot in the screwhead. When it did, the screw sheered sideways. "Shit," Tyler whispered.

Don't curse, Sissy scolded him.

There was a knock at the door. Joey's voice: "Colonel? You still in there?"

Three twists of the wrist to drive the screw home. A couple of seconds to clear Joey's toolbox off the table. Couple more to yank the chair away from the doorknob.

"Dark as a bitch in here. Sorry." He let Joey in.

Joey sniffed the air. "What's that stink?"

"Had some trouble with the radio," Colonel Tyler said.

■ ■ ■

"Thing's totally fucked," Joey said when he had examined the molten interior. "Transformer must have shorted. Though I don't know how it could of."

He offered to drive into Cheyenne and get a replacement.

"Fine," Tyler said. "But not yet."

How come, Joey wanted to know.

"I'm calling a meeting tonight. It's important, and I need you there. As a vote and as sergeant-at-arms."

"I could be back by dark."

"I don't want to risk it." Tyler drew himself up. "Let it ride, Mr. Commoner. Take my word on this."

Joey nodded.

Good soldier, Tyler thought.

■ ■ ■

Matt was compiling a pharmaceutical wish list to transmit to the Ohio people—he didn't know about the radio problem yet—when he heard Abby's anguished voice from the parking lot.

He hurried out of his camper into the rough circle of trucks and RVs, knowing what the problem was and dreading it.

Tom Kindle had climbed into the cab of his lumbering RV and was cranking the motor. Abby had stepped out of her own camper. She wore a denim skirt and a loose blouse and carried a hairbrush in one hand. Her feet were bare and she'd been crying. She ran a few steps across the hot, midday tarmac toward Kindle's vehicle.

"You CAN'T!" Stopping when it was obvious that he *could* and *was*. "OOOOH!"

She threw the hairbrush. Her hard overhand toss sent it pinwheeling at Kindle's camper; it rang the side panel like a bell.

Kindle leaned out the driver's window and gave her an apologetic wave.

"YOU COWARD! YOU SELFISH OLD *COWARD!*"

The camper rolled out onto the highway and began to pick up speed.

Matt took Abby by the shoulders. She pulled away and looked at him bitterly. "Matt, *why did you let him do this?* We *need* him!"

"Abby, Abby! I *know.* But he had his mind set on it. I couldn't stop him. I don't think anybody ever stopped Tom Kindle from doing what he wanted—do you?"

She sagged toward him. "I know, but . . . oh, *shit*, Matt! Why *now?*"

He didn't know how to console her. He had lost too much of his own. But he held her while she cried.

Joey Commoner came running from the truckstop, Tyler and Jacopetti a short distance behind.

Joey cupped a hand over his eyes and watched Kindle's camper disappearing down the highway. Then he looked at Abby. Figuring it out.

"Son of a bitch," Joey said. "He's fucking *AWOL!*"

Abby regarded Joey as if he'd descended from Mars.

"Calm down," Colonel Tyler said, to no one in particular.

"Sir," Joey said, *"he didn't ask permission to go somewhere!"*

"Quiet," Tyler said. In the sunlight, the Colonel was silver-haired, imperial. His eyes lingered a moment on Matt. "We'll discuss it at the meeting tonight."

Matt cleared his throat. "Thought you didn't believe in meetings."

"Special occasion," Tyler said.

▪ ▪ ▪

Tyler put his motion to the Committee before everybody was finished sitting down.

The meeting was held in the truckstop restaurant under a bank of fly-spotted fluorescent lights. Tyler stood against a window with the dark behind him and tapped a knuckle against the glass for attention.

"News over the radio," he said. "We've got some heavy weather across the state border along the Platte. Ohio thinks we ought to stay put for a while, and I agree—but I want a vote to make it official."

He paused to let this sink in. Everybody was still a little dazed by the departure of Tom Kindle, wary of another crisis.

Matt Wheeler said, "I thought the radio blew up."

"Call came early this morning, Dr. Wheeler."

"Did it? Who took it?"

"I did."

"Did anybody else hear this call?"

"I'm sorry, Dr. Wheeler. I didn't feel it was necessary to have a witness."

Jacopetti laughed out loud.

Wheeler said, "It would be nice to be able to confirm the message, Colonel Tyler."

"Mr. Commoner offered to find a replacement for the radio. I'm sure we'll be up and running in due time. Until then, let's keep a lid on the paranoia, shall we?"

Abby raised her hand: "A truckstop is hardly a place to spend time. . . ."

"Agreed. In the morning, we can take a look at the farmhouse to the south of here. I'm sure it'll be more comfortable."

Tyler registered, but didn't understand, the sudden look of concern from the boy, William.

Wheeler again: "Maybe we ought to keep moving—we can always find shelter if the weather turns bad."

Suspicious son of a bitch refused to drop the issue.

"After what happened to Buchanan," Tyler said, "I don't think we want to take any chances with a storm, do you? And there's another consideration. One of our company chose to leave us today. A particular friend of yours, Dr. Wheeler. All things considered, maybe we should stay in the neighborhood long enough to give Mr. Kindle a chance to change his mind. If he elects to come back to camp, at least he'll know where to find us."

This hit home with Abby Cushman, a potential swing vote; she folded her hands in her lap.

"All in favor of staying," Tyler said. "Show of hands."

It was an easy majority.

Chapter 31

Night Lights

They filed from the restaurant, subdued and silent, until Tim Belanger stabbed a finger at the sky: "Hey—anybody *notice* something?"

Tyler looked up. "The Artifact," he said, and calmly checked his watch. "It should have risen by now."

By Christ, Matt thought, for once the bastard's right. That ugly alien moon was overdue.

Missing. Gone.

"Dear God," Abby said. "What *now*?"

There was nothing in the sky but a bright wash of stars—no Artifact but the second one still grounded on the southern horizon.

The Earth was alone again. Matt had wanted it so badly, for so long, he hadn't allowed himself even to consider the possibility. It was the kind of desire you could choke on.

But here, mute testimony, was an empty Wyoming sky.

Too late, he thought bitterly. If they left, they left because their work was finished.

The starlight on the second and motionless Artifact, the so-called human Artifact, was cold and merciless. In scale and design, Matt thought, that object was wholly *in*human, no matter who owned it or what went on inside.

"The aliens are gone?" Abby asked, and Matt said, his voice a whisper, "Why not? We have our own aliens now."

■ ■ ■

It was an auspice that couldn't be read, an indecipherable portent, and they went to bed weary of miracles.

Deep in the cold Wyoming springtime dark, sooner or later, each of them slept. . . .

Except one old woman, one ageless boy.

"William?"

His eyes were wide and moon-bright. "Yes?"

"Don't you *ever* sleep?"

He smiled. "Sometimes."

Miriam's battery-operated bedside clock bled numbers into the night. 3:43. 3:44. There was a fresh new pain in her belly.

"The Travellers are gone, aren't they?"

"Yes."

"But you're still here."

"*We're* still here."

Humanity, he meant. The polis, he had called it, the world contained in that blister on the horizon: Home.

"William?"

"Yes?"

"Did I ever show you my journals?"

"No."

"Would you like to see them?"

His smile was unreadable. "Yes, Miriam, I would."

She left her bed and took down from their shelf the fat scrapbooks full of clippings from the *Buchanan Observer*. They had gotten wet in that terrible winter storm and the pages were thick and warped. But the clippings, for the most part, were still legible.

William sat up in his cot and leafed through the books one by one. It was a strange history contained there, Miriam thought. She remembered how everyone had been frightened by the first appearance of the Artifact in the sky. It had been enigmatic, terrifying, an emissary from another world. Now, less than two years later, it was these clippings that seemed like messages from another world.

The universe, Miriam thought, turned out to be a more peculiar place than any of us expected.

William said, "You obviously worked hard at this."

"Yes. It seemed important at the time."

"Not now?"

She had fought to protect these journals. But what were they? Tonight they seemed like so much paper and ink. "No . . . not now."

He looked at them carefully and then put them aside.

Miriam steeled herself to ask the essential, the final question: the question she had postponed, had dared not ask.

Give me strength, Miriam thought. *One way or the other. Give me strength.*

"William . . . is it too late for me?"

She trembled in fear of his answer. She closed her eyes, squeezed them tight, tight.

"No, Miriam," the boy said gently. "It's not too late. Not yet."

A chaste kiss on the lips.

The neocytes, he said, would work quickly inside her.

■ ■ ■

Before dawn, when Miriam was finally asleep, the boy crept out of the camper into the chill air.

A fingernail moon rode low in the sky. His breath made plumes of frost, and there was frost on the tarry surface of the parking lot, sparkling in the fragile light.

The Artifact had left orbit hours ago, resuming its long itinerary through the unexplored spiral arms of the galaxy. Its physical presence wasn't necessary any longer. The collective knowledge of the Travellers had been duplicated and stored in the human Home, and Home would begin its own journey soon—once certain controversies had been resolved.

William's bicycle was roped to the back of Miriam's camper. Silently, he untied it and examined it.

The trip from Idaho had coated the bicycle with dust. The action of the chain and the derailleurs sounded thick and gritty. But he didn't have far to go.

He climbed on the bike and pedalled down I-80, a young boy, legs pumping in the moonlight, the banner of his breath streaming behind him in the chilly air.

He turned left past an open gate, down a private road to the Connor farmhouse.

Rosa, hurry, he thought. *They're coming in the morning. Hurry now.*

Chapter
32

Release

William was with her as the sun rose.

Rosa lay on the farmhouse bed. The winter's cold and wind had given the bedroom a dishevelled look. The oaken dresser had faded and its mirror had dulled; the curtains had tangled on the rod. The single large window looked southeast, where Home occupied a portion of the sky. Sunrise was a faint vermilion on those distant slopes.

The gray cocoon on the bed had cracked on its long axis and the two pieces had begun to separate. William gazed without visible emotion at the pulsating mass inside.

Rosa—they'll be coming soon.

Help me, then, Rosa said.

William moved to the bedside, considered the problem, then grasped the two chunks of dense, porous material and began to pry them apart.

Hurts, Rosa said.

William broadcast a voiceless apology.

No. It has to be done.

The boy agreed, and grasped the cocoon again and strained his thin arms until he heard the material split along its back seam—a dry, fibrous sound like the crack of a walnut shell.

He felt her relief.

William stood away as Rosa began to unfold.

■   ■   ■

The sun was well above the horizon when she stood at last beside the bed, her enormous wings trembling in the cool air from the window.

Rosa Perry Connor, in her present incarnation, weighed less than fifteen pounds. Her new body was a hollow shell of what had once been human bone and tissue, transformed by the action of the neocytes into something more brittle and much less dense. Her features were diminished and compressed but still recognizable. She had an attractive face, William thought. Her eyes were large and bright.

She blinked at him, still mute. Her lungs were a fragile bellows, her vocal cords a memory. Her pupils, unaccustomed to the light, were black pinpoints. Her wings were a double ellipse around the axis of her body, and sunlight through the moist tissue made bright moires of blue and purple.

William felt her exhilaration. Curious, he thought, the way some of us manufactured these destinies for ourselves—these last, brief incarnations on the surface of the Earth. She didn't seem strange at all. Only a stubborn dream given fleeting substance.

The membranes of the wings needed to dry before Rosa could use them. William didn't hurry her—there was nothing she could do to speed the process.

He tore the drapes away from the window, the only practical exit. It was an old-fashioned window, one fixed pane and one counterweighted pane to slide up in front of it. Rosa's body was tiny now and her wings were flexible, but she would need more space than this.

He shattered both panes and carefully, meticulously, plucked away the splinters of glass and tossed them to the dry earth below. Then, with surprising strength for a boy of his size, he grasped the obstructing arm of the wooden frame and pulled until it cracked and came away.

Some splinters remained in the wood despite his effort. The palm of his right hand was scratched; the blood that oozed out was dark and viscous, almost black.

▪   ▪   ▪

Tyler looked up as he crossed the truckstop parking lot with Joey Commoner beside him. "Joseph? Did you hear that?"

"Sir? Uh—no."

"A sound like breaking glass?"

"No, sir."

Sound carries a distance in this still air, Tyler thought, across this dry prairie. He took a shallow breath, listening, but there was only silence.

"Hurry everybody along," he said. "Breakfast is over. We have business to attend to."

"Sir," Joey said.

▪   ▪   ▪

William heard the engines come to life one by one, though he couldn't see the truckstop from this window.

I know, Rosa assured him. *Soon now.*

There was not much margin, the boy thought, on this brink of time.

▪   ▪   ▪

The caravan of RVs made its way up the private road and parked in a ponderous line outside the Connor farmhouse.

Abby Cushman liked the look of the house. It was a fancy two-story frame house, a comforting contrast to the range land all around it. It occupied its space with a doughty colonial dignity.

The front door was unlocked. Abby filed in behind Colonel Tyler and his lieutenants. The inside of the house was nice, too, she thought—though a broken window in the living room had let in the wind and tumbled some of the contents.

This big, central room was decorated in a southwest/Hopi style that had been fashionable some years ago and seemed curiously misplaced on a northern prairie. Pattern rugs, beige walls, a long sand-colored sofa, and Kachina dolls on a sideboard; squat porcelain lamps. She wondered who had lived here. Someone dislocated, Abby thought. Someone out of place.

Colonel Tyler had gone off to investigate the kitchen and the cellar for supplies. Abby said, "I'll check upstairs," to Matt Wheeler, who was helping a breathless Miriam Flett into a chair.

It was odd that William wasn't with her. The old woman and the boy were almost inseparable these days. Come to think of it, Miriam had been acting strangely for days.

She thought of asking, thought better of it. *Mind your own business, Abby.* There had been much discontent in camp lately, and none of it was mysterious. This journey had demonstrated all too graphically the emptiness of the world and the inadequacy of the human temperament. America is as empty as an old cup, Abby thought, and the best we can do by way of survivors is a cowardly old man like Tom Kindle.

Unpleasant thought.

She hurried upstairs to a carpeted hallway, cool and dim, and three closed doors—the bedrooms, Abby supposed.

■   ■   ■

William heard the rattle of the doorknob behind him.
Rosa—
I know, she said. She took a step—a delicately balanced pirouette—toward the window. He felt her unsteadiness.
Thank you, she said. *Whatever happens.*

■   ■   ■

So accustomed had Abby grown to the vacancy of the world that she was astonished, above all else, to find the second bedroom occupied.
"William!" she said.
Then she looked at the window . . . at the thing *in front* of the window.
It was a delicate silhouette in the morning light. She thought at first it must be a kind of decoration—some eccentric assemblage of cellophane panels meant to break the morning light into these fractions of purple and blue. But then it moved. It was alive, somehow organic . . . she discovered eyes, a sort of face.
William raised his fingers to his lips, a child's *Be quiet!* And Abby stifled an urge to cry out.
"Don't be afraid," the boy whispered.
But *of course* she was afraid. She saw the broken cocoon on the faded bedspread. It was an insect thing. Abby had never liked insects. Her older brothers used to torment her with caterpillars. The cocoon on the bed implied that this creature was a kind of *human bug,* and the idea was so distasteful that Abby wanted to flee the room or call out for help.
William appeared to sense her distress. "Abby," he said—it was the first time William had called her by her given name, as if he were an adult—"this is Rosa Connor. She can't speak. But she won't hurt you. All she wants to do is leave. She's fragile, and I'm afraid she'll get hurt if the others find her here. Abby, do you understand?"
Of course she did not. How could one understand such things?
But she recognized the sincerity in William's voice. He was an odd child, Abby thought dizzily. Abby knew children. She had raised a daughter of her own and had been raising her daughter's two boys when Contact took

them away. William looked a little like Cory, her oldest grandson. Cory had always been bringing things home. Stones, bottletops—cocoons. She had tried to share his interest, at least from a distance; had tried to enter that child's world where everything was a mystery and a fascination. Perhaps William was fascinated with this—creature.

Abby's heart was pounding desperately against her ribs. But she thought of Paul Jacopetti in the basement of the Buchanan hospital, and she resolved to quell her panic this time, not make the same mistake.

She closed her eyes and swallowed hard. "If it wants to leave," she said, "why *doesn't* it?"

"Abby, did you ever see a butterfly when it's new? The wings are wet. They have to dry. Otherwise it would just fall."

"I see. How much longer?"

"Minutes."

"William—I can't stop anyone from coming upstairs."

"But if you don't call out—"

"I won't." She was steadily calmer. "But Colonel Tyler is searching the house."

"We only need a short time, Abby."

"A short time is all you may have."

■　　■　　■

Even in this extremity, William was impressed by Rosa's grace. She grasped the window frame with arms as delicate as strings, fingers like threads. She pulled herself up, paused on the sill facing inward, then unfolded her wings behind her, stretched them to their full span, wide sails, coral-patterned, the blues and purples a lighter hue in the sunlight. She was like an enormous orchid blossom. When the wind blew, she trembled.

Almost, Rosa told him. *Now.*

Then Abby gasped, the door opened: Colonel Tyler.

■　　■　　■

It was remarkable, Abby thought, how quickly Tyler seemed to grasp the situation. His eyes flickered from Abby to William to the insect woman. He was obviously shocked. But not shocked motionless, as Abby had been. His hand was suddenly active.

He drew that pistol he always carried.

"No," Abby said.

The Colonel paid her no attention. His attention was wholly focused on the creature William had called Rosa, and his face was a twisted grimace of distaste. Abby had been afraid, but the Colonel—the Colonel, she realized, was *offended*.

He stood with his legs braced apart and aimed the pistol at Rosa with both hands.

Abby felt as if time had slowed to a miserly crawl. There was time to see *everything*. See William's sadness and concern. See the insect woman arching her impossible wings against the morning sky. See Tyler's pistol in all its intricacy, a complex steel-gray machine.

She heard the rasp of her own breath in her throat like the tick of a metronome. Time to *see*; no time to *act*.

But now William was moving.

For all the compression of time, Abby thought, the boy was quick. Impossibly quick. Inhumanly quick.

He threw himself at Tyler's body. The impact turned the Colonel's pistol toward the ceiling. Tyler fired, and the sound in the enclosed room was an insult to the ears, cruelly loud. Plaster rained from the ceiling. There was a hole there, ragged and small. "Christ!" Tyler raged.

Abby looked to the window, where the insect woman's wings lifted, caught air, rippled; and then Rosa was away, dropping in a long trajectory, a glide . . . then rising. . . .

Tyler staggered to the window, raised his pistol once more.

William was beside him, tugging his arm down.

Tyler pushed the boy aside. Abby heard William's head crack against the wall.

"No!" she cried.

It was not a decent way to treat a child.

William straightened, unhurt; but Tyler's gun was pointed at him now.

"No!" Abby said furiously. "Colonel, *stop!*"

Was he deaf?

William turned his face toward her. It was absurd, but Abby felt he wanted to *reassure* her. To tell her he would be all right.

He was not all right.

The boy looked at Colonel Tyler and said, quite clearly, "I know what you are."

Colonel Tyler pulled the trigger. William's chest exploded.

"NOOOO!" Abby's voice was a wail of grief.

Tyler fired again, now at William's head, where his eyes were still blinking. Abby could not bear the sound of the shot or the result of it. So much blood. She could not help thinking of Cory or her other grandson,

Damian; of her daughter Laura. She had lost Laura to an airplane tragedy and Cory and Damian to the Greater World and although William wasn't family Abby could not tolerate the loss of another child, any child, for the sin of impeding Colonel John Tyler's line of fire. So she did what William had done, hurried across the room through slow-motion time, knowing it was too late, seeing but not seeing the impossible amount of blood, and threw herself at Colonel Tyler, who fell backward. Then they were wrestling for the pistol, Abby surprised by her own physical strength and the strength of her hatred, eyes blurred by tears, wanting to rip the pistol from Tyler's hand and punish him with it but managing only to twist it in his grip, and Tyler pulled the trigger twice more, both shots wild, chipping paint and dust from the wallboard, until at last her strength and courage ebbed and Tyler thrust her aside and sat with the pistol aimed at her—Abby thinking *Shoot me, go ahead, you child-murdering bastard!*—then someone was holding her from behind, and Tyler, horribly, was pointing his pistol at the boy's corpse:

"Abby, *he's not human.* Look!" Nudging the limp body with his foot. "This isn't blood! Christ's sake! It looks like thirty-weight motor oil! *Jesus!*"

Did any of that matter?

No, Abby thought.

In a gesture that surprised even herself, Abby collected all the saliva that remained in her dry mouth and spat into Colonel Tyler's face. Her aim was precise.

Tyler froze.

Everyone in the room—a crowd, now, including Bob Ganish, Paul Jacopetti, and Joey Commoner, who was holding her from behind—froze and waited.

"Take her to her trailer," the Colonel said. The spittle ran down his cheek, and his voice was a razory whine. "Take her there and *keep* her there. I'll deal with this later."

■   ■   ■

Rosa Perry Connor rode the morning thermals up long inclines of warming air until the ranch was far below her.

She moved in the sky with an easy familiarity. The sky was not an empty space, not a vacuum; it was an ocean, Rosa thought, rich with currents, inviting discovery, appreciation, acrobatics: glides and sweeping, sensuous curves. It was intoxicating.

She watched her shadow flow across dry rangeland, over scrub and cheat grass like ocean swells far below. The sun was warm on her wings.

She knew what had happened in the Connor house. She felt William's release. It was premature. He had been a sojourner like herself, an old man in a boy's body. She broadcast her sorrow in the direction of Home. The ecstasy of flight and this unhappiness mingled in her. William accepted her consolation, but lightly; he was also sharing her pleasure in the flight.

It was the human tragedy that saddened him.

Tragedy is what they live in, Rosa thought. *Tragedy is their ocean, William—their air.*

He touched her with a sad rebuke that was not quite contradiction. *You were human once.*

Yes, Rosa acknowledged. She fixed her attention on the far peak of Home, china-blue in the morning light. *Human once,* she thought. *But not anymore.*

■   ■   ■

Abby Cushman was confined after some struggle in her camper with Joey standing guard at the door.

Dazed beyond thinking and weak with grief, she pressed her face against the window and watched Rosa's orchid-colored wings grow small in the southern sky.

Chapter
33
Provocation

Beth came out of her camper at the sound of the gunshot and hurried into the farmhouse. She found Abby Cushman in tears, Joey and Bob Ganish leading her away.

Upstairs, Matt Wheeler was arguing with Colonel Tyler. Beth stood at the stairway end of the corridor, too far away to hear the argument clearly, but she was startled by the ferocity of it and by the way Colonel Tyler's hand hovered near his pistol.

The unexplained violence in the air made her dizzy. These two admirable men, Matt in faded jeans and shirt, the Colonel in a threadbare officer's jacket, looked used-up, worn out by their own anger.

She heard Matt say something about *killing*. And Colonel Tyler, fiercely: *He was some kind of spy.*

Not human, she heard Tyler say.

Who were they talking about?

Then Matt told Tyler he couldn't make a prisoner of Abby Cushman, and Tyler said the doctor wasn't in a position to give orders, and there were more of these bitter, clipped words, until Matt stalked away—Beth concealed herself in an empty bedroom as he passed—and the argument was finished.

She was surprised by a sudden thought that both of these men had touched her: Tyler with his large hand, Matt more intimately. Somehow, she was a party to this.

She walked down the corridor to Colonel Tyler.

He registered her presence, though his eyes were distant.

Beth said, "What happened?" Peering past him into a room where the window was open, broken, and there was an acrid smell— "Is that blood in there?"

The Colonel put his hand on her shoulder, another touch, and steered her away.

"I'll explain," he said.

It was William who had been the spy. The boy was dead.

• • •

The Colonel explained, and Beth retired to her camper.

They had acquired all these vehicles at a dealership in the Willamette Valley, on the eastern side of the Coast Range where the storm hadn't done as much damage. It was strange, Beth thought, everybody driving these $40,000 Travelaire and Citations with connections for running water and TV sets, these fancy boxes on wheels.

Everything we ever made, Beth thought—we human beings—most of it was boxes. A house is a box, she thought; an office building is a box. A TV is a box, and a microwave oven is a box of radiation. All these boxes. Nobody made boxes anymore. All the boxes we'll ever need, Beth thought idly, people left them lying around for free.

Alone, she listened to the morning's violence echo and rebound through the camp. Footsteps, doors slammed, angry voices now and then.

She wasn't accustomed to violence. Her family had never been violent, unless you counted her father's occasional deer hunts. Her mother was a careful, prim woman who left home and moved to Terre Haute with a new husband when Beth was fifteen years old. Her father was often angry, but he never actually hit her. Since that trouble when she was fourteen, her quick D&C at a Seattle hospital, he had seldom even looked at her. Nobody had looked at her, except to laugh or make fun—except Joey.

She dozed through the afternoon, afraid of what might be happening outside. At dinnertime, she left the camper and found Tyler and Joey and Paul Jacopetti building a fire in a barbecue pit behind the farmhouse: people didn't want to eat a meal inside the house where William had died. The Colonel ignored her; Jacopetti ignored her.

Joey watched her the way he always watched her—following her with his eyes, not making a big deal of it, but relentlessly. She felt his attention like a toothache. He had been watching her like this every day since they had left Buchanan, a casual proprietary surveillance that made her itch with indignation.

She decided she wasn't hungry. She turned her back on the men and walked to the front of the farmhouse and inside, although the hot-metal odor of this morning's bloodshed was still hanging in the air. Miriam Flett was inside, sitting in a chair doing nothing. Watching the dust float. Beth approached her with caution. She imagined the old woman must be horribly sad. It was obvious she'd liked that boy; even if he was a spy, not human.

Miriam looked up at Beth's approach, her face crowded with wrinkles.

"I'm sorry," Beth said. "I didn't mean to startle you."

"It's all right." Miriam's voice was a dry whisper.

"You must—" Was this the right thing to say? "You must feel terrible. I'm sorry about what happened."

"They told you about it?"

"The Colonel did. He said William was—uh—"

"Not entirely human," Miriam supplied. "But I knew that about him."

"Did you? Still . . . he died. It's sad."

"If he wasn't human," Miriam said primly, "he didn't die."

It took Beth a moment to interpret this. "I guess not. It's hard to get used to the idea, though."

Then Miriam did something Beth had not seen her do before: She smiled.

"It was hard for me, too," she said.

■ ■ ■

There was some talk of moving on, or back to the truckstop, some place away from this unhappy house, but Colonel Tyler vetoed the idea, at least until morning. They could sleep in their vehicles; there was no real urgency. Beth supposed he was right. But the encampment that evening was steeped in an ugly silence.

Just before dark, while there was still a rosy light around the high slope of the human Artifact, Tim Belanger unhooked the camper-trailer from the rear of his pickup truck and went roaring away east. He escaped, Beth thought, just like Tom Kindle—another refugee.

Another one gone, Beth thought sadly.

Nine of us left altogether.

She wished it had been Joey who left.

■ ■ ■

She found him damping the fire in back of the farmhouse. The fire had been the only significant light on this prairie, and she was sorry to see it flicker out.

Joey wore his ancient skull-and-roses T-shirt and a leather jacket to keep away the night chill. His pistol was tucked under his belt. It was a small-caliber pistol, but Beth thought it was reckless of Colonel Tyler to have given Joey any kind of gun. It was a miracle Joey hadn't blown his own balls off with it.

She hadn't come looking for him. She wanted to walk a distance into the Connors' grazing land and be by herself . . . watch the stars come out and try to make some sense of everything that had happened. But Joey waved her over.

"Sit down," he said.

"I was going somewhere," Beth said, aware of how pathetic it sounded.

"Taking in a movie? Goin' down to the mall, Beth?" He laughed. "It's a fuckin' desert out here. Everywhere we go is some kind of desert or other. Doesn't it rain anywhere but Buchanan?"

"It rains in Ohio."

"Ohio," Joey said scornfully.

He poured another bucket of sand over the embers until even that faint light was lost. "Some wild events this morning."

She nodded.

"I saw the whole thing. Two shots." He cocked his index finger. "*Bam,* the chest. *Bam,* the head. You don't want to *know* what it looked like. It was obvious the kid wasn't human. Inside, he was like—shit, I don't know. Like a watermelon full of motor oil."

"Christ, Joey!"

He smiled at her. "Facts of life."

"Is Abby Cushman still under guard?"

"Jacopetti's outside her door. Not that he could stop her from coming out. I take over from him when I'm done here. It doesn't really matter— where's she gonna go?"

"Like Tom Kindle or Tim Belanger, maybe. Just leave."

"Nope. I pulled the distributor cable out of her engine."

"Does Colonel Tyler know that?"

"He said it showed initiative." Big grin.

Beth resented Joey's access to the Colonel. It was Joey's influence that had caused most of their problems, she was sure of it. She remembered Tyler's hand on her shoulder this morning. Familiar hand. She had memorized the sensation.

His touch was like a token of everything she'd gained since Contact, and Joey was everything she wanted to forget. The two of them together . . . it was an unbearable combination.

"*Bam*," Joey said, reminiscing. "I'll tell you one thing there's less of now. There's less bullshit."

It was a callous, stupid thing to say, and it made her angry. "The end of the world is a good thing because you get to carry a gun for the first time in your life? Sounds like bullshit to me."

"If the world hadn't ended, I wouldn't be carrying a pistol. True. If the world hadn't ended, you wouldn't be fucking a doctor."

She flushed with anger. "You don't know who I sleep with. You don't have a clue."

"All I'm saying is don't act superior when you're out there with a 'For Sale' sign between your legs."

Maybe the rage she felt had been inside her all along, and maybe it wasn't even Joey she was mad at. But, oh, Christ, after a long and fucked-up day when somebody had *died*, for God's sake, to have Joey Commoner call her a slut, to be *sneered at* by him—it erased everything she had pretended to achieve; it was unspeakable, and she hated him for it.

She blinked back tears. Joey was watching her, was maddeningly attentive, his face calm and slack in the starlight, and suddenly Beth recalled a dream she had once had:

Joey as a wild horse. Beth the rider. She rides him to the top of some high cliff. He balks, and she spurs him. And he jumps.

Shut up, Beth. Just close your mouth. Don't make it worse.

She felt light-headed, utterly weightless.

This cliff, she thought. *This desert.*

"Bastard," she said. "You don't know everything that goes on in this camp."

"Try me," Joey said.

Chapter
34
Precipice

Matt was not quite asleep when the knock came at the door of his camper.

He sat up and peered out the window at prairie night. The stars were the color of ice and there was a milky glow on the eastern horizon where the moon was about to rise.

Beth? he wondered. But it was late even for Beth.

And it hadn't sounded like her knock. Not that reckless. Three discreet taps. Dear God, he thought wearily, what now?

He pulled on a T-shirt and briefs and stumbled to the door.

Tap tap tap.

"All right! Christ's sake! Hold on!"

He opened the door and stood mute in a river of night air.

"Matthew," Tom Kindle said. "Lemme in before I freeze my balls off."

.   .   .

Kindle didn't look good. He wasn't hurt, but he looked chastened. Matt tried to remember where he had seen that look on Tom Kindle before.

Of course: it was when he came into the hospital with his broken leg, raving about monsters. About a thousand years ago.

Matt kept the light low and poured his friend a cup of lukewarm coffee from a thermos. "You didn't get too damn far, did you? Not much farther than Laramie, I'll bet."

Kindle put aside his rifle and shrugged. His eyes were lost among wrinkles like crevices. "I took a little trip south. Toward that, uh, that thing—"

"The new Artifact."

"I admit I was curious about it. Aren't you? Even sitting on the horizon, it's big enough to fill half a sky." He took a long, noisy sip of coffee. "And it's strange, Matthew. It draws the attention. You ever been down to Moab? The canyonlands around there? Same kind of strangeness. Red rock, blue sky, and everything's too big. Maybe a person loses some judgment. I looked at that thing a long time, and then I started to wonder if I could get up close to it."

"Did you?"

"Get close? No, not very." He shook his head. "Close enough, though. The air gets foul. It smells like sulphur and it burns your lungs. The ground isn't too steady, either. Matthew—the thing is rooted to the earth! Literally, it looks like it put down roots, roots made of some kind of stone. Black sandstone or maybe pumice. Miles wide. And, Matthew, in the shadow of those roots, there were certain things *moving around.* . . ."

"Things?"

"Machines. I guess. Or animals. Or both, somehow. But they were big enough to see from miles away. Hazy in the distance, the way you might see a city from across a lake—they were as big as that. Big as a city and taller than they were wide, and different shapes, like giraffes, or gantries, or spiders, or cranes." He shuddered. "They must have built that entire thing since last August—have you *thought* about that? A thing the size of a mountain in half a year? God Almighty! And, Matthew . . . while I was watching those creatures move around, a thought occurred to me. They must be about finished their work, I thought. It doesn't look like a half-made thing. And it's a spaceship, right? When it's ready, it goes into orbit. Spaceship the size of Delaware. And here we are sitting practically on its tail. I came back north this morning and found you folks still parked here, and I don't think that's too intelligent."

"It's Tyler," Matt said. "He claims there was a radio message. Some bad weather east of here. So we're staying put."

"There was a vote on this?"

"One of the Colonel's votes."

"Bullshit and gerrymander."

"Yeah, basically."

"He *claims* there was a radio message?"

"Well—the radio blew up."

"While he was using it?"

"Supposedly."

"Any witnesses?"

"Nope."

"You put up with this horseshit?"

"He's not a stupid man, Tom. He had the Committee rolled up like a carpet. Made me look paranoid."

"A little paranoia's not a bad thing. I was careful coming toward camp. Left my camper in back of a billboard and hiked away from the road. I spent most of the afternoon hidden behind a rise south of here watching folks mill around. Am I crazy, or is Joey Commoner standing guard on Abby's trailer?"

Matt told him about the insect woman, about William's death and Abby's altercation with the Colonel.

Kindle listened carefully, eyes wide. "She had *wings*?"

"I saw her in the air," Matt said. "Yes, she had wings. They looked like butterfly wings."

"Oh, Matt . . . too many fuckin' miracles," Kindle said.

"Uh-huh." That about summed it up.

Kindle held his rifle in his lap. "The question is, what are you planning to do about it?"

"He can't keep Abby in her trailer indefinitely. Weather or no weather, we'll have to move on soon."

"Might not be time. I don't know why Tyler's stalling, but I don't think it matters. That mountain on the horizon isn't going to wait for us. It's not just Tyler's risk. There's Abby—and that old lady, Miriam—"

And Beth, Matt thought. "But Tyler's still got the Committee wrapped up."

"I'm not talking about a *vote*, I'm talking about *leaving*. Bugging out. Soon. Say, *tonight*."

"You just got back."

"I mean everybody. Everybody who isn't playing handmaiden to Colonel Tyler. I saw Tim Belanger headed east by himself. Obviously he's got the right idea. So we round up Abby, we get Miriam—"

"Beth," Matt said.

"And Beth, and we take one of these big RVs and leave before the Colonel gets his act together."

"It would have to be *this* camper. I don't want to leave my medical supplies behind."

"Okay, this camper. There's room for everybody until we can find more transportation. We're only a couple of days from Ohio if we keep moving."

"I thought you didn't want to go to Ohio. I thought you wanted to see the Wind River Range."

"Maybe I just want to see the last of Tyler. Maybe I don't like the fact that he locked up Abby Cushman." Kindle lifted his rifle and sighted down the length of it. "Or maybe some asshole talked me into thinking of this fuckin' trailer camp as a town."

■   ■   ■

Beth was ashamed of what she had told Joey . . . but tantalized by it, too.

He had reacted with an enraged denial, and here was the scary part: she *liked it*.

She had always liked her ability to rouse Joey from his slumberous complacency—to make him horny; to make him mad. Poke the tiger and see if he bites. Even if it was her he bit. Maybe *especially* if it was her.

She had left Joey by the dead fire in back of the house, had left him stewing in his own anger, and it was only fair, Beth told herself; not nice, but fair; now they were even.

She was restless in her bed with the memory.

You want to know where I'm spending the night?

In that camper, Joey had said. Like you always do.

Not every night. Not the whole night. Listen—

Remembering it made her weak-kneed. And hot. In every sense of the word.

If she left her camper now . . . would Joey notice?

He was guarding Abby Cushman. With her cheek pressed against the rear window, Beth could just see the light of the burning Sterno he used to keep himself warm. Joey took his guard duty seriously. He hardly ever slept anymore. He didn't seem to need to.

He was crouched against the meager light like a troll.

Beth thought, *If I leave on the other side of the camper and circle around toward the house* . . .

It might be possible.

She put on her old jeans and a blouse. Then she took three deep breaths and opened the door into cold prairie night. She stepped out barefoot with her long hair loose, like a country girl.

There was more light than she really liked. The moon had just come up. And was it a reflection of the moonlight or was the earthbound Artifact glowing with some subtle light of its own? A pale white pulsation, as if it were storing up some peculiar kind of energy?

Beth moved lightly, silently, in the radiant night.

• • •

Miriam, back in her camper, understood that distant glow. It registered on her eyelids and behind them as she lay in bed, her body eroding from within.

Miriam was two places now: here and Home. The neocytes had worked quickly. Miriam at Home was not made of blood and skin, was not even altogether *material*, and Miriam became more wholly *that* Miriam with every tick of the clock, as *this* Miriam—the old and used-up and ailing Miriam—grew increasingly hollow and fragile.

She turned her head to the window and saw Home bathed in a ghostly nimbus, summoning the energies that would lift it free of the Earth.

Summoning the energies, Miriam thought, that would carry it to the stars, a human *epistemos* in the growing awareness of the galaxy.

Very soon now, Miriam thought.

• • •

Colonel Tyler had occupied a downstairs room in the Connor house—a room that once had been Vince Connor's study, with a filing cabinet full of deeds, insurance documents, and bookkeeping ledgers, and a leather sofa long enough to stretch out on.

Colonel Tyler sat in what had been Vince's favorite chair: a high-backed recliner finished in olive-green Naugahyde. Although it was very late, the Colonel was awake. He hadn't slept for three nights now—a bad sign.

He hated the dark. In the dark, Sissy tended to disappear; and as bad as her presence was, to be alone was often worse. The days were all right. In the day there was sunlight, a horizon. At night, doubts came swarming.

Doubts . . . and sometimes madness.

It seemed to Colonel Tyler that his madness, which had once been a sealed box, had spilled out into his everyday life. Madness was everywhere: in Sissy, whose persistence was probably not normal; in the derangement of the world; in the appearance of the insect woman and the death of the pseudo-child William.

And today Tim Belanger had left camp, and that seemed the worst omen of all, the symptom of a disintegration that had begun to move from the peripheral Tom Kindle to the more central Tim Belanger and would eventually strike at the core: Ganish, Jacopetti, Joey, even himself. . . .

"Colonel Tyler?"

He looked up, startled.

Beth Porter stood in the doorway. He hadn't heard her knock.

He cleared his throat. "Beth?" He summoned up the daylight Colonel John Tyler.

She glanced at him and then at the service revolver he had placed on the arm of the recliner. "Are you okay?"

Who had last asked him that? A.W. Murdoch, he thought. In that little town in Georgia. In Loftus. "Certainly I am."

"May I come in?"

He nodded. She stepped into the meager light of a single lamp and closed the door behind her. She was not a child, Tyler thought, nor yet quite an adult; she still moved like a teenager, with a teenager's unconscious coltishness. "What brings you out so late?"

"Just that I was lonely," Beth said. "I thought it might be warmer in here."

■　■　■

Matt and Kindle approached the Sterno fire in front of Abby's trailer expecting a brisk who-goes-there from Joey. The fire cast tall, nervous shadows on the aluminum wall of the camper. The camper was dark and the door was closed, but Joey wasn't there.

"Maybe he got tired and found somewhere to sleep," Matt said. "Or took a bathroom break."

Kindle shook his head. "Joey doesn't sleep, and he pees in the bushes when he figures he's alone. This is peculiar." He rapped his bony knuckles on the door.

Abby's voice, sleepy and chastened, came from inside: "*Who's there?*"

"Me," Kindle said. "Me and Matt. We need to talk."

A few seconds later, she was at the door in an old blue nightgown, looking at Kindle with sleepy eyes and a stew of emotions. "You selfish son of a bitch—you *left*."

"Selfish SOB came back," Kindle said. "Abby, I didn't know he was going to lock you up."

"Where *is* Joey?" Abby wondered.

She turned her head at the sound of the gunshot.

■　■　■

"Hold up!" Kindle said. "Christ's sake! Hold up!"

He stopped Matt and Abby before they ran across the open space to the

Connor house. The shot had seemed to come from there. "Think about this. Who's in the house?"

"Tyler, probably," Matt said. " I don't know who else."

"Which room is Tyler using?"

"Around the side."

"Show me. But stay back from the house."

They circled clockwise in the dark behind the row of RVs, where lights had begun to come on.

"That window," Matt said.

It was a small side window with a roll blind across it. They saw a second flare of light in that confined space, a second gunshot; and moments later, a third.

■   ■   ■

Rosa Perry Connor didn't hear the shots. She was far away, attending to another summons.

She had flown miles from the Connor farmhouse. Carried more by wind than volition, she had flown south past the Artifact, had soared high above the faint smudge of Denver, an abandoned city, and then away from the mountains and across the plains in a wordless ecstasy of flight.

Her lifespan in this altered body was short but sufficient. Night fell. She approached the stars on gusts of colder, darker air. She grew lighter as her physical resources were exhausted.

It was time to go Home. The summons had gone out all over the world. Sojourners in the air, the sea, on the land: come Home, come Home now. Time for the great departure. But like a guilty child at bedtime, Rosa lingered a moment longer.

The moon rose over the lightless immensity of the high plains. *One wingbeat more*, Rosa thought, *one more*, savoring the brisk night wind that would carry her dust away.

Chapter 35

Wounds

Joey had been doing sentinel duty every night since they crossed the Snake, and he had learned how to listen to the dark.

Every night, he made a fire to keep himself warm. It was spring and the days were often hot, but after dark the heat bled into the sky, the air grew cold, and the wind cut close to the bone.

Make a fire too big, though, and the sound of it would obliterate every other sound. At first he burned windfall, roadside trash, loose barn boards or stick furniture from wasteland shacks abandoned long before Contact. Pine knots in the old wood exploded like gunshots, and their sparks threatened to ignite the dry sage beyond the blacktop highway. It was Colonel Tyler who showed him how to light the little cans of Sterno jelly, and Joey had begun to collect them from the sports-supply and general-merchandise shops in the towns they passed. The Sterno burned almost silently, just a whisper as the wind whipped the flames. It gave off precious little heat—with luck, enough to warm his hands. But in his leather jacket he was generally okay.

The campers were lined up outside the Connor house, and Joey sat minding his Sterno fire on the concrete drive at Abby Cushman's door, listening.

He had honed his listening skills quickly. The world might seem empty, but Joey knew it wasn't. There were animals, for one thing. Dogs: ex-pets, maybe, learning how to survive in the wild; or wild dogs; or wolves—he had heard some howling the last couple of nights. And people. It was amazing, the variety of noises people made on a still night. These camper-trailers had thin walls, and he often heard the murmur of night talk. People talking to themselves, talking in their sleep. Or rolling over in bed, rocking the RV a little. Maybe somebody trotting into the house to use a toilet; somebody else, restless, stepping outside to look at the stars.

Tonight he tried to calm himself, to make his ears come alive.

But he couldn't help rerunning his encounter with Beth.

It was stupid, what she had said. Joey knew what went on in this camp, especially at night. He knew all about Beth and what Beth did at night: slept alone, mostly; snuck over to the doctor's RV sometimes.

Which was bad enough. The mystery of Beth was that he simultaneously wanted her and didn't. Sometimes just looking at the way she moved across the tarmac in her blue jeans was enough to give Joey a raging hard-on. Other times she was as appealing as a day-old cut of meat. Sometimes he hated to think about her; sometimes he hated to think of anyone *else* thinking about her.

He guessed she was fucking the doctor; and as bad as that was, he had begun to live with the idea.

But the thing she had told him tonight—her dirty comments about Colonel Tyler—

No.

It was impossible. Colonel Tyler, Joey thought, was like an avenging angel, a pure and powerful force from far beyond the limits of this ratty trailer caravan. It was Colonel Tyler who had come into the ruins of Buchanan with clean clothes and a pistol on his hip and asked to talk to Mr. Joseph Commoner. It was Tyler who had trusted Joey to walk the perimeter, Tyler who had trusted him with a gun.

The idea that the Colonel would stoop to some furtive little night fuck with a nonentity like Beth—it was *obscene*, and he didn't believe it.

But the night wore on, and the moon began to rise, and the new Artifact radiated a pale light of its own, and Joey heard Beth's door ease open—the whine of the hinges above the moth-flutter of the Sterno flame—and he stood and took three silent steps to the corner of Abby's camper, helplessly curious, and watched Beth moving, a shadow, to the front door of the Connor house and inside.

Probably she was just using the toilet. But Joey itched with the insult of what she had told him, and he circled around the house to the side, to the window where Colonel Tyler's light was still burning. The blind was down, but Joey put his face to the glass and was able to capture an angle of vision where the blind gapped against the sill. Colonel Tyler sat motionless in a chair. His pistol rested on the arm.

Joey touched his own pistol, snug against his belt. He knew the Colonel couldn't see him, that the lamp and the blind would have made a mirror of the window on a night this dark, but his face was hot with shame and suspicion and his heart was beating wildly.

He saw Colonel Tyler look toward the door, saw his lips move but couldn't make out the words.

The door was at the wrong angle and Joey wasn't able to see who had arrived . . . but who else could it be?

He began to take small, sharp breaths.

Colonel Tyler spoke, paused, spoke again.

Joey registered these images but ceased to think about them. He couldn't think any longer; could only watch.

Now Beth moved into his range of vision. She was dressed too lightly for the weather. She was blushing a little. She looked nervous and aroused, her hair hanging loose around her shoulders.

She came and stood beside Tyler's chair. Tyler didn't move. Beth spoke. Words inaudible. She reached for Tyler's huge hand and took it in her own. She put his hand on her blouse, on her breast, and moved against it in a way that seemed to Joey brutally obscene.

Joey took his pistol out of his belt and hurried to the front of the house.

■   ■   ■

Once it was obvious why Beth had come, Tyler felt in control of the situation.

She wasn't much different from the hundreds of such women Tyler had hired at various times in his life, and there was nothing very surprising, he thought, about her presence tonight. Apparently he had inherited more than a gavel from the deposed Matt Wheeler.

She put his hand against her blouse and he felt the shape of her breast, the hard nugget of the nipple. He admired the sight of his hand there, the creviced skin against the flimsy cloth.

He stood up and pressed her against him. She wasn't very tall. Her head was tilted back, her eyes half-closed, expecting a kiss. Tyler didn't kiss—it was a dirty habit. Instead, he tangled his right hand in her hair and pulled.

Her eyes widened. He warned her not to speak, not to say anything. He didn't like women who talked.

He pressed his hips against her, put his left hand under her blouse and explored. He pulled her head back until her throat was exposed in a fine white curve. She wasn't sure what to make of the pain, seemed to hover between arousal and fear.

Her blue jeans were closed with a row of buttons. Tyler had opened two of them when Joey kicked open the door.

▪   ▪   ▪

Colonel Tyler had never been wounded in combat—he had never experienced combat firsthand—and he was surprised when the bullet hit him.

There was pain and anger but first of all, above all else, an enormous surprise, as if it were an act of God, a causeless momentum that tumbled him backward.

He caught himself against the recliner with his right hand. The left hand, his left arm, in fact, wouldn't answer to the helm. It felt as if someone had cut off the arm and replaced it with a fleshy, useless slab of rubber. There was blood all over his shoulder.

Beth was still standing, though the shot must have come very near her head. Tyler realized that she was screaming, that the sound was exterior to him.

"Move away," Joey was telling her—the Colonel recognized Joey's petulant whine. "Get out of the way."

Tyler braced his hip against the recliner and reached for his own pistol.

He had loaded it earlier tonight. He had meant only to touch its cold steel against his forehead, perhaps taste the barrel with his tongue, as was his habit. Never to pull the trigger. Sissy always talked him out of that. But now someone else had pulled a trigger, someone else had shot him. Joey had shot him.

He grasped the pistol and swiveled around.

One foot slid against the polished oak floor and Tyler bumped to a sitting position with his back against the recliner. Joey must have tracked this motion as a fall, or ignored it altogether; his attention was still on Beth. To the Colonel's eyes Joey looked grotesque, inflated with jealousy to bullfrog proportions.

"Move aside," Joey repeated, and Beth seemed finally to understand; she took two steps toward the window and turned to look for Tyler. Perhaps she saw the blood for the first time; her eyes widened and Tyler wondered if she would scream again. Beth looked a little ridiculous, too, with her smooth belly showing through the gap of her unbuttoned pants.

Joey looked at the Colonel and the Colonel shot him in the head.

There was no precision or elegance in the act, only the raising of the pistol and the pulling of the trigger and Joey falling down and convulsing for a horrible thirty or forty seconds before he died.

358 • Robert Charles Wilson

Beth went to Joey and knelt above him and made a choked sound at the sight of his injury. Her hand rested on the pistol Joey had dropped beside him. Colonel Tyler watched that hand. *Watch that hand,* Sissy instructed him. Sissy was a sudden, nebulous presence hovering near the ceiling of the room, but Tyler didn't look for her, merely followed her advice, watched Beth's hand on the pistol.

She took up the pistol and turned it toward Tyler.

Was she offering it? Threatening him with it? The expression on her face was unreadable, opaque with grief. There was no way to calculate the danger.

So Colonel Tyler shot her, too.

■   ■   ■

At the sound of the third gunshot, Matt ran to his trailer and collected his Gladstone bag.

Kindle tried to restrain him at the door. "It's stupid to go in there, Matthew. We don't know what happened. Matthew! Just *wait,* for Christ's sake!"

Matt ignored him, ran past him to the Connor house in its patch of moonlight, and inside, where it was dark.

Chapter 36

Prophylaxis

The girl was a mistake, Sissy said.

Colonel Tyler, weak with blood loss, climbed from the floor into the recliner and gave his mother's ghost a weary look.

It was unusual for Sissy to be out after dark. But she was not merely present tonight, she was almost tangible. Her layered skirts billowed around her large body; her skin was fish-white and her eyes were crazed and attentive. If I walked over to that corner of the room, Tyler thought, I bet I could touch her.

You shouldn't have shot the girl. You might have been able to explain about the boy. You might have gotten away with that. But not the girl.

"You told me to watch her hand."

Not to shoot her.

"She picked up the gun!"

She wouldn't have used it.

Tyler began an answer but stopped as the door opened.

Matthew Wheeler stood there with his Gladstone bag and a dazed expression, obviously struggling to sort out what had happened. His eyes flickered from body to body—Joey, Beth, Tyler.

Tyler raised his pistol, an action that was almost reflexive, and aimed it at the doctor.

Now listen to me, Sissy said. *If you don't do this exactly right, everyone will come in here. Everyone will come nosing into this room to see what you did. They'll know what you are. And we'll be lost. So listen to me. Listen.*

"Colonel Tyler," the doctor said, "I can't treat anyone if you're pointing a gun at me. Let me come in."

But his attention was obviously on Beth. The girl's breathing was wet and loud in the room. It reminded Tyler of the sound bathwater made as it ran down the drain.

Tyler held the pistol firmly and listened to Sissy's urgent whispers. Then he answered the doctor.

"Come in. Close the door behind you."

"I'll come in if you put down the gun."

"You'll come in or I'll shoot you, Dr. Wheeler. It's as simple as that."

Wheeler hesitated, but he entered the room after another long look at Beth.

"Now close the door," Tyler said.

Wheeler did so. He moved to lean over the girl, was fumbling with his bag, but Tyler said, "No—not yet."

The doctor's irritation was obvious. "She needs attention. She's badly injured."

"Of course she is. I shot her. Now go to the window."

Wheeler looked skeptically at the pistol.

"I won't hesitate to use this. Does it look like I would? We have two corpses here already."

"One corpse," Wheeler said. "She's still alive."

Tyler nodded impatiently and took more silent advice from Sissy: He leaned forward, though it hurt his bad arm, and trained the pistol on the girl. "So she is. I guess you want to keep it that way. Now *go to the fucking window.*"

Wheeler stood erect, finally, and did as he was told.

"Pull up those blinds. All the way. Good. Now open the window. Good. And turn off the lamp."

"I'll need the lamp to work."

"You're not working yet, Dr. Wheeler. Turn off the lamp, please."

Wheeler switched it off. Now the room was dark, no light but moonlight and a fainter, bluer radiance that might have come from the direction of the human Artifact. Tyler looked out at the space beyond the Connor house. The last RV in the caravan, Bob Ganish's big Glendale, was framed in the window.

"I want everyone assembled where I can see them."

"How am I supposed to manage that, Colonel?"

"Use your well-known powers of persuasion. Tell them I have a gun on you."

Wheeler leaned through the open window and signaled to Abby Cushman, who was standing not far away.

Sissy was distracted by the light from the Artifact, which flared brighter as Tyler watched.

That mountain may be ready to rise.

Good, Tyler thought. Then we can go to Ohio.

And no one will know what we are.

Except these few.

Who mustn't go with us.

How to stop them?

You know how.

It's an awful lot of people to kill, Tyler thought.

We'll be clever, Sissy said. *We'll think of something.*

■   ■   ■

Matt waved over Abby Cushman and told her to assemble everyone in the space between this window and Bob Ganish's Glendale. "Have them stand there where the Colonel can see them, Abby."

She stood a wary distance from the window, squinting at him. "What's this all about? Matt? Is anyone hurt?"

"I can't talk about it."

She took another step forward. Her eyeglasses reflected the moonlight. She looks like an owl, Matt thought. A frightened owl.

He thought of vaulting this windowsill, joining her outside and leaving the Colonel to tend his own injury. But Beth was under the Colonel's gun and badly hurt. He heard her terrible, stertorous breathing. He wanted to finish with all this menacing foolishness and get on with the business of helping her.

Abby came close enough to see Tyler in the dim room, the pistol aimed at Beth.

"Dear God."

"Just do as he says, Abby. Get everybody in one place. And try not to worry."

She pressed her fist to her mouth but nodded and turned away.

"Now stand back from the window, Dr. Wheeler," Tyler said.

He did so. "May I treat the girl?"

"Not yet."

"She may be dying."

"Probably," Tyler said. "But let's get our ducks in order first."

"Jesus Christ, Tyler!" It was too much.

The Colonel gestured with his pistol at Beth's prostrate body. "If you mean to be uncooperative, it would be easy to resolve the issue right now."

Looking at Tyler was like peering into an open cesspool. In a single day this man had killed two people, and he might be killing a third by delaying medical attention. Obviously, some internal restraint had snapped. Obviously, Tyler was mad.

It was vital to watch what he said, to weigh his words before he spoke. "I'll need more than what I have in my bag. I'll need bandages—"

"In due course. Be quiet."

The Colonel's attention was focused beyond the window. Abby had begun lining up people in front of the aluminum moonglow of Ganish's RV. Matt counted them off impatiently. Abby, Bob Ganish, Chuck Makepeace, Paul Jacopetti . . . the count seemed short.

Kindle, he thought. Where was Tom Kindle?

But wait: Kindle had come back into camp only an hour ago; Tyler wouldn't expect to see him in the line up. As far as the Colonel knew, Tom Kindle was still absent.

Okay—nevertheless, *where was he?*

Abby gestured for his attention.

"Go back to the window," Tyler said. "Slowly."

He did.

"Wave her over." Matt waved. "Tell her there's someone missing."

Matt gave Tyler an involuntary stare. *Somehow he knows about Kindle.* Tyler said, "The old woman—Miriam Flett."

■ ■ ■

He relayed the message to Abby.

"I know!" Abby said. She stood at the window with her eyes fixed on Tyler's pistol, obviously hating it, hating *him.* "That's what I wanted to tell you. Miriam's in her trailer. We can't wake her up."

Christ almighty! The last thing he needed was another casualty—and where was all this *light* coming from?

"Very well," Tyler was saying. "Tell Mrs. Cushman to take everyone inside that Glendale and close the door."

Abby said, "I can hear you quite well, Colonel Tyler. For how long?"

"Until further notice."

"Go on, Abby," Matt said. "Everything will be fine. I promise."

She stalked off and herded three sullen figures into the RV: Ganish, Chuck Makepeace, Jacopetti, the last sullen remnant of Buchanan, Oregon. The door closed behind her, and Matt felt suddenly much more alone.

He was about to turn away from the window when his eye tracked a glimmer of moonlight (or whatever peculiar light this was) at the right rear corner of the Glendale. He might be mistaken . . . but it looked like the barrel of Tom Kindle's rifle.

Had Tyler seen it?

Apparently Tyler had not. Tyler's uniform was sodden with blood. He must be weak, Matt thought. He ought to be in shock, by all rights. There was something more than frightening about the Colonel's calm facade; it was almost supernatural.

"I'll need bandages," he said.

"I don't want you going out there where those people are."

"I can't work miracles, Colonel. These wounds need bandages. Your wound, for instance. I need—well, at least, clean cloth."

"There should be such a thing in the house. I think there's a linen closet in the upstairs hall."

"You trust me that far?"

"Don't be asinine. If you're not back promptly, I'll shoot the girl. Or if I see you out that window, I'll shoot the girl. Get what you need. But hurry."

Tyler's face was pale and glassy with sweat.

■   ■   ■

Matt was out of the room for five minutes. He came back with a stack of clean white linen, a box of Kotex from Rosa Connor's bathroom cupboard, and a plan.

The plan was ugly, and the plan was dangerous, but it was the only way Matt could see into a future that contained both himself and a chance, at least, for Beth.

The room, which had been Vince Connor's study, was bathed in bright blue light from the window. Matt was conscious of the light but couldn't spare any thought for it. He had achieved a narrow, intense focus of attention. It reminded him of his days as an intern. There were times, at the end of a long shift, when he would be sleepless and vague and running on empty, and some emergency would arise. And either he would screw it up, maybe threatening somebody's life, or he would force himself into this condition of unnatural clarity, this bright bubble of concentration.

He concentrated on Tyler and Beth, the angle of his approach to the problem, the geometry of life and death.

He went to Beth first; but Tyler said, again, "Not yet. I'm losing considerable blood. I don't want to pass out."

"She's in worse shape than you are, Colonel."

"I know that," Tyler said irritably. "I want you to stop this bleeding from my shoulder. Then you can attend to the girl."

Matt didn't argue. *Focus*, he thought. Any distraction was too much distraction.

Tyler trained his pistol on Beth but allowed Matt close enough to examine his wound. There was enough light to see that the bullet had passed through fairly cleanly. "Joey shot you?"

Tyler nodded. "He found me with the girl." He watched for Matt's reaction. "Does that shock you?"

"Not especially."

"She was—what's a polite word for it? Loose."

"Maybe you aren't too tightly wrapped yourself, Colonel."

"What?"

"Nothing." Matt took his pulse. It was rapid but not weak. "Are you nauseous? Dizzy?"

"Not particularly."

"The wound isn't as bad as it looks."

"I can't feel anything in the arm."

"Damaged a nerve, maybe. Under the circumstances, I can't do anything about that. You understand?"

Tyler nodded.

Matt tore away the shirt and packed a sanitary napkin against the entrance wound and a second behind the shoulder where the bullet had come out. The Kotex was absorbent and wouldn't stick to the wound. He improvised a broad bandage and wound it around Tyler's shoulder. Tyler winced. The pain was beginning to break through his defenses.

When the dressing was secure, Matt opened his bag. He took a disposable syringe out of its wrapper and thumbed the plastic protector off the needle.

His attention kept wandering to Tyler's pistol, aimed almost casually at Beth. How much pressure was necessary to squeeze that trigger? How much awareness to keep it aimed?

He put the hypodermic needle through the rubber seal of a small brown vial and drew up a measured amount of clear liquid.

Tyler was watching him. "What is that?"

"A systemic antibiotic. Bullets aren't especially clean."

"Is it necessary?"

"Depends. Do you want to risk gangrene? We're a long way from a hospital, Colonel."

Tyler regarded him silently for a time. Oddly, he seemed to be *listening*. To what voice, Matt wondered. What invisible third party?

"Can you inject it into the bad arm? Because I'm not putting down the pistol. I'm not that stupid."

"How about the leg," Matt said. "The thigh."

"I'm not taking off my pants, either."

"It's a broad weave. The needle will pass through the cloth. It isn't very sanitary, however."

Tyler shrugged, distracted by his pain.

Matt flushed air from the syringe, flicked away bubbles, then pushed the needle into the meat of Tyler's leg and forced the plunger down.

"May I tend the girl's wound now?"

"Very well," Tyler said.

▪ ▪ ▪

Sissy, Colonel Tyler pleaded. I'm too weak.

You're not, his mother's ghost insisted. *Stay awake! Stay awake!*

She hovered in the corner and she smelled like stale blood—or perhaps it was the room.

You're not hurt bad! The doctor said so.

You trust him?

He took an oath. They all take an oath.

But I'm so tired, Tyler thought.

You have it all, Sissy said. *You have all the guns. All the guns are in this room. Joey's gone, the girl is gone, Tom Kindle is gone, Tim Belanger is gone. The old woman is no threat. You can kill the doctor whenever you like. And there are only four in that trailer, and they're unarmed, and one of them is a woman, and one of them is an old man. Four would be easy to kill.*

All this killing, Tyler thought. He was a little dazed by it.

You must, Sissy scolded him. *Or people will know.*

Tyler guessed he could do it. Shoot Wheeler. Walk out to the trailer. Walking would be the hard part. Open the door and shoot until everybody was dead.

It wasn't complicated, but it would be difficult. And he was so very tired.

He lifted the pistol, which had drooped away from its target, Beth, but the pistol was oddly heavy—and a new suspicion entered the Colonel's mind.

▪ ▪ ▪

The light was much brighter now.

Matt crouched over Beth. He was afraid of the wound, but he forced himself to look at it. He unbuttoned her blouse and pulled it away, exposing her small breasts, her pale skin freckled with blood.

The bullet had penetrated the chest wall and allowed air to flow into the chest cavity. Each time she exhaled, bloody bubbles formed on the wound. Her inhalations were labored, choked, and liquid.

He couldn't find an exit wound. The bullet was still inside her, might have been deflected by a bone.

He took a carotid pulse. It was weak and irregular. She was clammy and didn't respond when he raised her eyelid.

He took another sanitary pad from the box and used the plastic wrapping to cover Beth's chest wound. It was urgent to seal this opening, and the plastic was reasonably clean, reasonably airtight when he fastened it with surgical tape. Then he lifted her into a semisitting position with her body inclined toward the injury, and her breathing seemed to ease a little.

Beth! he thought. Her head lolled to one side.

He needed to keep her blood volume up, and he needed to get her to a hospital. Even then, with modern equipment at hand, he wasn't sure of his ability to treat the wound singlehandedly. He might have to explore for the bullet.

He looked at Tyler.

Tyler's eyelids were drooping. His mouth moved, but soundlessly. Who was he talking to?

Matt watched the Colonel's hand sag until the pistol was aimed, not at Beth, but at the floor. Tyler's mouth hung open now; his eyes were nearly closed. Matt turned his attention back to Beth.

She'll need an improvised stretcher, he thought, and which would be the fastest vehicle? And where was the nearest hospital? Laramie? Cheyenne?

He stood up and turned to the door . . .

But here was an unhappy miracle: *Tyler stood up, too.*

He came out of Vince Connor's old recliner like Neptune from the briny deep. His eyes were wide, his pupils small, and the blue light from the window made an eerie halo around him. "It wasn't an antibiotic," Tyler said.

It had been morphine, perhaps enough to kill him, certainly enough to sedate him, and what miracle of will or sheer evil had allowed him to resist it even this long?

Tyler's good right hand came cranking up, the pistol in it.

I'm going to die here, Matt realized. In this stupid room. For this stupid reason.

Then Tyler looked puzzled, turned his head aside, and vomited massively across Vince Connor's desk.

Matt dropped to the floor. He wanted just a little time, time enough for the morphine to do its work, as it inevitably must. He rolled into the corner of the room, knocking over a table lamp.

At the sound, Colonel Tyler jerked his head.

The pistol swiveled with his look.

Simultaneously the door crashed open.

Tom Kindle stood in the dark hallway with the barrel of his hunting rifle sweeping the room.

Tyler pivoted to face the motion.

Kindle fired.

Tyler fired his pistol.

The two sounds, in this confined space, battered the ears. Even Beth, deeply unconscious, gave an involuntary twitch.

Kindle cried out and fell back in the hallway.

Colonel Tyler fell, but soundlessly, with Tom Kindle's bullet lodged in his heart.

■ ■ ■

John! Sissy said as he fell.

It was the first time she had said his name, the first time since he was a child.

Tyler looked at her as the life went out of him in a powerful sigh. It was as if he had been holding his breath for fifty-two years, and his breath was his life, and now he just opened his mouth and let it go.

John, she said, her voice grown faint. *Now you can come to live with me again.*

■ ■ ■

It's over, Matt thought. The words seemed to circle in his head. It had been vile and ugly and there was still Beth's terrible wound demanding his attention, and Kindle in the hallway, but Tyler was dead: that impediment was gone.

It's over.

He must have said the words aloud as he bent over Tom Kindle, who had been shot in his bad leg and was bleeding from the calf. "Matthew, it's *not,*" Kindle said through gritted teeth.

Matt wrapped the injury. "What do you mean?"

"Are you blind? It's bright as day out there! Two A.M. and bright as day! And the sound! Jesus, Matthew, are you *deaf?*"

Not deaf, merely distracted.
He heard it now, a faraway rumble.
It came through the air. It came up through the bedrock.
It began to shake the house.
The Artifact was leaving the Earth.

Chapter
37

Ascension

From the doorway of Bob Ganish's motor home, Abby was able to see the Connor house—the dark window where Colonel Tyler was holding Matt hostage—and beyond it, on the horizon, the disc of the new Artifact, glowing like a floodlight or a bright new moon.

Paul Jacopetti had taken a propranolol and was resting in the camper's narrow bed. Ganish and Chuck Makepeace sat stiffly at the table in the kitchenette. They had grumbled at this confinement, but not too loudly; it was Tyler's idea, and they were Tyler's constituents; they seemed to think their docility would win them some brownie points when this was all over. "We don't know for certain what's going on," Makepeace said. "It would be premature to pass judgment."

Idiot, Abby thought.

She worried about Matt, and about Miriam, grown so strangely thin, and about Tom Kindle, hiding in the shadows with that hunting rifle of his. But her eyes kept straying to the Artifact. She had grown so accustomed to that presence on the far prairie that she had forgotten what an astonishing thing it really was. It was a spaceship, she thought, as round as a marble and as big as a mountain. It was affixed to the Earth like a tick on the skin of a dog . . . it had fed on the Earth, filled itself with humanity, and now, sated, it was apparently ready to leave.

It was almost too bright to look at.

Abby shaded her eyes and stood at the door of the Glendale waiting for a resolution. For more gunfire, or for Matt to emerge from the house. Or

Colonel Tyler. Or for the world to end: with this peculiar blue light radiating across the prairie, she guessed that was a possibility, too.

"You hear something?" Bob Ganish said.

The car salesman had cocked his head to listen.

Chuck Makepeace looked up sullenly from a game of solitaire. "No."

"Like a rumble," Ganish said. "Like a truck going by. You really don't hear it?"

Abby pressed her face against the cold window glass and felt another caress of the fear that had not left her for a day and a night.

"I do," she said. "I hear it."

The noise was faint but distinct, like thunder, like the artillery of a faraway war.

Then it was as if the cannons had come suddenly much closer, as if the caissons had rolled up behind the Connor house where the grazing land began. The Glendale motor home began to yaw and pitch.

Abby braced herself against the frame of the door. Jacopetti began shouting from the bed, shouting a single word over and over. The sense of it was lost in the roar; she looked at him and tried to read his lips. But he wasn't speaking to her, he wasn't speaking to anyone in particular; he was speaking to God, Abby thought. His eyes were wild with panic. The word was, "*Earthquake!*"

Chuck Makepeace fell to the floor and pulled the table down after him. Playing cards fluttered through the air like wounded birds. Bob Ganish gazed around himself in mute startlement, then slumped into a crude duck-and-cover with his hands clasped behind his neck. He had stocked this camper with every conceivable necessity, and the floor was suddenly awash with canned goods, bottled water, spare propane tanks, and plastic jugs of gasoline.

Somehow, Abby managed to stay upright.

She saw the Artifact begin to rise. The horizon had obscured its lower circumference, but now a gap began to widen there.

The spaceship rose with a gentle, impossible buoyancy.

At its base, a dome of hot volcanic gases exploded after it.

And the cannonfire became a deeper, more frightening growl; and the floor dropped under Abby, and rose and dropped again, until she lost her footing and fell.

■ ■ ■

Home had driven its roots deep into the lithosphere. Its central artery, its umbilical connection to the Earth, was a vent that reached below the basaltic crust to the fluid magma.

Home's departure fractured the substrate beneath it into floating chonoliths like so many loose teeth and exposed a reservoir of liquid rock to the cold night air.

The mantle shook with protest. A tectonic shockwave radiated outward from its epicenter in northern Colorado and was followed immediately by a second shock and a third.

The hole in the earth vented a cloud of luminous gas, a phenomenon geologists called a *nuée ardente*. The cloud emerged at enormous speed and pressure. It carried volcanic ejecta at high velocity, peppering the retreating Home with rock fragments. It unfolded around the newly opened crater and set fire to the prairie in an expanding ring miles in diameter.

Home rose at the crown of this maelstrom and accelerated toward the high atmosphere, toward the stars.

From an altitude, the caldera on the land below resembled a flower: a stamen of boiling lava, petals of gray smoke touched at their tips with flame.

Home rose silently beyond a thin waft of cloud, rose brightly and silently in the thinning air. Its motive force was silent; it transformed its few gigawatts of waste energy into a blue-white wash of photons.

In the space inside it, deserts shimmered in virtual sunlight; alpine meadows bloomed at the approach of a virtual spring. New oceans lapped at the shores of new continents.

Below, in the darkness, a blister of ash and fire expanded over the cold Colorado tableland.

■　■　■

The first shock knocked Matt to the floor beside Tom Kindle.

He guessed it was an earthquake. It felt as if the Connor house had grown legs and begun to take long, bounding leaps across the prairie.

Maddeningly, there was nothing to hang on to. He was as helpless as a mouse in a rolling barrel. After what seemed like an endless pummeling, he managed to grab a doorjamb and brace himself firmly enough to raise his head and look around.

The air was full of dust. The quake seemed to raise dust from every surface. Above the roar, he could hear the joists twist in the ceiling. He wondered how long the house would last.

Tom Kindle writhed on the floor with one hand clutching his bad leg.

Matt pulled himself into the room where Colonel Tyler had died. The shaking seemed progressively less intense, though it had not entirely stopped. He looked for Beth. The Colonel's body and Joey's had been thrown into a ghastly embrace, Tyler's limp arm draped over Joey's shoulder and his hand pawing at Joey's ruined head. Beth was approximately where he had left her but no longer sitting up against the foot of the recliner; she had slid back to the floor and her breathing—she was still breathing—sounded tentative and very wet.

The floor bucked again, and Matt braced himself until it steadied. He heard what must be the sound of the Connors' front porch collapsing: a series of dry, woody explosions. The window popped out of its frame and shattered on the ground outside the house.

When the trembling eased, Matt pulled himself up to the empty sill and took a hurried look outside.

He couldn't see the Artifact—the window faced the wrong direction— but he knew it must be rising. It was still radiating that vivid blue-white light, casting sundial shadows from the RVs and the prairie scrub, but now the shadows were growing shorter and inclining to the west.

The door of the Glendale opened, and Abby stood in it looking bruised and bewildered. She raised a hand to shield her eyes against the light. Matt heard someone crying out from inside the vehicle—Jacopetti, he thought. He wanted to tell Abby to stay away from the house, it wasn't structurally safe . . . the walls were inclining and it was a miracle only the porch had collapsed. The urgent thing was to get Beth outside, get Kindle outside, before the next shock or aftershock. . . .

But he couldn't speak or wave or make any coherent gesture before Abby opened her mouth in an O of dismay and clutched at the door of the motor home.

Matt supposed—much later—that there must have been a sinkhole under the RV, some old hollow in the bedrock that had been opened by the violence of the quake. All he knew as it happened was that the big Glendale tilted leftward, and the camper in front of it—Matt's camper—tilted right; one tumbled frontward into a sudden depression that might have been five or ten feet deep; the other tumbled back. The two vehicles collided, made the shape of a flattened V, and the Glendale began to slide sideways.

Abby fell back into the dark interior. Jacopetti's strained shouting ceased abruptly.

The exposed engine of the Glendale ground against a torn flank of Matt's camper and sparks fountained into the night air.

"Christ, no," Matt whispered.

The motor home was on fire as soon as that terrible possibility entered his mind.

Events were outrunning him. The fire didn't spread. It was much quicker than that. There *was* no fire—and then the fire was everywhere.

The side door of the Glendale rolled up to an impossibly steep angle.

Matt vaulted through the window and ran across the Connors' dry garden to the burning vehicles. Both were on fire now. A propane tank popped, and Matt heard shrapnel scream past his ear.

The subsidence wasn't deep. He scrambled down toward the Glendale just as flames licked up the undercarriage, forcing him back.

He called Abby's name. She didn't answer. He ran to the rear of the Glendale. There were no flames here—not yet—but the paint was peeling off the aluminum, and when he tried to climb up to the window, the skin of his hands sizzled on the metal.

■   ■   ■

He dropped to the ground and crawled away until the heat from the burning vehicles was no longer painful.

The Artifact, shrunken by altitude, dropped away beyond the western horizon. Its light faded.

It left behind the light of the burning campers, and a more baleful light from the caldera far away, a column of smoke impossibly wide, fan-shaped where it had risen into the dark sky.

The prairie was still undulating, Matt thought. Long, low-frequency waves. Like the swell of the ocean on a gentle night. Or maybe it was his imagination.

There might be stronger aftershocks.

He thought about Beth. Still work to do.

■   ■   ■

Time lurched forward in a drunkard's walk. Somehow, he dragged Beth away from the Connor house. Somehow, he went back for Tom Kindle, who had pulled himself most of the way to the door before passing out.

He remembered Miriam. The old woman had been too sick to be sequestered with the others. Her small camper was still intact. Matt hurried to the door and forced it open.

But Miriam wasn't inside—only a relic of Miriam. Only her empty skin.

■   ■   ■

In that interval, the sun had risen.

The southern horizon was a bank of roiling gray smoke larger than the Artifact had been. The sky was grayer by the minute and a gray ash had begun to fall like snow.

Beth continued to breathe. But each breath was a miracle; each breath was a victory against great odds.

Somehow, he lifted Beth and Tom Kindle into the coach of an undamaged camper.

Somehow, he began the longest journey of his life.

Chapter 38

Eye of God

It was cold in the shadow of the volcanic cloud.

The sun was a tenuous brightness in a dark sky, pewter or brass on a field of featureless gray. Matt drove with the camper's high beams on.

He drove toward Cheyenne on I-80. The place where the Artifact had been anchored to the Earth was sometimes visible on his right—not the caldera itself, but the glow of distant fires, of lava flows, a second brightness, not sunlight. Periodically, the road shook under his vehicle.

The road was difficult to follow. Ash fell from the sky in a continuous sheeting rain. It collected on the tarmac and drifted across the highway in charcoal dunes. At times the road seemed to disappear altogether; he navigated by the vague shapes of retaining walls, by road signs and mile markers transformed into gray cenotaphs. The camper's wheels spun in the drifts, grinding for purchase on the buried blacktop. Progress was slow and painful.

He passed through Laramie, a landscape of hopeless ruins. At noon—he supposed it was noon—he stopped at a gas station that had lost its windows but was otherwise reasonably intact. He fought through a drift of ash, his shirt tied over his mouth and nose. The volcanic ash was a fine-textured grit that smelled a little like rotten eggs. He stepped through the space where a window had been, and in the meager shelter of the depot he located a road map of Colorado and Wyoming.

The camper could have used some gas, but the pumps were dead.

Matt shivered in the cold. Across the highway, a charred frame building smoldered. All else was ash, a concealing darkness, a smudged snowfall.

Time to check on Kindle. Time to check on Beth.

■   ■   ■

He had left them in the coach, bandaged and wrapped in blankets against the cold. All his medical supplies, carefully hoarded, had been destroyed in the fire. But he had treated both patients with the antibiotics in his bag.

Kindle was occasionally conscious. Beth was not. Her breathing was terribly, desperately faint. Her pulse was rapid and weak. She was bleeding internally, and she was in shock.

He checked her bandage, decided it didn't need changing. There was so little he could do. Keep her warm. Keep one shoulder up so her good lung wouldn't fill with blood, so she wouldn't drown in blood.

He worked by the light of a Coleman battery lantern. The daylight that penetrated the ash-caked windows was powerless and bleak.

He turned to Kindle next. Kindle opened his eyes as Matt examined the leg wound.

The injury didn't appear serious but the bullet might have taken a chip from the fibula—and this was the leg Kindle had broken last fall. It would need to be immobilized until he could make a more thorough evaluation.

He looked up from his work and found Kindle staring at him. "Jesus, Matthew—your hands."

His hands?

He held them up to the light. Ah—his burns. He had burned his hands trying to get Abby out of the Glendale. The palms were red, blistered, peeling—weeping in places. He took a strip of clean linen and tore it in half, wrapped a piece around each hand.

"Must hurt like hell," Kindle said.

"We have painkillers," Matt said. "Enough to go around."

"You been driving since last night?"

"Mm-hm."

"Taking painkillers, and you can drive like that?"

"Painkillers and amphetamines."

"Speed?"

He nodded.

"You carry amphetamines in that black bag?"

"Found them in Joey's trailer," Matt said.

"You crazy fucker. No wonder you look like shit." Kindle moaned and moved a little under his blanket. "Beth alive?"

"Yes."

"Where are we?"

"A few miles out of Cheyenne."

Kindle turned his head to the window. "Is it dark out?"

"Day."

"Is that snow?"

"Ash."

"Ash!" Kindle said, marvelling at it.

■ ■ ■

But Kindle was right: he had gone without sleep for too long. When he looked at the map, all the names seemed obscurely threatening. Thunder Basin. Poison Spider Creek. Little Medicine Creek.

We have very little medicine at all, Matt thought.

Progress was maddeningly slow. The ash continued to fall. Hard to believe the earth could have yielded so much ash, the refuse of such an enormous burning.

Volcanic ash was rich in phosphorous and trace elements. He had read that somewhere. The rangeland would be fertilized for years to come. He wondered what might grow here, next year, the year after.

The speedometer hovered around ten miles per hour.

■ ■ ■

He was overtaken by a thought as the afternoon lengthened: *Beth might die.*

He had hesitated at the brink of this idea for hours. He was afraid of it. If he allowed the thought into his head, if he spoke the words even to himself—would it affect the outcome? If he named death, would he summon it?

But in the end it was unavoidable, a contingency that demanded his attention. Beth might die. She might die even if he found a source of whole blood, even if he found a functional hospital . . . and those things seemed increasingly unlikely.

He should be ready for it.

After all, he had chosen to live in this world: a world where people not only *might* die but inevitably, unanimously, *would* die. The mortal world.

He remembered Contact. The memory came back easily in this desolate twilight. He could have chosen that other world, the world of mortality indefinitely postponed, the world of an immense knowledge . . . the Greater World, they had called it.

The world of no murder, no fatal fires, no aging, no evil. There was a poem Celeste had loved. *Land of Heart's Desire.* He couldn't remember who wrote it. Some sentimental Victorian. Matt gripped the steering wheel with bloody hands, and the memory of her reading it aloud took on a sudden tangibility, as if she were sitting beside him:

> *I would mould a world of fire and dew*
> *With no one bitter, grave, or over wise,*
> *And nothing marred or old to do you wrong . . .*

He guessed that was what they had built out on this prairie: their curious round mountain, their world of fire and dew.

> *Where beauty has no ebb, decay no flood,*
> *But joy is wisdom, Time an endless song. . . .*

It was tempting, Matt thought. It was the ancient human longing, a desire written in the genes. It was every dream anyone ever hated to wake up from.

But it was bloodless. Not joyless, nor sexless; the Contactees had preserved their pleasures. What they had given up was something more subtle.

It had taken Matt most of his life to learn to live in a world where everything he loved was liable to vanish—and he had never loved that vanishing. But he had learned to endure in spite of it. He had made a contract with it. You don't stint your love even if the people you love grow old or grow apart. You save a life, when you can, even though everyone dies. There was nothing to be gained by holding back. Seize the day; there is no other reward.

But the price, Matt thought. Dear God, the price.

All our grief. All our pain. Pain inflicted by an indifferent universe: the cruelties of age and the cruelties of disease. Or pain inflicted, as often as not, by ourselves. Grief dropped from the open bays of bombers, grief inflicted by scared or sullen young men coaxed into military uniform. Grief delivered by knife in dark alleys or by electrode in the basements of government offices. Grief parceled out by the genuinely evil, the casually evil, or such walking moral vacuums as Colonel John Tyler.

So maybe they were right, Matt thought, the Travellers and Rachel and the majority of human souls: maybe we are irredeemable. Maybe the Greater World was better for its bloodlessness, its exemption from the wheel of birth and death.

Maybe he had made the wrong decision.

Maybe.

▪   ▪   ▪

He came into Cheyenne at what he calculated was nightfall.

The streets were all but impassable. In this darkness, it was too easy to lose the road. He turned off 80 onto what he guessed was 16th Street and faced the necessity of stopping for the night.

But then, as he was ready to switch off the engine, he peered up at the sky and saw, by some unanticipated miracle, the stars.

A wind had come up from the north. It was a cold wind, brisk enough to stir these ashes into more dangerous, deeper drifts. But the ash itself had ceased falling. There was a little light, blue shadows on a gray landscape.

He took his hands off the steering wheel, an experiment. It didn't hurt. He was beyond hurting. But he left some skin behind.

▪   ▪   ▪

Much of the city had burned.

He passed ash-shrouded rubble, strange columns of brick like broken teeth, the shells of empty buildings.

Two hospitals were marked on the map.

De Paul Hospital: a smoking ruin.

And the V.A. Medical Center, not far away. It hadn't burned—but the earthquake had shaken it to the ground.

▪   ▪   ▪

He checked on Beth and Kindle once more.

Kindle drifted up from sleep and nodded at him. Kindle was okay.

Beth, on the other hand—

Was not dead. But he couldn't say why. Her pulse was impossibly tenuous. She wasn't getting much oxygen; her lips were faintly blue. Her pupils were slow to dilate when he lifted her eyelids.

Still, she continued to breathe.

There was something awe-inspiring about each breath. For Beth, each breath had become a challenge, a kind of Everest, and it seemed to Matt that she met the challenge bravely and with a fierce resolve. But no single breath would meet the needs of her oxygen-starved body, and each breath must be followed by the next, a new mountain to scale.

She wasn't dead, but she was plainly dying.

What city might have an intact medical center? He looked at the map. His eyes seemed reluctant to focus. Somewhere beyond the range of the ashfall. But what *was* beyond the range of the ashfall? Denver? No: He would have to travel too close to the caldera itself; the journey might be impossible and would surely be too long. North to Casper? He wasn't sure what he might find in Casper; it was still a long distance away.

Everything was too far away.

She might not last another hour. Two hours would surprise him.

"Sleep," Kindle said. "I know how it is, Matthew. But you won't gain anything by killing yourself. Get some sleep."

"There isn't time."

"You've been looking at that map for a quarter hour. Looking for what, someplace to go? Someplace with a hospital? Not finding it, I bet. And you can't drive in this." He had pulled himself to a sitting position. "Looks like Armageddon out there."

Matt folded the map meticulously and put it aside. "Beth is badly hurt."

"I can see that. I can hear how she breathes."

"I don't have what I need to help her."

"Matthew, I know." Gently: "I'm not telling you to give up. Just we can't work a miracle. And it does no good to beat yourself for it. Look at you. You're a mess. Lucky you can walk."

It was true that they couldn't reach a hospital. He might as well admit it.

But something pushed forward in his mind, an idea he had not wanted to entertain.

"There's another possibility," he said.

■ ■ ■

He explained to Kindle, and listened to Kindle's objections for a while, but grew impatient and fearful for Beth and hurried back to the cab of the vehicle and turned it around.

He glimpsed the new Artifact as it finished a quick eastward transit of the sky. But the sky was closing in again; most of the stars had disappeared; and it was not ash that began to fall but a brutally cold rain.

The ash on the ground absorbed the water and became a slick, intransigent mud. He was forced to drive even more slowly, and even so, the rear end of the camper fishtailed now and then on what seemed like a river of liquid clay.

But he didn't have far to go.

He found the state capitol building, or what was left of it, at the end of a broad avenue lined with ash-coated trees and fallen limbs. Three-quarters of the dome had collapsed. One section of it, like an immense splinter, remained in place, lit from below by fires still burning in the shell beneath. The broad space in front of the building was a field of ash, and the rain had given it a wet sheen, and the firelight was reflected there.

Matt wasn't certain he would find what he wanted. But the capitol buildings were the centerpiece of the city, like Buchanan's City Hall, the most logical place, therefore, to find a Helper.

He parked and climbed out of the cab. There was blood on the steering wheel, blood on his pants.

He struggled for footing on the slick, compressed ash beneath his feet. The rain on his skin was not only cold, it was dirty. It carried soot out of the air. It turned his skin black. Matt realized he had left his jacket in the coach, with Kindle. He went to fetch it.

Beth's breathing was barely audible.

"Don't do this," Kindle said.

Matt shrugged into his jacket.

Kindle sat up and took his arm. "Matthew, most likely it won't work. And that's bad enough. But if it does—have you thought about that?"

"Yes."

"That's not a hospital out there. That's not a doctor. It's something from outer space. Something we never did understand. And that thing in orbit isn't humanity. How could it be? And what you're doing, it's not asking for help. It's praying."

"She'll die," Matt said.

"Christ, don't I know she'll die? Haven't I been listening to her die? But she's dying like a human being. Isn't that what we decided to do last August? When it comes down to it, what we said was no thanks, I'll die like a human being. You, me—even Colonel Tyler. Even Beth."

"That's not the issue."

"The hell it isn't! Matthew, listen. The Travellers left. They went away. Best thing that could happen. And that new Artifact, probably it'll go away too. Go star-chasing or whatever it is they do. And that's fine. Because we'll be left here with some human dignity. But if you go out and pray to that thing for help—my fear is that it *will* help, and it *won't stop* helping, and we'll have a new God in the sky, and that'll be the end of us, one way or another."

"I'm only one man," Matt said.

"Maybe one is all it takes. Maybe they can look at a thousand things at once—maybe *everything* matters."

"I have to help her." It was the only answer he could formulate.

"Why?"

"Because sometimes we help each other. It's the only decent thing we do." He turned to the door.

"Matthew!"

He looked back.

"Don't let that thing come near me. I don't care how badly off I am. I don't want it near me. Promise me that."

He nodded.

▪   ▪   ▪

The Helper was at the foot of the stairs of the Wyoming state capitol building.

Scabs of wet ash clung to it in the frigid rain. Matt reached up and brushed away these impediments.

He was a little feverish and immensely weary. It was strange to be standing here at the foot of this alien structure in the ash, in the rain, with the domeless capitol building burning fitfully in the dark.

He shivered. The shiver became a convulsion, and he bent at the waist until it passed and hoped he wouldn't faint.

Rain settled on the Helper in thick, dark drops. This Helper seemed to Matt less tall, less perfectly formed than the one at the City Hall Turnaround. He wondered whether it might have begun to erode. Perhaps it would eventually sink into the earth, a shapeless mound, discarded.

It didn't develop eyes. It didn't look at him. It remained impassive.

He told it about Beth. He described her wounds. Some part of him listened to the sound of his own voice and marveled at the melancholy note it added to the rainfall and the wind. He felt like an intern on rounds, reciting a patient's symptoms for a hostile resident. Was this necessary? It seemed to be.

He said, "I know what you can do. I saw that woman. That insect woman. If you can change a human being from the inside out, you must be able to heal a chest wound. And Cindy Rhee, the little girl with the brain tumor. She was cured."

The Helper remained impassive.

Was it dead? Deaf? Or simply not listening?

"Answer me," Matt said. "Talk to me now."

The cold seemed to claw inside his body. He knew he couldn't stand out in this night rain much longer. He put his hands on the body of the Helper. The Helper was as cold as the air. He left bloody prints on the alien matter.

It didn't speak.

▪ ▪ ▪

He carried Beth from the camper.

He knew this bordered on the insane, taking a dying woman into the cold night. But he seemed to be out of options.

There was no reasoning, only a slow panic.

Beth was heavy. He held her with one hand supporting her shoulder and the other under her knees. She was a small woman, but he was terribly tired. He staggered under her weight. Her head lolled back and her breathing stopped. He waited for it to resume. *Breathe*, he thought. She gasped. A bubble of blood formed on her lips.

He told her how sorry he was that all this had happened. She didn't deserve it. She wasn't bad. It was one of those unforeseeable tragedies, like an earthquake, like a fire.

He put her down in front of the alien sentinel. She was pale and limp in the wet gray ash. Rain fell on her. Matt put his jacket over her. He pulled away one limp strand of hair that had fallen across her face.

Then he addressed the Helper.

"Here she is," he said. "Fix her."

Was this too peremptory? But he didn't know another way to say it.

From that black obelisk: nothing.

"I *know* you can fix her. You have no excuse."

An infinitely long time seemed to pass. A gusty wind turned the rain to needles on his skin. The wind made a sound in the ruins of the capitol building. It sounded like whispering.

The Helper was connected to the Artifact, he supposed, and the Artifact was full of humanity—or something that had once been humanity. "Are you all in there?" Several billion human souls. "Can you hear me?"

Nothing.

He was light-headed. He leaned against the Helper to steady himself. The Helper was cold, substantial, inanimate.

"Everybody in there?" He was hoarse with all this talking. "Jim Bix in there? Lillian? Annie, are you in there? Rachel?"

Silence and the sound of the spattering rain.

"You have no excuse. You can help this girl. Rachel, listen to me! This isn't good at all. Just standing there letting this girl die. We didn't raise you to do that."

He closed his eyes.

Nothing had changed.

He felt himself sliding down, felt himself sitting in the wet ash beside Beth. He couldn't hear Beth anymore. He wondered if she had stopped breathing. There was a buzzing in his ears that drowned all other sound.

"If you were human," he said, "you would help."

He fought to cling to his awareness, but the sense was eroding from his words. There was nothing left inside him but a weary frustration.

"If you were human. But you aren't. I suppose we don't matter anymore. This girl doesn't matter. This dying girl. That offends me. Fuck you. Fuck all of you."

He wanted to open his eyes but couldn't. Time passed.

He roused for a moment.

"Rachel! Come out of there!"

He felt the stony body of it cradling his head.

"*Rachel!*"

▪   ▪   ▪

Asleep, he dreamed that she *did* come out.

He dreamed that the Helper changed, that its contours melted, that it became the shape of his daughter, Rachel, as if carved from black ice, black against a gray sky, rain on the polished skin of her like dew.

He dreamed that she touched Beth, touched Matt himself, and the touch was warm.

He dreamed that she said a word to him: some wonderful, comforting word he could not understand, because the language she spoke was not a human language.

Chapter
39

Direction

As soon as he thought it would be safe to leave Matt for a few hours, Tom Kindle located a functioning automobile—a Honda that had been buried under ash but washed more-or-less clean by the rain—and drove north to Casper.

His leg nagged him relentlessly. The bullet wound was a knob of fire in the meat of his calf. But it had been a clean wound, and Matt had bandaged it well, and Kindle found he was able to move around all right if he favored the leg. He wondered how he looked with a limp.

Like a lopsided old son of a bitch, he supposed. Which was approximately true.

A wave of cool, dry Canadian air had chased the rain away. He drove an empty road north beyond the limits of the ashfall. He marveled at how good it was to see some green grass again. Wildflowers were blooming in the gullies.

He saw a number of dead animals along the way. The departure of the human Artifact had killed a lot of livestock. Did they know? Did they care, the so-called heirs of mankind? But Kindle guessed it was no worse than a natural disaster—a unique event, unlike the perpetual hardships human beings had imposed on the animal kingdom since the year zip. The herd animals would come back quickly now that so many of the range fences were down.

In Casper he picked up a ham radio he believed would operate from a twelve-volt car battery. He wasn't sure how to hook it up, but it came with instructions—he could probably figure it out.

He could have used Joey's help, however.

As daylight faded, Kindle hunted for water. Water was a scarce commodity since the taps had ceased to work. A supermarket, its big windows shattered in the quake, yielded a dozen plastic gallon jugs of distilled H_2O.

He loaded them into a new car for the trip back: a Buick wagon with a nearly full tank of gas. Gas pumps didn't work any better than the plumbing, but there was plenty of this old Detroit rolling stock free for the taking.

Night fell. He drove with the Buick's heater running, with the smell of hot metal and a pine-scent air freshener, south toward that glow on the horizon, the smoldering volcanic crater, as if I-25 crossed a border into the western precincts of Hell.

▪ ▪ ▪

In Cheyenne the next morning Kindle assembled two wooden crosses from lumber stock and loose nails.

When the crosses were solid, Kindle used a nail to scratch a letter deep into the horizontal board of the first of the two markers. It was awkward, clumsy work. But he persisted.

He wrote the letters A, B, B.

Then he paused to think. Would she prefer *Abigail* or *Abby*? Or *Abbey*, or *Abbie*, come to that?

He had only ever known her as Abby, and in the end he inscribed the simplest version of her name:

ABBY CUSHMAN

And on the second cross:

JOSEPH COMMONER

And he took the two crosses out and hammered them into the ash-gray lawn in front of the ruins of the Wyoming state capitol building, next to the statue of Esther Hobart Morris. Of course Joey and Abby weren't buried here; their bodies were lost. But they deserved some memorial more dignified than the burned-out hulk of a Glendale motor home.

As for Jacopetti, Ganish, Makepeace, Colonel Tyler—
Let 'em rot.

■   ■   ■

He went back to the camper and stood vigil over the inert forms of
Matthew Wheeler and Beth Porter.

Matthew seemed to be asleep. His hands appeared to be gloved: they
were encased in a glossy substance the color of bituminous coal.

"Matthew?" Kindle said. "Matthew, can you hear me?"

But the doctor didn't answer—as he had not answered yesterday or the
day before.

Beth was covered from the waist up in the same inert black material.
Kindle didn't speak to her. Why bother? Her head was all enclosed. Her
nose, her mouth.

■   ■   ■

He built a fire and watched the smoke rise up into the blue twilight.

Probably no one would recognize the signature of a campfire in
Cheyenne. Much of the city was still smoldering. But he would have to be
careful out on the rangelands where it would be easy to spot a man's fire at
night. There might be other people who hadn't chosen the option of Ohio.
There might be more like Colonel Tyler.

■   ■   ■

Matt was awake in the morning.

The black substance had left his hands. Kindle wondered where it had
gone. Had it been absorbed by the body? Had it evaporated into the air?

"Thirsty," Matt said.

Kindle brought him some water. The skin on the doctor's hands was
pink and new.

"I dreamed about Beth," Matt said. "I dreamed they fixed her."

"Maybe they did," Kindle said.

■   ■   ■

Matt helped him build the evening's fire. They brewed coffee and sat
huddled at the flickering warmth.

"I thought maybe you had gone over," Kindle said. "Maybe you'd end up an empty skin, like everybody else."

Matt shook his head: No, that wasn't the decision he had made.

Kindle allowed the silence to grow to its natural length. The stars had come out tonight, all these bright Wyoming stars. He said, "I talked to Ohio."

"Hooked up a radio?"

He nodded. "Their Helpers are working again. I gather they weren't for a while. Everything went down when the Traveller Artifact left. Power went down. The Travellers had been running all the turbines and so forth, keeping electricity on line, I guess all over the country—all over the world. Now it's back on. But only in Ohio, the man says, a certain perimeter around that encampment. And a few similar places on other continents."

"A perimeter?"

"Not a fence. But I gather, if you stray too far, you're on your own. No power, no water, no guarantees."

"It's a safe place," Matt said.

"Eden," Kindle said. "Can you think of a better name for it? Kind of a garden. Live there, you're taken care of. God looks after you for your natural span. God makes the sun shine, God makes the grass grow."

"They're not God," Matt said.

"Might as well be."

"But only in Ohio," Matt said. "Maybe only as long as the Artifact stays in orbit."

"Artifact might not leave. Guy in Ohio says it's not decided yet, according to the Helpers."

"War in Heaven?"

"An argument, at least."

Matt looked across the gray lawn of the capitol building, at the local Helper, *their* Helper—the pillar to which he had prayed. "If we talked to it—"

"It was alive for a while, Matthew, but I think it's not anymore. I think if you want to talk to a Helper you have to go to Ohio."

Matt nodded. Periodically, he looked at his hands—his new, raw hands. He said, "You think I'm responsible for this?"

"For keeping the Artifact here?" Kindle shrugged. He had thought about this. "Who knows? We're talking about the collective decision of ten billion souls—I don't think Matthew Wheeler tipped the pot. But you walked into their debate, I think. Made them look at what they left behind. And maybe you weren't the only one. Maybe the same scene got played out a thousand times, different places on the Earth. People saying: If you want to be God, show a little compassion. Or if you're still human, some *human* compassion."

"You blame me?"

"No."

"But you don't like it."

"No." Kindle sipped his coffee. It was hot and bitter. "No, I do not."

▪ ▪ ▪

Beth woke up groggy the next morning—groggy but well. There was only a pucker of healthy skin where the bullet had entered her chest.

She asked about Joey and Colonel Tyler. Matt explained, not gently because there was no gentle way to say this, what had happened.

She listened carefully but didn't speak much after that.

She sat at the evening fire hugging herself and drinking coffee. The talk flowed around her silence like a river around a stone.

Periodically, her hand strayed to her right shoulder and touched her jacket above the place where her tattoo had been—where it remained, Matt corrected himself; the Helper had not taken it away. He supposed some wounds were easier to heal than others.

▪ ▪ ▪

She slept that night curled around herself on a mattress on the floor of the camper.

In the morning they began the journey east, across the border from Wyoming into Nebraska.

Tom Kindle said he would ride along for a while. But only a while.

▪ ▪ ▪

Nebraska was a half-and-half state—arid in the west, wetter in the agricultural east. Interstate 80 joined the Platte River east of the Kingsley Dam, and the Platte fed a valley of rich alluvial soil where acre upon acre of corn, beets, potatoes, and beans had grown wild and high in an empty springtime.

Matt drove most of the time. Tom Kindle's leg was still bothering him; it tended to cramp after a time behind the wheel. So Matt drove through these empty agricultural towns, pretty little towns made ragged by a hard, windy winter: Brady, Gothenburg, Lexington, Kearny. Sometimes Kindle rode in the cab beside him; mostly it was Beth.

Out of Kindle's earshot, Beth talked a little more about what had happened—and what *might* happen.

"They're still inside us," she said. "The—what are they called? Neocytes."

He nodded.

"They'll be with us for a long time."

He nodded again.

She said, "You know about this, too?"

"Yes."

"Same as me? I mean . . . nobody told you, you just *know* it, right?"

"Right."

"They're inside us. But dormant. Not doing anything. Until . . ."

"You can say it," Matt told her. There was a potent magic in saying things out loud.

"Until we die," Beth said. "And then they'll give us another chance to say yes. To go with them."

He nodded.

"Like heaven," she said.

"A little like."

"And not just us. Everybody in that town on the river, that town in Ohio."

Everybody in Eden, Matt thought.

■   ■   ■

They did some night driving.

It was Kindle who pointed out the line of division that had appeared on the orbiting Artifact, a dark equator on that bright circle.

"It's dividing," said Kindle, who had been talking on the radio again. "That's what Ohio tells me. It'll be two Artifacts, not one. One to go roving among the stars. One to stay here."

"Like a custodian," Matt said.

"Or a local god." He gave Matt a long look. "You don't seem surprised."

He admitted, "I'm not."

"You knew about it?"

"Yes."

"How?"

He shrugged.

Kindle turned away. He watched the road pass. He said, "You're not what you used to be."

"Not entirely."

"God damn," Kindle said. It was not a particular lament. It wasn't aimed at Matt. It was just a sad curse to rattle away in the chilly night air. "God *damn*."

Epilogue

As wise as they were, the Travellers had come to the Earth with their own assumptions and for their own reasons. They were benevolent but clumsy giants; and the human polis, alone in orbit, began to tinker with certain changes the Travellers had made.

In the oceans, the population of Traveller phytoplankton dropped to a fraction of its earlier numbers. The work continued—there was still much excess CO_2 to be bound into the sea—but it needn't be done in a season, and it needn't inject so much violent energy into the atmosphere.

Nor was it necessary to maintain power and water in every city on the Earth. That had been the Travellers' fumbling reaction to the phenomenon of human obstinacy: the puzzling willingness of so many people to accept their own mortality.

The human polis fashioned better and more compact alternatives: in Ohio, in Ukraine, in Hunan and Kenya and a dozen other places.

And outside those boundaries was simply the wild Earth, for those who wanted it.

Home divided itself into two entities: one to journey outward into an awakening galaxy; one to cherish its own past, its birthplace and its parent species.

After a harsh and stormy winter, the spring of the year was mild— oceans calm, skies blue.

■   ■   ■

Kindle stopped at the Iowa border and refused to go any farther.

He was away from camp for a day and when he came back he was riding a gaunt saddle horse that had survived the winter but was not entirely wild. Over the course of a dry season, Kindle said, most of the gas might evaporate from all these abandoned automobiles, or the hoses rot or the oil thicken or the pistons seize—or some damn thing. A good riding horse was a better bet, over the long run.

"You going west?" Matt asked.

Kindle said he was.

"Wind River? Whiskey Mountain?"

Somewhere through there, Kindle said.

▪   ▪   ▪

Beth, watching the two men shake hands, thought there was something similar in the way they looked at each other. Something more than friendship, more than sadness.

Each one seemed to look at the other and see what he might have been—what he could have been or maybe should have been—but would never be.

Two roads parted here, and they would not run together again; both men seemed to know it.

Kindle rode off down the ragged highway in the hot part of the afternoon.

Matt stood a long time watching.

▪   ▪   ▪

She was with him that night when the Artifact passed overhead.

It was almost two things now, a massive figure eight on the verge of separation: two parts of humanity.

She warmed her hands at a fire that seemed lonely without Tom Kindle. She hadn't wanted him to go. But things change whether you want them to or not.

"Things change," she said, needing to communicate the thought but daunted by the lonely sound the words made on this vacant plain. Wasn't that what everyone was afraid of? Things change. The past drifts off until it's irrecoverable and strange. And the future is a mystery. And nothing stands still. Not for us, not for those people in the sky. Nothing is solid. Not even trees or mountains or planets or stars. Look long enough and they all boil away, boil away. She had seen it as long ago as Contact. She had seen it in her mind's eye. "It's a dance," she said. You can't cling to what you love because it's all a dance, love and friendship and men and molecules, all dancing in a brief light.

She looked helplessly at Matt. Did he understand?

But he seemed to. She thought perhaps he had known it all along.

She looked east, where the stars were rising in a dark sky. "It's been getting greener as we go," Beth said. "And warmer."

These nights weren't as cold as they had been. Matt said, "Maybe it'll be a gentle summer."

Gentler in Ohio? Greener, warmer?

"I think so," Matt said.

"I would like that," Beth said, wanting to cry for no particular reason. "I think that would be good."